Withdrawn/ABCL

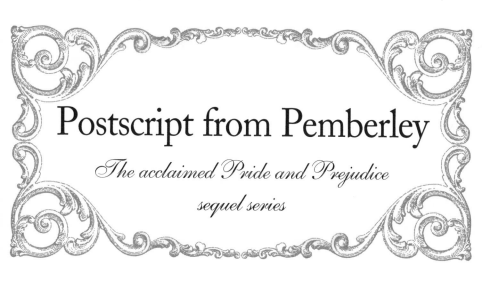

Postscript from Pemberley

*The acclaimed Pride and Prejudice
sequel series*

*The Pemberley Chronicles:
Book 7*

DEVISED AND COMPILED BY

Rebecca Ann Col

D0972114

SOURCEBOOKS LANDMARK™
AN IMPRINT OF SOURCEBOOKS, INC.®
NAPERVILLE, ILLINOIS

By the Same Author

The Pemberley Chronicles
The Women of Pemberley
Netherfield Park Revisited
The Ladies of Longbourn
Mr Darcy's Daughter
My Cousin Caroline
Recollections of Rosings
A Woman of Influence
The Legacy of Pemberley

Copyright © 2009 by Rebecca Ann Collins
Cover and internal design © 2009 by Sourcebooks, Inc.
Cover image © Getty Images

Sourcebooks and the colophon are registered trademarks of Sourcebooks, Inc.

All rights reserved. No part of this book may be reproduced in any form or by any
electronic or mechanical means including information storage and retrieval systems—
except in the case of brief quotations embodied in critical articles or reviews—without
permission in writing from its publisher, Sourcebooks, Inc.

The characters and events portrayed in this book are fictitious or are used fictitiously.
Any similarity to real persons, living or dead, is purely coincidental and not intended
by the author.

Published by Sourcebooks Landmark, an imprint of Sourcebooks, Inc.
P.O. Box 4410, Naperville, Illinois 60567-4410
(630) 961-3900
FAX: (630) 961-2168
www.sourcebooks.com

Originally printed and bound in Australia by SNAP Printing, Sydney, NSW, October
2002. Reprinted November 2004.

Library of Congress Cataloging-in-Publication Data

Collins, Rebecca Ann.
  Postscript from Pemberley : the acclaimed Pride and prejudice sequel series / devised
and compiled by Rebecca Ann Collins.
    p. cm. -- (The Pemberley chronicles ; bk. 7)
  Originally published: Sydney : SNAP Printing, 2002.
  Includes bibliographical references and index.
  1. Bennet, Elizabeth (Fictitious character)--Fiction. 2. Darcy, Fitzwilliam (Fictitious
character)--Fiction. 3. England--Social life and customs--19th century--Fiction. I.
Austen, Jane, 1775-1817. Pride and prejudice. II. Title.
  PR9619.4.C65P67 2009
  823'.92--dc22
                                        2009038825

Printed and bound in the United States of America
VP 10 9 8 7 6 5 4 3 2 1

To

Anthony & Rose,

without whom I could not have come this far

Withdrawn/ABCL

Author's Note...

IT IS NOT ALWAYS necessary to introduce readers to the characters or circumstances of a story; indeed, it seems to be the modern practice to leave them guessing or, better still, confused, about the author's intentions.

However, many readers of the Pemberley Chronicles series have written to ask if I intend to leave Julian Darcy out in the cold, as it were, following his failed marriage and the subsequent death of his wife, Josie.

Put like that, it sounded callous and though he was never a favourite of mine, it did seem hard-hearted not to give him another chance.

In *Postscript from Pemberley*, he has that chance.

Darcy Gardiner was quite another matter.

I will admit I did agonise about him for a while. What to do with a handsome and amiable young man, without a large fortune and not much chance of a substantial inheritance? He does have a will to work for the betterment of ordinary people and a deep sense of family loyalty.

So, should I make him a politician? Some might say, *God forbid.*

A preacher addicted to high moral sententiousness and a desire to convert everyone to his personal view of the world? Never.

A playboy who marries some rich mill owner's daughter? Over my dead body!

Darcy Gardiner is one of my favourites—cast in the mould of some of Jane Austen's most admired young men, with many of the qualities that distinguished his grandfather, and more to say for himself than Mr Darcy had at his age, besides. He was the chief raison d'etre for *Postscript from Pemberley*, and like the best characters any writer creates, he virtually wrote his own story.

I hope my readers will enjoy reading it as much as I loved the telling of it.

RAC / 2002
Website: www.geocities.com/shadesofpemberley

For the benefit of those readers who wish to be reminded of the characters and their relationships to one another, an *aide-memoire* is provided in the appendix.

Prologue

JESSICA COURTNEY COULD RECALL very clearly the moment that had changed her life. It had come upon her quite without warning and had caused her to regard very differently the course that her life might take in the following years.

While it did not bring either immediate or unalloyed happiness, Jessica realised that it could have been much worse, and she could have been drawn into a period of self-indulgent depression and complaint about the vicissitudes of life. But, despite her youth, for she was only eighteen years old, being possessed of both sense and sensibility, Jessica determined not to allow herself that dubious luxury.

It was all very well for heroines in popular novels to spend hours, days, months even, surrendering themselves to the melancholy contemplation of what might have been, she thought—they did not have a school to run.

The previous year, 1865, had not been an easy one for any of them, more particularly for members of the family of Mr and Mrs Darcy at Pemberley. Since the beginning of the year, news of the problems, which beset the marriage of their son Julian Darcy and his wife, Josie, had been filtering through to them in letters and whispered conversations. Not everyone was agreed upon who was to blame in the matter, but almost everyone had claimed to know something was amiss.

Jessica's mother, Mrs Emily Courtney, was too deeply involved in her commitments to the hospital at Littleford and her charitable work for the poor of the parish of Kympton to participate in such gossip, but whenever her aunt Caroline Fitzwilliam or their young cousin Lizzie Gardiner visited, they would share their news with her. They had no doubt at all that Julian and Josie were not happy.

Jessica had not wished to ask too many questions, lest they thought she was prying. Which was why she had been wholly unprepared for the dramatic news when it came, late one afternoon, that Julian Darcy had arrived from Cambridge at the home of his sister Cassy and Doctor Richard Gardiner, bringing with him his son Anthony and young Lizzie Gardiner, who had been staying with them in Cambridge at the time.

As her aunt Caroline told it, it seemed his wife, Josie, had left their home and had gone to live with a Mr Barrett, who had supposedly promised to publish her book! Incredible as it seemed, that was what Caroline had learned from her brother Richard Gardiner.

"It must be true, Dr Gardiner would not repeat such a story if it were not," thought Jessica. So appalled was she, that she had spent the rest of the evening in a state of shock, unable to speak of the disastrous news to anyone, while the rest of family had expressed consternation and grief.

On the following day, Jessica had gone into the village and met young Lizzie Gardiner at Mrs Hardy's bookshop, whither they had both gone in search of copies of a new novel by Mr Dickens. After making their purchases, they had repaired to a tea shop, where, as they took tea and sampled the shortbread, Lizzie was more forthcoming than Caroline had been.

Her aunt Caroline had been quite critical of Josie, especially of her decision to desert her little boy.

"It is beyond belief that a woman would leave a kind husband and her young child in this way," she had said, but Lizzie, with the advantage of having spent most of Spring in Cambridge with Julian and Josie, seemed to have more understanding of the reasons for her conduct. She knew more also about Mr Barrett, who had been a frequent visitor to the couple's home.

"I do not believe that Josie has done this lightly and only because of wanting to have her book published," she had said, adding, "I could not help feeling that Josie had been lonely and rather neglected by my uncle Julian, whose concentration upon his research work, almost to the exclusion of every other interest, may have left her open to deception by Mr Barrett and his friend Mr Jones, who are both guilty of great duplicity."

Jessica found it easier to ask her cousin the questions that had occupied her mind for some hours.

"And Julian, do you believe he still loves her, Lizzie? Will he have her back, do you think?" she asked.

Lizzie's answer had been unambiguous. "I am certain of it—he never looks at anyone else. He does love her, but is so completely wedded to his work, he has little time to tell her so or to pay any attention to her interests. Poor Josie, she cares little about the strange microscopic creatures he examines in his laboratory and I am convinced she felt she was no longer loved, when the opposite is probably true."

Though Lizzie's explanation would have been more painful for Mr and Mrs Darcy to bear, it made more sense than the notion that Josie, who only a year ago had appeared to be a loving wife and mother, could have been so altered in character as to behave in such an outrageous fashion. Lizzie had also revealed that Josie had left a note for her husband, in which she had declared that she did not love Mr Barrett, but needed the freedom he had offered her from her unhappy marriage.

Jessica had expressed disbelief at this, but this time Lizzie had been sympathetic to her uncle. "I have never seen anyone so distraught as my uncle Julian, when he read it. It was as though he had been struck dumb. He did not say a word against her—it was so sad to see him accept it, as though he believed he deserved it," Lizzie had said as they walked home, leaving Jessica wondering at the reasons behind it all.

Writing in her diary, to which alone she confided her innermost thoughts, she mused:

> Poor Josie, what could she have wanted? How much unhappiness must she have suffered to leave her husband and son for a man she did not love? I cannot even begin to comprehend her mind.
>
> As for Julian, how wretched must he feel to accept without protest such a situation, and yet he still loves her and would have her back! Love seems such a complicated emotion; I wonder if I shall ever understand it.

The shock and pain this unfortunate episode had inflicted upon Mr and Mrs Darcy, Jessica had seen firsthand. She had gone to Pemberley, to the church where she had promised to help the rector with the choir, and there she had met Mrs Darcy coming away from the rectory, a veil concealing her tear-stained face.

They had embraced without saying a word, but Jessica's warmth and sympathy had drawn Elizabeth out, and she had told her as much as she had learned from her son.

Elizabeth did not conceal her anger at Josie's behaviour, and Jessica took care not to mention what she had heard from Lizzie Gardiner. It would not do to admit that they had been discussing her son's circumstances.

Later, Mrs Darcy had insisted that Jessica should accompany her home to Pemberley and stay to tea. Making her excuses to an understanding rector, Jessica had done as Elizabeth had asked, not knowing then that they were to be joined by Julian, who was staying at Pemberley for a few days.

He was late coming downstairs, and when he arrived, Jessica, who had seated herself at the far end of the room to get the benefit of the afternoon light, had wished sincerely that he would not notice her. She had hoped that he, being understandably pre-occupied, would pay little attention to her as she sat reading by the window.

But, despite her intention to draw no attention to herself at all, he had seen her. When he had finished his tea, he had put down his cup, walked over to where she sat, and drawing up a chair, had seated himself beside her.

Jessica had known Julian Darcy all her life, they had been childhood friends, but now, she feared there would be some degree of awkwardness between them; it was the first time they had met since his arrival from Cambridge.

When they had finished their customary greetings and said all the usual things people say on such occasions, they had sat looking at one another and neither had said a word, until Jessica asked gently, "What will you do, Julian?"

He had shrugged his shoulders and smiled, a funny, crooked little smile, before saying softly, "Why, Jessica, you are the only person who has asked me that question. I am touched by your concern. However, if I am to be completely honest, I have to say I do not rightly know how to answer you."

Jessica had hastened to reassure him that she had not meant to pry and he should not feel he had to provide an answer. But then, in a voice heavy with resignation, he had said, "Well, I must return to Cambridge and complete my work there, but then, perhaps I shall go to France. I have an appointment with one of the medical schools in Paris."

"Do you intend to work there?'" she had asked, and he had replied, "I do, if they will let me continue my research into tropical diseases. I had intended to travel to Africa later in the year, but now, I may go a little earlier than planned."

"To Africa?" she had been unable to conceal her surprise.

"Yes, there is a great deal of work to be done and much to be studied there. A group of French scientists has invited me to join them—perhaps they will be pleased to see me earlier than expected," he had said, and as a rather mirthless smile crossed his countenance, Jessica thought she had not seen such anguish upon anyone's face before.

Lizzie Gardiner had been right; Julian Darcy was truly miserable, of that there could be no doubt. He must have loved Josie very much, she thought.

Some days later, Julian had left Pemberley to return to Cambridge.

No more was heard of Josie for several months, and Julian subsequently went to work in France. Jessica, though concerned to know how matters stood, preferred not to speak too openly about the subject, lest she upset Elizabeth, whose heightened anxiety seemed to increase by the day.

Later in the year, news had come that Josie had been found. Lizzie Gardiner had brought the news which gave everyone hope.

Unhappy and unwell, Josie had left Mr Barrett, whose promise to publish her book had evaporated as swiftly as his professed affection for her, over the months she had been with him. Her faithful maid Susan had stayed with her and brought word of her desperate situation to Cassy and Richard Gardiner, who had gone to London immediately to recover her. They had sent word to Julian, who had returned from France to be with his wife. While Josie was diagnosed as being very sick indeed, her husband would not give up hope.

"Julian is so generous, he has forgiven Josie everything and wants only for her to be well again," Lizzie had said, and Jessica, like the rest of the family, had hoped and prayed it may all come right.

⚘

Meanwhile, Jessica's own circumstances had begun to change.

Mr Darcy, now dependent mainly upon his daughter Cassandra and her husband Richard for advice on matters pertaining to his estate, had announced the extension of the small parish school at Pemberley to accommodate older pupils from the area.

"Hitherto, these children have had no education beyond a level so elementary, it fits them for little more than menial work," he had said. "Sir Thomas Camden and I have decided to extend the buildings and facilities of the parish school at Pemberley to provide an opportunity for them to be better taught.

"Furthermore, I have asked Miss Jessica Courtney to manage the school for me and hire two new teachers for the new term. I am delighted to say that she has very generously consented to accept the position and will soon move to live here at Pemberley, so as to be near the school. It goes without saying that her parents, Reverend James Courtney and our dear cousin Emily, have agreed to this arrangement as well."

Jessica had been overjoyed. It had seemed as if at last, with the New Year approaching, some changes were taking place, bringing hope back into their lives.

But, shortly afterwards, things had got much worse again, when even as they awoke to a new year, news came from London that Josie, who had never been very strong, had suffered a relapse and passed away in the night.

On a bitter January afternoon, the family had gathered for her funeral at Pemberley and Jessica could not help noticing the coldness that had appeared to exist between Mrs Darcy and Josie's mother, Mrs Rebecca Tate. Clearly, Elizabeth still blamed Josie for all that had happened.

Not long afterwards, Julian Darcy had announced his intention to renounce his inheritance in favour of his son, Anthony, and quit his position at Cambridge. Despite his disappointment, Mr Darcy seemed able to accept his son's decision with a level of stoicism and resignation. Elizabeth, however, had continued to suffer and not always in silence, while it had seemed to Jessica that Julian still wore a heavy cloak of misery.

She had chanced upon him once in the library at Pemberley, a book open in front of him, his eyes staring out of the window at the far horizon.

It had been plain to her that he was deeply distressed.

When she had apologised for disturbing him and tried to leave, he had assured her she was not and urged her to stay.

"Don't go, Jessica; stay and talk to me. No one else does," he had pleaded, and she had stayed. It was soon clear that he longed for some company.

They had spoken variously of her work and the hopes she had for the school, now it was to take in older children too. She was excited and looked forward to the new term.

"It will be a great opportunity for them," she had said and he had asked, "Will you teach them to read and understand more than just the Bible?"

"Oh yes indeed," she had replied, "we do so already, both at Kympton and at Pemberley, even to the younger children. They learn to read, write, and count at an elementary level."

She wanted very much to convince him of the value of their work, "Much as my father wishes them to read the Bible, he insists that while they remain untutored and ignorant, they will grow up unable to improve their lot in life. He is dedicated to the improvement of education for all children as I am and as your father Mr Darcy is. It is his generosity that has enabled us to do this good work."

When she stopped to draw breath, Julian smiled and nodded. "I am aware of that, Jessica. I know also that my father values your dedication highly. Do you intend to teach as well?" he asked.

Jessica was modest, "Only the little ones; I have not the skills nor the experience to teach the older children, but we do intend to employ a school master from Matlock who will. He is well spoken of and seems a good man. The rector knows him and recommends him highly," she had explained, and Julian had surprised her by saying, "Well, Jessica, it sounds a very good scheme. I shall look forward to hearing about the progress of your school. Indeed, I have long had an interest in public education and wrote a paper on it once, at Cambridge. I hope you will write to me and tell me how you get on."

Before she could respond, they were interrupted by the bell that summoned them to dinner.

They had met again when Jessica was returning from visiting a patient at the hospital in Littleford, and Julian had talked with a marked lack of reserve about his decision to relinquish his inheritance.

They were both bound for Pemberley and the question came up quite naturally as they crossed the footbridge and took the path leading to the house.

"And do you, like some members of my family, think me selfish and irresponsible for giving up Pemberley as I have done?" he had asked quite suddenly.

Taken aback by the directness of his question, Jessica had been unable to answer him immediately, but when she did, having gathered her thoughts, she made it clear that not only was it not her place to make such a harsh judgment, but she did not share the opinion of those who had.

"It is not a matter upon which I need make a judgment—I am unaffected by your decision," she had said, adding when he pressed her for an opinion, "But, since you have asked me, I would not condemn you for giving up Pemberley, if you honestly believed you were unable to give it the time and attention it deserved. After all, Pemberley is far too important to be left in the hands of a manager alone."

Julian seemed pleased and said, "Indeed, you are right, Jessica, my research work is my highest priority—it can save thousands of lives—and I would not wish to be an absentee landlord. My father appreciates that, but I fear Mama's disappointment in me cannot be assuaged. She feels I have let Pemberley and Papa down. I wish I could persuade her to see my situation as you do, Jessica. It is comforting to know I am not universally condemned."

"You are certainly not," she had protested. "I am well aware that your sister Cassy understands too, and so do Doctor Gardiner and young Lizzie."

"Ah yes, Cassy and Richard do understand. They always have. I should have been lost without them throughout last year. And Lizzie has been wonderful with Anthony—I could not have coped without her help," he said, and Jessica had been flattered by the confidence he placed in her, discussing his situation with her so unreservedly and openly.

Julian was almost twelve years older than she was, and she had always regarded him with a degree of awe and respect. His learning and erudition, which was far in advance of anyone in her immediate family, had set him apart from them, but more recently, especially since Josie's illness, Jessica had been surprised to find him approachable and genuinely friendly. She had expected that he would be withdrawn and reserved, and would have understood if he had been, but in fact, the reverse had been true. She had found herself feeling some measure of sympathy and understanding for him.

When they reached Pemberley House, they had learned from the housekeeper that Mr and Mrs Darcy were dining with Sir Thomas Camden, leaving them to dine alone. Afterwards, they had repaired for coffee to the smaller private sitting room rather than the formal drawing room, and there, Julian asked if Jessica would read to him, as she did to his mother.

"My mother says you are the best reader she has known. Would you read something for me, Jessica?"

Temporarily surprised by the request, Jessica had hesitated but momentarily, before agreeing, "Of course, what would you wish me to read?" she had asked.

Selecting an anthology of poems from the collection of books that lay beside the chair in which Elizabeth sat each evening, listening to Jessica read before dinner, he had handed it to her, saying, "I am no connoisseur of poetry, Jessica, I shall let you choose something you would enjoy reading."

She was happy to oblige. It was a popular anthology and she loved many of the poems of Keats, Coleridge, and Shelley it contained. Choosing a favourite of hers, she had read John Keats' Ode "To a Nightingale" and as he had listened to the rich, mellifluous words of the poet, it had seemed from his expression as if he was, for the first time in many long months, at peace. Julian listened, his eyes closed, his head thrown back. When she had finished, he thanked her sincerely for the very special pleasure and commended her selection.

"It is a most sonorous and memorable piece," he had said. "I shall read it again myself and remember it always. You read very well, Jessica. I am not surprised that Mama delights in having you read to her."

Jessica thanked him and assured him she had enjoyed reading to him, but as he helped himself to more coffee and port, she had begged to be excused on account of an early appointment at the school and retired to her apartments upstairs.

She had been convinced more than ever that Julian's present melancholy was the result of loneliness and want of companionship, rather than excessive grief.

Before leaving Pemberley for Cambridge, Julian had sought out Jessica, whom he found at the schoolhouse, busy making preparations for the new term. He had brought her some books, which he hoped she would find useful. "They are old schoolbooks of mine, which I have preserved for many years, and I thought they may interest you," he had said, handing over a large canvas satchel, which Jessica opened with gratitude, exclaiming at the treasures it held.

She was eager to build a collection for the school's library, she told him.

"I have already begged for books from Pemberley and Camden House; these will do very nicely, it was kind of you to think of us at such a time," she said, pleased when he added, "Well, if you need more, you must ask my father. He has agreed to have the rest of my books placed in storage at Pemberley. You are very welcome to have them; I shall not have much use for them myself and there will be very little room in my luggage for books, apart from those

I require for my research. Besides, they would deteriorate very quickly in the humid heat of Africa."

It was the first time he had mentioned Africa since the funeral, and Jessica asked if he still intended to go and if a date had been agreed.

"Yes indeed, I do, but we have no fixed date for our departure because there is as yet some work that must be finished before the medical board will release the funds for our project. I wish we could go sooner, but we have to await their approval," he had replied in the most matter-of-fact manner, as though he were merely leaving for the next county.

"Shall we see you again before you leave England?" she had asked, and when he had smiled and said, "You certainly shall, if young Lizzie's wedding date is settled. Cassy tells me she expects her to be engaged to Mr Carr very soon and their marriage may follow not long afterwards. Should that be the case, I have promised to return for the wedding," she had detected real pleasure in his voice. Changing the direction of their conversation, he had asked, "But you will write to me, Jessica, will you not? I look forward to hearing how you get on with the school and if the children are as eager to learn as you are to teach them. I hope, amidst your many important duties, you will find the time to pen an occasional letter with news of home?"

"Of course," said Jessica, more than a little surprised at his request, to which he replied, with a smile, "Good, I shall look forward to that," and taking a card from his pocketbook, he gave it to her. "That direction will always find me. It is a *poste restante* order."

She put it away and was preparing to close the schoolroom.

He had assumed that she would be returning with him to dine at Pemberley and had seemed disappointed when she had said, "It's Friday, I always return to the rectory at Kympton on Fridays. Mama and Papa will be expecting me to dine at home."

"May I walk with you then?" he asked, and she was pleased to agree.

"Thank you, that would be nice; it is such a mild evening, we could walk through the park. When I am alone, I use the road—it's a shorter route but much less pretty," she said as they set out.

The setting sun had caused the woods around Pemberley to glow in its golden light, and the lake below gleamed like a jewel. The beauty that surrounded them had made Jessica catch her breath, and for a moment they were both silent.

"I can see you love Pemberley," he had said, to which she responded without hesitation, "I do indeed. I cannot imagine that anyone could not."

They walked on, and as they did so, they had spoken not of his work or hers but of their hopes. Julian, now seemingly more at ease than before, had asked, "And what do you do with your time, that is when you do have time for yourself, when you are not teaching the children or reading to my mother or training the choir—with all these duties, you must have very little time for leisure."

Jessica had assured him that she had plenty of time to herself, explaining that she enjoyed her own company.

"I read a great deal and play the recorder and practice on the piano-forte, which I must confess I do not do as often as I should... but that is a matter of application, not lack of time. I have never found it difficult to entertain myself, even as a child."

When he looked a little perplexed, she added, "Perhaps because my sister and brother were a good deal older than I was, I was frequently alone, left to my own devices."

"It is a singular blessing to be happy in one's own company. I wish I could make the same claim for myself. I too was a solitary child, but I must admit that now, without my work to occupy me, I should have become a very dull fellow." He had sounded quite envious, and Jessica had looked askance at him.

"That cannot be true," she had protested, and he'd quizzed her, playfully, "Do you think not?"

"No indeed, I should never have said you were dull; reserved perhaps, but not dull. Why, you know so much about things that are hidden from the rest of us, you have studied and opened up whole worlds of knowledge that have been closed to us all these years, how could that be dull?"

Even as he laughed at her enthusiasm, he seemed quite delighted.

"Jessica, my dear, you must be the first young lady I have met who has thought so. Most women I know would rather not know that microbes and bacteria exist, much less desire to have a conversation about them! I cannot think of anyone, apart from another scientist, who would have expressed such an interest. Creatures who only come to life under the microscope are difficult to describe and not a lot of fun!"

At this, she had laughed too and admitted that perhaps they were not much fun, in the way that dogs and horses were, but surely they would be fascinating to study and understand.

"I should have thought there would be a special fascination in the very fact that we cannot see them, but we know they are there, mysterious and strange..."

Before he could respond, Jessica, who had looked up at him as she spoke, had stumbled, catching the heel of her shoe on the root of a spreading oak that jutted into their path, and her companion had hastened to catch her before she fell, holding her until she had regained her composure and ascertaining that she had not suffered any injury to her foot.

Flustered and shaken, she thanked him and they walked on; this time he took from her the case she had been carrying and offered her his arm for support, which she took gladly.

The light had been fading fast as they approached a stile, which separated the park from a narrow lane leading to the Kympton rectory. He had helped her over it before climbing over himself.

"We are almost there; I think I will not come in with you, Jessica; I have some work to complete at Pemberley."

She was disappointed. "Mama and Papa will be happy to see you," she'd said, but he had pleaded to be excused.

"I did call on your parents after church on Sunday and said my farewells; besides, there are matters to be settled before I leave early tomorrow. I hope to take the morning train to London."

This time it was she who had said, "If I write to you in France, will you write too?"

"Certainly, though I must warn you I am not an interesting correspondent, as my mother and sister will surely tell you. My letters will probably bore you with accounts of failed experiments and unidentified bacteria."

Jessica protested, "I promise I shall not be bored. I should like very much to learn something of France—I have never been outside of England and have heard much of the beauty and elegance of France. It has long been an obsession of mine."

"Then you shall receive letters full of the delights of Paris and the French countryside, which, though it is very different to ours, has a rustic charm all its own; it has grown on me each time I have visited there," he had said, and Jessica had made no attempt to hide her pleasure at the prospect.

"I shall look forward to reading them. My mother had a small farm in France once, left to her by Monsieur Antoine, but I believe she sold it and used the proceeds for the extension to the hospital at Littleford. I think I should have loved to have travelled to France and spent some part of my life there. But, as it is not to be, I shall have to console myself with your accounts of it."

With the rectory in sight, they had stopped, and as she had moved to reclaim her case, he had taken her hand in his and said, "Dear Jessica, let me thank you for your kindness to me these past days. For being so open, honest, and friendly, as few others have been. I am truly grateful. I had wondered, after all that has happened, how I should endure staying at Pemberley, but your companionship as well as the kindness of my family has rendered it more enjoyable than I had ever expected it to be. I shall not forget your generous heart."

"Not even if you go to Africa?" she had quipped softly, hoping to sound lighthearted.

"Especially not if I go to Africa, it will be my happiest memory of home," he had said, and as she remained silent, unable to think of anything to say, he had bent and kissed her very gently on the cheek, saying good-bye, not once but twice

Then reminding her once more of her promise to write, he had retraced his steps along the lane to the stile and entered the park.

As Jessica had stood watching him, he had turned once and waved; then he was gone, hidden from her sight by the gathering darkness and the trees.

Jessica had felt her cheeks burning. Nothing like this had ever happened in her life before. As she had walked quietly into the garden of the rectory, she had hoped no one would notice anything unusual about her appearance or demeanour.

Her mother certainly had not, as she greeted her affectionately, and later her father, returning from visiting a parishioner, had welcomed her with just as much enthusiasm, but had seemed not to notice anything different about her.

Jessica alone had been acutely conscious of the change in herself, the warmth that had flushed her cheeks and the racing of her heart which made her breathless were so obvious to her, that she had thought they would surely be as conspicuous to her family. Would they not wonder at the reason for them?

After dinner, her youngest brother Jude had monopolised everybody's attention with his clever recitation of a song he had learned by rote, and Jessica, glad of the distraction, commented upon how he had grown.

"He seems taller each time I see him" she had said and both their parents agreed.

"Jude is going to learn to be an altar boy soon," said her mother.

"And help me with distributing the prayer sheets and hymn books, aren't you, Jude?" said his father, and to Jessica's great relief no one had asked about Julian's plans. She had been especially pleased at not having to reveal her meeting with him that afternoon.

Later that night, back in her own small bedroom, the one she had occupied all her life until moving this year to Pemberley, Jessica had wondered at her own feelings, trying to comprehend them.

Unused to dealing with such situations, she had found it a difficult exercise, to explain even to her diary. *How is it that I feel this way?* she had written, struggling to understand.

> *It cannot be that I am suddenly in love with Julian Darcy. I have known him all my life and never felt a particular partiality towards him before. He has been a friend of my childhood, a cousin, and chiefly a rather remote, learned person who engendered feelings of esteem and even awe, but never love.*
>
> *When he married Josie, I was probably not old enough to experience jealousy, but I felt no loss. So how do I feel this way now? What has changed between us? Why am I all a-tremble because of a single, chaste farewell kiss, and why do I want to hug this feeling to myself and tell no one?*

And what of his feelings? She could not help wanting to discover what they might have been.

> *It is surely not possible that he, in so short a time after Josie's death, would be ready to feel anything akin to love for someone else. Or is it?*
>
> *Lizzie Gardiner was certain that he loved Josie dearly and grieved deeply for her. If this is true, as she believes it is, he would probably be outraged and embarrassed should he learn that I harboured some childish affection for him. It would probably ruin our friendship.*

I must therefore ensure that whatever happens, he does not discover my secret.

Concluding her note, she had locked her diary away in her case and as she retired to bed, resolved that in everything she did and especially when she wrote to Julian, as he had asked her to do, she would quite deliberately steer well away from personal matters that might lead her to betray her affections, however unwittingly.

She had determined that her letters would be friendly in style, informative in content, and lighthearted in tone.

That way, she had decided, she would be in no danger at all of giving herself away.

Of Julian, she knew only that his present plans, which he had revealed quite candidly, meant he would spend most of the rest of his life abroad, in France or Africa. There had even been some mention of a French Colony in the South Pacific, where the team may venture to study some particular tropical pest. Unlikely then, she thought, that he would ever spend sufficient time in England, much less in Derbyshire, to have any chance of falling in love with her.

Yet, as she lay sleepless for almost an hour, her mind rehearsed their last conversation: the walk through the park, the manner of his parting from her, that very gentle kiss upon her cheek, and a bewildering array of feelings crowded in upon her. Uniformly pleasurable, they stayed with her until sleep claimed her, recalling just before it did that Julian had given his word that he would attend his niece Lizzie Gardiner's wedding.

There would be time enough to prepare for that occasion, she thought.

Jessica knew, no matter how eventful her life might be in future years, she would never forget the events of this day.

END OF PROLOGUE

POSTSCRIPT FROM PEMBERLEY

Part One

Chapter One

JESSICA'S MEMORIES OF LIZZIE Gardiner's wedding day were filled with myriad impressions that crowded upon one another.

The happy lovers and their contented families predominated, coming together for a great celebration at Pemberley, where Mr and Mrs Darcy watched with pleasure as their granddaughter was married to Mr Michael Carr, a gentleman they had come to admire and respect. There were other recollections too, not all of which she wished to share with the rest of her family.

Jessica had dressed with some care for the occasion, in a becoming but simple gown, resisting the temptation to have a new one made. She knew that Julian was expected, although there had been some concern that he may not arrive in time, since he had to travel all the way from France; nevertheless, she was confident he would be there.

Several months had passed between the time of his departure from Derbyshire and Lizzie's wedding in the Autumn of 1866. To her surprise, not long after he had left Pemberley, a letter had arrived for her from Cambridge and upon her having sent a short reply, she had received another from Paris, whither he had gone to attend an urgent meeting of the medical board.

Both communications had been completely devoid of any descriptions of experiments, successful or otherwise, or microscopic bacteria, for that matter.

Instead they contained references to many matters of mutual interest, including quite a detailed description of the part of Paris in which his lodgings were situated. Jessica had been delighted.

The first, which had arrived barely a week after his departure, began with the usual courtesies but then went on to speak of the arrangements he was making at the university as well as his attendance at a concert of chamber music, which he had greatly enjoyed. She recalled that he had confessed to a growing interest in music, which, he said apologetically, he had neglected all his life. Jessica, a proficient and keen student of music, had encouraged him.

"I cannot imagine life without music; I lay no claim to great talent but I have an abiding love of music that sustains me at all times; without it my life would be poor indeed," she had said and he, inspired by her enthusiasm, had promised faithfully to maintain his interest.

His letter had concluded with a paragraph of such warmth and sincerity that she returned to read it again and again.

He wrote:

Finally, I cannot send this away without telling you of the happy discovery I have made, when packing my things to be sent over to France. There among my personal papers and books was a collection of poems presented to me by your aunt Caroline Fitzwilliam and in it is Keats' "Ode – To a Nightingale," which instantly brought back delightful memories of your reading it at Pemberley.

It was a recollection replete with feelings of gratitude for your generosity and kindness to me, during a time that was particularly painful for me and indeed, distressing for us all.

I shall be happy to take it with me to France and look forward to the day when I may have the pleasure of hearing you read it again.

In her response, which had taken Jessica quite some time and many sheets of notepaper to compose, she had striven to appear detached though friendly. She had written of their preparations for the start of the school term and the arrival of the new schoolmaster, Mr Hurst, who was to teach the older boys. She wrote:

Mr Hurst is an interesting man, though he must surely be quite old (Mama

thinks he could be forty five, but I believe he must be fifty years old at least).
He is surprisingly unlike any of the teachers one reads of in Mr Dickens'
books. He is soft spoken and considerate and does not appear to have that
accessory of all school masters: a cane.

What is more, he is a veritable treasure house of information on every
subject under the sun. For instance, I did not know that Mr Darwin,
who wrote the Origin of Species, had married the daughter of Mr Josiah
Wedgwood, the owner of the great Staffordshire potteries. Did you? Nor
was I familiar with the name of his ship, The Beagle. *Is that not an odd*
name for a ship?

Mr Hurst knows all the details of the ship's amazing voyage to the
other side of the world and the excessively weird and wonderful creatures
they saw there!

In answer to a question, he informed Mr Darcy very gravely that he
intended to teach the boys more than reading, writing, and numbers—he
plans to satisfy their natural curiosity by introducing them to Science and
Nature through everyday things in their lives, he says. Mr Darcy seemed
rather puzzled by this approach, but I must admit I look forward to seeing
the results of Mr Hurst's work.

Thank you for reminding me of Keats' "Nightingale," I am glad to
learn that you have a copy to take to France; it is a beautiful piece and
a favourite of mine, as you know. I am sure you will find time to read it
yourself in Paris; it will remind you of home.

I trust you are well, as we all are.

God bless you,

Jessica Courtney

Then, as if suddenly deciding to abandon the pretence of being cautious and
impersonal, she had added a postscript, in which she said she had heard he was
arranging to travel from France to attend Lizzie's wedding in the Autumn.

If this is the case, I expect we shall meet at Pemberley. I did so enjoy our conversa-
tions when you were last here and hope there will be time to talk some more, she had
said, hoping it would not be considered too forthright.

To this there had been no response for some weeks, leaving her anxious and
concerned lest she had offended him, however unwittingly.

She had waited daily for the post in a state of anxiety and no letter had been delivered, until a few days before young Lizzie's wedding day, when it had arrived, postmarked from Paris.

Late, short, but to her exceedingly sweet, it brought an apology for the delay in responding to hers and assured her that he would indeed be seeing her at Lizzie's wedding, adding also that afterwards, he expected to stay a few weeks at least at Pemberley before returning to France, during which time, he supposed, there should be plenty of time for the happy conversations they had both enjoyed so much.

It was a prospect that filled her with a confusion of delight and trepidation.

Julian Darcy's stay at Pemberley, at first set to be a fortnight, was extended to three weeks and more, as he surrendered to the persuasive arguments of his parents and the ambient pleasures of Pemberley in late Autumn. He spent much of the time with Mr and Mrs Darcy and his son Anthony, thereby bringing much happiness to all of them.

Elizabeth was especially pleased to see how much calmer and more confident her son had become since the previous year, when beset with a plethora of troubles, he had appeared to lose both direction and interest in his life.

As his sister Cassandra wrote to her cousin Emma Wilson:

Since Lizzie's wedding, Julian has been at Pemberley and he is a man transformed! He seems far more at peace with himself and at times appears almost happy to be here with us. I can only pray he will remain so...

As for Jessica, the period of his stay proved to be one of particular pleasure. While her days were spent chiefly at the school, she would frequently return in the afternoon to Pemberley, where Julian would join her for tea in the sitting room. The hours were filled with long, relaxed conversations on every subject available for discussion or readings from books, which they selected at random, mainly to please one another, often continuing until the servants came to light the lamps and it was time to dress for dinner.

At dinner, when they were joined by Mr and Mrs Darcy and, occasionally, the Bingleys, Fitzwilliams, or Cassy and Richard Gardiner, Julian would be the centre of attention, called upon to satisfy their guests' curiosity and answer questions about his work and the political situation in France, while Jessica listened. Later, however, he would join the ladies in the drawing room, usually leaving the gentlemen to their port and discussions of political and commercial matters, which seemed not to hold his interest at all. Then, his attention was all hers, as she played or read to please the company.

Jessica had many happy memories of these evenings, of conversations all invariably interesting to her, filled as they were with tales of people and places she had never seen or heard of before. He had told her so much about France, which she had not known before. She was as much enthralled by its recent bloody history as by its ancient culture and current sophistication.

Julian had detailed to her the idealism as well as the ferocity of the French revolution, yet balanced them with pictures of French music, art, and architecture that were the envy of Europe.

"It is indeed a place of great contradictions, Jessica, yet one that has an undeniable grasp upon me. I realise that it is not fashionable in some circles to profess admiration for the French—we have had some bitter battles in the past—but the country fascinates me like no other place on earth."

"It is well that it does, since you are determined to live and work there," she had remarked, and asked, "Do you expect to spend much more time in France?"

He had replied, "No, not unless something untoward occurs to thwart our plans. We expect to leave for Africa in Spring, before the rains begin. Arrangements are already afoot for our journey and I expect to know a firm date for our departure very soon."

"And you are looking forward to it, of course?"

"Yes indeed, it will be the culmination of more than a year's preparation."

Jessica had expressed some apprehension. "Will it be a dangerous expedition?" she asked.

His reply, though calculated to allay her fears, had been honest.

"All expeditions to places such as Africa or South America, where so little is known of the environment, are fraught with some danger. But I am assured by my French colleagues that the native peoples of the areas we intend to study are generally friendly. They are familiar with foreigners, and unlike some of the coastal tribes, whose experience of Europeans is tainted by the memory of the slave trade, these places are free of that scourge, thank God."

Despite these assurances, Jessica remained concerned.

One afternoon, when they had met as she had walked home through the park to Pemberley, she asked, "I cannot help wondering if you will be safe in Africa—I know your mama worries, too. Will you write, if only to reassure us that you are well?"

He had smiled and replied, "Of course, it is kind of you to be concerned; but be aware there is no penny post and letters must be carried to the ports and be shipped out to England. I mention this because I should not wish you to think, if there were to be a long delay in the arrival of a letter, that I had not kept my word."

She had protested strenuously, "I should never think that—but I am glad to be forewarned of the difficulties, else I may have thought that the letters had gone astray and been anxious. Now, I know I shall just have to be patient."

"Are you always so patient, Jessica?" he had asked, with some degree of amusement, to which she replied candidly, "Indeed, I am not. Not always, at any rate. I am patient when circumstances are so fixed, there is no help for it and nothing will change the situation. But I have to confess I am impatient when unnecessary obstacles arise; I am eager to learn and discover new ideas and long to see and experience what I have read. Yet it is often impossible. I am far from being patient about such matters."

"Such as?" he persisted.

"All sorts of things—things that excite my imagination, I suppose. I should love to feel the salt spray of the sea in a storm or the bustle of London streets, perhaps to walk those beautiful boulevardes of Paris with their elegant buildings and see the great works of art in their galleries. You and others have spoken of these things—I long to know how it feels to be there. Men are so very fortunate, to be able to travel and work where you please. I do envy you and I am impatient that we have not the same freedom."

Julian had seemed fascinated as he watched her eyes shine and heard her voice rise gently as she spoke. Clearly, Jessica was growing a little restless with the sheltered existence she led in Derbyshire, and he sensed a desire for something new and perhaps a little more exotic than her present life afforded her.

He understood her inclinations but was conscious of the need to be cautious in encouraging such yearnings. Remembering another young woman, whose desire to break out of the narrow confines that had circumscribed her life had led not to satisfaction and happiness as she had hoped, but disappointment and disaster, he had paused awhile before speaking.

His memories of Josie, still too fresh and painful, had made him somewhat more circumspect in his response. Reminding Jessica that she was young enough to look forward to all of those things she had mentioned, and many more experiences besides, in the years that lay ahead, he had said, "There will be time enough for you to enjoy all these experiences and more; I do not doubt that you will find time in your life to do so. Remember only, dear Jessica, that life is best enjoyed at leisure, without undue haste or desperation, with time for judgment and discrimination as well as enjoyment. We are not all blessed with the capacity of John Keats to drain life's cup to the lees in a single draught."

Surprised by his words and the quiet intensity with which they were spoken, Jessica had asked, "Do you merely advise me in a general sense against haste, or do your apprehensions arise from a perception that I am too bold in dreaming of discovering and experiencing what is new? Is it because you think I would act rashly in attempting to grasp what is outside my reach?" and her voice trembled a little, as though she had felt chastised.

He responded directly, "Certainly not. Your dreams are not too bold, far from it. What would we be if we did not dream, however impossible the goal? Much of my own work is built upon a dream that we may find something that is hidden from us; something that might change the lives of millions of people. I merely wished to remind you of the great gifts of youth and enthusiasm, which are yours, which I pray you will hold on to for many years, expending them sparingly and with care as you enjoy all that life will offer you in the future."

She looked unconvinced. "And do you really believe that my life lived here, in Derbyshire, is likely to hold such promise in the future?" she asked, with an astonishing degree of frankness that compelled his own reply to be equally honest.

"It could, but if it did not, it does not follow that you should remain all your life in Derbyshire. Jessica, our lives are circumscribed not by geographical boundaries, but by the limits of our minds and our capacity to persevere in pursuit of an ambition. There is no obligation that we should continue to live out our lives only in the place of our birth, is there?

"Nor is there any reason to suppose that your life will be so constrained— after all, mine was not. I was born and bred here and rarely left the county except to accompany my parents to London or Scarborough or some such place, until I went to Cambridge. Well, you see me now..."

"I do indeed, on the verge of a great adventure in the unknown depths of the African continent! A considerable transformation by any measure! Would that we might all aspire to such an exciting achievement," she declared, making him laugh and breaking the tension of the moment.

Postponing any further argument that she might have mounted, as they approached the entrance to Pemberley House, Jessica threw one last pebble into the pool of their discussion and waited for the ripples.

"If it had been at all possible, I should have wished very much to go to Africa with you," she said in a teasing kind of voice and was surprised when he said, quietly but very seriously, "If it had been possible, Jessica, I should have liked it too, very much."

When she turned to search his face, she saw not a trace of equivocation upon it. She had then to accept that he had meant every word.

That night Jessica recorded her thoughts in her diary, admitting to herself for the first time that she was falling in love with Julian Darcy.

There can be no other explanation for the way I feel—feelings of panic alternate with delight on each occasion that we meet, and I struggle to appear disengaged and untouched, when I am often filled with the strongest possible feelings of affection and pleasure, such as I have not known before.

Oh, how disadvantaged are women—a man may openly acknowledge his pleasure in a woman's company, admire her beauty, or pay her a compliment, without raising any criticism, but were a woman, especially one of my age, to betray such feelings, she would be immediately accused of lacking good manners and being deficient in decorum. We are pitiable creatures indeed.

⭒

On the afternoon before he was due to depart, Julian had been to see his sister Cassy and her family and say his farewells to young Anthony.

Returning to Pemberley, he had found Jessica in the sitting room, curled up on the couch in front of the fire, a rug over her feet. The weather had changed from mild to blustery, and Julian appreciated the welcoming warmth of the room. It was the place where they had been most companionable together over the last three weeks.

That afternoon, however, they seemed unable to steer the conversation away from the weather, almost as though it provided a safe haven from more personal waters, which could prove difficult to navigate.

Following several attempts, which had led nowhere, Jessica had fallen silent and sat gazing into the flames, when Julian had said, in a voice whose gravity was unmistakable, "Jessica, I owe you an apology. I cannot leave without saying how very sorry I am for having lectured you two days ago. It was quite arrogant of me—you must have thought me overbearing and patronising, and if I have offended or hurt you, please believe that it was unintentionally done and I am deeply sorry."

Completely astonished and unable to make an immediate response, Jessica remained silent and he, assuming her silence meant that he had been correct to suppose he had offended her, continued, "Perhaps if I were to explain, you may understand and find it easier to forgive my unpardonable presumption, in trying to instruct you on how you should conduct your life. I, who have made such a mess of my own, have no right to lecture you on such matters.

"But, if there is one excuse I might offer, in mitigation, it is that I have endured the most painful experience of watching one young woman, for whom I had the greatest affection, destroy her chance of happiness and finally her life itself in a wasteful expense of spirit. I have suffered for many agonising months, wondering if my inaction, my silence, my reluctance to interfere in her life, made me complicit in the tragedy that befell her and all our family. I have not acquitted myself as yet of that guilt and may never do so.

"She too was talented and lively, impatient to discover and grasp all that life had promised her, all she thought she was entitled to enjoy, but in her haste to do so, she fell into the trap that awaits the innocent and unwary and lost her way. Jessica, you know of whom I speak; pray try to understand my reasons for speaking to you as I did."

Jessica, who had listened with increasing astonishment, had risen from the couch and, throwing aside the rug, approached him, her hand outstretched. At first, too choked with emotion to speak, she had gradually found the words to reassure him, to say she had taken no offence, felt no anger or hurt; indeed she had been deeply touched by his concern and felt only gratitude.

"Julian, you must not believe that. It is not true. I was neither grieved nor angry and you certainly owe me no apology. I was touched by your concern and shall value your advice, always. As for your reason for speaking as you did, it speaks to me only of kindness, not arrogance or presumption. Pray do not waste another moment in disquiet or anxiety on that score, for there is no need."

When she had finished speaking, there were tears in her eyes and his relief was palpable. Taking both her hands in his, he had drawn her to him and held her in an embrace, as though she were a favourite child from whom he could receive the kind of instinctive comfort that words could not adequately impart. It had seemed the most natural thing to do.

When they moved apart, they did so without haste or awkwardness and nothing more was said between them. There was no further need for words. It seemed there was sufficient understanding and affection to fill the void.

~✦~

At dinner, they had been joined by Caroline and Colonel Fitzwilliam and their son David. The latter had kept Julian busy answering questions about his proposed journey to Africa. Later, Julian had retired to his room, citing his need to be awake early on the morrow, while the Fitzwilliams, always welcome guests at Pemberley, had stayed on awhile.

Despite her own preoccupations, Jessica had noticed that her cousin David had seemed unusually distracted that evening. Aware that he had recently decided against a military career, Jessica wondered if he was perhaps somewhat restless and discontented with his present role in the family's business at Manchester.

Jessica had often felt some sympathy for David, a pleasant and easygoing young man whose parents, bereft of their eldest son Edward when David was but a little boy, had been for many years inconsolable, leaving David and his sister Isabella to struggle on alone with their grief. While Isabella had found the inner strength to sublimate her own sorrow in work at the children's hospital, David, who had been sent off to boarding school, had grown more isolated from his family.

Jessica had often regarded her cousin with sisterly compassion, but the opportunity had never presented itself to do more than sympathise with his plight. David, like Jessica herself, was reserved and solitary by nature.

When the Fitzwilliams were leaving that night, however, he seemed to make a special effort to single her out, promising to call again before returning to Manchester later that week. Jessica had responded with sincerity.

"I shall look forward to that, David, I am always here in the afternoons—why don't you come to tea?"

"Thank you, I shall," he said, with a degree of alacrity that surprised her somewhat and then he was gone to join his parents in their carriage.

On the following day, Julian Darcy had risen early and left Pemberley to get the train to London.

Jessica ensured that she was not alone with him for long. She wanted to hold on to the memory of the previous afternoon and was determined that nothing should spoil it, which is why she had waited together with Mr and Mrs Darcy and Cassy, who had come to say her farewells to her brother and wish him Godspeed.

There was time only to say a quick good-bye and raise her hand to his lips, before he entered the carriage and was driven away.

That afternoon, as she sat rapt in quiet contemplation of the possible direction her life might be taking, there was a knock on the door of her sitting room and David Fitzwilliam was admitted. Jessica could not conceal her surprise—she had not expected he would take up her casual invitation to tea with such speed, and it was possible she had appeared taken aback at his appearance, which was a little informal, to say the least. He had plainly ridden over from Matlock, and it being a windy afternoon, he appeared somewhat dishevelled.

Sensing her discomposure, David apologised. "I am sorry, Jessie, clearly I have surprised you. I should have sent word; perhaps you would prefer me to go away and return tomorrow?" he asked awkwardly and quickly, as though trying to undo some *faux pas*, but Jessica, having already recovered her composure, came forward to welcome him and reassure him she was not at all put out by his arrival. Asking for tea to be sent up, she urged him to be seated and waited to learn the reason for this sudden visit, for she was sure there had to be one.

Sure enough, after some initial stumbling efforts at small talk, David came to what was plainly the purpose of his visit, although it took Jessica some little while to deduce the exact nature of his concern.

On the previous evening, they had, while at dinner, spoken of the work she did at the school at Pemberley, during which mention had been made briefly of a Miss Fenton, who had been governess to the younger children of Dr Richard and Cassandra Gardiner some years ago.

"I wish we had been able to persuade Miss Fenton to return to Derbyshire, she would have made an excellent teacher for the older girls," Jessica had said, "but Aunt Cassy tells me she is now settled in Manchester, with a family that likes her so well, they will not easily agree to let her go. Besides, I believe her niece Lucy Longhurst has found a position there as well, which must be very satisfactory for them."

Jessica had noticed then, that David had seemed well aware of the facts and had nodded agreeably and said, "I believe you are right. I am told that Miss Longhurst is preparing to be a teacher herself."

Jessica expressed much pleasure at this.

"Indeed? Well, if she follows her aunt's excellent example, she should do very well I'm sure. Miss Fenton has a remarkable reputation."

It was at this point in the conversation that Colonel Fitzwilliam, sitting across the table from them, had chimed in with the news that David was taking a closer interest in the business and would be moving to live in Manchester, where he planned to share accommodation with the new manager of the company, Mr Philip Bentley.

"They are getting to be good friends, David tells me, which is quite fortuitous, since David is keen to learn more of the work at the Manchester office. Caroline believes Mr Bentley will be an able teacher."

"He most certainly will. He has a wealth of experience in matters of commerce and trade, of which David has a lot to learn, now he has abandoned the cavalry!" said his mother.

"I certainly do," David agreed, adding, "It is exceedingly decent of Bentley to spend time on training me, but he has extracted a promise from me that in return, I will assist him with the housekeeping!"

At this revelation, everybody laughed and thereafter, the conversation had become fixed upon Mr Bentley, who, it was generally agreed, was proving to be an excellent manager.

Jessica recalled that she had not exchanged another word with David on the subject of Miss Fenton. Indeed, she had never discovered how it was that

David Fitzwilliam knew so much about the affairs of Miss Fenton and her niece, Lucy Longhurst.

That was until he had walked into her sitting room on the following day.

Returning to the subject of Miss Fenton, and more specifically to her niece Miss Lucinda Longhurst, who was engaged as a companion to two young ladies, the daughters of a Mr Winter, David confessed he wished to ask for his cousin's advice on a private matter of some delicacy.

"It is a matter on which I am sadly deficient in information and would very much appreciate your opinion," he said.

Jessica admitted to being surprised, but added she was proud to think he would believe that her advice might be more appropriate than that of his sister, Isabella.

"I would not trouble you, Jessie, but I think I am right in assuming that you, being closer to the age of the lady concerned than my sister, would have a far better notion of how she would respond," he explained and proceeded to ask, "In your opinion, how would a young lady in pleasant and gainful employment, preparing for a career in teaching, respond to an offer from an educated gentleman of good family, but with no visible means of support other than his income from shares in the family company?"

Jessica was astonished, not only by the directness of his approach, but also because it was a matter about which she'd had no previous warning whatsoever! Nothing he or anyone else had said or done before had allowed her to contemplate that David Fitzwilliam was about to propose marriage to Lucy Longhurst. Yet, there he was sitting in front of her, sipping tea and calmly discussing the proposition.

Jessica recalled Lucy Longhurst clearly. She had been quite young, maybe a year younger than herself, rather shy, studious, and very pretty. When her aunt Miss Fenton had brought her to stay with the Gardiners at Christmas and Easter, Lucy had joined the children in the Pemberley choir, and Jessica remembered her clear, lovely voice, which had lifted the quality of their singing to an entirely new plane. After a few moments silence, she asked, with a smile, "Lucy Longhurst, tell me, does she still sing as sweetly?"

"Like an angel," David replied without a moment's hesitation and added that she was the chief reason he attended church on Sundays.

"Jessie, she *is* an angel. I have met dozens of other young ladies but none to compare with her in gentleness of disposition, accomplishment, and education; what's more, she must be the loveliest girl I have ever seen."

Even allowing for his obvious partiality, this was high praise. David was either deeply stricken or very much in love, thought Jessica, regarding her cousin with some amazement.

If it was the first, it would probably pass in time, even if he were to be disappointed; if the second, well, that was much more serious and Jessica had little experience in handing out advice on such matters.

"How long have you had this determination to propose to the lady?" she asked, and David, predictably, bridled, thinking she was not taking him seriously, which in truth she was not inclined to do.

"Jessie, I met her almost a year ago at a ball in Derby, and though I was struck by how elegant and ladylike she had grown from the little girl we used to tease in church, I did not seriously believe she would be interested in me. Anyway, I was still trying to get into the cavalry and had little time for young ladies. However, this year, since I have been in Manchester, we have met on several occasions—usually by chance but occasionally by some judicious planning on my part—and each time, I felt she paid me great courtesy and attention. The Winters are friends of Mr Bentley, and we are often asked to dine with them.

"Just last week, we were invited to dinner at the home of a mutual friend, who had also asked Misses Deborah and Sarah Winter. Miss Longhurst was there with them, and I was privileged to spend an hour or more in her company, while the others played a game of whist. I am now convinced she is the one girl I wish to marry, if she will accept me. Will she, Jessie?" he asked, and there was such a plea for hope in his voice, Jessica relented and decided to be kind.

"David, I cannot speak for Lucy Longhurst, I would not be able to predict what her response may be to your proposal, because I have no means to discover what her aspirations are in life. You say she is happily employed with the Winters, I believe her aunt Miss Fenton is there too as governess to the two younger children, and I understand Lucy is preparing to be a teacher. Putting all those facts together, I would say that in normal circumstances, such a young lady may think twice about accepting an offer from a gentleman who has no fixed occupation or estate."

Then seeing the look of sheer devastation upon his countenance, she added, "But, if she loved you and if you could persuade her that your interest in the business at Manchester is likely to lead to a more permanent position in the company, with the hope of advancement in the future, then even a happily situated young lady like Miss Longhurst may be persuaded that your suit was worth considering."

And as a smile suddenly lit up his face, she said, "Besides, David, you are educated and handsome and your parents are the best regarded family, outside of Pemberley, in the county. If I were Miss Lucy Longhurst, I would certainly not be refusing you."

It was a piece of friendly impertinence, which surprised him.

"Would you not?" he asked, eyebrows raised.

Jessica smiled; he must know she was teasing.

"No, but, David, I am not Lucy Longhurst..." she began and he interrupted, "Of course not, and I am not Julian Darcy!"

Jessica held her breath and in that second, he smiled and looked rather nervous, letting her see that he knew something of her secret. Then, as they both dissolved into laughter, it became clear that they had unwittingly exchanged confidences, which neither wished to reveal to the rest of their family at this time.

"I hope I can depend upon you to say no more on that subject, David?" said Jessica, and the quiet, serious tone of her voice convinced him he had been right.

"Of course you can—my lips are sealed."

"And mine—except to wish you every success."

He rose then and kissed her cheek and said very quietly in her ear, "If I am, you shall be the first to know, Jessie. Thank you and may I wish you every happiness too."

Jessica bowed, acknowledging his words, but said nothing.

It had been a week of surprises, and mostly they had been pleasant ones.

But, sadly, the same could not be said of events that followed later that year. Amidst the chill Winter darkness of the coal pits of South Wales, Dr Henry Forrester, the husband of David's sister Isabella, succumbed to a putrid fever, believed to be typhus.

A relentless campaigner for the improvement of health care and sanitation for the poor, he had gone to Wales to work with the Reverend Jenkins, helping the children of the pit villages survive the appalling insanitary conditions in which many were condemned to live out their often short and joyless lives.

He had been engaged in a very worthwhile project, yet, after only a short period of hard work, Henry Forrester himself had become infected with typhus—probably carried by the lice on the children he treated.

The suddenness of the blow had left Isabella a stunned and grieving widow and her family dismayed by the injustice of it all.

Jessica could hardly believe that in so short a time their family had suffered two such tragic losses; first young Josie then Dr Forrester, closing the year as it had begun—with woeful, untimely death.

Unwilling to speak of her fears to anyone, she wrote in her diary:

If those who try to help them die also, who will be left to tend the poor and the sick? What unknown dangers will Julian face in his quest for new cures for dreaded diseases? I dare not think. All I know is I am very afraid.

Chapter Two

I T MAY HAVE BEEN surprising to some that Mr Darcy Gardiner was almost
as well known and equally as well regarded in Derbyshire, particularly in
the districts around the estate of Pemberley, as was the owner of that great
estate, his grandfather Mr Fitzwilliam Darcy, after whom young Mr Gardiner
was named.

They may have been even more surprised to learn that young Darcy
Gardiner was no less respected at Westminster, where he had several friends
among the parties of the Whigs and Liberals, who would have had no trouble recommending him, despite his relative youth, for a seat in the House
of Commons.

To be involved in the political life of the nation, to debate the policies of
a government, to become a member of the British Parliament, had for years
been the pinnacle of Darcy Gardiner's ambitions, in pursuance of which he had
worked assiduously to understand, explain, and promote the ideas that had fired
his enthusiasm from a very early age.

"It is not good enough that Britain is rich and powerful, that her ships carry
her goods to every continent and corner of the earth and her Treasury is full
from the proceeds; I believe she must also regain her reputation for justice and
fairness for all her people, nurturing and educating every child and listening to

the voice of every man and woman in the land," he had declared, while campaigning for the reform program of his hero Mr Gladstone.

It was a stirring speech that had earned him the applause of many and special notice from the leader himself. Many of those who knew him well and had observed him over the years had assumed he would stand for Parliament, at the earliest opportunity.

That had been in the Autumn of 1865.

A great deal had happened since then, at Westminster and in the family of which Darcy Gardiner was a member. His parents, Sir Richard and Lady Gardiner, were proud of their son, who had been recently appointed to manage the Pemberley estate. His mother Cassandra knew that her favourite son, though occasionally restless for the city, was both conscious of his duty and devoted to his family. Well educated, handsome enough to be attractive without arousing envy, and generally respected for his honesty and intelligence, Darcy Gardiner at twenty-six years of age was surely one of the most eligible young men in the county. His family certainly thought so.

Yet, to the chagrin of about half a dozen anxious mothers with daughters of marriageable age, the subject of matrimony seemed to be farthest from his thoughts. Indeed, while he was unfailingly polite and attended the balls and parties at which he was introduced to several eligible young ladies, none had ever reported that he had paid them anything more than friendly attention and courtesy.

He danced with all of them and complimented them upon their performance at the pianoforté or the harp and had even been known to sing a duet with one or two of them.

But, none of the ladies had ever felt he had shown a deeper interest, which might signify a special partiality. He was gallant, behaving with perfect decorum at all times, but was seemingly unwilling to be drawn into any situation which had the merest suggestion of intimacy or flirtation.

His sister, Lizzie Carr, who had observed this phenomenon for a while, was concerned. Her fondness for the younger of her two brothers led her to take a special interest in him and, while she was generally satisfied that Darcy had developed into a particularly pleasing and amiable gentleman, who carried out both his familial and social obligations in an exemplary fashion, she had to confess she was somewhat anxious about his future happiness on account of his continued single state.

Since her marriage, Lizzie had felt sufficiently qualified to take her brother to task, if only in the gentlest possible way. The opportunity arose when he called to see her husband at their home, Rushmore Farm, and since Mr Carr was away at a yearling sale, Darcy stayed to take tea and keep his sister company awhile.

They were walking in the grounds together when with very little warning, Lizzie said, "Darcy, you must forgive my question, but it is only my affection and concern that makes me ask. Have you no wish to settle down at all?"

Her question, coming with no prior notice of such concern, seemed to take him completely by surprise. He stopped and stood silent a moment before resuming their walk, and it was only after a further pause of a minute or two, during which his sister feared she had offended him, that he said, "Lizzie, that is a most unusual question. May I counter with another? Would you reveal what has prompted you to ask it? Has Mama or perhaps my grandmother expressed some anxiety about the matter?"

He seemed quite genuinely puzzled, and Lizzie, though relieved she had not angered him, was cautious in her response.

"No indeed, Darcy, I cannot know whether they have been concerned since neither has mentioned the matter to me. I ask only because I have wondered whether you had not given it some consideration—after all, you are twenty-six and..."

He interrupted her with a teasing laugh, concluding her sentence, "...and will soon be an aging bachelor with a reputation for being rather pernickety and difficult to please? Is that what you fear for me, Lizzie?"

Lizzie was pleased to be able to lighten the tone of their conversation. "Now you are teasing me. Of course I do not believe any such thing, but I did think and even hoped last Summer that you showed some interest in Miss Teresa Marchant. Perhaps I was wrong and it was not your real inclination; it is no matter."

The lady in question had been introduced to their family by their brother Edward's wife, Angela, who had certainly promoted the advantages of her friend. The daughter of a surgeon, Miss Marchant, who was both handsome and wealthy, had proved very popular at parties and picnics through the Summer. For a little while then, Lizzie had believed that Darcy may have been attracted, too—they had appeared to get on well together.

Her brother smiled. "Miss Marchant is certainly charming and pretty, but, Lizzie, apart from her talent for learning all the newest dance steps and painting innumerable pictures of pastoral scenes, there was little to recommend her as a wife for a fellow like me. She has very little knowledge of the predicament of the poor in our community and no understanding at all of the processes of politics. When I had finished admiring her art and needlepoint and she had told me how much she liked Tennyson's verse, we would have soon run out of intelligent conversation, not to mention space on the walls to hang her water colours, of which she is quite understandably proud."

Despite the lightness of his tone, Lizzie understood his reservations. "Darcy, you mean she has no interest in public affairs, do you not? Because that is where your heart lies; you do not wish to be involved with someone who does not share your passion for it?" Lizzie asked, looking up at his face.

Darcy was unabashed. "Do you blame me, Lizzie? I have never hidden my enthusiasm for it and I confess, I do still harbour some ambition to return to Westminster in the future, though that would depend upon the wishes of my grandfather and the political fortunes of Mr Gladstone. It will always be my hope that I may one day enter the Commons to support Mr Gladstone's Reformist government. I have no other obvious talents and no profession.

"But, Lizzie, consider this, a partner who has no interest in the concerns that I take so seriously, whose life is centred around purely domestic and artistic matters, would soon lose patience with me. Let us never forget the tragic consequences of the marriage of Jonathan Bingley and Amelia-Jane Collins and the manner in which a similar situation was the cause of so much misery."

Not wishing to appear unfair to Miss Marchant, he added, "I do not mean to suggest that Teresa Marchant is deficient in any of the standards that are usually applied to young ladies; merely to explain why she would not be happy married to me nor I to her. Besides, I am in no danger at all of falling in love with her, so the question does not arise."

"Indeed, it does not," replied Lizzie quickly. "I would not have you marry anyone, however suitable or well connected, whom you could not love as deeply as I do my own dear husband. To marry without love would be inconceivable."

Darcy's hand tightened upon hers as he said quietly, "Exactly so, Lizzie. Such a proposition would be utterly abhorrent to me. I knew you would understand."

His voice was grave and left Lizzie in no doubt of the sincerity and seriousness of his words. She was silent, unable to find the right words to continue, when Darcy, sensitive to her change of mood, attempted to reassure her, saying in a lighter tone than before, "You must not be too anxious about me, Lizzie. I am grateful for your concern and I know it flows from your affection for me. Our brother Edward has been so much better at finding a suitable bride, he must be a source of great satisfaction to you and Mama. I am sorry I have not been more accommodating. But, let me assure you, when I do find the lady of my dreams and she accepts me, you will be the very first to know."

They laughed together and turned at the end of the path, intending to return to the house, and as they did so, saw approaching Lizzie's husband, Mr Michael Carr. The two men had been firm friends for some years before Mr Carr had met Lizzie and lost his heart. The marriage of his sister to his friend had delighted Darcy, even though he had done nothing directly to secure the outcome. The two men greeted each other with warmth and pleasure.

"It's good to see you, Darcy, I had no idea you were coming over today," said Mr Carr, as they shook hands.

"I had business in Matlock and called in to see you and Lizzie," Darcy explained as they walked together towards the house.

Mr Michael Carr, an Irish-American gentleman with a deep love of England and an interest in horse breeding, had, over a few years, become Darcy Gardiner's closest friend. He knew more than most people his friend's thoughts and hopes and even some of the disappointments that had beset his young life. While he did not always burden his wife with such matters, Michael Carr was her brother's trusted confidante.

They were close enough, the three of them, for Lizzie to say in a playful tone of voice, as he took her hand, holding it in his as they retraced their steps, "Dearest, I have been reproaching my brother about his apparent unwillingness to fall in love with a young lady good enough to be his wife. You must speak to him, for he will not take me seriously."

She spoke in jest and hardly expected to receive a serious response, which was why Lizzie was surprised by the sudden change in the expression that crossed her husband's countenance and the swiftness with which he turned to regard Darcy.

Almost as though he sought to shield his young brother-in-law from some embarrassment, he laughed and then swung the conversation around to the yearling sales from which he had just returned. Darcy too was quick to respond, asking with exaggerated eagerness about the horses—a subject in which he generally showed little interest.

They were neither of them quick enough, however, to conceal from Lizzie their keenness to change the subject.

When the two gentlemen had concluded their discussions and Darcy had departed, her keen observation of their mutual desire to avoid the subject of her brother's matrimonial prospects led Lizzie to pose a more direct question to her husband.

"Dearest, would I be wrong in thinking that my brother has some secret of which you are aware and I am not?" she asked innocently and her husband was so taken aback that he was momentarily lost for words.

Then, seeing her regarding him with a very quizzical expression, one he knew would soon lead to even more questions, he said, "Why, Lizzie, my dear, what sort of secret would I have with your brother that you could not share?"

Lizzie shrugged her shoulders and said with a degree of insouciance that was more calculated than spontaneous, "Well, it may be that he is in love and does not want us all to know lest we tease him about it. Am I right? Is that it?" Then, seeing a look of utter consternation upon her husband's face, she went to him and said, "It would not matter, except that if I knew the lady, I might be able to help. On the other hand, if I were to be kept in the dark and being ignorant made some embarrassing *faux pas*, it could cause him a great deal of grief, could it not?"

Lizzie sounded very convincing.

Mr Carr was at a loss to know how to deal with this utterly unexpected situation. What he knew of his brother-in-law's particular circumstances had been told him in confidence, and Darcy had begged him to speak of the matter to no one.

"Especially not Lizzie, because she will feel bound to tell Mama, and then my grandmother would know, and soon enough all of Pemberley will be talking about it. I could not bear that, and it would be most unfair to the lady," Darcy had said, swearing him to secrecy.

Yet, now Mr Carr knew with absolute certainty that unless he told her something of the truth, to satisfy her curiosity, Lizzie would wheedle it out of him over the hours, days, and nights that followed, until it was all known. Better, he thought, to involve her in the secret pact he had with her brother and ensure she said nothing to him or anyone else.

He spoke rather hesitantly and with a degree of gravity that was unusual between them. Lizzie was at first surprised by the seriousness of his tone, "Dearest, if I tell you, you must give me your solemn promise never to say a word to anyone, not to your mama or your cousins and especially not to Mr and Mrs Darcy. Your brother must never know that I have told you—indeed, I would not have, except I do realise the danger of your saying something in ignorance which may have quite unforeseen consequences. Will you promise me, Lizzie?"

By now Lizzie was speechless, astounded by the response that her teasing remark had elicited. She had only half believed what she had said about her brother being in love, yet now here she was drawn into sharing his secret!

She could not begin to imagine what revelation was to follow.

She nodded and said very softly, "Of course, I promise. No one shall ever know."

They were in their bedroom and it was almost the time when the servant came in to light the fire. Mr Carr went to the door and locked it. It would ensure they would not be disturbed.

In the next hour, as Lizzie listened with increasing astonishment, he recounted the story her brother had divulged to him some months ago. He did not dwell too long upon the details of how it had all come about, saying he was certain that Darcy would, one day, confide in her himself.

"When he does, you must not betray the fact that you already have some knowledge of this matter; if you do, Lizzie, your brother's trust in me as a friend and confidante will be totally destroyed," he said and once again, she solemnly gave him her word that her brother would never know.

As it was told, Lizzie could not help feeling some degree of guilt at having forced her husband to break his promise to Darcy.

"I would not have pressed you about it, if it were only a question of idle curiosity," she explained, attempting to convince herself as well as her husband of her motives. "Indeed, had you refused to tell me, I should have accepted your decision and asked no more. But I could see that there was something that troubled my brother; there is a look of gravity, even a little melancholy about him, which is unusual. I have thought it was the result of other disappointments—in politics, perhaps. I know he had hopes of seeing Mr Gladstone become Prime Minister and was very unhappy when he did not. But I had not thought it possible that he should be crossed in love."

By this time, Lizzie was looking so distressed that her husband had to reassure her that her brother was not in any danger of going into a decline as a consequence of his unhappy experience, although he did admit that Darcy had been extremely dejected at the time.

"When he told me of it, I think he did so because he needed desperately to talk to a friend he could trust. Clearly, he did not wish to reveal the matter to his family; besides, I gather he gave the lady his word that he would not, since it would have entailed explanations that may have compromised her. He was in the unfortunate position of a man who must bear his own disappointment alone, because to speak of it would be to betray another's secret. It was a difficult and painful time for him."

"Poor Darcy," said Lizzie, still close to tears, "how is it possible for someone so universally loved to fall in love with the one woman who will not have him? It must have been a grievous blow. Does he still love her, do you think?" she asked.

"Perhaps he does," said Mr Carr, adding, "but I do believe he has since made some progress in gaining control of his feelings. He no longer suffers each time they meet, and I understand their present association is as between two good friends. Darcy speaks very highly of the lady and assures me that she has behaved at all times with the utmost care and consideration towards him, being particular to avoid situations in which he may be embarrassed or pained by her presence."

"I can well believe that," said Lizzie, "but I cannot help feeling for him. My brother is the kind of person who will suffer in silence rather than betray a confidence. What must he have gone through all these months? I wish he had spoken of it to me, I may have been able to offer some comfort as a sister; now I must remain silent and pretend I know nothing of his disappointment. It is so unfair!"

Afraid that his wife would indulge her sorrow to the point of becoming depressed, which, in her condition, would not have done at all, Mr Carr looked for a way to lighten her mood.

"Lizzie my love, do not worry on that score. Your brother's general disposition is strong and resilient, able to overcome disappointment with little or no permanent scars. You may depend on me to help him in every way I can and to keep you informed of his progress.

"Perhaps, one day in the future, when he falls in love and weds another young lady, one who will welcome his attentions, we may recall this time and smile that we took it all so seriously."

Lizzie was not at first easy to convince, but her husband, whose devotion to her was unqualified, could always rescue her from a melancholy mood and did so, quite successfully, on that occasion too.

The warmth and sincerity of his love had sustained her before in the midst of crises and would do so again. Before long, she relaxed and agreed with him that her brother was unlikely to suffer permanent damage.

"Darcy is too sensible and well disposed towards the world to be embittered by disappointment," she said. She was persuaded, also, that she need feel no guilt about enjoying what was their moment of deepest happiness, as they anticipated the arrival of their first child. One quite positive consequence had come about, following her husband's revelations. Though she continued to be concerned about her brother's future, Lizzie resolved never again to tease or scold him about his lack of interest in the eligible young women of the district. Darcy would be relieved, she was sure of it.

Darcy Gardiner, though he knew nothing of the reason for this relief, would, in the coming months, be very grateful indeed.

There were, he believed, very good reasons for not revealing to his sister, or any other member of his family, certain matters involving a young lady of their acquaintance. Lizzie's teasing remarks about his single state, however lightly made, had caused him some disquiet, and he had been glad of his brother-in-law's discretion in helping to extricate him from the situation in which he had found himself.

His friend, Michael Carr, was the only person who knew the truth and even he did not know the whole of it.

❦

Recalling with some chagrin the unhappy episode which had taken place some months ago, Darcy Gardiner could not avoid a feeling of dejection. His friend had found him then in just such a mood, when the two men had met at the inn, whither Darcy had gone to be alone and had confided in Mr Carr, having first sworn him to secrecy.

"Michael, I must have your word that nothing of this will ever be revealed to anyone else; I should not have spoken of it even to you, except as you can see, I have been so downcast, I had need of a friend I could trust, in whom I could confide. But you must promise me the lady's name will never pass your lips. I ask it chiefly on her account, rather than my own."

Eager to assuage his friend's undeniable disappointment, Mr Carr had promptly obliged, promising secrecy even as he wondered at the depth of young Darcy's attachment to the lady in question. He did not know her very well, but from the extent of their short acquaintance, he would not have judged that she was the type of person likely to attract the romantic interest of his brother-in-law.

There was, however, no doubting Darcy's distress at being rejected by her, and Mr Carr had listened very attentively and sought to ameliorate his condition with encouraging words and the suggestion that the young lady may perhaps be persuaded to reconsider her refusal of his offer, if applied to again at a later, more appropriate time.

But Darcy had been quite adamant. "No, Michael, she will not. I cannot say more for fear of compromising her, but she has assured me that she cannot change her mind, because her heart is already given to another. So you see, it is quite hopeless."

Which is all he was prepared to tell Mr Carr, and having begged him once more never to reveal his secret, he had departed and taken himself home in an extraordinary state of despondency.

Chapter Three

C OMING AWAY FROM RUSHMORE Farm, with the setting sun filling the meadows with pools of light and shadow, Darcy Gardiner could not avoid reliving that unhappy episode. His sister's teasing words had brought it back to the surface, and he recalled it as if it had been yesterday.

It had been an evening very much like this one, some weeks after his sister Lizzie's wedding. The couple had not as yet returned from their wedding journey and Darcy had been busy, keeping a promise to his brother-in-law that he would watch over the management of the Rushmore Farm and Stud in their absence.

Returning to Pemberley, having spent the afternoon at the farm, he had surrendered his horse to the groom who had accompanied him to Rushmore Farm. It had been a particularly fine day, and Darcy had decided to take a walk through the park to Pemberley, not expecting to meet anyone else there at that hour.

It was already late afternoon and the sun was warm upon his back as he traversed the woods, alive with birdsong and filled with the scents of Spring. The very day, he thought, for a quiet walk during which he could think upon some aspects of his future life. Recently, he had begun to think about matters other than politics and the fortunes of Mr Gladstone, which had rated very high on his list of priorities the previous year.

As manager of the Pemberley estate, he had been successful, at least in satisfying the concerns of their tenants and, more importantly, pleasing his grandfather Mr Darcy, who was a very meticulous employer. It was a source of some satisfaction to him that his grandfather had accepted his advice on matters affecting the diversification of crops on the estate, which had proved to be quite profitable.

As he strode along the path winding through the great trees arching overhead, he heard the voices of young women, two at least, and they seemed to be approaching. He slowed his steps as they came nearer and then realised it was Jessica Courtney and another young person—Nellie, eldest of the rector's daughters.

They seemed to be in very good humour, and Jessica appeared especially happy; he heard her laugh ring out as they crossed the footbridge and entered the park. She had a pretty, infectious laugh, which always made him smile. They walked towards him, then, seeing him, they stopped.

Jessica spoke first, "Why, Darcy, what a surprise. I had understood that you were away today at Rushmore Farm."

He explained that he had been at the farm in the absence of his brother-in-law Mr Carr. "Finding everything in order, I decided to return earlier than expected."

"Did you walk all the way from Rushmore?" she asked, and he explained again, "No, I rode over, but it is such a beautiful day, I could not resist the prospect of a walk through the park."

Jessica agreed, "Nellie and I were saying much the same thing; it has been wonderful weather," and he noticed as she spoke how her eyes shone and the sun on her skin made it glow. She was wearing a new gown of fine soft cotton in a pretty peach colour, which enhanced her complexion, and he could not take his eyes off her.

Striving to be polite and natural, he asked, "And are you ladies going to Pemberley, too?" to which Jessica replied, "I am, but Nellie is returning to the rectory. We have been to the hospital at Littleford to see a patient—one of the boys at the school had a nasty fall and cut his knee," she explained.

Darcy was solicitous. "I am sorry; he is on the mend, I hope? No broken bones?"

"No, none, but he is bruised and shaken by his unhappy experience and feeling very sore. I doubt he will attempt to climb upon the roof of the church again!" she replied, and they laughed together.

They had reached a fork in the road, where Nellie said good-bye and took the path, which led to the rectory, leaving them to walk on towards Pemberley.

Engaged in the usual casual exchanges about one thing and another, they had not gone far and were passing through a grove of elms, which sheltered them from the sun and concealed their presence from anyone at the house looking out across the park.

Jessica had been recounting for Darcy's entertainment a story about Mr Hurst, the new schoolmaster, and one of the students. A young boy from Lambton, having learnt of the work of Charles Darwin, had told his father about his great voyage to the Galapagos Islands.

"And Mr Hurst was horrified to discover that the boy's father had threatened to beat him if he ever mentioned Mr Darwin in the house again, 'because he were an evil Godless man and taught that us and the monkeys is brothers, sir!'" she had said, mimicking the little boy's voice.

Darcy could not help but laugh with her, and Jessica was still laughing, about to continue with her story, when suddenly, unaccountably, he had stopped and turning to her said, "Dearest Jessica, I should like very much to say something, which I want you to hear, and I must beg you to listen, please."

Her astonishment had been plain to see, as she looked at him in some confusion, unable at first to understand the import of his words, unwilling perhaps to believe what must surely have been obvious—that Darcy Gardiner was about to propose to her in the middle of Pemberley Park. She said not a word, standing quite still, too surprised to speak.

He had reached for her hand, begged her pardon for surprising her in this manner, and then, in the clearest way possible, declared that he loved her dearly and asked if she would agree to marry him.

Jessica's initial surprise had by now turned to complete amazement.

"Darcy," she had said, "please forgive me, I do not at all mean to sound facetious, but is this not a little sudden? We have known one another all our lives and been friends for years, but never before have you hinted or shown in any way at all a particular partiality for me. I do not mean to suggest that I am not honoured by your proposal, but may I ask, please, what has brought you to this sudden declaration?"

Except to reiterate in even more ardent terms his love for her, Darcy gave no reason for the suddenness of his approach.

He was still holding her hand, and as they stood there amongst the trees in dappled sunlight, he looked startlingly handsome and yet uncertain and vulnerable. Jessica wondered at his impetuousness. She could not understand it. It was not like him at all. Even though she had always enjoyed the openness and energy that marked all his dealings, rashness had not been a character trait she had associated with him. She liked him and had no wish to hurt him. She was puzzled and not a little troubled by this development and wished with all her heart it had not occurred.

Darcy Gardiner was without doubt a most eligible young man and one of the most agreeable of her acquaintance. That she could not deny. In other circumstances, there was no knowing if she may have been persuaded to consider his proposal more favourably. But, on that perfect spring day, Jessica was in no state to consider the advances of any gentleman, no matter how eligible or agreeable he may be. Although he could not have known it, Darcy had probably picked the very worst day of all to propose to Jessica.

On that morning, the post had brought her a letter from Julian Darcy. Sent from London, shortly before embarking for France, it had so lifted her spirits and enhanced her hopes, that marriage to any other man was the last thing she could contemplate. Indeed, she had carried it with her all day and could scarcely wait to get home and read it again.

Julian's handwriting, not very elegant at the best of times, was difficult to read. He had plainly written the letter in haste, prior to his departure for France. Yet, even this was to Jessica an advantage, since it gave her a good reason to linger over each line and read it over again, more carefully than before, savouring every one for the sentiments it conveyed.

He wrote:

> *Dearest Jessica,*
>
> *It would be quite useless for me to pretend that I could leave England for France and proceed to Africa thereafter, without telling you how I feel. If I did, I should neither sleep nor concentrate upon my work over the next few months.*
>
> *I do not know, because I was too afraid to ask, if you had been sensible of my growing fondness for you and if you were aware that your friendship meant so much to me. I hoped you had, for had you appeared indifferent, my spirits would have been low indeed.*

"Oh yes," she said softly, "but I thought that was all it was. I too was afraid even to think there was more than simple friendship between us."

I should have spoken sooner, whilst we were together at Pemberley, except that it would not have been seemly. I think both our families may have looked askance at any proposition that seemed to come too soon after Josie's tragic death, and I am almost certain it would not have made you happy either.

I shall not be other than honest with you, Jessica; so let me admit that I did try, on first becoming aware of my feelings for you, to suppress them, to tell myself you would not care for someone like me, that I was too old or too dull for you, and then, when it seemed you might, I tried to explain it away as the natural affection between two people who had known one another since childhood and had become good friends.

But, increasingly, I have come to the realisation that in truth I love you dearly, Jessica, and must acknowledge it before I leave for France tomorrow morning.

At this admission, Jessica had been unable to read further, as tears of joy had filled her eyes and she had to put the letter away until she could compose herself. When she did so and read on, there was more to delight her.

I hope, my dearest Jessica, that I am not being presumptuous in believing that those tender affections I have detected are similar to mine and will allow you to accept and return my love.

I leave for France tomorrow and thence to Africa within the fortnight. If all goes well with our journey and our plans are accomplished and I return safe to England as I hope and pray I will...

(at which Jessica stopped reading and closed her eyes to add her prayers to his)

...I shall, on my return to Pemberley, ask you to be my wife.

If you accept, it will make me happier than I have been in all my life so far, and I shall promise to do everything I can to ensure your continuing happiness for as long as I live, including the fulfillment of those very special dreams we spoke of recently.

Meanwhile, may I ask that you keep our secret, for I should prefer that it did not become the subject of gossip between our families and friends.

Only send me word—just a line or two will suffice to set my heart at rest—that I do not hope in vain.

I shall count the days and months until we meet.

Till then, God bless you,

Julian Darcy.

And below he had given her the address in Paris to which she could send a letter. He expected to remain there a fortnight, before leaving for Africa.

⁓❦⁓

Throughout the morning, which Jessica had spent at the school and later with Nellie, visiting the boy at Littleford hospital, the letter had lain in the pocket of her gown as she went about her work.

From time to time, she would touch it as if it were a talisman, and when she had a moment to spare and was certain she would be undisturbed, she had taken it out and perused it again, to renew the joy she had felt on receiving and reading it.

As she and Nellie had made their way home that afternoon, she had looked forward to the moment when she could go to her room and read it once more, enjoying in private the pleasure it gave her, before composing the reply Julian was waiting for. Walking through the park, she had hardly heard Nellie's chatter; she had been busy fashioning in her mind the lines she intended to write.

"Only send me word," he had said, and she had intended to do just that, as soon as she had returned to Pemberley and could put pen to paper.

She had hoped it would tell him what he wished to know, and she had decided she would send it by express on the following morning.

She had been pre-occupied also with the vexing problem of getting it to the mail without the servants at Pemberley seeing the address, when suddenly, Darcy Gardiner had appeared on the path in front of them.

At first, she had wanted only to be rid of him, wishing above all to get back to Pemberley and write her letter. She feared that a delay may mean that her letter may not reach Julian before he left Paris and he would go to Africa, believing that she cared nothing for him. It was therefore with some degree of impatience that she had first responded to his totally unexpected proposition.

But Jessica was nothing if she was not tender-hearted. When she had said, "Darcy, you are very kind and I thank you for your proposal, but I cannot marry you," she saw the pain upon his face, and when he asked, "Why, Jessica, may I ask for a reason? Have we not always been friends?" his eyes had betrayed the sense of shock and confusion he obviously felt at her rejection. Clearly he had not expected this response.

Jessica, unhappy to cause him so much hurt, had struggled to explain. "We certainly have been good friends, and I have only warm and affectionate feelings for you. It is not that I do not respect and admire you, Darcy, but oh dear, this is too difficult for me... I do not wish to mislead you, yet I am not free to tell you the reason... in any detail..." she concluded rather lamely, and he was utterly perplexed.

"Not free? Jessica, what does this mean? Could it be... Have I understood you correctly? Are you secretly engaged to someone else? If that were the case, I should not press you, it would not be right or fair..."

He was clearly taken aback, yet she surprised him even more, when she replied, "No, Darcy, I am not secretly engaged, but you are right; there is someone else I love, and while there is no engagement at present, there is a possibility, indeed a very strong possibility, that we may be engaged in the future."

Darcy had stepped back to look at her as she spoke. If he had been surprised at being rejected and astonished to hear there was someone else she loved of whom he knew nothing, he was truly perturbed to hear her say there was no engagement, yet she had hopes of one eventuating in the future.

He had seen and heard of too many such situations to be sanguine about it. He had known of young women who had waited years for some man, who had promised to marry them and never returned to keep his promise. He was deeply concerned lest Jessica had fallen in love with some such heartless blackguard, though he could not recall anyone of their acquaintance who might fit the role.

When he spoke, he tried hard not to sound pompous and self-important. Rather it was with sincere concern that he asked, "And if you cannot tell me who he is, will you at least say if he is from the district or does he come from Derby or London?"

Jessica seemed a little unsettled by the question, causing him to say, "Forgive me, Jessica; I ask not out of idle curiosity, but only because I have heard of young ladies who have been deceived by fellows—London toffs—who never intended to keep their word. I am sure you would not fall in love with such a man, yet I am concerned…"

She interrupted him, but spoke gently, "You are right, Darcy. I would not fall in love with such a person. This man is no London toff, I assure you. However, I am conscious of the kindness that prompts your concern for me, so although it is not my secret alone, I *shall* tell you, to set your mind at rest. He is your uncle, Mr Julian Darcy."

Then seeing the look of complete amazement upon his face, she continued, "There, I should not have revealed his name, but I had to say it, else you would have been convinced that I was about to do something stupid and perhaps told your mama, and she would have told cousin Lizzie, and there would have been a great to-do over it. I hope now that you know the truth, you will be satisfied that I am not about to throw myself into the power of some perfidious scoundrel!"

Darcy had been silent, still unable to comprehend how this had come about. The surprise had temporarily blotted out his own disappointment and uncharacteristically, he had been lost for words.

Finally, he stammered, "Jessica, what can I say? I knew nothing of this, else I should not have dreamed of imposing myself upon you. I am truly sorry if I have offended or embarrassed you…"

Her compassionate heart would not let him take the blame. Placing her hand upon his arm, she said, "Darcy, please do not apologise—you did nothing wrong and I am not offended. You were not to know and there was not the slightest trace of presumption or arrogance in your approach to me. Indeed, I am not unconscious of the honour and I thank you again for your offer, but I hope you will understand when I say that Julian and I have been falling in love over the last few months. It came upon us so gradually, we scarcely knew it ourselves, until a few days ago, when he was preparing to leave.

"For myself, I can truly say I have not felt such a strong attachment for anyone in my life. It will be obvious to you that after the dire circumstances of last year, we could not let it be generally known now, at least not for a few more months. I have received a letter from him today, in which he declares his feelings and the hope that we may be engaged when he returns from Africa."

She smiled then and said in a lighter tone, "There, you are the very first to know. I have told no one else our secret."

At this, young Darcy Gardiner, despite his disappointment, could only offer his heartfelt congratulations and wish them every happiness.

Jessica then extracted from him a solemn promise that he would tell no one until Julian returned and their engagement was revealed to the family.

"It would preserve us from the gossip and rumour which will start should even the smallest hint of it be known. Please keep our secret as I will keep yours. No one shall ever know of our conversation this afternoon, not even Julian, I promise. We have been friends for long enough to keep each other's secrets, have we not?" she asked, and he was adamant that no one should ever learn of her secret from him.

"Indeed, and you may be assured of my absolute secrecy. But let me be the first to wish you and Julian the deepest and most lasting happiness. I know no two people more deserving of it," he said, his voice decidedly lighter than his heart.

As they reached the entrance to Pemberley House, they noticed that the Bingleys' carriage was standing in the drive, and Jessica remembered that Jonathan Bingley and his wife, Anna, were visiting his parents, and the entire party were dining at Pemberley that evening.

Turning to Darcy, she said in a whisper, "I have a letter to write that must go tomorrow morning. Will you be so kind as to make my excuses and tell Mrs Darcy I shall join them at dinner?"

So saying, she slipped away through the rose garden and up the steps leading to the private apartments, leaving him to enter the saloon and make her excuses to Elizabeth, before making his own excuses and withdrawing to dress for dinner.

The presence of Jonathan and Anna Bingley greatly eased the strain upon Darcy Gardiner and Jessica that evening. While Anna Bingley and Elizabeth had a great deal to talk about, Jessica obliged the party with some music on the pianoforte. She had, while Julian was staying at Pemberley, played for him often and enjoyed reliving the pleasure of those times, playing the same compositions he had chosen for her.

There was a special delight in knowing that no one, other than Darcy of course, knew her secret. Unlike many others, being a rather solitary young woman, Jessica suffered no loss by not sharing her happiness with a confidante. Indeed, her greatest pleasure was in contemplating it alone.

As for Darcy, he was glad indeed to have Jonathan Bingley beside him at dinner, and afterwards the two men continued their discussion of the political landscape. Jonathan, whose interest in politics had survived his resignation from the Commons, thanks largely to the involvement of his brother-in-law, James Wilson, had some interesting news.

"It would seem, Darcy, that Disraeli and Lord Derby are planning to outfox Mr Gladstone and the Whigs again. Having defeated Lord Russell's reforms, this time, they mean to bring a reform bill of their own making into the Parliament when it next meets, and having got it through, with the support of a motley coalition of members, they intend to claim the credit for reforming the system."

Darcy expressed his disgust at the news. "What? I had heard from friends at Westminster that Derby was talking of 'dishing the Whigs,' but I did not take it seriously. I am appalled to hear that they propose to bring down a Reform Bill of their own. They do not have their hearts in it. What sort of reforms would they propose? Who would support them?"

Jonathan was older and took a calmer but no less critical view of the cynicism of Disraeli, a politician whose word he had never trusted.

"Oh, no doubt they will cobble together something, anything, so long as they can claim credit for it. It is an unprincipled political stratagem but a clever one, you must admit; Disraeli has proved he can run rings around Gladstone," he said, and poor Darcy was well nigh incoherent with anger.

"But they do not believe in the reforms at all. It is opportunism at its worst—" he raged, and Jonathan agreed, though adding with some humour, "It certainly is that, Darcy, I grant you, but it is partly built upon the failure of Russell and Gladstone to use the opportunity they had last year to convince their party to pass their bill. They must bear some of the blame. I do not believe that Lord Derby will last long as PM—mark my words, Disraeli will lead the Tories before long."

Darcy was outraged at the prospect. "And become Prime Minister?"

"Indeed," said Jonathan, with some genuine distaste for the proposition, "and unless Mr Gladstone is very careful, he may find he has missed his chance altogether."

Darcy shook his head in disbelief. He was glad now that he had postponed his political ambitions and accepted the job as manager of the Pemberley estate.

"It will not be much fun being at Westminster while Mr Gladstone and the Whigs languish in opposition and Disraeli occupies the treasury benches and struts the political stage," he said, unable to hide his dismay.

Jonathan agreed; though he was out of it now, he could appreciate Darcy's disappointment.

Presently, Anna Bingley came to urge the gentlemen to join the ladies around the pianoforte, where she hoped to involve them in some entertainment. "Jessica will play for us, and if you gentlemen will support me, I may even be persuaded to sing," she said, and, turning to Darcy, invited him to join her in a duet. He went, even though he did not feel like singing. It had been a very trying day and he was glad indeed of the light relief.

The rest of the company enjoyed the performance, especially the ladies, who had grown bored with the political discussion. Elizabeth was heard to draw her sister Jane's attention to the very becoming glow upon Jessica's countenance.

"Doesn't Jessica look particularly lovely tonight, Jane?" she asked. Jane agreed that Jessica did, and both her husband and Mr Darcy, when asked for an opinion, agreed with their wives that young Miss Courtney was looking remarkably well. They thought the colour of her gown must have something to do with it, or the mellow lighting in the room.

But none of them could guess the real reason for her well-being.

On the morrow, Darcy Gardiner had risen early and made his way to the stables, hoping to ride out before the rest of the household was about.

His head still filled with the disappointments of the previous day, he had hoped to enjoy a solitary gallop to the crest of the hill. As he urged his horse out of the paddock and along the road leading from the park, he came upon Jessica, in cape and bonnet, walking briskly down the road that led to the village of Lambton.

Dismounting, he greeted her and asked, a little awkwardly, what had brought her out so early. At first, she was reluctant to say anything, pretending she was out for a walk in the fresh morning air, but then, perhaps seeing his sceptical expression, she relented and confessed that she was on her way to Lambton, from where she hoped to send a letter by express to London and thence to Julian in Paris.

"And you plan to walk the five miles to Lambton?" he asked, astonished, and when she nodded and said, "I have no other means to despatch it without arousing the inevitable interest and gossip that will arise as soon as it is seen by one of the servants at Pemberley. I have told my maid that I am going to visit my grandmother and that is all."

Darcy had looked at her and said in a quiet voice, "It will take you half the day to walk to Lambton and back, and you will be exhausted. What's more, they will all wonder what has become of you and send out a search party! Will you not let me take it for you? I could direct it to Julian as though it were a business matter, and no one would be any the wiser."

Jessica had been surprised; it was the very last thing she had expected. She could never have asked him herself.

"Would you?" she had asked, almost in disbelief, whereupon he had smiled and said, "Why would I not, Jessica? If you will entrust your letter to me, I should be happy to despatch it for you. I can be there and back before they finish breakfast and no one will know about your letter." She had handed him the letter and, reaching up, kissed him on the cheek and said, "Dear Darcy, thank you. I shall not forget your kindness. You are truly a good friend."

She stopped and, as he was about to mount his horse, began again rather clumsily, "Darcy, there is something else... about yesterday... I am very sorry if I seemed ungrateful... I did not mean to be unkind or unfeeling, but I was truly surprised... I had no idea..." She had tried to say something to help him understand, but he touched a finger to her lips.

"You are not to blame, Jessica; you have nothing to regret. I am sorry too, only for myself, because I love you, but I am happy as well for you and Julian. I pray you will both enjoy all the happiness you deserve."

And putting the letter away in the inside pocket of his jacket, Darcy had mounted his horse, waved good-bye, and ridden on, leaving Jessica to retrace her steps and return to Pemberley, in time to join the rest of the family at breakfast.

❧

Later, Darcy told Michael Carr, recounting his impetuous proposal, "I cannot explain it, Michael; it all came upon me very suddenly; it was an irresistible impulse... I have long admired her and enjoyed her company; we are cousins and good friends, but I have never thought of her as I did at that moment.

"It is impossible to give you a reasoned account of my behaviour; I have not been able to explain it even to myself. Perhaps it was how she looked; she had a glow about her and a look of such serenity and joy, which, at that moment, convinced me she was the girl with whom I could spend the rest of my life!"

Noting his friend's rather condescending smile, Darcy looked a little sheepish and added, "It's all very well for you to smile, Michael; you are a happily married man. I confess I feel a little foolish—but she was very kind and ladylike, as she always is; she listened to me, and when I had finished, said in a very gentle voice, 'Dear Darcy, I am very fond of you and honoured that you should ask me, but I cannot marry you.'"

"And did she give you a reason? One you could accept without bitterness?" his friend enquired, and Darcy nodded sadly.

"Indeed she did, the only reason against which there can be no argument. She told me her feelings were already engaged. She is in love with another man, Michael, and while I can never break a confidence and tell you his name, I am able to say that he is a man well worthy of her!"

Michael Carr was sincerely sorry for his friend. Darcy Gardiner was the sort of young man who could have expected to marry any one of a number of eligible young women, who would have been privileged to have been asked. Yet, here he was, a rejected suitor!

Observing his friend's anguish, Mr Carr felt great sympathy for him, but had taken comfort from the fact that Darcy Gardiner at twenty-six was unlikely to be permanently scarred by his disappointment. Handsome and amiable, he was almost certain to be in love again, within the year.

He did not dare say so at the time to the melancholy young man before him, however, trying instead to offer some temporary solace. Alas, without much success, for there is little one can do to assuage the self-inflicted sorrow of unrequited love.

END OF PART ONE

POSTSCRIPT FROM PEMBERLEY

Part Two

Chapter Four

JULIAN DARCY WAS ABOUT to leave his lodgings in a quiet suburb of Paris and travel into the city, to complete the arrangements for his sojourn in Africa, when a packet was delivered to him, inside of which was Jessica's letter. He noticed that the direction had been written by his nephew, Darcy Gardiner, but paid little attention to the fact.

He was appointed to travel with two distinguished French scientists, a chemist and a biologist, with whom he had planned to meet at L'Ecole de Saint Martin, where they were to receive their travel papers.

He was late, and stopping only to break the seal on the packet and extract the letter within, he climbed into the carriage that waited for him in the street and read the letter as they made their way into town.

Jessica had been brief, but in a few words she had so completely met his expectations, that he could hardly restrain himself when they reached his destination and alighted from the vehicle with the alacrity of a schoolboy. His two colleagues, noting the spring in his step, put it down to his eager spirit of scientific enquiry and enthusiasm for their journey; it suited Julian to let them believe it was so.

Later, on returning to his rooms, Julian read the beloved letter again.

Jessica wrote:

My dear Julian,

First let me thank you for your letter, which arrived in time to bring me such happiness that I am unable to stop smiling, and everyone I meet must think I am gone suddenly silly, for I cannot explain my cheerfulness!

You asked me to send you word and said I could be brief. I shall do as you have asked and say with all my heart—I love you too, Julian. I have known this for some time now and long for your return so I may tell you so myself. It will be my greatest pleasure to do so. Will that do?

Please, dear Julian, keep safe and write me when you can, but I do understand it may not be often, for you will be busy with your work. Besides, I needs must pretend that my interest is chiefly in your research, so do remember to fill at least half the page with useful scientific information, which I may relate to the rest of my family, who will undoubtedly expect to be informed of your progress.

I am, of course, interested in your research too, but I love you and miss you so, I shall not be entirely at rest until you are safely home in Derbyshire.

Till then, God bless you,

Yours ever, Jessica.

Julian smiled as he put it away in his pocket book, knowing he would take it out and read it again and again in the days to come. Nothing in his life so far had stirred him as deeply as the realisation of his love for her. That she returned his affections and had said so in words so simple and sincere, with no qualifications or conditions, was almost more than he could believe. That it had all come about so unexpectedly only enhanced his joy.

Julian Darcy had long come to an acceptance of a position of secondary importance in every sphere of his life, save his profession, in which his preeminence had been established by patience and hard work and was recognised by his peers. Yet in his personal life, the reverse had been true.

Since early childhood, he'd been aware that nothing he did or achieved would ever compensate his parents for the loss of William, his elder brother, whose death in an horrific riding accident had desolated their family. His sister Cassandra—intelligent, beautiful, and happily married—had always seemed the more likely heir to Pemberley than he was. It had been with some relief that, after Josie's death, he had relinquished his inheritance to his son, making young Anthony his grandfather's heir.

In his marriage to Josie Tate, entered into at an early age, he had very quickly come to comprehend that his aspiring young wife placed greater value upon the opportunities she hoped to find at Cambridge and in London for pursuing her career as a writer than upon their marriage.

When his own work had engrossed his attention and taken up a good deal of his time, Josie had appeared to lose interest in their marriage and their son, leaving herself open and vulnerable to the deceits of those who would lead her astray. She had ceased to confide in him or seek his counsel, and he had been certain she no longer loved him.

With Jessica's letter in his hand, he recalled that never, even in the most intimate moments of their married life, had he and Josie been able to make as open and artless a commitment to one another, as Jessica and he had done in the last fortnight. It was the recognition of this that afforded him the greatest pleasure and gave him more hope for happiness than he had dared to expect.

He would go to Africa not just with the zeal of the scientist, but with the inspiration of a man who had every reason to return safe to England.

It was a complete reversal of his former frame of mind.

Before leaving France, he despatched a note, addressed to his nephew, Darcy Gardiner, in which he acknowledged receipt of the packet sent from England under his name, including the letter enclosed therein. Having thanked him for his kindness, Julian asked that this information be passed on to Miss Courtney together with a sealed note. Clearly, he believed that Darcy was in his Jessica's confidence.

Of Darcy Gardiner's own feelings Julian knew nothing.

When, on receiving the letter, Darcy took the enclosed note to Jessica, he could not fail to notice how her eyes devoured the few lines Julian had written and with what sincerity she thanked him for being the bearer of good news. If he'd had any doubts about her feelings, they were swiftly dispelled.

Meanwhile, Jessica had spent a good deal of time contemplating the future and wondering how her life might change, were Julian to return from Africa and ask her to marry him. She had no confidante but her diary, in which she faithfully recorded her thoughts.

I wonder, would he expect us to be married right away or would it be a long engagement? I do not believe he will wish to wait too long.

Will he choose to settle here at Pemberley? I think not; having relinquished his inheritance to Anthony, it may prove awkward for him to live here.

Perhaps he may wish to move to another part of England, though it is unlikely that will be Cambridge—too many harrowing memories there! Maybe he would return to France and travel again to Africa or the South Pacific colonies, and when we are married, he could take me with him. I think I should like that, very much.

She mused upon the prospect, and it excited her a great deal. Jessica had never left England, not even to visit Scotland or Wales, and having read widely about foreign lands and their people in the ample collection of traveller's tales available to her in the library at Pemberley, she had journeyed far in her imagination and longed for some real experience.

It would be good to live somewhere that was not confined by the fences and hedgerows of a farm or the walls of a rectory in Derbyshire, where the trees, flowers, and creatures were exotic rather than familiar, she wrote, for much as she loved her home and enjoyed the grace and elegance of Pemberley, Jessica's vibrant spirit yearned for new horizons.

Yet, she worried about her work at the school and wrote an *aide-memoire* to herself, underlining the necessity to recruit a suitable teacher, who if the need arose, could take over the administration of the school in her absence, were she required to accompany Julian on his travels.

I owe that to Mr Darcy and to the pupils. She must be capable as well as personable, else the children will not pay any attention to her, she noted, wondering even as she did so, how and where they would find such a person.

Putting away her diary, she rose and stood before the looking glass in her room, surveying herself with a critical eye. Slender, of medium height, with pleasing features, a well-formed figure, and a warm smile, Jessica was not a great beauty, but then neither was she plain.

Like her mother Emily, whose intrepid, generous nature had won her universal admiration, Jessica paid not a great deal of attention to fashion; her clothes were mostly simple and unfussy, but there was about her an extraordinary quality that caught the eye, no matter how simply she was dressed. Quite free of affectation, she possessed an intensity of purpose and a guileless honesty, which was quite disarming.

Young Darcy Gardiner had noticed and admired it since she had come to live and work at Pemberley, and Julian Darcy had found it irresistible.

Writing later to Julian, she mentioned her desire to travel and her hope they could do so together.

Would it not be exciting to taste the dust of the desert, experience the heat of the African sun and the warm tropical rain on one's skin, while observing those graceful birds you have described, skimming the surface of the water? I can think of nothing I would like better. I have seen so little of the world, I hardly feel I have lived at all, and I should love to see it with you...

Stirred by her words and grateful for the exhilaration they brought him, Julian responded usually in like manner, sending her detailed descriptions of the myriad of matters that occupied his days, as well as the hopes and dreams that filled his nights. Unable to confide in anyone else, they poured their thoughts and feelings into letters, which became gradually more openly affectionate, until neither could endure the thought of separation for much longer.

Do you know when your work in Africa will be concluded? I pray it will not be long, for it is such an agony to keep a secret, even such a wonderful, joyous secret as ours is, when I want to tell everyone I meet how happy I am, she wrote, and he concurred, declaring that their separation was fast becoming intolerable.

Understandably, Julian wrote more discreetly than she did, for she knew her letters were for his eyes alone and could write as she felt, while he was aware that his may well be delivered to her at breakfast and would have to be opened and probably read aloud to the family; every scrap of news would have to be shared. Which is why his warmest, most tender sentiments were usually well-embedded in the midst of a letter filled with descriptions of the African landscape—its sudden storms and stunning beauty. No detail was too small, no incident too trivial, but she would share and enjoy it, knowing he was both safe and happy. The brief, personal lines she treasured and read over and over again, having mastered the art of skipping over them as she read her letters to the family.

For Jessica, Julian's letters brought a fresh sense of purpose, as she thought of him and their love for one another. They promised a more mature, deeply passionate life than the predictable pleasures that marriage to Darcy Gardiner would have offered her. Though he had said not a single word against Josie, Jessica knew from the comments of Cassy and Mrs Darcy that Julian had been deeply wounded by his wife's conduct; the thought of loving him and healing that pain appealed to her and imbued her with a very special happiness.

However, Jessica knew also that she had to be cautious; it would not do to arouse the interest of others in the family before his return. She was devoted to Elizabeth, yet feared that Mrs Darcy may not view her relationship with Julian in quite the same light and strove to maintain the impression of an easy friendship, which would not arouse any suspicions.

She was confident that once Julian returned from Africa and declared his intention to marry her, all would be well. It was an indication of her modest nature that it never occurred to her that Mr and Mrs Darcy may welcome the prospect of the marriage as being beneficial for their son.

~⚓~

For Darcy Gardiner, the return of his sister and brother-in-law from their wedding tour of Ireland had brought both relief and a new dilemma.

He had missed them and welcomed them back, but how to keep Jessica's secret and yet explain with any credibility his own melancholy mood caused some considerable soul-searching. Even though he had accepted without rancour the fact that Jessica was out of his reach, he could not forget the mortification her rejection had caused, leaving him dispirited and averse to indulging in those popular pastimes that he had enjoyed so well. Picnics and parties were suddenly far less attractive than they had been before, and an explanation would be called for. It would not be plausible, he knew, to lay the entire blame for his dejection upon the recent accession of Mr Disraeli to the Prime Ministership!

His brother-in-law Mr Carr had detected the condition and diagnosed it correctly as a more personal malaise. Having questioned Darcy, he elicited at first some evasive answers, followed by a full confession and some friendly counsel.

"You will promise never to breathe a word of this, Michael," he had pleaded, and Mr Carr had given his word.

His sister, who had long teased him about the need to "settle down," seemed suddenly to have grown tired of the game, and Darcy assumed that Lizzie, who was to have her first child within the year, must have turned her attention to more practical matters and decided to leave him to his own devices. For this relief, Darcy was profoundly grateful.

When Summer arrived, his sense of deprivation increased as he looked forward to a rather dull season, enlivened only by the first cricket match on the calendar and Caroline Fitzwilliam's chamber music concert.

It was at this point that two events occurred to compel his attention to the exclusion of all else.

The first came without warning on the day that Camden Park hosted the cricket match between the teams from Pemberley and Ripley. On what was a picture-perfect day in early Summer, with all of the families and many of the workers from the two estates gathered to cheer them on, Darcy Gardiner led his team to an unexpected victory.

As he walked off the ground to the applause of the spectators, he was unaware that an urgent message had been received from Oakleigh and his father, Sir Richard Gardiner, had left the match to travel to Lambton to the bedside of Mrs Gardiner, who had suffered a spasm.

Dr Gardiner had asked that Darcy, who was batting at the time, be not informed until the match was over, and had left with the servant from Oakleigh. When Darcy, flushed with success, came seeking his parents' approval, he found only his mother waiting for him.

Seeing her countenance, tense and pale, he knew at once it was bad news.

Cassandra spoke urgently, "Darcy, we must go at once—Mrs Gardiner has been taken ill, and your papa has gone to her, about an hour ago. I have the carriage waiting."

Darcy did not wait to hear more; returning instantly to talk to his team and make his excuses to the visitors from Ripley, he rejoined his mother and they set out at once for Oakleigh.

Elizabeth had wished to accompany them, but the weather was changing and a cold breeze presaged rain on the way, which prompted Cassandra to persuade her mother not to venture out that afternoon.

"Darcy will return and bring you word, Mama, and you can go over to see Mrs Gardiner tomorrow morning," she promised, and together with her husband's persuasion, it was sufficient to change Elizabeth's mind.

Arriving at Oakleigh, they found that Dr Gardiner had already successfully treated his mother, and having revived her spirits as well as her body, he had sent for the physician from Littleford to provide a second opinion. Mrs Gardiner, who had not been in the best of health ever since the death of her husband, was still rather weak. Richard was concerned to ascertain that the problem was not with her heart.

"I do not know what came over me," she said, as they gathered around her bed. "There I was, one minute writing a letter to Robert, and then without any warning, I found myself falling out of my chair... It was most peculiar..."

Cassy and Richard exchanged glances as Darcy poured his grandmother more tea, which had always been her panacea for all ills.

Mrs Gardiner was especially partial to this grandson among all her grandchildren, and it was clear that she enjoyed his attentions.

When Cassy and Richard left the room for a few minutes, she said, "My dear Darcy, there is some thing I would like you to do for me," and as he attended upon her, added quickly, "The letter I was writing to Robert, when I was taken ill, it is on my bureau over by the window. It is almost finished, but I had not written the direction. Could you please complete it and have it sent on tomorrow? There is no need to trouble him unnecessarily by mentioning this little problem of mine—poor Robert has troubles of his own, and I do not wish to add to them."

Darcy agreed. "Of course, I shall attend to it right away. But are you sure you do not wish me to tell him? I could add a line or include a note explaining you were quite recovered. My uncle may wish to know surely..."

"No, no, he will want to rush over to England to see me, and that will make matters worse between him and Rose; they are rather short of money, and the expense will be too great," she said, then added cheerfully, "Besides, as you can see, I am quite well now, right as rain. Just send him the letter, and, Darcy, I have written out a cheque—it is under the note pad? Would you fold it in and enclose it with my letter, please?"

Darcy did as she asked, but noting the cheque was for a sum of two hundred pounds, he could not help wondering what had prompted this largesse. He was surprised, too, that Mrs Gardiner had asked him and not his father to attend to the matter.

That night, despite the victory in the cricket match, Darcy's mood was sombre when he returned to Pemberley. Mrs Gardiner, like her husband, was much loved, and both Mr Darcy and Elizabeth were anxious about her. When Darcy arrived, before he was allowed to go up to his room to bathe and dress for dinner, he had to satisfy their concerns and reassure them that she was out of danger.

"My father has asked a colleague to give him a second opinion," he explained, "but my grandmother has declared that she is perfectly well and requires no further medication. She seems to have made a remarkable recovery, and Mama believes it was probably a fit of dizziness or fatigue."

Elizabeth agreed, pointing out that her aunt was always busy whether in the house or the garden at Oakleigh and may have become over-tired.

At dinner and afterwards, the conversation was dominated by many reminiscences. Elizabeth and Mr Darcy were feeling especially nostalgic; the Gardiners meant a great deal to them. Mrs Gardiner's devotion to her family and especially to her sons was well known. When someone mentioned Robert, the youngest of the Gardiners' four children, Jessica's mother, Emily Courtney, who was dining with them, advised that she had despatched a note to her brother advising him of their mother's sudden indisposition.

This piece of news left young Darcy speechless for a moment, as he recalled Mrs Gardiner's particular instruction that Robert was not to be told. Having pondered for a moment whether he should mention the matter, he decided against it. If what Mrs Gardiner said was right, and Robert was short of money, it was unlikely he would consider travelling to England at short notice, he thought, and decided to despatch Mrs Gardiner's letter to Robert on the morrow, by the earliest post.

No doubt it would reassure him on the question of her health.

Despite Darcy's best efforts, however, Robert Gardiner, alerted by his sister Emily's note, arrived unannounced at Oakleigh the following week, accompanied by his wife Rose, their children, two servants, a small dog, and a carriage full of luggage.

It was the very thing poor Mrs Gardiner had sought to avoid.

❦

Jessica awoke to the sound of rain.

It had been raining all night long. She had heard it drumming on the roof and the window panes, and looking out of the window at the small sodden garden of the Kympton rectory, she sighed. It was the same little patch of ground, with the clump of blue bells under the apple tree, she had looked out on every year since childhood. Over the years, nothing had changed.

Nothing, that is, except herself.

In the months just gone, since admitting to herself that she was in love with Julian Darcy, Jessica had changed to such an extent that what had been to her familiar and ordinary was no longer. Even the people she had known and lived with all her life seemed rather remote from her, because they had no knowledge of her present situation and could not share with her the multiplicity of feelings that flowed from it.

As she turned away from the window, she caught sight of herself in her mirror, stopped, looked, and shook her head, as she contemplated her parents, her siblings, and Mr and Mrs Darcy.

"If they knew how I feel, they would not know me!" she said to herself.

Having regarded the bleak scene outside, she went back to bed, recalling that her mother had returned from Oakleigh the previous evening, with news that her uncle Robert and his wife Rose had arrived together with their servants and children. Jessica was not at all certain that a visit from Robert and Rose was what Mrs Gardiner would welcome just now. While she was quite partial to her younger son and had often protected him from the consequences of his own foolhardy conduct, her daughter-in-law was quite another matter.

An attractive, aspiring young woman, Rose Fitzwilliam had surprised many people when she had accepted Robert Gardiner's offer of marriage. Not that there was any doubt she was fond of him, but equally there was no question that she completely dominated him. She was ambitious for her husband and expressed her disappointment in no uncertain terms when circumstances did not always fall into place as she had hoped.

Jessica had memories of the recriminations that had followed the death of Mr Gardiner a few years ago, when Caroline Fitzwilliam had inherited control of her father's business. It had seriously discomfited both Robert and his wife, and to her even greater chagrin, Rose had discovered that she was not to become the mistress of Oakleigh either.

Rose's mother, now Lady Fitzwilliam, had declared that Rose and Robert had been unfairly dealt with in Mr Gardiner's will.

"It is not fair, surely, that not only should Robert be deprived of the right to run the Commercial Trading Company, for which position he has the best qualifications, but to add insult to injury, Rose and he must rent expensive apartments in London and Paris because the future of Oakleigh is left up in the air," she had declared.

It was of no use whatsoever to point out that Mr Gardiner had purchased Oakleigh for his wife, who had been born and raised in Lambton, and he had wished that the house should be hers until her death, when she could will it to anyone she chose.

Lady Fitzwilliam had been overheard to say that Mrs Gardiner was in such excellent health, she may well live to be a hundred, and then where would Robert and Rose be? Caroline's comment that it mattered not a fig, since they lived chiefly in London, Paris, or Timbuctoo, had not been very well received.

The recollection made Jessica laugh, but then quite suddenly, she sat up again, and this time she was not amused.

"Good Lord, is it possible they have arrived so suddenly because they think Mrs Gardiner is at death's door?" she asked herself, as she pulled on a robe and ran downstairs. She found her parents having breakfast and, begging their pardon for her dishevelled state, she asked, "Mama, is it possible that my Uncle Robert and his wife are here in the hope of occupying Oakleigh until they can take possession of it?"

Emily smiled and shook her head, "Jessica, you do surprise me, my dear; one minute you do not seem to hear what I say, and the next you are racing in with some dramatic notion in your head," she said. "I did point out last night that I thought they had arrived with a very particular purpose in mind and that was to ensure that Rose could establish herself in the household, while Mama was too ill to attend to her duties. I have no doubt that she thought it would be a good opportunity to take charge, and I am certain she must have been exceedingly disappointed to find Mama quite recovered and well able to manage her own household."

"Do you suppose they will stay, regardless?" Jessica asked, and when her father, in his customary charitable way, suggested that perhaps Mrs Robert Gardiner was genuinely concerned about the state of her mother-in-law's health, both mother and daughter exploded with laughter.

"Oh Papa, you are too good—indeed you are. If my Uncle Robert's wife could ensure that her interest and that of her husband and family could be satisfactorily served by staying on in Paris, I think we might never have seen her spend a day longer than was necessary in Derbyshire. That she has arrived complete with her servants and, I understand, sufficient luggage to last until Christmas if need be, must signify her determination. What do you make of it, Mama?" she asked.

Her mother hastened to say that her husband's Christian charity would probably preclude his seeing anything but the noblest of motives in the actions of her sister-in-law.

"Thank you, my dear," said James Courtney, rising from the table. "No doubt Jessie and you will together find sufficient evidence to contradict my thesis. When you do, I shall be happy to hear it."

They were about to launch into a further examination of the motives of the lady concerned, when a loud knocking on the door heralded an early caller. Expecting it to be a parishioner seeking her father's help and unwilling to be found in her nightgown and robe, Jessica retreated upstairs as the maid answered the door and admitted Darcy Gardiner.

She was on the stairs when she heard his voice, as he handed his coat to the servant and greeted her parents. They invited him to join them and partake of tea, which he accepted with alacrity. It had been a damp ride over from Pemberley, he said, and tea would be most welcome.

Not waiting to hear any more of the conversation, she shut the door of her bedroom and hastened to complete her toilette. Jessica wondered what could have brought him to the rectory at this early hour. Surely, she thought, with some anxiety, it cannot have been to do with Mrs Gardiner? Could it be she had been taken ill again?

This thought alone drove her to rush through the rest of her preparations, and having put on her gown, she decided not to spend more time on arranging her hair. Braiding it quickly and tying it with a ribbon, she went downstairs, just as the maid came up to say that Mr Darcy Gardiner was about to leave and her mother asked if she would come downstairs.

Darcy Gardiner was standing in the hall; it appeared he was ready to depart but had delayed leaving, hoping to see her before he went.

As she approached, he came towards her. "Jessica, I leave for Derby in an hour and expect to take the train to London and thence to Westminster.

I received the news from Colin Elliott by electric telegraph last night; there appears to be much unrest in London over Mr Disraeli's proposed Reform Bill; meetings are being held everywhere, and there may well be an election. If the Bill is defeated in the Parliament, I hope to work with Elliott and his group to ensure a victory for Mr Gladstone and the Reformists," he said, and she could hear the excitement in his voice.

She knew how much this meant to him and expressed her pleasure without reservation. "Darcy, that is excellent news. It must make you very happy and no doubt you are looking forward to it. Let me wish you and Mr Gladstone the very best of luck. Do you mean to stay on in London for the campaign?" she asked.

"I have no firm plans as yet—it will depend upon many things, including the date of the election. But I have promised Colin Elliott I will help all I can, and my grandfather Mr Darcy has kindly permitted me to use his townhouse while I am in London. I may have to travel to the country if need be. Mr Gladstone will surely wish to campaign in the towns like Leeds and Birmingham," he explained, and Jessica was genuinely pleased that something had turned up to capture his attention.

The fact that he had been remarkably quiet since their unhappy encounter in the park at Pemberley had not escaped her; yet despite her concern for him, she could summon up no more than a sisterly interest in his welfare.

Compared to her emotions whenever she contemplated her reunion with Julian, these were jejeune feelings indeed. She grew more certain, each time they met, that she could not have decided differently.

"You will keep us informed, will you not? We shall all await your news with interest, I am sure," she said, holding out her hand, which he took and held for a moment before moving to the door.

Reverend Courtney expressed an interest in receiving information about Mr Gladstone's proposals for the Irish Church, and Mrs Courtney asked to be remembered to Mr and Mrs Elliott. Darcy promised to oblige them all, and bidding them farewell, he was gone, riding into the rain, which was falling less heavily now.

Knowing how very keenly Darcy felt the need for his hero Mr Gladstone to win the election, Jessica was particularly pleased. This had been a difficult time for both of them. Neither of her parents knew anything of Darcy Gardiner's impulsive proposal, nor the reason why their daughter had turned it down. Only Jessica knew her own heart and as she went upstairs and prepared to return to Pemberley, she reflected upon the events that had so altered her life in so short a time.

Jessica's diary recorded her feelings:

It is almost beyond belief that in a single season, I have gone from a state of happy indifference to all gentlemen, to an ardent attachment to one of them. Whether this turns out in the end to be a blessing or an affliction, bringing more pain than pleasure, remains to be seen. Some might believe it is better to love less passionately, for there may be less to lose; but, for the moment, I must confess, I feel that I am the happiest creature on earth.

With Darcy Gardiner gone to Westminster and Julian still in the depths of Africa, life may have returned to a fairly predictable routine over the Summer, except for the presence of Mr and Mrs Robert Gardiner at Oakleigh. Their continuing occupation of her home presented a problem not only for Mrs Gardiner, who though discomfited made no mention of it, but for all of her other relations and friends.

For a start, the two young boys and their governess appeared to be constantly in the way, using the morning room for their lessons or the sitting room for their games, whenever Jessica or her mother went to call.

Her aunt Caroline was especially put out, complaining that on two separate occasions, Mrs Hunt, the children's governess, had remained in the room whilst she was visiting her mother.

"It is quite aggravating enough to have the children—who must be the noisiest, most boisterous boys in the county—and their dog racing through the house with no consideration at all for poor Mama, but to have Mrs Hunt, who is a complete stranger to me, sitting with us while Mama and I took tea together was too much," Caroline complained to Elizabeth.

"On the first occasion, I assumed it was on account of the weather, which was a little damp, but yesterday, the sun was shining and the birds were singing, but alas, Mrs Hunt showed no inclination to leave us and step into the garden."

"Do you suppose, Aunt, that she has been asked to sit in with you?" asked Jessica, aware that relations between her aunt Caroline and Rose Gardiner were not entirely cordial.

"Who by?"—Caroline seemed astonished—"And to what end?" she asked.

Elizabeth, with an eager eye to a conspiracy, enquired, "Is it possible that Rose wishes to discover whether your mama has made any arrangements regarding the disposition of her estate? We do know that she was particularly peeved that Mr Gardiner did not leave Oakleigh to Robert. Lady Fitzwilliam has never ceased to complain on that score."

Caroline's countenance revealed her contempt for the moans and machinations of Lady Fitzwilliam and her daughter. When she spoke, she dropped her voice so that only the three of them could hear her words.

"I know she does. Well, she is in for an unpleasant shock; sometime in the future, when dear Mama is gone, it is Emily who will inherit Oakleigh, not Robert. Then we shall see some real hostilities break out!"

Both Elizabeth and Jessica were so shocked by her revelation, they were speechless for a few minutes, before Jessica said in a quiet voice, "Mama will inherit Oakleigh? But does she want it? She seems so content at the rectory, I cannot believe she will wish to move."

"Content she may be, but it is not a permanent home. One day, Jessica, your papa will retire and a new rector will be appointed to Kympton. Where will they live then?" asked her aunt.

Elizabeth, while agreeing that this was indeed the case, was not entirely satisfied that Caroline had her facts right.

"Are you sure, Caroline? How did you come by this information?"

Caroline, still keeping her voice low, answered confidently, "There is no doubt at all—Mama herself spoke with Richard and me, as she must do according to the conditions of Papa's will. She wanted to ask us how we would feel if she left the property to Emily. You see, she argues that when Dr Courtney must inevitably retire from living at Kympton, they will have no home to go to. Mama had always assumed they would come to live with her. But I do believe she has been apprehensive, ever since Papa's death and all the fuss Rose and Robert made at the time, assuming that they would take over Oakleigh, not to mention Lady Fitzwilliam's complaints. With her own health failing, she fears that Emily may not be made welcome there."

"And did Aunt Gardiner consult Richard and you *before* coming to a decision?" asked Elizabeth.

Caroline smiled, "No indeed, I thought you might have known that she consulted Mr Darcy." And seeing Elizabeth's expression of complete amazement, she added, "It was what my father wanted her to do, and she was happy to comply. She informed Richard and myself and asked if we would be unhappy with her decision—we were not, of course," Caroline declared, adding, "I had spent years worrying that Robert and Rose would get a hold of the place and sell or sublet it without our consent. Neither Richard nor I wanted it for ourselves, so we were happy to agree that Emily should have it. I understand Mama has since instructed the attorney Mr Jennings to make the necessary changes to her will."

"And how long have you known this, Aunt Caroline?" asked Jessica, who was beginning to see some exquisite ironies in the situation.

"Not very long—I think it was not more than a month ago that we were summoned to Oakleigh on a day when Robert and Rose were visiting her parents in Staffordshire. Mama told us of her decision, and when we agreed, she was delighted, of course—she has been concerned about Emily for some time; she knows that most of the money Papa left her has been spent on their pet charities."

"What?" Elizabeth could not believe her ears.

But Caroline was quite serious. "Did you not know, Cousin Lizzie? How do you suppose the children of all those Irish families in the village are clothed and sent to school? And who do you suppose pays for the repairs on their roofs and windows?"

"I had no idea," said Elizabeth, shaking her head. "Does Mr Darcy know of this too?"

Caroline was unsure. "I cannot tell; he may, and again, Mama may not have told him, anxious not to embarrass Emily and Dr Courtney. But she did tell us—Richard and me—that the rector's stipend is all they use for their own living, and Emily, who is very thrifty, manages very well and never complains or asks for money."

Jessica did recall that she had found her mother picking berries on the common and wondered why she was doing it.

"Everyone knows the rectory had the best kitchen garden in the district and Mama's jams and preserves always sell out first at the church fête. But it did not occur to me that it was because they needed the money," she said, feeling particularly guilty that she enjoyed a life of comfort and some luxury at Pemberley, whilst her parents scrimped and saved at Kympton.

Caroline reassured her, "Don't worry, Jessica, your mama is not about to take in washing. It is not that they are so poor, but they will not spend all their income upon themselves. They have always been frugal and lead simple lives, and they use their money to help the poor and the sick, because they believe they must. My dear mother's anxiety stems from the fact that Emily and James own no property and have no savings, which means, when Dr Courtney retires or, God forbid, should he die before he retires, Emily and young Jude will be both poor and homeless."

"Caroline, do you mean she has used up all of her share of the money your father left her?" asked Elizabeth, quite unable to believe this.

Caroline shook her head, "No, Lizzie, but every last penny is invested in a trust out of which the Littleford hospital and the Irish children are the main beneficiaries. All Emily holds now are her shares in Papa's company, which she cannot dispose of without our consent. She receives her share of the company profits twice a year, and since she sold the farm in France, that is the sum total of her income. "

"Do you know what became of the money from the farm?" asked Elizabeth.

"I believe most of it was used to extend the services at the children's hospital, as Paul Antoine had desired in his will. Emily would not hear of the money being used for any other purpose."

As both Jessica and Elizabeth sat silent, Caroline rose and made ready to leave. The sun was setting, and it would soon be dusk. Plainly she was not displeased with her mother's plans for Oakleigh; Elizabeth and Jessica could not help wondering at the response they would get from Robert and Rose and Lady Fitzwilliam of course! But, that was for another day, and they all prayed it would be very long in coming.

However, later that evening, when they were at dinner, just Mr and Mrs Darcy with Jessica, Elizabeth was determined to introduce the subject of her cousin Emily's financial situation. She wished to discover how much Mr Darcy knew of the matter and what opinion he had of it.

Waiting until the servants had left the room, she began, "Caroline believes my aunt Gardiner intends that Emily should inherit Oakleigh rather than Robert. I had always thought she would favour Robert. Do you know anything of this, Darcy?"

Mr Darcy put down his knife and said, in a voice that reflected hardly any surprise, "I do, because Mrs Gardiner asked my advice, in confidence."

"And did you advise her to follow that course?" his wife asked, to which Mr Darcy smiled and said very quickly, "Certainly not, my dear. Your aunt was not asking for my opinion on *whether* to leave her property to Emily; she had decided that already. She wanted to know *how* to set about arranging it, without alerting Robert or Rose. My advice was limited to legal matters concerning the disposition of the estate, not the choice of beneficiary."

Elizabeth, finding herself stymied, pursued the matter down another track.

"May we assume, then, that you agreed with her proposition?"

"You may, Lizzie, but even if I did not, it would have made no difference—Mrs Gardiner was quite determined that she wanted it done. She has been concerned about making provision for Emily against the time when Dr Courtney retires from the living at Kympton. She is well aware that neither Emily nor her husband have much in savings and has decided to help them in this way."

His voice suggested he was quite comfortable with the proposition.

"Is that because Emily has spent most of her patrimony on charitable causes and the children's hospital?" asked Elizabeth.

"Indeed, and as a result they lead quite simple lives, as I am sure Jessica will testify," said Mr Darcy, looking across at Jessica, who remained silent, "and while neither you nor I may wish to follow their example, it is their choice and one that compels admiration. I have a great deal of regard for Dr Courtney—he is a man of erudition and principle. As for Emily, you and I, Lizzie, know well her generosity of heart."

Turning again to Jessica, Mr Darcy added, "Your dear mother was a source of strength and comfort to us in a time of great sorrow; we could never adequately repay her kindness."

Jessica knew something of what he spoke; she had heard her mother and her grandmother speak in whispers of the death of her cousins, William Darcy and young Edward Fitzwilliam, and the toll it had taken on the entire family. Emily, whose own life had been in turmoil with the loss of her beloved husband, had become Elizabeth's friend and confidante.

After a few minutes of silence, Elizabeth said very quietly, "Sometimes, Emily makes me ashamed; I think of all the pleasures we enjoy, yet she and Dr Courtney, by their acts of charity, deprive themselves of far more modest comforts."

Jessica recalled her own feelings on hearing of her parents' situation and waited to hear what more Elizabeth would say, but Mr Darcy intervened, speaking more gently, this time.

"They do not regard it as deprivation, Lizzie. I have spoken privately with Dr Courtney when last we discussed an increase in his stipend, and while he thanked me for my concern and appreciated the extra money he would receive, he assured me that Emily and he did not feel they were making any extraordinary sacrifices; rather they saw their work as enhancing their lives. When I asked if I could assist, he asked only for permission to use some of the men and materials on the estate to repair the houses of the Irish families who are settled on Litton Common. Naturally, I urged him to use whatever he needed and have instructed Mr Grantham to make the men available to do the work. He asked nothing for themselves."

There was silence around the table, as the servants entered to remove the dishes. Jessica was thoughtful, and Elizabeth asked no more questions.

She had learned over the years of her life at Pemberley that Mr Darcy was a man of compassion and generosity; indeed, she who before her marriage had done little in the way of charity had been encouraged by her husband to become involved and had gained considerable satisfaction from her work in the community.

Clearly, Jessica thought, Mr Darcy admired the work of her parents in the parish. While she had some knowledge of their activities in the community, Jessica had had little insight into the consequences, financial and otherwise, of their efforts and felt, as Elizabeth obviously did, somewhat ashamed of her ignorance. She determined that this at least would change in the future and was grateful to Mr Darcy for affording her the opportunity to do her share, by placing her in charge of the parish school at Pemberley.

In the weeks that followed, Jessica turned her mind to the business of hiring a new school teacher. She consulted Mr Hurst, the school master, and Mr Darcy, who had been exceedingly keen that they obtain the services of "an educated and well-read lady of exemplary character and with experience in teaching young women."

He was particular that she should not be "of the old school," pointing out that outdated ideas in educating girls would be a waste of money.

"I believe, Jessica, that we should aim to do more than prepare these young women for marriage or domestic service. I should like to think that at Pemberley we would teach them to aspire to better things," he had said, and Jessica agreed without reservation, deciding to place advertisements in the *Matlock Review* and further afield in the *Courier*.

She was determined to have it done before the end of Summer, in case her hopes that Julian would return in Autumn were fulfilled. It would not do to be unprepared for such an eventuality, although she could not possibly reveal that to Mr Darcy!

Armed with a list of the desirable qualifications and a description of the duties of the position, she went in search of Mr Darcy, before setting out for the offices of the newspaper.

She found him in the library and placed before him her material.

"Will that do?" she asked simply.

She was hoping for his approval or, at the very least, his advice. She was not ready for his response, when he, having read the document, leaned back in his chair, laughed, and said, "My dear Jessica, where do you suppose you are going to find this paragon?"

Taken aback and not a little hurt by his riposte, she drew away and said, "You did ask that she be of exemplary character and experience, sir."

Whereupon, hearing the injured note in her voice, he relented, "Of course I did, and I am sorry, Jessica; I did not mean to vex you—I was only teasing. You have done well to define your high expectations; I hope you will find someone who fits them. She will need to be a very special lady. I cannot help wondering if such a person may be found in the county, much less in the district."

Relieved, Jessica smiled and agreed that she had set a high standard.

"It is only because I sincerely believe we must get the best possible teacher for the children at the Pemberley school. I am determined we shall find her."

Mr Darcy had always valued the commitment of Jessica's parents to their community; now it was clear his regard had to extend to their daughter as well. There was certainly no doubting her dedication.

"Well, my dear, when you have found her, I assure you we will assist you to keep her by offering an attractive salary. I believe that a good teacher is a valuable asset and should be well rewarded."

Jessica thanked him and went away delighted with his response.

Chapter Five

THE FAMILY OF O'HARE had been settled for several years on the free-hold property of Colley Dale, situated on the far side of the Great Common, within a reasonable walking distance from the village of Kympton, on the Pemberley estate.

The O'Hares had moved to England after the end of the war with Napoleon and before the great potato famine in Ireland. Mr Daniel O'Hare, then a boy of fourteen, had found work at the Rushmore Stud, first as a strapper and later as horse trainer. Several years later, he had married a young woman from Chesterfield, who had been the children's governess at Rushmore Farm, and together they had purchased Colley Dale farm, where they now lived in retirement.

They had three children, two of whom were now young adults.

The eldest, a daughter, Kathryn, had shown early promise in her studies, and when sent to a ladies' seminary in the south of England to continue her education, she had so exceeded the expectations of her teachers, they had selected her to receive a scholarship to attend a college for young women in Belgium. There she had pursued further studies in French as well as art and music, with a view to becoming a teacher herself.

Their son, Stephen, was apprenticed to a firm of transport engineers in Birmingham and had spent many years overseas, working on building bridges and roads in the colonies.

Elena, their youngest, had been born several years after her siblings and lived at home, where she had the benefit of being the sole object of her parents' attention for most of the year. Taught chiefly by her mother, she was a bright, cheerful girl who spent most of her mornings helping her mother in the house and around the farm and all the rest of her time reading anything she could lay her hands on.

"Elena, you will surely ruin your eyesight," her mother would warn, finding her daughter reading in fading light, and Elena would promise faithfully not to read for much longer, but she would soon forget the time and go on until it was too dark to see the words on the page.

A regular borrower of books from the community library established by Mr Darcy, young Elena O'Hare was well known to Jessica Courtney, who helped out at the library twice a week. Indeed, it was through her that Jessica learned that the elder Miss O'Hare was returning permanently to live at Colley Dale.

Handing in two books, which she had finished reading in less than a fortnight, Elena was borrowing two more. When Jessica, surprised at the speed with which she had read them, remarked upon it, she had said, "I must have twenty on my list before my sister Kate arrives next week, else I shall be mortified, for she reads so well and knows so many books, I shall never catch up."

Jessica had tried to point out that reading was not some kind of competition in which the race was to the swift, but it had no effect. Determined, Elena had carried away two large tomes by Mr Fielding and Mrs Gaskell, vowing to read them within the fortnight.

Before she left, she revealed that her elder sister Kate would be arriving by train on Saturday, by which time Elena hoped she would have got at least halfway through Joseph Andrews. She had to, she insisted, if she was to impress her sister, declaring earnestly, "She is a teacher and knows a great deal more about books than I do."

Jessica was all ears. "Is she a school teacher? Where does she teach?" she asked.

Elena was a mine of information. "Yes, ma'am; that is, yes, she was a school teacher, ma'am, at the convent school at East Grinstead. She then went to Lindfield to teach the daughters of Lord and Lady Denny, but she didn't enjoy it, ma'am, and she has given it up now and is coming home to stay."

If these were not the mere ravings of a thirteen-year-old, they could be quite interesting, thought Jessica, who made a mental note to make further enquiries about Miss Kathryn O'Hare. A school teacher, considered suitable to tutor the daughters of Lord and Lady Denny, had to be worth investigating. Especially if she was returning to live in the district.

⁓᭝⁓

The O'Hares did not always attend the church at Kympton.

In fact, Mr Daniel O'Hare, being somewhat inconvenienced after a riding accident which had left him with a painful limp, hardly came to church at all. Mrs O'Hare did, though, and when Jessica accompanied her parents to church on the Sunday, she noticed Elena and her mother occupying a pew some little distance from their own.

With them was a lady, whose face was half hidden from view by a very pretty hat and whose gown was of an elegant simplicity that bespoke a woman of taste and fashion.

"That must be Kathryn O'Hare," Jessica whispered to her mother, and Emily Courtney, who had noticed the little group as she entered the church, nodded.

"Yes, it is. I met Mrs O'Hare in the village and she did mention that her elder daughter was coming home after several years away. I understand she's a very clever young lady and highly educated," she said.

Jessica could not wait to see what Kathryn O'Hare looked like; she hoped they would meet outside the church, when the service was over.

Impatient, she waited only until her father had left the sanctuary after the customary blessing before slipping out into the vestry and thence through the side door and around to the front of the church. There, Reverend Courtney was greeting members of his congregation.

As Jessica waited, she saw first Mrs O'Hare and Elena emerge from the church and then Kathryn, who was introduced to the rector. They spoke briefly, and as the ladies moved down the steps and into the churchyard, Jessica moved towards them, and catching Elena's eye, she smiled.

Elena, who obviously adored her elder sister, could not resist the opportunity to introduce her, and when Kathryn turned to her, Jessica was struck by the remarkable brilliance of her smile and the easy friendliness of her manner as they greeted one another.

Having exchanged the usual pleasantries, they were about to part, when Mrs O'Hare, clearly proud of her daughter and happy to show her off to the notable families of the village, invited Jessica to join them for afternoon tea at Colley Dale.

"If you are not busy, we would be honoured, if you are able to come, Miss Courtney; I am sure Kate and you will have a great deal to talk about. Kate dear, Miss Courtney is in charge of the parish school at Pemberley," she said, at which Miss O'Hare regarded Jessica with new interest.

"Are you really?" she asked, probably wondering at Jessica's youthful appearance. "That must be very interesting indeed. I understood from Elena that you worked at the library, Miss Courtney."

Jessica admitted that she did help at the library, but added, "That is only a hobby; my chief preoccupation is with the school. Elena tells me you are a teacher; would you like to visit our school? It is probably not as grand as the schools in the south of England..."

Miss O'Hare laughed, "They are not very grand at all—especially those like the convent school of St. Margaret's that takes in the children of the poor and the orphaned. I should like very much to see your school, Miss Courtney; perhaps when you come to tea we could arrange a convenient time?" and so saying, she said good-bye and slipped away to join her family, leaving Jessica to wonder at the fortuitous circumstances that had brought them together.

There was something about Kathryn O'Hare, a vivacity and energy, as well as her elegant appearance, that immediately appealed to Jessica. She was quite certain Kathryn would be an interesting and rewarding acquaintance and had accepted Mrs O'Hare's invitation to tea with pleasure.

Rejoining her family, Jessica related the detail of her conversation with Mrs O'Hare and her daughter, declaring that she intended to get to know Miss Kathryn O'Hare better. Her mother, who had always wished that her daughter would make more friends outside their family circle, encouraged her to do so.

"She seems a very agreeable and pleasant young person, and seeing you are both interested in teaching, I do believe she would be a good companion for you, Jessie," she said, adding, "She cannot have too many acquaintances in the district—she has been away so long in Europe and then again in Sussex."

"Well, I am pleased she is back, and I mean to get to know her well. She looks and sounds both intelligent and amiable, and that is a good start," said

Jessica, to which her mother replied, "It certainly is. Besides, she is bound to be interested in your school."

Jessica nodded, and though she said nothing of her hopes, she saw Kathryn O'Hare as much more than an engaging companion.

That afternoon, she left the rectory earlier than usual to return to Pemberley and made her way across the common to Colley Dale.

A picturesque place set in a broad meadow with the river behind it and the house built upon rising land backed by woodland, it was an attractive and valuable property. Jessica was quite familiar with the farm, although she had never been inside the house. She was pleasantly surprised to find it was both more spacious than it appeared from without and quite tastefully appointed. There was none of the clutter that characterised the usual farmhouse parlour, and unusually, there were several glass-fronted cabinets well stocked with books. Clearly there were other members of the family who shared Elena's passion for reading, she thought.

Mrs O'Hare, a pleasant woman, well known and respected in the village, had greeted Jessica, and in the parlour, Kathryn presided over the tea table. She rose and came towards Jessica, welcoming her warmly and inviting her to occupy the chair beside the fireplace, for which Jessica was grateful. Though it was not a particularly cold day, there had been a brisk breeze blowing as she crossed the common, and it was good to feel the warmth of the fire. Sensing this, Kathryn hastened to pour out a cup of tea, and Mrs O'Hare pressed upon her a piece of dark fruit cake of her own making.

While they were taking tea, Mrs O'Hare left them to take her husband a cup of tea and some cake, explaining that Mr O'Hare did not always come downstairs to tea.

"I hope you are not offended, Miss Courtney," said Kathryn. "My father has not fully regained the use of his leg since his accident; he tries to avoid going up and down stairs too many times a day. He joins us at dinner every evening, but prefers to take his breakfast and tea upstairs. It is hard for my mother, but there is not a great deal to be done; he is often in pain, and she will not press him to come downstairs."

Jessica noticed a gentleness in her voice when she spoke of her father's pain and her mother's efforts to care for him, which suggested a degree of sensibility and compassion. There was simultaneously a marked softening of the expression upon her handsome countenance as she spoke.

"I understand completely, and I am not at all offended," Jessica said quickly, wishing only to reassure them. "We do not stand on ceremony at home, my father is frequently out doing parish work, and we would rarely see him when he leaves after breakfast until he returns at dinnertime. My mother complains that he is often too tired to appreciate his food."

"Mama tells me that you live at Pemberley," said Miss O'Hare, and Jessica felt the need to explain.

"I do, ever since I was appointed by Mr Darcy to take charge of the parish school at Pemberley. Mrs Darcy and my mother are cousins," she said. "Besides, it is more convenient—being only a short walk from the school, it enables me to spend more time there. However, I return every Friday night to Kympton and stay over Saturday with my parents, and I help Papa with his parish work, too."

By this time, Mrs O'Hare had returned and settled into her own chair with a cup of tea, and Jessica had the opportunity to ask if Mr O'Hare was well. Having assured her that he was, Mrs O'Hare proceeded to hand the plate of cake around again and sent Elena to get a fresh pot of tea.

While Jessica commented on the excellence of the cake and took another cup of tea, Kathryn turned the conversation to books.

"With your work at the library and the parish school, you must do a lot of reading, Miss Courtney," she remarked, and Jessica confessed that it was, apart from music, her chief pastime.

Rising from her chair, Kathryn went over to one of the bookcases, from which she extracted a slim volume bound in leather. Putting it in Jessica's hands, she said, "Tell me, Miss Courtney, have you read this?"

Jessica saw it was an unusual book indeed, though one she had certainly heard of before. She recalled hearing Mr Darcy and Julian discuss it with her father, but had not paid much attention at the time.

Published in 1859, it was Charles Darwin's *The Origin of Species*.

Looking up at Kathryn, Jessica shook her head. "No I have not, Miss O'Hare, though I have heard of it. My cousin, Julian Darcy, who is himself a scientist, has spoken of it; but it is not widely read, is it?"

"Indeed it is not, except among men of science, and that is a pity, since it is the kind of book of which many people speak without understanding it and, even worse, not having read it at all. It is only recently being read more widely and understood by people other than scientists and scholars," she said very decidedly, and Jessica was again surprised by the intensity of feeling in her voice.

It was quite plain that Kathryn O'Hare had strong views and was not reluctant to express them. Whether they extended to subjects other than books was not immediately clear to her.

Meanwhile, Jessica was delighted to discover that Miss O'Hare was as enthusiastic a reader as herself and, on asking her opinion of Mr Darwin's work, received an answer given in very clear terms.

"It is a most absorbing document, Miss Courtney, albeit one that the church and some others have condemned out of hand, in most cases without fully understanding its purpose. I can find no harm in it; it records Mr Darwin's observations of creatures that many of us have never seen and his conclusions as to how much of the natural world came to be as it is today," she explained, adding generously, "Should you wish to read it yourself, I should be happy to lend you my copy."

Jessica was unsure how much she would comprehend of the scientific work, but eager not to appear indifferent, said quickly, "I should like that very much, thank you," and then not wishing to sound ignorant, but wanting to acquire a better understanding of a work of such obvious importance, she made a suggestion.

"Perhaps, when I have read it, we could talk about it together, and I may discover more about it and understand why it is of such great significance."

To her surprise and delight, Miss O'Hare readily agreed. "Certainly, that would be a very good scheme. There is nothing better to improve one's understanding than a good discussion. When I used to teach at St Margaret's convent school, there was a nun, a woman of great intelligence and perspicacity, who used to organise the recreational activities for the staff. They were always very interesting, thought-provoking ideas—often we would read a book as a group and discuss it together between evensong and dinner. I looked forward so much to those evenings; surprised at the varying views of my fellow teachers, it taught me to look at things from more than one point of view and to consider the reasons that lay behind another's opinion."

"It must have been very enjoyable," said Jessica.

"It certainly was and I think it greatly increased my appreciation of literature."

"Do you believe that to encounter contrary or opposing views is beneficial to one's understanding?" asked Jessica, beginning to enjoy this discourse. Miss O'Hare responded without hesitation.

"Indeed, I do. I think the more open one is to new ideas and the more opinions one hears on a work of art or literature, the better will be one's understanding and ultimately one's appreciation of it. It stands to reason—if one sees a work only from one point of view, one may well miss the great richness of interpretation that comes from sharing other perspectives. It is easily demonstrated when admiring a vista from a window," she said, moving to the window and looking across the dale to the woods beyond.

"Here you see the frame and walls limit one's vision of the scene, whilst stepping outdoors, to see it as a whole, surrounding one, immediately enhances the prospect."

So saying, she took Jessica by the hand and moved to the door that led out into the garden, and it required no further explanation, for there before them was the entire panorama of Colley Dale cradled by the rising hills, a lovely vista that had not been visible from the window.

Jessica listened, fascinated, and agreed that yes, she did really understand better now and was positively excited by the prospect of further conversations along these lines. But it was growing late, and she had to be back at Pemberley before dark.

When she made to leave, both Mrs O'Hare and Kathryn seemed reluctant to let her walk home alone across the common, especially as the sky had clouded over and the evening was drawing in.

Fortuitously, as they were thinking of sending for the carriage, a young gentleman arrived in a hired vehicle and alighted outside the gate. It was Kathryn's brother Stephen, back earlier than expected from Birmingham.

Jessica knew him slightly, having met him at one or two functions in the neighbourhood, and he greeted her cordially. When appealed to by his sister, he was happy to oblige, which meant that both Stephen and Kathryn O'Hare accompanied Jessica as she made her way home, insisting on seeing her safely into the park and within sight of Pemberley House, before turning back.

It was almost dark, and Jessica was grateful for their company. When they parted, she thanked them both and arranged to meet with Kathryn on the following Tuesday, at the library, from where they could proceed to the Pemberley

Parish school. It was a meeting both ladies seemed to anticipate with a great deal of pleasure.

For Jessica, holding the copy of Mr Darwin's famous work, it was the beginning of an entirely new and promising friendship.

She knew no other woman like Miss Kathryn O'Hare. Not even her aunt Caroline, whose grasp of matters political and commercial was quite remarkable, could compare in poise and erudition with Miss O'Hare.

The following Tuesday turned out to be not as pleasant a day as one might have wished for in the middle of Summer. Following a week of fine, warm weather, the temperature fell, and though there was as yet no rain, the sun seemed decidedly reluctant to appear and grey clouds hung low over the distant peaks, when Miss O'Hare and her young sister Elena arrived at the library.

Jessica noted that Kathryn was well prepared for inclement weather, being armed with a large umbrella. She was relieved to hear that Elena intended to spend the next hour at the library, before returning home, while her sister accompanied Jessica to the school. She had hoped to enter into a serious conversation with Miss O'Hare and the presence of young Elena may well have interfered with her plans.

Following a quick tour of the library, which Kathryn agreed was very well stocked and organised, they left together to walk the short distance through the park to the parish school at Pemberley.

Arriving at the school, they found everything in readiness for their visit.

Mr Hurst had been forewarned and urged to ensure that Kathryn had an opportunity to see the students at work.

They were duly busy at their lessons, and Mr Hurst was at pains to assure their guest that they were both keen to learn and generally well behaved. She appeared impressed and asked many questions about the work the children did and the way their lessons were planned.

So genuine did her interest seem that Jessica began to believe there was a good chance Kathryn would be interested in a position at the school, if an offer was made. She was, however, unwilling to take the plunge and introduce the subject, until she had consulted Mr Darcy. She wished now that she had arranged for Miss O'Hare to visit Pemberley House as well.

As often happens in these matters, the weather intervened to bring about an unforeseen resolution to the problem. Having spent the best part of an hour at the school, they were about to leave when a cloudburst brought a drenching shower of rain that made it quite impossible for them to return to the library through the park. It was not only very damp underfoot, a stiff breeze blowing from the hills meant it was a lot colder than before.

Waiting until the rain had eased, Jessica suggested that they try to reach Pemberley House, where there would be a welcome cup of tea and the possibility that a carriage would be available to convey Kathryn to Colley Dale. The prospect certainly appealed, and both ladies agreed it was the best thing to do. Setting out under a shared umbrella to walk the short distance, they arrived well before the next downpour.

The housekeeper at Pemberley was surprised to see them, but that did not prevent her producing a repast of tea, cake, and fruit, which she sent into the sitting room, where the fire was stoked up to a lively blaze.

Later Mr and Mrs Darcy joined them, and to Jessica's delight, Miss O'Hare seemed quite at ease, not in the least intimidated by her distinguished host and hostess. Kathryn had heard a great deal about the Darcys and even more about Pemberley. Her mother had spoken with great respect and admiration of the elegant Mrs Darcy and the wealth and influence of her husband.

Determined not to be daunted by these accounts, Kathryn had been prepared for a somewhat more formal reception than she received.

Both Mr and Mrs Darcy were friendly and welcoming.

She noted that Mr Darcy had remained a most distinguished-looking man despite his years, while his wife had lost none of the lively wit and enthusiasm for which she was renowned. There was between them, Kathryn thought, the kind of understanding and warmth that one saw only in couples whose love and esteem for one another had survived the familiarity of a long marriage.

The Darcys too appeared ready to be impressed by their unexpected guest.

She had admired the beauty of the park and the elegance of their home, without resorting to effusive praise or flattery. A short tour of the rooms downstairs, followed by an invitation from Elizabeth to call again and visit the library and picture gallery, was to Jessica a clear sign that Kathryn had made a favourable impression upon Mrs Darcy.

Jessica was very pleased.

During tea, a general discussion about the parish school led to questions from Mrs Darcy about Kathryn's sojourn in Europe and one from Mr Darcy about her present preoccupation.

"Do you maintain a continuing interest in teaching, Miss O'Hare, or have you decided you have spent enough time in the profession?" he asked, and Jessica, meeting his eye, clearly understood the point of his question.

Kathryn was quick to declare that she was still committed to educating the young, but had needed to take a rest after a couple of difficult and tiring years.

"You found teaching at the convent exhausting?" Elizabeth asked.

"Oh no," replied Kathryn, with a light laugh, "the orphans at the convent school were no trouble at all; in fact, they were absolute angels. No, it was my work at Lindfield Towers I found far more arduous. I was governess to the three children of Lord and Lady Denny, and I regret to say they were the most intractable charges I have ever had to teach. Her Ladyship was keen they should study literature, history, drawing, and music, but none of the children wanted to learn anything at all. Try as I might, I could not interest them in study; they preferred to believe that continued ignorance was a blissful state! Camilla, the youngest, was not so great a problem, except she was easily led and would be drawn into every prank the older pair devised. My efforts to teach them were so wholly unsuccessful, when at last I decided to leave, I felt a great sense of relief."

Elizabeth appeared to sympathise.

"It must have been very frustrating for you," she said, and Mr Darcy concurred, "There cannot have been much satisfaction in it, if the children were so difficult. Were not their parents aware of the problem?"

Kathryn did not wish to criticise her former employers directly.

"I believe they were, but then Lord Denny was often away on business or at Westminster, while Lady Denny was frequently indisposed and had neither the time nor the inclination to discipline the children. Not, I must say, that it would have made a great deal of difference. I knew that no matter how much effort I put into teaching them, they had decided they did not wish to learn."

"Which is a pity, because they will most likely grow into stubborn and ignorant adults; hardly a good example to the rest of the populace, especially as the eldest probably expects to sit in the House of Lords one day!" said Mr Darcy, and at this everybody laughed.

Then Elizabeth asked, "And when you decided to leave Lindfield, did you give them a reason?"

Kathryn smiled and cast her eyes down for a moment.

"I did, but it was not the right one. I did write a long letter once, about the children's problems, but I tore it up. My courage deserted me, and I told them my father's condition had worsened and my mother needed me at home, which wasn't untrue. They knew already about his accident, so it served my purpose to exaggerate it a little. I'm sorry, but I had to get away; I could not go on much longer."

Listening, Jessica felt enormous sympathy and admiration for her new friend. Clearly an educated and intelligent young woman, Kathryn must have endured a good deal of discomfiture, she reckoned, yet she had not lost her interest in teaching. To Jessica, this demonstrated great strength of character and purpose.

Then Elizabeth asked a further question, "Was that the only reason you wished to give up your position at Lindfield Towers?"

Kathryn looked a little surprised at the question, but answered promptly, "No, but it was the chief reason, Mrs Darcy. I had studied to be a teacher and I wasn't enjoying it, nor was I doing any good. But I will admit that I wished also to emancipate myself from the boredom of life at Lindfield. Neither my employers nor any of their visitors appeared to have any interest in life, beyond the most superficial. No one reads or sings or plays an instrument with any enthusiasm. Everyone eats, drinks a great deal more than is good for them, gossips and plays cards, or sleeps! It was a dull life, and I had long wearied of its sameness."

A wry smile crossed Mr Darcy's face at the candid picture. He recalled his cousin Colonel Fitzwilliam complaining about similar evenings at Rosings, over which their aunt Lady Catherine de Bourgh presided in days gone by.

However, he kept his counsel and asked, "And would you wish to teach again, in a school perhaps?"

Kathryn's eye's brightened. "I certainly would, should the opportunity arise, but I am not hopeful. There are not too many schools requiring teachers in this part of the country, and those that do expect one to live in. I am committed now to looking for work I can do while living at home for a while at least; I have been away too long, my mother and sister need me. My mother in particular has grown very tired these last few years attending upon my father since his accident, and I think I have a duty to do my share."

Elizabeth smiled approvingly.

Jessica met Mr Darcy's eyes and read his mind directly. She decided it was time to ask the all-important question. "Miss O'Hare, would you consider teaching at our parish school?" she asked tentatively.

As Kathryn turned to answer, a smile lit up her face. "Would I? If there were a position available, I most certainly would. May I ask if there is such a prospect?" She sounded keen and interested.

Jessica looked again at Mr and Mrs Darcy, and this time, drawing courage from their apparent approval, as evidenced by their smiles, she said, "Well, we have been considering the appointment of a lady, who will teach the older girls. Mr Hurst, who joined us some months ago, teaches Maths and History; we wondered if the second position teaching Language and Art may be of interest to you."

"Thank you, it certainly would, and I should like very much to try," said Kathryn, and Jessica, delighted by her response, immediately suggested that they could meet again at the school to discuss details of work hours and remuneration. Kathryn appeared pleased to agree, and with the tacit approval of Mr Darcy, matters were soon set in train.

Jessica, who was fascinated by her new acquaintance, was keen to have the consent of Mr and Mrs Darcy, and it seemed to her that, at least on the question of teaching at the parish school, Miss O'Hare's credentials were quite acceptable to them.

Later, a carriage was summoned to convey Kathryn to Colley Dale, and the Darcys, returning to the sitting room, took up the subject again.

Mr Darcy, obviously pleased, turned to Jessica. "Congratulations, Jessica, that was very well done."

"Do you believe she will suit?" Elizabeth asked, and Mr Darcy had no doubt at all.

"Miss O'Hare seems both well qualified and keen, two essential attributes for a successful teacher. I am confident we shall find her quite satisfactory. But, I am certain also that Jessica will ensure her certificates and references are all in order. Thus far, she has done very well indeed, I think."

Jessica smiled and thanked him, assuring them that she would do all that was necessary. She was pleased indeed to have the blessing of Mr Darcy for her plan, but was impatient to be gone to her room.

Time was when she would have wanted nothing more than the approbation of Elizabeth and Mr Darcy; now she could not rest until all her thoughts had been set down and despatched to be read by Julian.

I know you will be pleased to hear that I have been making a new and very interesting acquaintance. She is a Miss Kathryn O'Hare, who has returned to live with her parents at Colley Dale after several years away. Miss O'Hare is a most elegant and charming person. In addition, she is also highly educated and has agreed to teach at the parish school. It is most wonderful news for our school and I cannot find words to tell you how delighted I am... she wrote, her pen racing to keep up with her mind, as she thought how much she wanted to have him understand her hopes and aspirations.

When she was satisfied that she had told him everything he needed to know about Miss O'Hare, she paused awhile, thinking of another matter she wished to mention in her letter.

While I know neither of us would indulge in idle gossip, I believe you will enjoy the information that I am about to relate, for it is certainly not malicious rumour.

Our cousin David Fitzwilliam is in love, and the lady, coincidentally, is also a teacher—or aspires to be one and is working to this end. I had best not detail her family name and circumstances, lest this letter should be mislaid and fall into other hands, but I can tell you that Lucy is exceedingly pretty, well read, and accomplished, and David declares she has the disposition of an angel. There, is that not sufficient evidence that he is in love with the lady?

David has not, as yet, told his parents, but I believe his sister Isabella, in whom he has confided, approves of the match.

Suddenly aware that she had filled a paragraph or more on the subject of David's romance, she apologized:

Dear Julian, forgive me if I seem to have run on about it, but I am at this time so very happy, that I seem to want everyone around me to be filled with feelings of delight as I am. Needless to say, I wish my dear cousin David every success with his Lucinda. If they could achieve but half our felicity, they will be happy indeed.

It was unlikely that Julian Darcy, on receiving such an explanation, would censure her for any previous shortcomings in her letter.

Having spent many of the years of his short, troubled marriage to Josie Tate, trying to persuade his wife of the worth of his affection for her and feeling, at its tragic end, that he had failed, Julian was discovering with Jessica the delights of shared love. Her letters conveyed a warmth and generosity of feeling that was entirely new to him and acted like an elixir upon his sense of self worth.

While there was much he wished to say and had perforce, to leave unsaid in his letters to her, there was by now, no doubt in his mind of the absolute rightness of his decision.

On his return to England, he would ask her to marry him, and they would announce their engagement to their families.

END OF PART TWO

POSTSCRIPT FROM PEMBERLEY

Part Three

Chapter Six

THE REFUSAL OF MR Disraeli to call an early election, despite being thwarted in the Commons, had consequences well beyond Whitehall and Westminster. There had been considerable agitation from organisations like the Reform League, which irritated the government, and Disraeli had vowed to produce a bill that would "destroy the agitators and extinguish Gladstone and Co."

To this end, he adopted a series of tactical measures, which stalled the entire process in the Parliament.

For Darcy Gardiner, who had come up to Westminster to help his friend Colin Elliott, MP, campaign for the anticipated election, it meant idleness and frustration. Mr Gladstone, to whose cause he was wholly committed, appeared not to mind the delay, being bent on developing an issue upon which he could unite his party. But for Darcy it was a singularly boring business, and after four weeks, when it was plain that Disraeli was going to tough it out, he returned to Derbyshire for the rest of the year.

He was warmly welcomed by his parents, friends, and grandparents, all of whom had missed him. Likewise, the tenants of the Pemberley estate had wished for the return of the energetic and amiable young man, whose capable management of their affairs had brought a high degree of prosperity and contentment to the community. For himself, Darcy, who had become bored and impatient awaiting political developments in London, found he was enjoying his return to Pemberley more than he had expected. The need to find solutions to the problems on the estate and the knowledge that his grandfather relied upon his judgment provided a very special satisfaction, well beyond the somewhat ephemeral excitement of politics as it was being played.

It was on the third day after his return that Darcy, having spent the morning visiting some of the tenants whose concerns were thought to be most urgent, was returning to Pemberley House shortly before midday.

It was a particularly fine, mild morning, and he, having handed the reins of his horse over to a stable hand, took the path across from the stables into the park. As he emerged from the grove of trees to the right of the drive, he glimpsed an unusual flash of colour and, moments later, encountered a young woman, attired in an ensemble of fine lilac linen and matching hat, standing in the drive, apparently in a state of some bewilderment.

It was difficult to tell who was more surprised by the encounter: she at seeing him emerge suddenly from the trees or Darcy finding himself face to face with a handsome and elegant but completely unknown young lady.

They stood silent for a few moments, then, there being no one available to effect the usual introductions, protocol gave way to practicality. He bowed, introduced himself, and asked if he may be of assistance.

She likewise acknowledged his greeting and told him she was Kathryn O'Hare, daughter of Mr and Mrs O'Hare of Colley Dale.

"I am on my way—or so I thought until I became lost—to an appointment with Miss Jessica Courtney at the Pemberley Parish school. I have been there before, a week or so ago, but we did not come through here and I must confess, this park is so large, I have completely lost my bearings," she said. Then, consulting her watch, she added, "I do believe I have walked about these grounds for the best part of half an hour and still cannot think how to find my way to the school. Would you, sir, be so kind as to direct me?" she asked.

Darcy smiled and assured her that it was not at all uncommon for visitors to Pemberley to lose their way in the park. As for the parish school, he said, it was not far and he could take her there.

"It is really only a short distance to the village church and the school, if one knows the way. We can either take the route over the footbridge and down the path through the woods into the village, or we can make our way up the drive to Pemberley House, which you see in the distance, and walk over to the rectory, which adjoins the parish school. The choice is yours."

She chose to go by the footbridge. "I think we had best take the shortest route. I must get to the school as soon as possible, else Miss Courtney will think I am unreliable, and that will not be a good beginning at all, if I am to work at the school. Punctuality is *de rigeur* in a teacher, do you not agree?"

Darcy agreed but added generously, "One cannot, however, be blamed if one has lost one's way getting there," to which Miss O'Hare replied, with a little grimace, "Except that it might be considered evidence of ineptitude in a grown adult; I should feel rather silly admitting to it, and I hope Miss Courtney will not be provoked by it."

She sounded genuinely concerned, and Darcy decided to reassure her. "On that score at least, I believe I can set your mind at rest. Miss Courtney is my cousin, and I can say with a fair degree of certainty that she is never provoked or aggravated and is both understanding and fair. You have no cause to fear her censure."

Miss O'Hare looked across at her companion quickly and said, "Thank you, that is good to know. It restores my confidence a little, especially since I have some hope that Miss Courtney and I will soon be colleagues. She has offered me a teaching position at the school, and I am on my way to tell her that I have decided to accept."

Darcy smiled, wondering why this revelation had brought such a feeling of pleasure. As they walked on through the woods, he wished he knew something more of Miss Kathryn O'Hare. She had said she was from Colley Dale, which was not a great distance from Pemberley, yet he had never seen her before in his life.

At the school, Jessica greeted them with a worried frown.

"Kathryn, I was most concerned, I thought you had been delayed by some dreadful misadventure," she said.

"I was," said Miss O'Hare, with a self-deprecating laugh, "by the common misadventure of losing my way; you did not warn me that I should make myself a map before undertaking the journey through the Pemberley grounds. I fear I have no excuse to offer except my own confusion."

Then, turning to Darcy, "However, thanks to Mr Gardiner here, you see me at last, else I should still be wandering around that magnificent park."

Jessica laughed, thanking Darcy for his help and, before escorting Kathryn into the school house, requested that he remind the housekeeper at Pemberley that Miss O'Hare would be joining them for afternoon tea.

It was an errand Darcy Gardiner promised to carry out with the greatest pleasure.

It was late afternoon when the two ladies arrived at the house, and Darcy had had time to change and await their appearance. He had lunched earlier with his grandparents and, on mentioning his chance meeting with Miss O'Hare in the park, had been informed of all the circumstances of her appointment to the parish school. Mr Darcy had described her as a remarkably well-educated young lady, whom Jessica had fortuitously discovered, while Mrs Darcy had noted that Kathryn O'Hare was, without any doubt at all, the most personable young woman she had met in many a year. "Truly, I cannot think of anyone who has so impressed me since young Anna Faulkner returned from Europe and your uncle Jonathan Bingley fell hopelessly in love with her!"

Darcy, who knew well the story of Jonathan Bingley and Anna Faulkner, agreed Miss O'Hare was certainly very elegantly dressed.

"I think when you get to know her better, you will find she is more than elegant, she is quite a remarkable person," his grandmother continued. "I was very impressed with her appreciation of art and music, too, which we discovered in the short time she spent with us on her last visit to Pemberley."

His grandfather concurred, adding, "And to all these accomplishments, she brings also an ability to speak with a certain confidence, a sense of understanding, that is doubtless the result of a good education and wide reading," he said, and Darcy was pleased to note that Miss O'Hare had found favour with both his grandparents.

He was well aware of the very high standards they set. He had heard Mr Darcy express his reservations about some young men and women in the district, and as for Mrs Darcy, she was known to be quite pernickety about partners for members of her family.

His mother had often laughingly admitted that it was fortunate his father, Doctor Richard Gardiner, had been a favourite of the Darcys well before the couple had fallen in love, and there had been no question of their disapproving of the match.

"I cannot imagine Mama taking very kindly to someone she did not approve of, however deeply I was in love with them," she had said, and Darcy knew, from some of Mrs Darcy's pointed comments about certain members of the family, that her approval was not easily given.

It was therefore good to know that they had no reservations about Miss Kathryn O'Hare; indeed, it was quite the opposite!

"I am sorry your mama is away this week; I should have liked her to have met Miss O'Hare," Elizabeth said. "I do believe Cassy will like her very well." His grandfather said nothing, seemingly preoccupied with his thoughts, but he smiled and nodded, and Darcy took this to signify agreement.

When the ladies arrived, he noticed that both Mr and Mrs Darcy greeted Miss O'Hare warmly and made her welcome.

At first, he was a little overawed, expecting this paragon of learning and artistic appreciation to have an opinion on everything, expressed without fear or favour. He had met one or two such women in London and had not enjoyed their company very much.

"I always feel inadequate, as if they expect me to be as erudite and knowledgeable on every subject under the sun, which I know I am not," he had once confessed to Jessica and she had laughed merrily and accused him of being very silly.

He certainly did not wish to be so regarded by Miss O'Hare.

He was relieved indeed to find Kathryn O'Hare quite amiable and far from being opinionated on every topic. In fact, she was exceedingly reasonable, willing to accommodate other points of view and to admit her own ignorance of matters political, of which she confessed she knew very little. She did, however, declare an interest in the possibility that Mr Gladstone may soon be Prime Minister.

"My father, who has a thorough dislike of Mr Disraeli, hopes that he will live to see the day; do you believe it possible?" she asked.

"Indeed I do," replied Darcy with some vigour. "If only it were possible to persuade Mr Disraeli to call an election, we may well see Mr Gladstone take the Prime Ministership quite soon."

While tea was being served, the topic changed, and talk was mainly of the school, and though Miss O'Hare was more experienced in teaching than was Jessica, she seemed especially keen to let Miss Courtney explain her plans. Jessica was eager to do so; "What we propose is…" she began, and Darcy listened as the two ladies talked as if they had known one another for many years. They seemed to understand and anticipate each other's ideas, and it appeared they would work well together.

Jessica especially seemed happier than Darcy had seen her in years. There was, of course, another reason for her felicity, to which no one else in the room was privy but himself, and he was sworn to secrecy!

When they had finished their tea and their discussion, Miss O'Hare rose and said it was time to leave. Mr Darcy offered to send for the carriage, but she thanked him politely and refused, declaring that she was looking forward to a walk on such a fine Summer's evening.

Darcy Gardiner, who had risen as she did and moved to the door, said, "Will you let me escort you to the gates of the park? Then at least, we shall not worry that you have been left to wander the grounds all night long."

She laughed then, a very light, pretty laugh, and thanked him for his concern, saying to the others with a smile, "I can see I am not going to be permitted to forget my lapse of this afternoon."

She thanked her hosts and promised Jessica that she would not be late on the morrow, before turning once more to Darcy, who awaited her at the entrance. "I think I shall write myself a set of instructions, so as not to lose my way again," they heard her say as they went down the steps, laughing together.

Jessica stood watching them. There was something about the ease with which they had come together as they walked across the courtyard and out into the park that made her smile. Perhaps, she thought, the lovely Miss O'Hare might help Darcy forget his earlier disappointment. She was very fond of her cousin and wished very much to see him happy again, but had no indication of his present state of mind.

The pair in question had walked on a while in silence.

The softness of the evening and the sheer beauty of the prospect before them, as they crossed the sloping lawn and walked towards the lake, with the woods and hills in the distance touched by the setting sun, seemed to render speech unnecessary.

He wanted to speak but was reluctant to break the silence with what might have been considered some banality, and she appeared only to want to absorb the scene that surrounded them. Her soft exclamations of appreciation as the sky blushed pink and then gleamed gold required no response from him.

They approached the bridge that spanned the stream and carried the road out to the main gate of the estate, and as they did so, Kathryn spoke, "Mr Gardiner, Miss Courtney tells me you are an acknowledged disciple of Mr Gladstone. Is this true?"

Darcy inclined his head and said, "To the extent that I am a Reformist by conviction and a believer in the cause that Mr Gladstone has stood for, I confess I am."

Looking up at him, she asked, "And do you seriously believe he will be Prime Minister soon?"

"I do indeed, just as soon as Mr Disraeli calls an election. I have no doubt of it."

At this response, Kathryn smiled and said, "My father will be pleased to hear that. Mr Gardiner, I should like very much for you to meet my father, who has for many years followed the progress of Mr Gladstone. Unhappily he does not get out and about much since his accident, and has very few opportunities to indulge his interest in politics. Many of his friends have moved away or passed on, and my mother and I have very little knowledge of political matters and cannot engage him in the kind of discussion I know he would enjoy...."

Waiting until she had finished, Darcy sought to assure her that he would like just as well to meet her father.

"It would give me great pleasure to meet him; it is always good to engage a fellow Reformist in conversation; there aren't many in these parts," he said.

Kathryn was smiling, and seeing she was pleased, he added quickly, "If you would let me know when it would be convenient to your father and yourself, I would be delighted to call on him. I shall look forward to it."

She thanked him, and they walked on.

Soon they were at the main gate, where, having said farewell without further delay, she walked briskly down the road that led out of the park.

Once, as she reached the spot where the road curved away, taking her out of sight, Kathryn turned to look and saw him standing at the gate, watching her progress. He waited thus for some few minutes longer.

Afterwards, as the sky darkened ahead and a flock of starlings flew across the lake, he walked slowly back to the house.

The rest of the year passed peacefully enough at Pemberley and equally, without an increase of tumult or turbulence, in the country at large.

Except, that is, for the rising impatience among the political fraternity at the recalcitrance of Mr Disraeli, who clearly meant to hang onto office for as long as possible.

At the parish school, Miss Kathryn O'Hare slipped with remarkable ease into her appointed role and, to Jessica's very great relief, appeared to get along exceedingly well with Mr Hurst, even though he was her senior by at least three decades. They clearly shared a sense of dedication and an interest in imparting knowledge, which made them thoroughly compatible colleagues.

The students liked her, too, and Jessica noted how meticulously she prepared her lessons and with what care she attended upon her charges, many of whom had had little or no learning at all. That she was a good teacher with a genuine love of her work was without any doubt, Jessica reported happily to Mr and Mrs Darcy, who seemed unsurprised.

Writing to Julian, Jessica observed:

> *The children obviously like Kathryn O'Hare and enjoy being taught by her, and I can see she takes much pleasure from their satisfaction. They are always bringing her flowers and once a basket of early fruit, which she very generously shared with all of the students and staff.*
>
> *I am particularly pleased to report that she seems to get along very well with our new school master Mr Hurst, who, being a quiet, old-fashioned man, may have been expected to be rather difficult, but happily, they seem to have taken to one another. She is in awe of his years of experience, and he appears to enjoy her bright, lively manner.*
>
> *It is a most happy coincidence, and I am so proud to have secured such a fine teacher for our own little school.*
>
> *The rector is excessively pleased, and both Mr Darcy and your mama are quite convinced it will do a great deal of good for the children of the parish to have as dedicated a teacher as Miss O'Hare.*

There was another matter too, of which she wrote:

> *Dear Julian, you must promise not to breathe a word of what I am about to*

reveal to you, but I think our dear cousin Darcy Gardiner is a little partial to Miss O'Hare. He quite clearly admires her, for she is both very handsome and exceedingly elegant, as well as remarkably well educated. I have caught him regarding her with a very curious look, as though he were trying to make her out, for she is at times serious and at others, rather pert and light-hearted in her manner and not averse to speaking her mind, much as your mama does.

There may be nothing to it, and certainly I cannot see anything on her part at this stage, beyond an amiable friendliness towards him, but if it were to grow into something deeper than a passing fascination that might happen between two attractive and intelligent persons, I believe I should be very happy for them.

However, it is not for me to say it should or should not happen, for I am definitely not a matchmaker, though it does no harm to hope, I am sure.

Both Darcy Gardiner and Miss O'Hare would have been somewhat diverted if they had been able to see what Jessica had written. In fact, neither had admitted to themselves the possibility of there being anything more significant in their association than the pleasant affinity of two people who appear to have a great deal in common and consequently enjoy the pleasure of each other's company.

That they met fairly frequently was not a matter for surprise or speculation, since Miss O'Hare came daily to the parish school, and Darcy, as manager of the Pemberley Estate, had charge of the buildings and facilities provided there.

It was a responsibility that had previously not lain very heavy upon his shoulders, but one which he now appeared to administer with particular zeal and dedication. The school wanted for nothing if he could provide it, and he ensured that any request for repairs or improvement was carried out most expeditiously.

Both Jessica and Mr Hurst were delighted by the attention their requests received, and the students, though unaware of this, were the greatest beneficiaries of all.

Moreover, Mrs Darcy's admiration for Miss O'Hare meant she was frequently asked to tea at Pemberley. On one occasion, Cassandra and Richard Gardiner were also present; consequently Kathryn was invited to dine with them later in the month, at Camden House.

In between times, Darcy Gardiner had, by discreet questions posed to his cousin Jessica, gleaned more information about Kathryn O'Hare.

Having arranged to call on her father, he reasoned that it was pertinent he should acquaint himself with the family's circumstances. They were not tenants, but they were neighbours, he argued, and it was only prudent to make some enquiries about them. While young Elena was frequently seen in the village, he had been puzzled by the fact that he had had no notion at all of the existence of their accomplished and charming elder daughter.

Where, he wondered, had she been all these years?

Jessica was not entirely surprised and not a little amused by Darcy's interest, but provided him with the information he sought, if she was in possession of it herself. She was able, therefore, to reveal that Miss O'Hare had been educated at a well-respected ladies' seminary in Sussex, in the district of East Grinstead, and had later been sent by the nuns there to a sister establishment in Brussels, for further study. She knew also of the position Kathryn had held at Lindfield Towers as governess to the three children of Lord and Lady Denny.

However, she was not able to assist him when he asked, "And why do you suppose she decided to return at this time to Colley Dale rather than continue with her work there?"

Jessica shook her head. "I did not ask her, and she did not tell me. It was not relevant to our current discussion. I do recall she claimed she had been bored with life at Lindfield Towers; besides, the children she was supposed to teach had no desire to learn," she replied.

Darcy was not unsympathetic. "I can appreciate that it must then have been a trying situation indeed, but enough to make one give up what must have been a prestigious and well-remunerated position?" he mused, but said nothing more about it.

He had already discovered something of her taste in literature and music from the lady herself, and her sister Elena had let slip the fact that Kathryn was twenty-five years old, a few years younger than he was, and that, in the intimate circle of her family, she was called Kate.

"Do you suppose she has a preference for it?" he asked Jessica with a degree of interest that amused her vastly, for why would such a trivial matter signify, she wondered, unless his partiality for the lady was on the increase. No young man who is a mere indifferent acquaintance would consider such a trifling detail to be of any consequence, she thought.

But she answered him honestly, "I cannot tell for certain, Darcy. She has certainly not indicated to me that she prefers one or the other. I do know Elena has always referred to her as 'my sister Kate,' which may indicate that where there is some closeness or intimacy in the relationship, as in a family or with a dear friend, the diminutive is preferred."

Darcy concurred, deciding he would observe how this played in the family when he called on them the following week. It was an occasion to which he looked forward with pleasure and some degree of trepidation.

The enquiries he had made at Camden Park about their former steward and trainer had revealed that Mr Daniel O'Hare was a man of very strong views and an uncertain temper.

There were stories aplenty of his remarkable prowess as a horseman and steward, but also a few about his Irish temper. Darcy was pleased to be fore-warned; he had no desire to anger the father of Kathryn O'Hare. It had been clear to him from the tone of her voice when she spoke of her father that there was a good deal of affection between them.

Darcy Gardiner called on the O'Hares on a fine, mild morning in late Summer, not long before Mr Disraeli, unable to hold out any longer, finally called on the Queen to dissolve the Parliament.

The invitation came through Kathryn, who had promised she would be there at their first meeting, but had assured him that there would be nothing to be concerned about, since her father had the highest regard for the Darcys of Pemberley as well as Dr Richard Gardiner.

"Dr Gardiner treated my father when he was first injured and has seen him often since. He is much loved in our family for his kindness and respected for his skill. Which means, Mr Gardiner, you can bask in the reflected glory of both your father and grandfather—in addition to the fact that my father has heard only the best reports of you."

Astonished at this candid remark, Darcy asked, "And pray from whom has he had these reports?" only to be fobbed off with a light riposte about not asking too many questions and not looking a gift horse in the mouth!

Clearly, he thought, he was not supposed to question her too closely on the subject. Deciding to comply, Darcy promised himself he would pursue the matter later and discover what claims had been made for him.

He had a general suspicion that the "reports" had come from her, but had no wish to disconcert her by pressing the matter now.

Mr O'Hare turned out to be a man in his late fifties, still handsome, with a clear, tanned complexion, a bright smile, and features that immediately recalled his elder daughter's countenance. His greying hair had traces of the deep auburn colour that was also her most striking feature.

But there the resemblance ended for he was tall, almost gaunt, while she was of medium height and her figure was well formed and graceful. His firm voice bespoke a man used to command, while hers had the gentle but persuasive tones of a teacher, who understood the need to explain and convince.

When they were introduced, Mr O'Hare stood up, using a sturdy cane to support himself, and was later helped into his chair by Elena, while Mrs O'Hare went to order the tea. Kathryn then busied herself handing out plates with slices of cake, looking from time to time to ascertain whether her father was comfortably settled, before getting him his tea.

In the intimate atmosphere of their modest parlour, Darcy was immediately aware of the closeness of the family group. Quite soon he learned the answer to one of his unanswered questions when both Mr and Mrs O'Hare referred to their daughter as Kate. He caught the lady's eye and observed that she was a little amused that he had noticed it.

Everyone having partaken of cake and tea, Elena removed the tea things and left the room with her mother, leaving Kathryn with Darcy and her father. Darcy was grateful for her presence; she stayed as she had promised she would and, in doing so, made their conversation much easier.

At first both men were hesitant and tentative as they groped their way through two or three topics. Having dispensed with the weather, the parlous state of the road between Matlock and Staffordshire, and the state of British agriculture, they were silent for a while until Kathryn informed her father that Mr Gardiner was the captain of the district cricket team. Mr O'Hare was interested, and there was something more to talk about, but with the season just ending, the conversation was about to lapse again, when the mention of the imminent election brought it back to life.

Mr O'Hare expressed his dislike of Mr Disraeli in no uncertain terms.

"I have to say, Mr Gardiner, I do not trust the man. They say the Queen likes him; well, if she does, she should tell him it is time to be gone. I cannot believe the people will vote him back in; even those to whom he has lately extended the franchise must by now be weary of him," he said, with unconcealed antagonism.

Darcy, meeting Kathryn's eyes, smiled and nodded, happy to have been forewarned.

"Indeed, sir, if they are not, then they ought be, for he has long outstayed his welcome. Mr Gladstone has been ready for an election for many months now; he waits only for a date to be fixed."

"Ah, Mr Gladstone, the people's William—now there is a man I can and will trust," declared Mr O'Hare, hastening however to add, "Well, I should say I would trust him more easily, if he were to pass a law giving all voters a secret ballot. There is too much opportunity for bribery and intimidation by landlords, mill owners, and the like now. Do you not agree, Mr Gardiner? What do you think, would Mr Gladstone support the secret ballot?"

Darcy had never given the matter much serious thought and was quite surprised to hear such a cogent argument in its favour. He took awhile to collect his thoughts and frame an answer, which gave Kathryn time to ask her father if he needed another cushion for his back. His response revealed a gentleness that had not been obvious to Darcy before.

"Thank you, Kate my dear," he said as she tucked a cushion behind him and settled him in. He stroked her hand as it lay on his shoulder and said simply, "I am glad you have come home, my love; your mother and I have missed you very much."

At this she coloured slightly and made an excuse to leave the room, leaving them together.

"She's a good girl, my Kate," he went on. "Her mother and I have missed her these last few years. Do you have sisters, Mr Gardiner?"

"Indeed I do, sir, two of them; one was recently married, to Mr Carr who has purchased the Rushmore Farm and Stud."

"Ah yes, I do believe Mrs O'Hare mentioned it. I know the stud well, and I understand the new owner has made some improvements to the place?"

Darcy told him yes, he had, and their conversation moved to other more mundane matters for a while before Darcy, realising that Mr O'Hare was probably tiring and quite possibly in some pain, rose to take his leave.

As he did so, Kathryn and her mother returned, and everyone thanked him for coming. Mr O'Hare urged him to tell Mr Gladstone, when he met him, that "he must bring in a law to enforce the secret ballot, else it will do no good at all to extend the franchise, because the same corrupt individuals will bribe their way back into the Parliament."

Promising to pass the message on, Darcy said his farewells.

Kathryn accompanied him into the hall, and as they stood there, she thanked him again for coming. "Do not feel that you have to take everything he says seriously," she added. "My father has been immersed in all of this for years; it must have been a great pleasure to be able to talk so openly and passionately about it with you," she said, and Darcy, making light of it, assured her he had enjoyed every minute of it.

"It is good to find a man as committed and keen as your father, Miss O'Hare, and I truly appreciate his sincerity," he said, adding quickly, "I shall certainly convey his views about the secret ballot to Mr Colin Elliott, MP, who is close to Mr Gladstone and quite likely to be in the ministry after the next election. Rest assured he will hear of it, as soon as I go to Westminster."

"Will that be soon?" she asked softly and he replied promptly, "It cannot be soon enough for me; Mr Gladstone and the party are ready and eager for the campaign to commence; only Dizzy, the old fox, delays us," Darcy replied.

When he took his leave of her and left, Kathryn thought about his words. Could he really have meant "it cannot be soon enough for me" because he was impatient to be gone to Westminster to join his friends, since life in Derbyshire had grown dull and boring? Or did he mean only that he wished the election would be brought on sooner, because as a loyal supporter of Mr Gladstone he wanted him to win. Kathryn had no way of telling, but she could not help feeling a twinge of disappointment that he would soon be gone. He was quite the most interesting young man she had encountered in years.

When they met again at Camden House, his parents' home, where Kathryn had been invited to dine, Parliament had been dissolved and the date for the election fixed. Darcy Gardiner was preparing to leave for London.

Jessica had suggested that Kathryn should come prepared to stay overnight at Pemberley after the dinner.

"It will be better than returning alone in a carriage at that hour of night," she had said. "We could convey you to Colley Dale on the morrow, after breakfast." Kathryn had thanked her and through her Mrs Darcy, who had suggested the arrangement.

"If you are sure it will not inconvenience anyone?" she said, and Jessica assured her she would not.

"Of course it will not, there are rooms aplenty at Pemberley House, and if you wish, you may use my room; it will be no trouble at all."

The dinner party was both pleasant and impressive. The guests, mainly family and close friends, had been gathered in the elegant Regency Room at Camden House and plied with a variety of refreshments before being invited to accompany their host and hostess into the dining room.

A pleasing degree of informality had permitted the guests to be introduced to each other and then to circulate and talk to those they knew best, but in the dining room, they sat at assigned places, which made Kathryn nervous, for she knew very few of the people present.

She gave silent thanks, however, and could not hide her pleasure when she found herself seated next to Mr Darcy with Jessica to her left and Darcy Gardiner opposite, with his grandmother beside him.

"In such good company," she thought, "I shall certainly not be bored through dinner."

And she was not, for between them Mrs Darcy and her grandson kept up a most interesting series of conversations, which, even when she was not participating in them, held her attention. Mr Darcy commented gently that his wife had lost none of her wit and their grandson had inherited some of it himself.

Encouraged by their response, Darcy Gardiner had provided a commentary upon many matters, all of which were either intriguing, amusing, or both. Diverting and intelligent observations on matters social and political, drawn either from his experience of life in London or his knowledge of the local area, kept them entertained throughout the meal.

Aside from the more serious aspects of his character, his sense of honour and loyalty, which were not immediately apparent to the casual observer, Darcy Gardiner's easy charm was his main asset, and Kathryn could see why he was so well liked within his family and among their general acquaintance. He did not stand upon ceremony and rarely intervened in a conversation with the sole purpose of asserting his opinion. On the contrary, he was a keen listener and frequently asked for the views of others on a subject, before offering his own.

Recalling the stifling formality of Lindfield Towers and the exasperating pretensions of her previous employers and their coterie of sycophants, Kathryn was delighted by the friendliness and hospitality of Sir Richard and Lady Gardiner and their charming family. They mingled easily with all their guests, and Kathryn found herself able to relax and enjoy the occasion to the fullest extent. With excellent food, fine wines, good company, and post-prandial entertainment of a high quality provided by a chamber music ensemble, everything was designed to enhance their pleasure through the evening.

Later, the company broke into small groups as tea and coffee were served, and seeing Darcy Gardiner at the coffee table waiting for his cup to be replenished, Kathryn took the opportunity to approach him.

She had hoped all evening for such a moment and he, sensing she was desirous of speaking with him alone, waited while she re-filled her cup and moved with her, indicating a seat beside a window at the far end of the room.

Some part of the way through dinner, as it became clear that Darcy would soon be leaving for Westminster, Kathryn had formed a resolution to speak with him that evening. She wished to express her thanks and that of her parents for his kindness in calling upon them and spending above an hour in conversation with her father.

It was something for which she had sought an opportunity and when it appeared, she took it. As they seated themselves, she said, "Mr Gardiner, I must convey to you my heartfelt thanks and those of my mother for your very generous gesture in visiting my father and spending time with him. I cannot tell you how much it has meant to him, how elated and gratified he has been since your visit."

"I am delighted to hear it," said Darcy, acknowledging her remarks, and she added, "It has been many years since he has been able to speak so openly and enjoy such a lively discourse with someone who shared his concerns and hopes. He has spoken of it often since that day and with so much pleasure; my mother truly believes it has been more efficacious than his medication in improving his spirits. I wanted very much to tell you how deeply your kindness is appreciated."

As she spoke Darcy had remained silent, though his countenance revealed clearly that he was not unmoved by her words.

When she had finished speaking, he said gently, "Miss O'Hare, please do not think me unappreciative of your kind sentiments, but you must not feel that you owe me any gratitude on that score. I called on your family and spent what was for me a most exhilarating hour in conversation with your father, whose knowledge of and dedication to the great Reformist cause, which I support, quite astonished me. I am pleased indeed, that he enjoyed our meeting, but the greater pleasure was mine, I assure you, for his is surely a far longer and more intense commitment to a great cause. It is not often that I meet someone in this district with the same passion and loyalty as your father has expressed."

Looking directly at her, he added, "Please tell him that I greatly appreciated the opportunity, and if he so desires, I should be more than happy to visit him again, when I am returned from Westminster, to acquaint him with the progress of our campaign."

As he concluded his words, Kathryn looked at his face, keen to ascertain whether he was merely being gentlemanly and polite.

His expression was open and sincere; from what she could see, there was nothing in his manner or tone to suggest that he was being other than completely honest with her.

She smiled and said, "Thank you, you are very kind; I shall convey your message to my father, and I know he will be delighted to see you again and will look forward to news of the campaign."

At which he inclined his head in acknowledgement, then, taking her cup, placed it and his own upon a side table and offered her his arm.

"Now, I believe there is to be some entertainment in the music room; my sisters have been persuaded to play and sing; they will be most displeased with me if I do not attend. Shall we go?" he asked, and Kathryn rose and went with pleasure.

Observing him as they watched the performance of Lizzie Carr and young Laura-Ann, she saw his expression soften with affection as he listened and his eyes light up with pleasure at the appreciative applause they received from the party. Plainly, he was quite devoted to his family.

Later that night, Jessica and Kathryn returned with Mr and Mrs Darcy to Pemberley House, in the carriage that took only a very little time to convey them the short distance from Camden Park.

Jessica had arranged for Kathryn to have a room opposite her own.

Since the hour was late, they spent only a little while in conversation, remarking upon the success of the evening and the enjoyment they had each derived from the occasion. Jessica had not failed to notice that Kathryn had spent some time speaking with her cousin Darcy after dinner and that she appeared very pleased and happy thereafter.

But, since Kathryn had made no special mention of it, neither did Jessica, before bidding her friend good night and sending a maid to attend upon her.

After the girl had helped with her toilette and withdrawn, Kathryn retired to bed, but it was a while before she could sleep.

Her mind was engaged in wondering at her good fortune in making such admirable friends. Their generosity and hospitality far outweighed anything she had known before. The atmosphere of well-being and congenial gentility that surrounded them was of a quality that she could never have found within her own small circle of friends. Mr and Mrs Darcy, as well as Sir Richard and Lady Gardiner, had extended to her a level of cordiality that she had never expected, when she had returned to live at Colley Dale, hoping to find there respite from the atmosphere of Lindfield Towers, of which she had grown so weary.

For Jessica Courtney and Darcy Gardiner she had developed a special affection. Their warmth, genuine kindness, and happy sense of humour had surprised and delighted her, adding a completely new dimension to her life.

By the time sleep came, in the small hours, she had determined that these new friendships were so precious to her, nothing should be permitted to tarnish them.

Chapter Seven

O N HIS RETURN FROM London, Darcy Gardiner called at the parish school, ostensibly to ascertain if everything was in order, but also to see Kathryn O'Hare, although he had not as yet admitted this even to himself.

Kathryn, who had been alerted to his return by Jessica, greeted him cordially. Darcy was quite clearly pleased to see her looking so well and said so. However, she had sad news for him.

"You find me alone today, Mr Gardiner, except for Mr Hurst. Your cousin Jessica was summoned this morning to Oakleigh, where Mrs Gardiner has been taken ill."

Darcy was immediately perturbed, as anxiety for his grandmother outweighed all other concerns. He wanted to be told what had occurred, when and where had Mrs Gardiner been taken ill.

"Is the cause of her illness known, and have you any news if she is recovered or is she still unwell?" he asked, and there was real urgency in his voice, while his usually cheerful, handsome face was darkened by a frown.

Kathryn could tell him little more than Jessica, who had received the news that morning from her mother, had revealed to her, before setting out herself for Oakleigh. It was enough for him to decide that he would travel thither himself, forthwith.

"I must discover if they need any help and make what arrangements may be necessary, especially now my uncle Robert and his wife have returned to London for the season. If my grandmother is seriously unwell, it will not be possible for Jessica to care for her alone."

Kathryn nodded in agreement, understanding his concern.

Before he left, he revealed that he had hoped to arrange to visit her father again, on a mutually convenient day, but that needs must be postponed, he said, until he knew more about Mrs Gardiner's condition. He apologised and said, "I promise to return as soon as I have ascertained how things stand at Oakleigh," and Kathryn accepted that Mrs Gardiner must have a prior claim upon his time.

When he had gone, Kathryn could not help wondering at his remarkable good nature and the deep concern he demonstrated for those he loved. She had not known a gentleman possessed of such a commendable sense of responsibility. It was not a common commodity in these times, when self advancement was the predominant concern of most young men.

As she returned to her young charges, who were becoming impatient and trying out the piano with very little success, Kathryn could not help feeling flattered by his attention, in coming so soon after his return from London to see her and arrange to call on her father. Yet, it was the impression of his kindness that stayed longest with her.

Two days later, Darcy revisited the school.

Kathryn was not entirely surprised to see him; Jessica was back too with the news that Mrs Gardiner's illness was not as bad as had been feared. Jessica's mother, Emily Courtney, had moved temporarily to Oakleigh to attend upon her mother until her condition improved.

When Darcy Gardiner arrived, Kathryn was preparing to leave and to Jessica's amusement, it seemed he had timed his arrival to coincide with her departure. Consequently, as he walked with her through the grounds, they were afforded plenty of time for private conversation.

Both Kathryn and her companion were pleasantly surprised at how easily they were able to pick up the threads of conversations on subjects which had been left unresolved, when they had parted some weeks ago.

After some initial pleasantries and light-hearted talk, she felt the need to ask how Mr Gladstone's campaign for the election was proceeding and did not anticipate his answer when he said, "I have to confess that I am not entirely sure how to answer you, because in truth, most of my time was spent working with Colin Elliott on a very parochial matter, the provision of money for a school in his constituency in Hertfordshire. I had hoped to be involved in some work on Mr Gladstone's policy on Ireland, concerning the matter of absentee landlords, which, as your father would know, is a vexed problem indeed."

"And were you not?" she asked, expressing some concern.

His voice reflected his disappointment. "Sadly no, I was not. Primarily because Mr Gladstone's present preoccupation is almost wholly with the disestablishment of the Irish church—a subject for which I can summon up no enthusiasm at all!"

If Darcy Gardiner had no enthusiasm for the cause of disestablishment, Kathryn O'Hare knew nothing at all of the matter and confessed as much. Raising her eyes to heaven in exasperation, she asked, "And was there really nothing else to involve you? No policy on public education or the funding of parish schools?" knowing these were areas of great interest to him.

She heard the frustration in his voice when he replied, "No, in fact, I spent almost an entire fortnight waiting to be asked to become engaged in some matter of policy, but no such call came!"

"My father will certainly be very disappointed," she said, explaining that Daniel O'Hare had been hoping to hear some good news of Mr Gladstone's campaign.

Darcy was about to respond when, as they approached the gate leading out of the estate, they heard the sounds of a horse being ridden at a very fast pace, approaching from the direction of Bakewell.

As the horse and rider came into view, Darcy saw but failed to recognise the man, who rode by, hardly glancing in their direction.

Kathryn, however, had been quite startled.

She had grown pale and drew back into the shelter of the trees beside the path.

When he turned to her, Darcy noted her pallor and obvious discomposure. Immediately solicitous, he asked, "Miss O'Hare, are you not well? Has something upset you?"

She hastened to deny that she was ill, but even as she spoke, her voice trembled and she swayed on her feet, which made him move swiftly to take her arm and steady her, before suggesting that she should not attempt to walk any further.

"You *are* unwell; I can see it, plainly. Please do not attempt to walk home alone, it will not be safe for you to do so. If you stay here awhile, I shall go round to the stables at Pemberley and return with a vehicle; I could bring it round by the road and convey you to Colley Dale," he suggested.

But, she was reluctant to put him to so much trouble, even though she was well aware that she could not undertake a walk of above a mile to Colley Dale in her present state.

Still unwilling to impose upon him, she said, "I think if I were to rest here awhile, I could go on."

He would not hear of it.

"No, I will not permit it. You must not put yourself in danger. Should you feel ill or faint on the way and suffer some accident, your parents will never forgive me nor will I forgive myself. I cannot agree to let you go on alone. Let me help you to that arbour over by the stream; if you would rest there awhile, just a very short while, I shall make my way across the park to the stables and return with a vehicle and all will be well. Trust me, Kathryn," he said, and looking up at him, she saw the concern and anxiety on his countenance, and suddenly, she was very grateful for his reassuring presence.

She agreed then, and he helped her over the very short distance to the arbour, where he waited until she was seated and, having assured her he would not be long, strode quickly away towards the house.

As Kathryn waited, she heard again the sounds of an approaching horse. This time, they were coming back along the road, and even though she was fairly well concealed from the sight of anyone passing beyond the boundaries of the park, she was apprehensive and was very still until the horse and rider had gone past. Then, she rose and looked at the figure disappearing up the road; it was the same man they had seen a short while ago; she recognised his jacket and hat, quite clearly. As she realised who it was, her knees trembled and she returned to sit again in the shelter of the trees, feeling quite miserable.

By the time Darcy Gardiner returned, bringing a small vehicle up the road that encircled the estate, she had attempted to compose herself, but she was so very grateful for his help, so relieved he was back, she could not help the tears that filled her eyes.

Her manifest distress convinced him that she was indeed ill and he had been right to fetch the carriage. He helped her in, placed a rug over her knees, and drove away, taking the fork that branched off the Matlock road towards Colley Dale.

When they reached the house, he helped her out and attended her to the door, where Elena, who was in the front room, saw them and came out to greet them, followed by her mother.

Darcy explained that Kathryn had been taken ill.

"While walking home, she felt faint and was unable to make the journey on foot; I think she probably needs to rest," and as Kathryn made to protest, he added, "Please do not be anxious, Miss O' Hare, I shall explain to Miss Courtney that you are not well enough to be at the school tomorrow. I am sure it will be best to rest for a day or two."

It seemed her mother agreed and while Kathryn did try to explain that it could have been the heat, since it had been an unseasonably warm day, neither Elena nor her mother would listen, and soon she was helped upstairs to her bedroom. Darcy said his farewells and left to return to Pemberley.

Later, alone in her room, after her mother and sister had helped her change and left her to rest, Kathryn went over the events of the afternoon in her mind. She could say not a word to anyone, but she had recognised the man on the horse. It was a Mr Gordon Hartley-Brown, with whom she had become acquainted during her stay at Lindfield Towers. A cousin of her former employer, Lady Denny, he was probably the one man in the world she had absolutely no desire to meet. Not at this time, not ever.

⚜

On the way back to Pemberley, Darcy Gardiner called at the inn in Bakewell. It had been a warm afternoon and he was thirsty.

There were a few men in the parlour, and Darcy, who knew the landlord well, had a jug of ale brought to him in the smaller, more private room, where he would be undisturbed. Seated in an alcove, which afforded him a clear view of the road, he saw a man ride into the yard, dismount, and having handed the reins of his horse to a stable hand, enter the inn.

Darcy recognised his jacket; it was cut in a fashionable London style of a deep burgundy-coloured cloth; the very one he had seen on the man who had ridden past earlier that afternoon. From his vantage point, he could see the man as he stood at the bar and ordered a drink; he was not anyone Darcy knew, nor was he a man from the district.

He spoke to no one and made no attempt to be sociable.

Not long afterwards, the man finished his drink and took himself upstairs. Darcy was puzzled.

Fashionably dressed and disinclined to mix with the locals, he was clearly a stranger in the area, and he must have rooms at the inn. Darcy was curious to know who he might be. There had been some talk in the village of speculators arriving to look over properties in the district. His grandfather, Mr Darcy, had heard from Colonel Fitzwilliam of extravagant offers being made to local farmers and was very much averse to the practice.

"It will destroy the land and impoverish the people," he had predicted.

When the landlord returned to refill his glass, Darcy asked discreetly if he knew what business the gentleman from London was doing in the area.

"I have seen him in the district and thought he may be looking at a property," he said, hoping by this means to lead the innkeeper on to divulging some thing he knew.

But in vain, for the landlord knew only that the gentleman, a Mr Hartley-Brown, was staying in the area for a while.

"You are right, sir; he is from London and is here on business, but I cannot say what his interest is. He has taken the room for a week and says he may stay longer if necessary…"

Darcy nodded and paid his bill. It was puzzling, but he knew it would soon come out. There were few secrets in a community as close-knit as theirs. Putting it out of his mind, he set off for home.

He found Jessica in the sitting room and told her of Kathryn's being unwell and unlikely to be at the school on the morrow. She was concerned and asked if he knew what ailed her. Darcy explained briefly and retired to his room.

On the day following, Jessica decided to call on her friend in the late afternoon. She went to Darcy and asked if he would drive her to Colley Dale, quite certain he would not wish to miss the opportunity to see Kathryn again. Clearly he did not and agreed at once to take her.

They were part of the way there, when a horseman passed them, riding at a furious pace towards Bakewell.

"There he is again, the fellow I saw at the inn yesterday," said Darcy, "The landlord tells me he has rooms for a week. I wonder what he wants."

"Who is he?" asked Jessica

"A Londoner, a Mr Hartley-Brown, or so the landlord told me, though he knew little more than his name. He is very flashy—probably with plenty of money to spend. I think he is probably looking to buy a property in the area," said Darcy, and Jessica laughed.

"Oh dear, Mr Darcy will not welcome that. You know how he resents outsiders buying up pieces of the district and developing them for resale. If that is what he is about, Mr Hartley-Brown will not find himself welcome in these parts," she said.

Darcy agreed wholeheartedly. "I know exactly how my grandfather feels; these men want only to make a fat profit. They have no interest in the land or the people who live here. They will cheerfully sell a village with all its houses, farms, and people as though they were cattle!"

"Are you sure that is what this man Hartley-Brown wants?" she asked and he shook his head, "I have no idea what he wants—I am only speculating, as I guess he is!" he replied. "He may be a perfectly innocent fellow, visiting the peak district on holiday, but somehow, I doubt it," and they laughed together as they approached Colley Dale.

Kathryn heard the carriage and, looking out of her window, saw them alight at the front door. She hurried to be ready to go downstairs. When she came down to meet them, Jessica and Darcy were seated in the parlour with her mother and Elena. Both rose at once as she entered the room.

Jessica's concern at her being taken ill so suddenly and Darcy's relief at finding her much recovered from the previous day were equally heartfelt.

Jessica conveyed also the wishes of Mr and Mrs Darcy, who had sent a basket of fruit, which was placed on a table in the parlour.

While thanking them all for their concern and generosity, Kathryn was conscious of some embarrassment, since she had had no appreciable degree of physical indisposition to speak of and no way to account to them for her sudden affliction. It was bad enough to suffer from an inexplicable attack of something, but to be unable to identify or show cause for it was quite discomposing.

Kathryn tried to make light of it, but she was not assisted by her mother's intervention, when she claimed that Kathryn had been working too hard and was probably exhausted. Her daughter rushed to deny this; speaking with a lightness of tone she did not feel, Kathryn said, "That is not it at all, Mama, I am certainly not overworked at the school; indeed, having been on call for my three obstreperous charges at Lindfield Towers for most of the day and part of the night, I feel as though my present occupation is a permanent form of recreation. So little is demanded of me and there is so much satisfaction to be had from teaching the children, I am enjoying myself to such a degree, I am certainly not suffering from exhaustion." Turning to Darcy Gardiner, she added, "It was, however, a rather warm day, and I confess I was feeling a little fatigued from walking. I was very grateful to Mr Gardiner for bringing me home in the carriage."

Darcy hastened to assure her it had been no trouble at all, asking afterwards, "And I trust you are feeling better today?"

"Yes indeed I am," she replied brightly, "and I expect to be at the school tomorrow."

"Kathryn, are you quite sure?" asked Jessica, clearly anxious she should not return too soon, but Kathryn was adamant; she was quite fit and well, she claimed, and would certainly be at the school on the morrow.

"If that is the case, we shall send a carriage for you. My grandfather, hearing of your illness, suggested it, at least until this very unseasonable warm weather ends. It can be quite oppressive for walking," said Darcy. When she protested that there was no need, Jessica supported her cousin and in spite of Kathryn's protestations, it was agreed.

Thereafter, they partook of tea and shortbread, which Elena and the maid had brought in and placed upon the table.

Relieved to change the conversation from the subject of her indisposition, Kathryn sought to engage her visitors in a discussion of the plans for the school. It was something they were all interested in, but before long, she was to find herself trapped again in another subject, not of her choosing, which threatened to take her to the brink of very troubled waters.

Speaking of the need for a playground where the children may take some regular exercise, Jessica brought up the matter of a piece of farmland, that had lain idle for many years on the boundary of a freehold property near Little Meadow, not far from the school.

"It would be a most convenient and appropriate place for a playground for the older children, being only a few minutes' walk from the school. We plan to ask Mr Darcy if he will purchase it for the school from the owner, who appears to have no good use for it."

"Do you think he will sell?" asked Kathryn.

Mention of this reminded Darcy of the man at the inn, who, he had assumed, was probably looking for a property in the district.

"Possibly; it is only idle land—unless our visitor from London has got in first. He has taken rooms at the inn at Bakewell, for a week or more; clearly he is looking for something or someone! I believe he is looking at saleable properties in the area.

"I saw him at the inn yesterday, and today, we passed him on our way here, riding like the devil was after him, with no care for anyone else on the road. A proper London toff, all style and no manners!"

Jessica intervened to explain, "The innkeeper told Darcy that the man was a Mr Hartley-Brown, but he had no notion what his business might be," she said, and even as she spoke, she noticed that Kathryn had gone very quiet and the colour had fled from her face. Yet, only a few minutes ago, she had seemed her normal lively self.

Jessica wondered what could have caused this sudden change. Could it have been the mention of Mr Hartley-Brown? Who was he?

Keen to discover the connection, if any, between the two, yet unwilling to expose Miss O'Hare to unfair scrutiny, she determined to observe her when they met again at the school on the morrow.

There was no doubt in her mind that something or someone linked to the strange Mr Hartley-Brown was behind Kathryn's distress.

Darcy meanwhile had not noticed the change in Miss O'Hare, except that she had been rather quiet, which he put down to her continuing indisposition. To Kathryn's great relief, they rose to leave and said their farewells quickly, urging her to take some nourishment and rest some more.

By the time Kathryn had got upstairs and back to her room, her distress was so great, she was forced to sit on her bed and stay still awhile to compose herself.

The chance discovery that Hartley-Brown was staying in the area had been shock enough, but the revelation that Darcy Gardiner had seen him at the inn at Bakewell, and the landlord had identified him, was even more troubling. It was possible, she thought, that Darcy may meet him, if he continued to ride about the district as he had been doing, or he may even be introduced to him, by some mutual acquaintance at the inn or elsewhere in the village.

Kathryn had never envisaged such a situation and had nothing in her personal armoury to help her deal with it, if it arose. She felt exposed and vulnerable. Why had he come? And why now?

Had she been able to confront him on her own terms and at a time and place of her choosing, things may have been different; but to have him intrude upon her life, where she had retreated for some relief from her experiences at Lindfield, was for her, inconceivable.

As tears stung her eyes, she wondered by what means she would cope, for she knew his presence in the district had nothing to do with property; she was quite certain he had discovered that she had returned to her parents' home in Derbyshire and had travelled here to seek her out. What he wanted from her or how she would negotiate with him she did not know.

As she grew increasingly apprehensive, her usual self-control deserted her. Locking her door, she broke down and wept, helplessly. It seemed to her Hartley-Brown would do everything to thwart her plans and destroy the peace of mind she had sought here.

There was nothing she could do to prevent it.

She had only to wait for it to happen.

The following day dawned cooler and brought with it the first serious signs of seasonal change, as though nature had decided to hurry Autumn along.

There was a welcome chill in the air.

Kathryn dressed with care and waited for the vehicle from Pemberley, which called to convey her to the school.

She was grateful indeed for the consideration shown her by Mr and Mrs Darcy, and her mother was eager to commend them also.

"It is very kind of them indeed, dear," she said and added, "There's not too many people of quality who will condescend to help others in this way. But I will say that it has always been said of Mr Darcy that he is a most generous man, and I think this proves it. Do you not agree, Kate, my dear?"

Kathryn agreed, of course, but had neither the time nor the wit to pay much attention to her remarks, so disturbed were her thoughts with the prospect that lay ahead. She had wondered how long it would be before either Jessica or Darcy Gardiner or both discovered her secret. She was sensible enough to know that concealment was no longer an option.

Her sister Elena wished to go to the library at Kympton and asked if she may come too. Kathryn, having ascertained that it was not much out of their way, agreed and they set off.

It was almost nine o'clock when she reached the school and Jessica was already there. Despite her best efforts, Kathryn failed to conceal the deep unease she was feeling. Within minutes of their meeting, Jessica knew there was something troubling her friend, which went beyond simple discomfort; she determined to discover its cause and help her if it were possible to do so.

Yet, it would have to wait, for the children awaited their teacher and Kathryn appeared keen to go to them. At least with the children she was safe.

It was past midday when Jessica was able to speak with her alone, once the children had gone to Mr Hurst for the rest of the afternoon. Jessica noted that Kathryn had been admirably composed throughout the morning, but there was no mistaking the look that crossed her countenance when Jessica asked her if she would join her for a cup of tea at the rectory.

"The rector and his family are away visiting another parish, and the housekeeper has invited us to take tea in the parlour," said Jessica, noting that her companion had seemed anxious and reluctant at first, but then appeared relieved that they were to be alone.

"Yes, yes, I should like that very much, thank you," she replied and a little while later they were seated in the warm comfort of the rectory, each with a cup of the comforting brew.

Kathryn was silent but Jessica, determined not to lose the opportunity, pressed on.

She spoke cautiously at first. "Kathryn, please forgive me for asking, but I cannot remain silent while you suffer such distress; I do want to help, but I will not intervene, unless you wish me to. You may well consider it impertinent of me to ask, but I could not avoid noticing how very distressed you became yesterday, at the mention of a certain person's presence in the district."

She waited, seeing again the same discomposure she had noticed on the previous evening, then added, in a quiet voice, "I wondered whether there was perhaps a connection between the same gentleman and yourself, which is causing you anxiety, and if there is anything I can do to help?"

At this, Kathryn put her cup and saucer down with a clatter and said, "You are mistaken, Jessica; there is no connection whatsoever between us, and he is no gentleman either!"

"Then you are acquainted with him? I speak of this man who has taken rooms at the inn at Bakewell and has been riding furiously around the district this week. We have all seen him. You do know him?"

Kathryn met her eyes directly when she answered, "Yes, I do. He is Mr Gordon Hartley-Brown, the cousin of my former employer Lady Denny. I have been acquainted with him in the past... a year or more ago to be exact, but have not seen him since."

"And it is obviously not an acquaintance you wish to continue?"

"No indeed!" she replied with great emphasis. "That is exactly the problem. It seems *he* does."

She was becoming agitated, and Jessica moved to sit beside her on the sofa and asked, "Is this why he has travelled to Derbyshire? Do you believe he seeks to contact you and continue his previous association with you?"

By this time, Kathryn's tears refused to be held back, and Jessica, driven by both compassion and concern, put an arm around her, at which she broke down completely and sobbed, hiding her face.

"I cannot know for certain, but I think so... I do not wish to, but Jessica, I really do not know what I can do to stop him... How is he to be dissuaded from following me or contacting me?... If only my brother were here, he might have helped, but I cannot tell my father... in his state... What could he do? What is to be done?"

So distressed had she become that it was some time before they could resume their conversation.

Jessica was very circumspect. She was young and inexperienced in such matters. She had no desire to interfere, yet knew she had to do something to ease the pain of harassment that Kathryn was clearly suffering. She let her compose herself, before she said anything more, and when she spoke, her voice was gentle.

"Kathryn, I should like very much to help you in any way I can, but to do so, I would need to know some pertinent facts. I have no desire to pry into your life before you returned to Colley Dale, but are you able to tell me a little about the reason why you do not wish Mr Hartley-Brown to contact you?" she asked, and the concern in her voice was so genuine, Kathryn could not refuse her.

Her sobs had ceased, she dried her eyes and straightened her clothes, yet to Jessica, she looked exceedingly vulnerable and apprehensive.

The violence of Kathryn's anguish had shaken her; as yet ignorant of all the circumstances, she was astonished at the depth of her friend's unhappiness.

But not for long.

When, over the next hour, she heard what Kathryn had to reveal, told slowly and with many pauses, to think, sometimes to weep and dry her eyes, blow her nose, and drink more tea, Jessica was no longer surprised at her desire to stay well out of the way of Mr Hartley-Brown.

Jessica's only immediate concern was for her friend's safety and peace of mind. The rest would have to wait.

She decided she would need to get the help of her cousin Darcy or Mr Carr to deal with the man Hartley-Brown; but before that, some means had to be found to preserve Kathryn from his unwelcome attentions.

Chapter Eight

JESSICA ARRANGED FOR KATHRYN to be taken home, before returning to Pemberley in time to escape a short sharp thunderstorm, which blew in from the northwest and drenched the area from Maclesfield to Matlock. Darcy Gardiner was not so fortunate.

He had just left Bakewell, where he had gone on business, and was on his way home on horseback, when the heavens opened, at which point, he was compelled to turn around and make for the shelter of the inn. The landlord, solicitous and friendly, provided him with a room to change out of his sodden jacket and shirt, had them sent to the kitchen to be dried and pressed, and, while he waited, sent up some hot food and brandy, which was very welcome indeed.

Some little while later, when the rain had eased, he returned with Darcy's clothes and, while assisting him into them, said in a confidential voice, "Mr Gardiner, sir, do you recall the gentleman Mr Hartley-Brown? You once asked if I knew what he was doing in the area."

Without turning around to face him, Darcy indicated his interest, "I did indeed, and do you have an answer for me?"

"I may do, sir," said the innkeeper, coming around to adjust the collar of Darcy's jacket and brush down the front of his coat. "I cannot be certain, you understand?"

"Of course," said Darcy, waiting patiently.

"But, there is talk in the village that he has been enquiring about the whereabouts of a family by the name of O' Hare. Irish, I think, sir, probably came over during the bad days of the potato famine."

Darcy had at first been shocked into silence, then he asked quickly, "And does he say why he wishes to find them?"

"No, sir, but I understand that he says he knew a young lady, a Miss O'Hare, and seems very keen to discover if she is here."

At this Darcy grew exceedingly angry, but with commendable presence of mind, did not betray his feelings to the innkeeper, nor did he ask any more questions. He paid the man well for the food and the services rendered, and set off, but not before saying, "I would prefer that Mr Hartley-Brown did not learn of our little exchange," to which the innkeeper responded cheerfully, "He will not, sir, not from me. He's moved to the inn at Lambton, where he expects to stay a further week."

Grateful for this unexpected information, Darcy left the inn and rode back to Pemberley, his mind in absolute turmoil. He was shocked and angry, and yet, there was nothing he could do. He was completely baffled.

His thoughts filled with a confusion of suspicion and assumption of which he could make no sense at all, he experienced a feeling of foreboding, the like of which he had not known before.

The weather had cleared following the storm, to a blue sky and crisp, sweet air. Yet Darcy Gardiner could appreciate none of this. He was aware only of a sense of impending trouble, linked to the stranger—Hartley-Brown.

On reaching Pemberley House, he went directly upstairs and, while making for his rooms, chanced upon Jessica coming out of the library. She looked worried, yet, on seeing the expression upon his face, stopped in the corridor and asked, "Darcy, whatever is the matter? Have you had bad news? Is it Mrs Gardiner? Is she unwell again?"

He shook his head. "No, no, my grandmother is quite well, or so I believe, having heard nothing to the contrary today. It's Miss O'Hare I am concerned for. Jessica, I do believe she is in some danger," he said.

"In danger? How do you mean?" Jessica was dismayed.

"Indeed, in grave danger of being importuned and harassed by a man she probably has no wish to meet, none other than our odd visitor from London, the man we saw the other day riding like the devil—Mr Hartley-Brown."

Jessica was stunned by the revelation that Darcy had discovered the connection between Hartley-Brown and Miss O'Hare. She could not imagine how he might have done so, since there was no possibility that Kathryn could have told him. After their talk together, Kathryn had begged Jessica to keep her secret safe, and Jessica had given her word that no one would know. Yet, here was her cousin Darcy speaking as if he knew it all.

She wondered how he had found out and how much he knew. When she responded, it was with a degree of circumspection.

"Darcy, are you quite sure? What makes you think Kathryn is in danger from Hartley-Brown?"

Darcy took her arm and drew her into the library, where they were unlikely to be disturbed, nor would the servants overhear their conversation.

"I've heard that he has been asking around the district for her family—he knows they live in the area but not where exactly. There has been talk in the village that he claims he once knew Miss O'Hare and wishes to contact her."

"How do you know all this?" she asked.

"I had it from the innkeeper at Bakewell. Hartley-Brown had rooms there and has just left the inn and moved to Lambton, closer to Colley Dale. I believe he means to remain in the district until he finds her. Jessica, I am convinced she is in danger from him. I do not believe she wishes to meet him."

This time, Jessica responded without thinking, "She most certainly does not," she said and then realised what she had said. Darcy was instantly alert.

"Has she told you so herself?"

There was no help for it, the truth was out now.

"She has, and, Darcy, there are things about their association which you do not know, which I think you must know, but since I have promised not to speak of them to anyone, you will have to ask her yourself," she said gravely.

At this, Darcy looked so shaken that Jessica, aware of his sensibilities, was concerned for him. He seemed unable to speak and his face was taut with the strain.

Then he said slowly and deliberately, "Jessica, I can do no such thing. I have no right to question her about any part of her life, especially about matters that may have taken place long before she came to Derbyshire. It would be the height of arrogant presumption for me to ask her to answer such questions in the present circumstances. I am neither her employer nor her lover. What right have I?"

Jessica was now in a quandary. Her dilemma arose from her desire to keep her promise to her friend not to divulge to anyone the story she had been told earlier that day, and her belief that Darcy Gardiner had to learn some of the salient facts regarding the association between Kathryn O'Hare and Mr Hartley-Brown, lest he took some precipitate action, which he may later have cause to regret.

As she regarded his face, she saw the expression change from concern to confusion. Quite clearly, he was not convinced they had the truth.

"Jessica, do you know what really lies behind all this? Has Miss O'Hare confided in you? Has she or anyone else told you why Hartley-Brown is looking for her, seeking to contact her? The man has come in search of her; is he blackmailing her? Why else would she hide from him? I have to know, I cannot remain in ignorance. Were I to meet him or run across him among our general acquaintance, unlikely as that may seem, it would be to my great disadvantage if I were unaware of the true state of affairs between them. I may well do or say something that may have unintended but distressing consequences for all of us, including Kathryn."

When Jessica remained silent, his voice became more serious; he was thinking of several possibilities, some worse than others.

"Jessie, I understand that you may not wish to break a confidence, but will you at least answer me truthfully on one matter? Is there some clandestine arrangement that I do not know of, between them? An understanding, an affair, an engagement even?"

At this suggestion, Jessica had to speak and she did so with vigour.

"Oh no, no, certainly not! There is no engagement, but they are acquainted. He is the cousin of Lady Denny of Lindfield, and I gathered they became friends for a time, when Kathryn lived there as governess to the children. But, she told me she has no desire to continue the association."

"Why?" he asked abruptly and Jessica, realizing she had to speak the truth, said, "Kathryn discovered something about him, which she did not detail to me; she had decided to end their association before she left Lindfield and returned to Colley Dale. Now, it appears he is pursuing her."

Darcy seemed ready to explode with anger.

"The scoundrel! And he comes all this way in search of her. Why? What sort of hold does he have on her?" his voice reflected his confusion.

"Truly, Jessica, I am at a loss to understand how Miss O'Hare—for whom I have great regard—how she would allow herself, with her education and understanding, to fall into the power of such a man."

Jessica, seeing his anger and astonishment increase at every moment as he contemplated the situation, knew it was vital that he learn the truth, not from her but from Kathryn herself. Else there was bound to be a series of misunderstandings and suspicions, which would seep like a poison through their friendship and destroy it.

Taking a deep breath, she said, "Darcy, I think it is time you spoke directly to Kathryn. It is neither fair to her nor sensible for you to continue this speculation. Let me go to Colley Dale and fetch her. We will meet you at Lady Anne's gazebo, by the yew tree overlooking the river. There we may all speak openly and without interruption or fear of being overheard."

Darcy thought this was a sound idea, but there was a question on which he wished to be quite clear before he agreed to the meeting.

"Jessica, before you go to her, I need to have you understand one thing. I do not wish Miss O'Hare to believe that I have taken it upon myself to make all these enquiries for some sinister reason. It will only increase her wretchedness, if that is how she feels," and on being assured by his cousin that "wretched" was possibly too mild a word to describe Kathryn's present state of mind, he continued, "Well then, it is neither fair nor appropriate to add to her tribulation with some inquisition into her past. It would only make matters worse for her."

Jessica threw her hands up in frustration. "Then what is to be done? How is this matter to be resolved?"

At first, Darcy made no answer. He walked up and down the room as if in deep thought, his brow furrowed, shaking his head as though every good idea had deserted him. Then, he stopped and approached Jessica. Standing directly in front of her, he said, "Jessica, I have an idea; you must go to Miss O'Hare and tell her exactly what I told you when I first saw you this afternoon and revealed what I had learned from the landlord at Bakewell."

"Do you mean I should tell her that you are already aware that Hartley-Brown is trying to find her?"

"Yes, and that I fear she is in some danger."

"How will that help?"

"Tell her that, having discussed the matter, we have decided that she should be alerted to the situation. Tell her I am concerned and that I wish to be better informed, should the need arise for me to have Hartley-Brown removed from the neighbourhood by the police, so he will no longer harass her with his attentions.

"She may then decide that it is best to reveal anything that is pertinent to us. That should convince her also of your sincerity in not wishing to divulge to me what she has told you in confidence. Yet it will allow her to reveal such matters as she feels it is necessary for me to know. What do you think?" he asked, hoping for her acquiescence.

After a few moments' reflection, Jessica agreed to the scheme.

"It sounds good; it may work. We shall have to see," she said and, going to her room to fetch her cloak and bonnet, bade him farewell and left to make the journey to Colley Dale, leaving Darcy to return to the stables and, as agreed, proceed on horseback to the meeting place.

The gazebo, where they had arranged to meet, stood on the edge of the Pemberley estate. Built on a rising piece of ground, in the lee of an old yew tree, it had been designed for Lady Anne Darcy, mother of Fitzwilliam Darcy, the present master of Pemberley. Lady Anne was said to have come there almost daily, when the weather was fine, to enjoy the vista across the river and write or read poetry.

It was a pretty, albeit melancholy, spot, since it was generally known that Lady Anne Darcy, who had died relatively young, had left several notebooks, containing scraps of poetry, touching little verses which dwelt mainly upon the beauty of her surroundings and the loneliness of her life.

Darcy Gardiner had been waiting awhile, when the small carriage from Pemberley came into view on the road below him.

The two ladies alighted and began to make their way up the bank, towards the gazebo. Darcy went down to assist them, helping each one in turn, supporting them until they reached the clearing on the edge of the woods, in which the gazebo stood.

Jessica had clambered up easily, being younger and somewhat lighter in frame than her companion. Kathryn, her face partly hidden by her bonnet, made slower progress. Her breath came quickly as she took his outstretched hand and climbed the last few steps to reach firm ground.

Finally, they were all seated on the old stone seats—a little breathless, their faces flushed from their exertions.

Jessica was the first to break the silence.

"Darcy, I have related to Kathryn all that you have told me today, of Mr Hartley-Brown and his activities in the district. Kathryn wishes to acquaint us with some facts of which we were not aware. I have told her she need not do so, but Kathryn insists…"

At which Darcy stood up and said in a very quiet voice, "Miss O'Hare, pray do not feel under any compulsion to speak of any matters that are not our direct concern. Such associations and friendships which you may have had in the past should in no way matter to us now.

"My concern has been primarily for your safety; that you may be importuned, harassed, and even placed in some danger by this man's efforts to see you, and that his widespread enquiries in the area, in which he mentions your name and that of your family, may become an embarrassment to yourself. I have some fears also, that if he discovers where you live, he may lie in wait for you and try to confront you as you walk to and from the school. I confess, I have based this only on the sundry pieces of information I have received; it is possible that I am entirely wrong about his intentions and you, knowing the man, will be able to reassure me on that score. "

Kathryn listened, hearing his words through a fog of her own confused feelings. Jessica already knew some of what she was about to reveal, yet now, she had determined, was the time to be completely open and honest with them, especially in view of their kindness to her.

There was no other way.

At first, when she began to speak, her voice was hesitant and soft, but Jessica seated beside her, lent her strength and resolution, as she endeavoured to explain the circumstances of her association with Mr Hartley-Brown.

"I wish it were possible, Mr Gardiner, as you have suggested, to reassure you, but as you will understand when you have heard what I have to say, I am unable to do so, because I could not vouch for Mr Hartley-Brown in any way at all," she said, and there was great sadness in her voice.

It was not an easy story to tell, yet she told it, making no attempt to conceal the facts or spare herself. Anxious above all, to be believed by both Jessica, for whom she felt warm affection, and Darcy Gardiner, whom she regarded with the deepest respect, Kathryn laid the facts before them in her own unembellished words.

"My own knowledge of Mr Gordon Hartley-Brown goes back to the days when I was in Belgium, studying music and French. During one of our Summer vacations, two of my fellow students and I were visiting Paris, staying at the home of a Mrs Dickinson, who had a villa just outside of town. There I first made the acquaintance of Lady Denny and her cousin Mr Hartley-Brown. He was then her escort, and they were both close friends of Mrs Dickinson.

"Our hostess, knowing I was soon to return to England, very kindly introduced me, and Lady Denny invited me to apply for the position of governess to her three children. She was very keen, she said, for them to be taught something of the arts and literature. I was pleased to be asked and agreed to consider it.

"Mr Hartley-Brown seemed a pleasant enough young man, very attentive to his cousin Lady Denny. I saw no more of him and had no further contact with him until a year or fifteen months later. Having returned from Europe to the convent school at East Grinstead, where I had been very happy, I taught there for several months.

"One morning, I was called to attend the Sister Superior, who said that a letter had been received from Lady Denny requesting a character reference for me. I was surprised, since I had made no application for the position, but also, I will admit, quite flattered that Lady Denny had remembered me.

"The reference was, I believe, gladly given, and a week or two later, a letter arrived inviting me to present myself at Lindfield Towers."

At this point, Kathryn looked around at her listeners and said lightly, "I will not take up your time with details of the occasion. Suffice it to say that I did as requested, was obviously judged to be satisfactory, and was engaged for a period of two years to teach the three children of Lord and Lady Denny. There were few questions asked, which I thought was due to the quality of the reference given by the Sister Superior.

"The conditions were reasonable and the remuneration generous, with the added attraction of living on the Lindfield Estate, which is a place of considerable beauty, though it is not as grand as Pemberley. My three young charges, at least at first glance, did not present any unusual problems, and I was generally regarded by my friends at the convent as being exceedingly fortunate to have secured such a position."

She smiled, and Darcy asked, "And did it live up to expectations?"

"Indeed, it did, at first. The children, I discovered, were not as keen to learn as I was to teach them—they were not nasty or incorrigible, just rather wild and untaught, but Lady Denny left them mostly to me, seeing them only twice a day, after breakfast and before bed."

"And Hartley-Brown?" he prompted.

"During my first six months at Lindfield Towers, though he visited occasionally, I hardly met him at all. However, later that year, he came more often and stayed longer. Lord Denny was often from home at Westminster when the Lords were sitting or in Scotland, where he had investments in ship-building. Mr Hartley-Brown, as her Ladyship's cousin, seemed to have a special status at Lindfield; he appeared to feel it was his duty to be there more often to support Lady Denny and the family in the absence of her husband.

"During this period, he began to pay me more attention than he had done on his previous visits. Some of my normal routines too were altered either at his behest or that of her Ladyship."

"How do you mean?" asked Darcy, not wishing to pry, but keen to understand her situation.

Kathryn explained, "I generally took all my meals with the children and only joined the family if invited to do so on some special occasion. But in time, and I became aware later that it was at his suggestion, Lady Denny invited me to join them every night at dinner after the children had gone to bed, and she would persuade me to play for them, especially if they had company. I play both the harp and the pianoforte, and Mr Hartley-Brown was very appreciative of my efforts. He led me to believe then that he had an interest in music and poetry, but that was an illusion," she said sadly, adding, "He was no more interested in the arts than the man in the moon, but I was too ingenuous to understand. I am now thoroughly ashamed of my naiveté."

Darcy shook his head, realising how difficult would have been her position in the household.

"You must not take all the blame upon yourself, Miss O'Hare. It is clear that they were both far more culpable; it was neither right nor proper that you should have been asked repeatedly to entertain them. It was surely not your role to do so," he said, and Kathryn shrugged her shoulders.

"It was not, but I did not mind at first. I suppose I was flattered, but later, I confess, it became a chore rather than a pleasure; I should have preferred to have the time to myself," she replied, before continuing her tale.

"Late last Summer, Lady Denny became unwell and took to spending much of her time in her apartments. Lord Denny was away in Europe, and Mr Hartley-Brown, who used to have rooms in Worthing, where he had many friends, moved to live at Lindfield Towers. He has a suite on the second floor, not far from the main apartments.

"Lady Denny did not wish to be disturbed by the children; instead, she would send him to the nursery or the schoolroom to spend time with them, reading to them and playing games with them.

"It was during this time that I, being thrown more and more into his company, began to believe that he had a strong partiality for me. It was, I realise now, a foolish and naïve assumption, based more on my susceptibility to flattery than reason. I have no excuse of any kind to offer, except my complete lack of knowledge of those types of people.

"I had no one to confide in and no one to advise me, except Mrs Ellis the housekeeper, who had warned me to be cautious and not let him be too familiar with me. Thankfully, I was in no such danger; the very strict schooling I had received at the convent ensured that. But I admit, I was flattered and having allowed myself to be persuaded that he loved me, I finally consented, after some initial reluctance, to a secret engagement!"

At this, she stopped speaking, rose, and walked to the entrance of the building, as though it was a point beyond which she could not proceed, and Jessica, who was hearing this part of the story for the first time, could not suppress a little gasp of astonishment.

Darcy remained silent, and after a few minutes, Kathryn returned to her place and resumed her story.

"Being inexperienced in their ways, I was unprepared for what followed.

"Mr Hartley-Brown confided in his cousin—or so he led me to believe. He said she approved and was very happy for us. Lady Denny sent for me and told me how very happy she was that I had found favour with her dear cousin. She said he had been very lonely of late, and since she was herself unwell, she was pleased I was there as company for him. She said he had confessed to her that he was very attracted to me. But she made no mention of an engagement between us, secret or otherwise, nor did she indicate that there would be any change in my status within the household as a consequence.

"Bewildered by this rather odd approach, spent several days in a state of uncertainty and confusion, before I discovered, quite by chance, the horrible truth—that I was a mere pawn in a cruel game of deception that Lady Denny and her cousin Mr Hartley-Brown were playing.

"I was soon to learn that Mr Hartley-Brown and my lady were in truth much more than cousins."

Jessica saw Kathryn steel herself at this point and continue as if she were describing a situation out of some nightmare.

"I should not have believed it, had I not seen it myself, when, quite by accident, I intruded upon them in her apartment.

"Late one afternoon, hearing voices in Lady Denny's bedchamber, I thought one of the children had gone in and disturbed their mother when she was resting. I knew she would be very annoyed by this and entered the room to take the child away, going in through her dressing room, before I realised who it was she had in her bed. His boots and clothes lay scattered upon the floor, and their voices and their laughter were unmistakable.

"Fortunately for me, the bed curtains were closed, and they were so engrossed in each other, they failed to notice my intrusion. I withdrew instantly, but not before everything I had been led to believe was shattered. I understood then his increased desire to visit Lindfield when Lord Denny was away. Clearly, I was not the reason, only the decoy, who would help allay any suspicions. They were both using me to deceive Lord Denny. They were probably laughing at me—at how easily I had fallen into their trap."

Jessica's expression of revulsion mirrored her thoughts.

Kathryn's voice shook as she continued, "I was so shaken, so totally morti-fied at having been duped and used as I had been, I fled and hid in the maids' quarters, unable to face either of them.

"Sarah, Lady Denny's personal maid, who knew everything that was going on between the mistress and her cousin, suspected from my distress and embar-rassment that I had seen something I should not have and delighted in telling me everything she knew. Their affair had been a long-standing one, dating back many years, and the rest of us, including Lord Denny, were all being deceived by them, she said. She explained that none of the servants would go into that part of the house unless summoned.

"Sarah had been bribed into secrecy, but she was not entirely the loyal servant—for it transpired that he had been previously responsible for despoiling the lives of two young chambermaids, one of whom, a childhood friend of Sarah's, had since taken her own life. I realised then why Mrs Ellis the housekeeper had warned me at the outset to beware of his attentions. She knew well his true character."

Even as she spoke, Kathryn could see the effect her story was having upon her listeners. Their expressions of acute pain and shock told her how deeply they were affected by these revelations.

Jessica sat fixed in astonishment, her eyes wide, unable to say a word. She had not expected anything like this; it was quite outside the realm of her experience. Her quiet life at the Kympton rectory and gracious living at Pemberley had not prepared her for this.

As for Darcy, although he was composed and made no immediate response, Kathryn saw he had been dismayed by her story. Even as she spoke, she could not help wondering if, after this recital, he would ever wish to speak with her again.

What must he be thinking of me? He may well judge my indiscretion so harshly, that this may be the last time I see him, she thought, and a sharp feeling of hurt cut through her at the prospect.

Nevertheless, knowing there was no going back, she continued as she had begun. "I stayed out of their way for the rest of the evening, feigning illness in order to avoid them. I knew he was leaving for London that night and determined that when he had gone, I too would leave Lindfield forever."

There were tears in her eyes as she explained, "It was clear to me that he never intended us to marry; he may well have hoped, if he had had his way, to abuse and abandon me as he had the other young women whom he had deceived. Worse still, my employer, Lady Denny, who should have been my protector, was probably complicit in the plan. How else could I explain her attitude to me, her encouragement of my association with him, when she knew exactly how things stood between them? Quite plainly, I was nothing to either of them; I have no words to describe my sense of hurt and humiliation."

Her voice broke and tears fell. Darcy produced a handkerchief, which was gratefully received.

She soon composed herself and resumed. "After a sleepless night, I decided to ask leave to visit my parents, on the grounds that I had received an urgent letter from my mother, asking me to return to help her with my father, whose condition had worsened. In this pretence I was greatly assisted by Mrs Ellis the housekeeper, a most wonderful woman, who attested to the truth of my story, saying she had seen the letter. She was the only person I could trust and turn to for help.

"When I saw her Ladyship and asked for leave of absence, I was quite astonished that she agreed readily. She was surprisingly sanguine about my sudden departure. Her maid Sarah believed she was pleased to see the back of me. She told me she thought Lady Denny was suffering some symptoms of jealousy. She probably didn't trust Hartley-Brown either," she said, and both Jessica and Darcy nodded. Their thoughts had run along similar lines.

Kathryn refused to speculate. "I cannot say if this was the case. I was so glad to be gone from Lindfield, I did not care. Only the housekeeper knew I was going to East Grinstead, where I stayed awhile, trying to restore my spirits. I told the nuns I had to return home to help my parents and wrote to Lady Denny that my father's condition was so much worse, I was unable to return to Lindfield in the foreseeable future. I asked also that my apologies be conveyed to Mr Hartley-Brown, because I did not think I would be able to see him again.

"Even as I wrote, I have never felt so mortified in all my life. I knew that it was only my exceedingly scrupulous upbringing by the nuns that had saved me from their pernicious schemes and the consequences of my own foolishness.

"Weeks later, when I felt I could face the world again, I left the convent, took the train to Derby, and returned to Colley Dale, hoping in time to forget that part of my life of which I was so ashamed. I knew it would not be easily done, but hoped that with my family around me, I would recover something of my lost self-esteem," she said.

Darcy looked grave and thoughtful. "Can you think how Hartley-Brown might have discovered that you were in this part of the country? Had you ever mentioned it to him?" he asked.

"No, never. Lady Denny knew my parents lived in the north of England, but not in which county. The only address she had was the convent in East Grinstead.

It is unlikely they would have revealed my parents' address to Hartley-Brown. Which is probably why it has taken him so long to discover where I live."

Darcy asked, "Do you believe he will try to persuade you to return to Lindfield?"

Kathryn nodded. "Probably, but he will not succeed. I could never go back."

"And if he does not succeed at first, is he likely to persist?"

"Very likely. I fear he is not easily dissuaded."

"Which is why we must find some means by which you may be protected from his unwelcome attentions and be able to come and go as you please. It is not right that you should be constantly in fear of being accosted or worse, when you are going about your business in your own village," he said, in a voice that expressed his determination to protect her.

The clear matter-of-fact tone in which he had spoken surprised Kathryn. It indicated that he was either so shocked, he had decided already to distance himself from her and the situation that was not of his making, or he was being calm and logical in order that a solution be found to an intractable problem from which he wished to free her.

She feared the former and hoped with all her heart it was the latter.

Darcy walked out of the gazebo to stand on the very edge of the clearing, looking out across the river to the peaks in the distance. It was difficult to believe that they were involved in this predicament, here amidst the peace and quiet of Pemberley. But, it had to be faced and something needed to be done and swiftly.

It being late afternoon, the setting sun was casting deep indigo shadows in the dales, ushering in the long Autumn twilight. There was not a lot of time.

Returning to the gazebo, he asked almost abruptly, "Miss O'Hare, I wonder if you will consider a temporary move to stay at Rushmore Farm for a short period? It will obviate the need for you to walk or travel any distance through the town and you will be completely out of the reach of Hartley-Brown. I will speak with my sister Lizzie and make the necessary arrangements. There is no need for Lizzie to know too many details; the fact that you wish to avoid the unwelcome attentions of a stranger should suffice. Lizzie will understand very well."

He seemed to be totally at ease as he outlined the plans and, turning to Jessica, added, "Meanwhile, perhaps, Jessica, you could return with Miss O'Hare to Colley Dale and help collect some of her things. I shall leave it to you ladies to provide some reasonable explanation for your parents. I would suggest also, Miss O'Hare, that you compose a letter of resignation to your former employer, Lady Denny, making it clear that you are unable to return to Lindfield ever, so there can be no doubt about your intentions."

Clearly, he intended to ensure that every aspect of the problem was secured. "We can have it sent to Birmingham or Liverpool to be posted there; that should help throw Hartley-Brown into some confusion, too."

Kathryn was astonished, not only at the suggestions he had made, but also at the swiftness with which he had assessed the situation and devised a solution, however temporary.

She was profoundly grateful that neither Darcy nor Jessica had tut-tutted and made censorious remarks about her indiscretion.

They had listened, for the most part in silence, except to ask the occasional question or, in Jessica's case, to place her hand upon Kathryn's as if to reassure her of her understanding.

Now, Darcy Gardiner was offering to make arrangements for Kathryn to stay with his sister at Rushmore Farm; she scarcely knew how to thank them. She did not wish to inconvenience anyone, but understood very well the risks she would face if she were to be accosted and confronted by Hartley-Brown in the village or as she walked alone to and from school.

The unpleasantness to her would be compounded by the inevitable gossip that would ensue, which would surely put an end to her work at the parish school and perhaps even her friendship with Jessica and others of the Pemberley circle. She could well believe that Mr and Mrs Darcy may never invite her to Pemberley again; and who could blame them, for why would they wish to be associated with such a person? Even the thought made her feel ashamed.

Expressing her gratitude as well as apologising for causing such a deal of inconvenience, Kathryn agreed and soon afterwards left with Jessica in the carriage. They had barely proceeded beyond the bounds of the Pemberley Estate, taking the road to Colley Dale, when a horse and rider travelling at a furious pace passed them going towards Matlock. Jessica and Kathryn looked at one another, and seeing the look in Jessica's eyes, Kathryn nodded—it was Mr Hartley-Brown.

Neither said a word, but both women knew clearly the implications of his presence in the district. Jessica's fingers tightened around her friend's, trying wordlessly to reassure her.

Meanwhile, Darcy rode on to Rushmore Farm, which lay within a mile from the boundary of the Pemberley Estate linked by a private road. It was ideally suited to their present purpose, in that Kathryn would have no cause to leave the confines of the two properties and take to the public road in order to reach the school.

Meeting with his brother-in-law Mr Carr and his sister Lizzie, Darcy explained his errand of mercy. A lady needed help to avoid the persistent and unwelcome attentions of a stranger. It was a simple tale and Darcy related it without fuss.

Lizzie, who had once been subjected to similar harassment, understood and sympathised at once.

Miss O'Hare, whom she had met on one or two occasions and admired for her spirit and style, was very welcome to stay as long as was necessary, she declared, and her husband went so far as to suggest that there were ways in which the unwelcome stranger may be persuaded to leave the district.

He was in no mood to be cautious, "I am quite certain that a visit from the local constabulary could have a very persuasive effect," he said, and Darcy thought about it and replied, "Indeed, and since we know where to find him, that gives us an advantage. I am sure we could find some good reason to suggest to him that he is not welcome. However, I believe that once he discovers Miss O'Hare is out of his reach, he will leave the area."

Not long afterwards, he went to meet with the ladies and accompany them to Rushmore Farm, where young Lizzie Carr did everything possible to make Kathryn feel welcome and at ease.

Returning later to Pemberley, Jessica and Darcy found Mr and Mrs Darcy back from Oakleigh, expressing some concern about Mrs Gardiner, who had been feeling rather melancholy again. In view of this, Darcy decided and Jessica agreed that 'twere best not to trouble them with the events of the day.

On the morrow, however, matters would come to their attention in a most unexpected way.

Chapter Nine

BREAKFAST AT PEMBERLEY WAS usually a rather leisurely affair.
Mr and Mrs Darcy came downstairs to read the newspapers and open their mail, which they did, having taken two cups of tea each and eaten rather lightly.

Young Darcy Gardiner, on the other hand, frequently rose early and completed a ride around the park on horseback, before he returned to the house, changed, and came down to a much heartier meal than his grandparents. Only Jessica flitted cheerfully in and out again, usually partaking of tea and toast, with a piece or two of fruit, before leaving for school. She was invariably punctual, almost obsessively so.

On that particular Autumn morning, however, with the hint of a wintry chill in the air, Jessica was late, and to everyone's surprise, when she came downstairs, she looked pale and unwell.

Elizabeth was immediately concerned. "Why, Jessica my dear, you look quite ill. Have you been sick overnight?"

Jessica nodded, unable to explain her state of ill-health. She had, she said, a headache and a badly stuffed up nose.

"It is probably a head cold," said Elizabeth. "This changeable weather makes it worse. Go back to your room, dear, and Mrs Grantham will send your tea up to you, but before that, let her get you some lavender oil in boiling water; inhale it, and it will clear your head. Do stay in bed and keep well wrapped up, Jessica, else you will catch a chill," she warned, and Jessica did as she was told, without protest, so unwell did she feel.

She did, however, remember to ask that they send a message to Mr Hurst at the school. Darcy volunteered immediately to take the message, and Jessica was packed off to bed.

That morning, the post was late, too, and Elizabeth, who had two or three letters, took her time with them. One came from a most unexpected source—Lady Fitzwilliam, wife of Mr Darcy's cousin, Sir James Fitzwilliam, and mother of Robert Gardiner's wife, Rose.

Elizabeth could not imagine why Lady Fitzwilliam would write to her—the two had been friends many years ago, but no longer. The Fitzwilliams had, upon inheriting a title, acquired also an attitude of social superiority, which greatly irked Elizabeth and amused her husband.

"I cannot think what she can have to say to me, unless someone is dead, of course!" she said, almost to herself.

Mr Darcy looked up from his newspaper, smiled, and made no comment. He could judge from her tone of voice that his wife was not expecting to be pleased with her correspondent, whatever her purpose.

Curious, Elizabeth opened up the letter and began to read.

At that very moment, Darcy Gardiner, who had earlier left the room, returned with some information he had received in the post and became involved in a discussion with his grandfather about a piece of farm equipment, which he proposed to purchase. They both knew that the farms on the Pemberley estate were in need of diversification, and Darcy had some interesting ideas, which he wished to talk about.

Meanwhile, Elizabeth read on.

After the usual perfunctory greetings, Lady Fitzwilliam claimed she had heard of Mrs Gardiner's indisposition and was writing to inquire after her state of health.

This unusual degree of solicitude for Mrs Gardiner, with whom her association had never been close, aroused Elizabeth's suspicions.

"Why do you suppose Lady Fitzwilliam would bother to write to me with such an enquiry about my aunt? Would it not be simpler to ask Robert, her son-in-law? I'll wager anything, she doesn't care a fig about poor Aunt Gardiner; she is probably fishing…" she said aloud, and her husband looked up and said with a sardonic smile, "Lizzie my love, you must at least acknowledge her right to ask the question?"

"I cannot abide such insincerity," Elizabeth retorted and read on, only to have her suspicions confirmed on page two of the letter, where the true motive of the writer emerged.

Lady Fitzwilliam wrote, *There is another subject on which I wish to ask your opinion, Mrs Darcy…* at which Elizabeth gave a most unladylike snort, and muttered, "More likely you wish to give me *your* opinion on the matter!" and read on.

Rose has told me of a young woman, a Miss Kathryn O'Hare, who has recently come to live in the area. I believe she lives with her parents at Colley Dale and has begun to teach at the Pemberley Parish School. I understand she is also a frequent visitor to Pemberley, having become quite a favourite of young Miss Jessica Courtney.

Elizabeth could not begin to comprehend where this was leading, as the writer went on.

My dear Elizabeth, forgive me for taking the liberty to pass on some information, which may throw a different light on this young woman's character. I understand that she was once the governess to Lord and Lady Denny's three children at Lindfield Towers and is said, while she was thus employed, to have inveigled Lady Denny's cousin Mr Hartley-Brown into becoming secretly engaged to her.

Since then, I believe she has left the position, having jilted Mr Hartley-Brown—perhaps for some other more prosperous gentleman. (It is well known that Hartley-Brown has no money or estate of his own and lives entirely off the benevolence of the Dennys.) Miss O'Hare may have discovered this and decided to end the engagement.

The story, in case you have doubts about it, comes from Lady Denny herself, who revealed the details to Rose and Robert when they met in London recently. Rose says her Ladyship was highly indignant on her cousin's behalf—said the girl had made a fool of him and he is very angry indeed.

I do not know if you and Mr Darcy are aware of this situation, Elizabeth, but I was sure you would not have countenanced the appointment of this person to be a teacher at the parish school, nor would you have permitted her to develop a friendship with young Miss Courtney, had you been aware of the facts.

No doubt, Jessica is as yet too inexperienced in the ways of the world to appreciate the import of such matters. Such an inappropriate association can seriously damage her own chances of advancement in society, not to mention those of making a good marriage.

But I know you will ensure that she is made aware of these considerations.

She rambled on for half a page or more on family matters, but Elizabeth, too astounded to read any further, put the letter in her pocket, glad of the fact that both her husband and her grandson were engrossed in their discussion. They failed to notice that she had become quite discomposed and had left the room without finishing her tea, to go upstairs to Jessica.

Having been put through the tedious business of an inhalation of herbal oils and having her feet immersed in a bath of hot water, before being tucked up in bed, Jessica was feeling slightly more comfortable than before. Her head felt lighter, and she managed a pale smile when Elizabeth entered the room. When the maid brought in a tray with tea and toast, she sat up without much enthusiasm, and Elizabeth, drawing up a chair beside her bed, helped her partake of it.

Jessica thanked her for her kindness and smiled as she said, "I feel like I used to when I was a little girl and Mama used to feed me when I was ill."

Elizabeth smiled and patted her hand; she was very fond of Jessica. Her mother, Emily Courtney, was Elizabeth's cousin and dear friend, while young Jessica was as warmly loved as her own daughter.

Waiting until Jessica had finished and the maid had removed the tray, Elizabeth fluffed up her pillows, tucked the bedclothes around her, and sat down again. Then, taking out Lady Fitzwilliam's letter, she put it in Jessica's hands, saying, "Now, Jessica, I should like you to read that letter carefully, and when you have done, please explain to me whether there is any truth in it, or is Lady Fitzwilliam completely demented? For my part, I am more inclined to believe the latter to be the case, but I am eager to hear your opinion on the matter."

Bewildered, Jessica took the letter and read it through quickly, skipping over the first page which held little information of interest to her.

When she turned it over, however, and arrived at the paragraph about Kathryn O'Hare, she gasped and cried out as if in pain, "Oh, the horrid, wicked woman! Why must she assume that everything Lady Denny says is true? Who would believe her, if they knew what she was really like?"

"What is she really like, Jessica, and what part of this letter is not true?" asked Elizabeth.

"Why almost all of it—or most of it anyway," Jessica replied, her voice rising with emotion. "Oh, cousin Lizzie, it is such a cruel, malicious letter... I cannot believe that Rose or Lady Fitzwilliam would accept such a story without question and then proceed to spread it around like this!"

Elizabeth was patient, but persistent. "Well then, will you tell me the true story?" she asked, and Jessica, despite her cold and discomfort, did so, omitting only those very intimate details that related to Kathryn alone.

Elizabeth asked if she would like her to go away and come back later, after she had time to rest, but Jessica would not hear of it.

"No, I must tell you the truth now—I cannot let you continue to believe such outrageous lies even for a few minutes longer," she declared.

Over the next hour, she gave Mrs Darcy an account of all she had learned from Kathryn O'Hare, whose insistence on telling them the facts without any attempt at prevarication had clearly stood her in very good stead. Jessica was able to provide Elizabeth with sufficient detail to convince her of the truth of Kathryn's story.

As Elizabeth listened in a state of complete amazement, Jessica revealed how Darcy Gardiner had, quite by chance, uncovered the presence of Hartley-Brown in the area and, having heard of his enquiries after Kathryn O'Hare, had warned her of his presence.

"Knowing he intended to find Kathryn, it was Darcy's idea that she move temporarily to Rushmore Farm, where she will be completely safe from his advances, and could come and go and continue her work at the school free of harassment," she explained.

Elizabeth could hardly take in the strange tale; she had no intimate knowl-edge of the Dennys, though like almost everyone, she too had heard of Lady

Denny's reputation. She was ready to accept that Kathryn O'Hare had been treated very ill by them.

While Elizabeth made no judgment upon Kathryn, except to commend her for having quit the position at Lindfield immediately upon discovering the deception practiced upon her, she was determined that Lady Fitzwilliam should receive an adequate response to her spiteful letter.

Leaving Jessica to rest and urging her to trouble herself no further about the matter, Elizabeth retired to her private sitting room, there to pen her reply.

My dear Lady Fitzwilliam, she wrote, and after the preliminary niceties, continued thus:

> *I am happy to reassure you that my aunt Mrs Gardiner is well, having recovered from her recent indisposition. While I do thank you for your concern, I am quite certain Mr Robert Gardiner is kept well informed at all times of his mother's condition by his brother, Sir Richard, who sees her daily.*
>
> *As to the second matter on which you have sought my opinion, concerning Miss Kathryn O'Hare, let me hasten to disabuse you.*
>
> *The appointment of Miss O'Hare to teach at the parish school was handled by both Jessica and Mr Darcy. The matter of her employment at Lindfield Towers by Lady Denny, as well as the circumstances of her departure from that position, are well known to us here, as are other matters relating to the conduct of certain persons in that household.*
>
> *I suggest that, should you make further enquiries, you may well find that Lady Denny's account, which Rose and you have clearly accepted without question, is coloured by her own relationship with Mr Hartley-Brown, whose probity is seriously under question at this time. Indeed, a cursory investigation may reveal that it is probably non-existent.*
>
> *If it is true they were secretly engaged, and you have only Lady Denny's word for it, then Miss O' Hare is to be congratulated for having extricated herself from a most unfortunate connection. If all we have recently learned of Mr H-B is true, he is surely not a man to be trusted.*
>
> *As for Miss O'Hare's friendship with my cousin, Jessica is well able to judge the character and reputation of people for herself, having had a most excellent example in her mother, Mrs Emily Courtney. I do not for*

a moment doubt her capacity to show both discernment and sensitivity when choosing her friends.

And I need not add that any friend of Jessica's will always be welcome at Pemberley.

I trust this adequately answers your enquiries.

Concluding with the usual formalities, Elizabeth despatched the letter to the post and went to tell her husband all about it.

She found him in the library and without more ado told him of Lady Fitzwilliam's letter and the entire tale that Jessica had related. Mr Darcy's initial response had been one of disbelief, followed very soon afterwards by anger.

"Does Darcy intend to set the police on him? He should. He has no business importuning young women and spreading gossip here. The constabulary will have him out of the county very smartly," he declared.

But Elizabeth explained that it was probably better not to involve the police at this stage.

"Jessica thinks that Darcy believes it would not be in Miss O'Hare's interest to involve the police. It may lead to the story being more widely known than at present and start some gossip. I believe Mr Carr has suggested that they pay the man a visit and let him see how much they know of his activities. They feel they can persuade him to leave."

Mr Darcy saw the wisdom of this course of action and said as much. "Very prudent indeed; and if, as you say, he is dependent upon the benevolence of the Dennys, a threat to expose him to Lord Denny may prove far more effective than anything the police can do to him. I have to say, Lizzie, my respect for young Darcy's good sense and discretion increases every day!"

There was certainly nothing that Elizabeth could disagree with in that remark.

Writing later to her sister Jane, Elizabeth recounted some of what she had been told by Jessica and drew an interesting conclusion.

You recall, dearest Jane, how mortified we as young girls used to feel at Mama's unceasing attempts at matchmaking and her constant efforts to draw every available young (and sometimes not quite so young) man into our circle, who might make a prospective husband for one of her daughters?

I know we used to cringe with shame at her blatant attempts to inveigle eligible men into dancing with us—ugh!

But I think you will agree with me when I say that, compared to the evil and sinister activities of women like Lady Denny, who will heartlessly manipulate and use young women, even at the risk of ruining their young lives, Mama's silly matchmaking was a far less heinous offence.

Foolish, yes, and certainly embarrassing to us at the time, but viewed in the light of the vile deeds perpetrated by Lady Denny and her cousin Mr Hartley-Brown, and their appalling consequences, I think I would find it hard to condemn Mama for hers.

Besides...

(and here Elizabeth knew her sister would smile, understanding that she spoke only in jest)

...as subsequent events have proven, Mama was perfectly right—at least about you and Mr Bingley!

END OF PART THREE

POSTSCRIPT FROM PEMBERLEY

Part Four

Chapter Ten

IN THE WEEKS THAT followed, neither Darcy Gardiner nor Jessica were fully aware of the matters that impinged upon the life of Kathryn O'Hare, chiefly because their own lives were so deeply affected by events quite outside their control.

First came the election, in which Darcy's hero Mr Gladstone and his party of Reformists and Liberals won a decisive victory. Darcy had been summoned to Westminster by Colin Elliott and others, who sought to involve him in the celebrations as well as the policy work that would inevitably follow their return to government.

He was keen to go and his family urged him to do so; he had worked hard for many years hoping for just such a day. Taking leave of them, he promised to return anon with news of Mr Gladstone's plans for reform and the investiture of a new government.

Idealistic as ever, he was certain much would be achieved. He wrote optimistically from Westminster of the dawn of a great new era of social and political reform, in which he hoped to play a small part. Mr Colin Elliott was to be in the ministry, and Darcy had been invited to work for him.

When he had visited Rushmore Farm to take leave of his sister and Mr Carr, he had also met with Miss O'Hare. He had spoken with her briefly, but long enough to ascertain that she felt secure and comfortable at the farm. She thanked him again, most sincerely, for his part in helping her avoid her tormenter. They said farewell, with neither yet certain of the other's feelings, nor even of their own.

Then, not many weeks after he had arrived in London and settled into work at Westminster, Darcy received news of the death of his grandmother.

After some years of struggling on without the husband she had loved and depended upon during a long and remarkably good marriage, Mrs Gardiner had finally slipped away, leaving her family and friends grieving and her devoted staff at Oakleigh desolated at their loss.

Advised by electric telegraph, Darcy Gardiner returned at once to find that his father and mother were to bear the responsibility of making all of the arrangements for the funeral as well as the weight of consoling members of their family. Richard and Cassy had the onerous task of supporting Mr and Mrs Darcy in their grief, while their own children and the families of Emily and Caroline drew together to mourn a beloved grandmother.

Mrs Gardiner had always been the preferred confidante of both Jane and Elizabeth, closer to both her nieces than their own mother had ever been. The two sisters were deeply saddened, and a good deal of Cassy's time was spent supporting them.

Mr Darcy, who had respected and admired Mrs Gardiner over the years, was similarly grief-stricken. It was difficult for him to accept that his esteemed partner, Mr Gardiner, and his wife were both gone now; the close ties between them at an end.

Darcy Gardiner, arriving the day before the funeral, was drawn in to help, and in the days that followed, found he had neither the time nor the opportunity to call at Colley Dale. Some weeks previously, having settled Kathryn O'Hare at Rushmore Farm with his sister, Darcy and his brother-in-law, Mr Carr, had sought out the man Hartley-Brown and warned him to leave the district or face exposure. Despite his initial show of bravado, Hartley-Brown quite clearly did not wish to be confronted by the police, nor, when it was put to him, did he relish the prospect of facing an irate Lord Denny once his relationship with Lady Denny was revealed. Given a few days to leave the inn, before which he would need to pay his bills and settle his gambling debts, he had sullenly agreed to depart, not before he had tried to brazen it out and even demanded money—a request that had been rejected out of hand.

While in London, Darcy had heard from his sister Lizzie that her husband had discovered that Hartley-Brown had left the inn at Lambton and, it was believed, the county. Lizzie wrote that Kathryn, having spent a couple of happy weeks at Rushmore Farm, had decided it was safe to return to her parents at Colley Dale.

I did say she could stay for as long as she wished, but she was keen to rejoin her parents, who she was sure were missing her, Lizzie wrote and Darcy was most relieved.

A note received from Jessica confirmed that Kathryn was now able to come and go without fear of harassment.

It is a great relief to all of us that the man is no longer in this district, she wrote and so it was to Darcy, also.

Some days after the funeral of Mrs Gardiner, Darcy went to Colley Dale. He found Kathryn at home, looking remarkably at ease. She was clearly pleased to see him, and they spent an hour or more in conversation, during which she thanked him once again for his part in saving her from the unwelcome attentions of Hartley-Brown.

"Mr Gardiner, I do not recall that I ever had the opportunity, while in a calm frame of mind, to tell you how very grateful I was for your intervention and for the kindness of your sister, Mrs Carr, and her husband. Jessica knows how deeply I appreciated it, for I have never ceased to tell her so, but you were gone too soon to Westminster, before I could compose my thoughts sufficiently to speak with you and I did not have an address to write you a letter either." She was particular that he should know how much she had appreciated his help.

"Jessica could have given you my address in town, if you had applied to her," he said lightly and though she looked up at him sharply, at what might have been a gentle rebuke, she could tell from his tone and expression that he was teasing her.

"I know, but I did not wish to make such a point of it," she replied and went on, "but now you are here, please accept my heartfelt thanks, even though they are later than perhaps they should have been."

Her sincerity was clear and it was all he could do to reassure her, that his pleasure flowed from seeing and knowing that her situation was much improved and she could move around the village as she chose, unafraid.

"Indeed I can and I hope and pray it remains so," said she.

When they parted, he gave her his card with his address in town, saying with a smile, "There, now you may write to me whenever you wish,"

She accepted it with thanks and bit her lip to hold back a light riposte. She was still a little confused by the tone of his voice, but happy indeed with the implication of his words. They had seemed to suggest that such a communication as she may choose to send would be welcome.

Some days later, on the eve of Darcy Gardiner's return to London, Mr and Mrs Darcy invited a few people to dine at Pemberley. Among them was Kathryn O'Hare, to whom the invitation had been delivered by Jessica.

"It is to be mostly family and since they all know you, you will be quite at ease," she had said, when Kathryn had seemed a little reluctant to attend, whereupon she had accepted with pleasure.

Edward Gardiner and his wife, Angela, were present also, having stayed on after the funeral to visit their respective families.

Though, out of respect for the late Mrs Gardiner, it was generally a quiet occasion, the guests enjoyed an excellent meal and interesting conversation. Darcy had many political tales to tell from Westminster, and Edward, who now practised in Harley Street, had his own news to give, though it was mostly of the eminent medical men he had met and the many worthy citizens he had treated. His wife, Angela, who did not trouble herself to engage in much conversation, sat mainly with Sir Richard and Lady Gardiner and the Darcys, and throughout the evening, addressed her rare remarks almost exclusively to them.

Being the only outsider in the party, Kathryn had felt a little awkward at first, until Jessica and Darcy joined her and, seating themselves on either side of her at dinner, kept her happily involved in their conversation. Elizabeth had been especially keen to ask Kathryn, to demonstrate her belief in her as well as to please Jessica, who had completely convinced her of their friend's integrity.

With dinner over, the company repaired to the drawing room, where Lizzie Carr and Jessica played and sang for them.

After which, Mrs Darcy, exercising her prerogative as hostess, invited Kathryn to sit down at the pianoforte. She was at first overcome with shyness, but when she was persuaded to comply, her performance of a charming nocturne by the Irish composer John Field was so exceptional, that it had everyone exclaiming at the skill and beauty of her playing and demanding she play some more.

When she left the instrument, Darcy Gardiner was not the first to congratulate her, but he was certainly one of the most appreciative.

"That was very beautiful, Miss O'Hare," he said, adding quickly, "I had no idea you played so well. I have heard no one in recent times who has performed with such delicacy and depth of expression. I must confess I am unfamiliar with the composer John Field, is he a favourite of yours?" he asked.

She thanked him for his kind words and explained her choice of the piece, after which they spent a little time together, as they took coffee, speaking more about John Field and his music.

"He is Irish but very well regarded in Europe, where he gave many concerts and lived for much of his later life," she said and he expressed his surprise that Ireland's major classical composer was so little known in England.

In the course of their conversation, Kathryn learned that Darcy had once studied music with his sister, thereby accounting for his sensitive and discerning remarks on her performance.

"I have always loved music, but had neither the talent nor the patience to become a proficient performer; I play for relaxation and pleasure alone; now Lizzie is much better than I am. She would practice a lot more than I did and has a real gift," he said.

"Indeed she has," replied Kathryn. "I had the pleasure of hearing her play often when I stayed at Rushmore Farm and was quite astonished at the facility with which she would pick up a new composition and play it with such confidence. It is an exceptional talent."

Kathryn revealed that she had studied pianoforte in Belgium with one of the finest musicians in the city of Brussels.

"If I could play only half as well as he could, I would be content," she said, to which Darcy replied, "I am quite certain that if he could hear you play now, he would declare himself well pleased with your performance. It was quite exquisite."

Unbeknownst to them, their conversation, which had become more intimate as it progressed, was being watched by Edward Gardiner's wife, Angela, herself a lady of some musical talent. She too had admired Kathryn's performance at the pianoforte and applauded politely, but unlike many others in the party, she had made no move to congratulate her.

The reason was a strange one. It lay in the fact that Mrs Edward Gardiner had, while living in London, become closely acquainted with Lady Fitzwilliam and her daughter Rose Gardiner. From them she had heard some, though certainly not all, of the story of Miss Kathryn O'Hare's stay at Lindfield Towers, which had diminished her opinion of the lady.

On returning to Oakleigh, where they were staying while in Derbyshire, Angela was moved to relate all this to her husband, with the added spice that she had observed his brother Darcy at dinner and afterwards deeply engrossed in conversation with Miss O'Hare.

"I think I would have to say, my dear, that your brother seems very taken with her. I wonder whether he is aware of her past conduct. Perhaps, Edward, as his elder brother, you may wish to caution him, urge him to beware of any deeper involvement. It would be most unfortunate, would it not, if Darcy were to make such an unsuitable match?"

Edward gave the matter some thought and agreed with his wife, as he usually did on such subjects. A keen and busy medical practitioner, Edward had little time to spend in the contemplation of such trivial matters, and like many active men, rather than argue the point with his wife, he preferred to take the simple way out by adopting her opinions. It required less effort and generally made for a more peaceful life.

Which is how he came to write to his brother Darcy on the subject of his friendship with Miss Kathryn O'Hare.

Two other observers had also noticed the happy flow of conversation between Darcy and Kathryn and drawn very different conclusions. Lizzie Carr, who, much earlier in the piece, had become aware of her brother's unrequited love for their cousin Jessica Courtney, had begun of late to hope that he had quite recovered from his earlier disappointment and was ready to open his heart to another young woman. And if that woman were to be Kathryn O'Hare, Lizzie's satisfaction would have been complete.

During the days she had spent at Rushmore Farm, Lizzie and her husband had improved their acquaintance with the lady and liked her very well.

Mr Carr, whose American heritage meant he was accustomed to personable and articulate women with strong opinions of their own, was very impressed with her erudition and general intelligence, while his wife declared her to be "a most interesting and witty companion, with a wide range of interests."

They were both agreed that she was also charming and talented. All these attributes combined to convince them that Miss O'Hare would probably make a very agreeable partner for her brother.

"If I were to say that I think my dear brother may be very close to falling in love with Kathryn, what would you say?" Lizzie asked her husband as they sat at dinner one evening.

He did not appear at all astonished by her question.

"Lizzie, if that is the case, then I believe he will be very happy with her, should they marry. I can see nothing adverse or disadvantageous in the match, can you?" was his reply, and they were agreed that Miss O'Hare certainly seemed a most acceptable young lady.

"She is both intelligent and charming, and should your brother decide to stand for Parliament, as he may well do, such a wife will be a considerable asset to him," Mr Carr added.

Meanwhile Jessica, who had by now become quite convinced that it was only a matter of time before Darcy and Kathryn would discover the true extent of their mutual affection, wrote to Julian, declaring that an engagement could not be far off and if a wedding were to follow, this was one occasion for which he must surely return to Pemberley.

Darcy is in London at present, but he will be back for Christmas and it is my hope they will become engaged then. Dear Julian, how I wish you too could be here at that time, but I know you must be very busy and will want to complete your work before the new year, she wrote and only just succeeded in holding back her tears, as she dispatched her letter to the post, unaware that the man to whom it was addressed was, at that very moment, embarking upon the journey that would bring him back to Pemberley for Christmas.

~❧~

On a cold morning in London, with not a great deal of enthusiasm for leaving his warm bedroom and setting out for Whitehall, Darcy Gardiner broke the seal on the letter from his brother Edward, casually and without thinking what its contents might hold.

His brother did not communicate with him very often, and Darcy assumed this would be a formal note of thanks for his part in making the arrangements for their grandmother's funeral. (Edward had been very busy at his practice and had arrived on the morning of the funeral.)

On opening the letter, however, Darcy was surprised to find it comprised of two pages, closely written and clearly of rather serious import.

My dear Darcy, it began, and then went on in a most unexpected fashion:

> *I am not unaware that most young gentlemen do not easily admit of any interference even from their nearest relations, into their personal affairs.*
>
> *Far be it from me, then, to attempt such interference or to dictate to you in matters of the heart, but I do hope, my dear brother, that you will accept my advice in the spirit in which it is proffered.*

Surprised, Darcy read on.

> *In the very important matter of matrimony, there is much to be considered before a final decision is made. Your family, especially your parents and siblings, must be considered, as well as the credit of your name and reputation in society, and, of course, there is your own prospect of happiness.*
>
> *All these are in jeopardy, should you make an error of judgment in the important matter of choosing a wife. One false step will bring misery to many, including yourself.*

Puzzled indeed by this line of argument, Darcy continued reading.

> *I know you will probably be well aware of all this and would surely not require to be reminded of it, but, I think also, and my dear Angela reminds me, that we men are weak creatures when it comes to the fair sex and when we are blinded by fascination, especially if the lady is both beautiful and talented. However, appearance, dear brother, is not everything and one must look to character and reputation.*
>
> *Now, I do not mean to suggest that the lady in question is wanting in character, but that it is best to make certain enquiries first and satisfy*

yourself, and your family, that she is all you believe her to be, prior to mak-
ing any commitment.

No doubt she is both attractive and elegant and, as she certainly
proved in her performance at Pemberley, exceedingly talented, but is she
right for you and your family?

Darcy read the letter through twice, before deciding that Edward was
warning him against making an offer to Kathryn O'Hare. Since he had not at
any time mentioned the lady's name, no doubt deeming it to be indelicate to do
so, the letter had seemed at first to be a general sermon on matrimony. Only in
the last two lines had his exact intention become clear.

When he realised the implications of his brother's words, Darcy was furious! His first response was, "How dare he?"

His immediate inclination was to sit down at once and write a curt note
requesting that Edward mind his own business.

But, on reflection, Darcy realised that it was possibly Angela, his wife, who
had urged him to write and it would be unfair to take it all out on Edward.

He decided then to ignore the letter altogether.

There was, however, one part of it he could not ignore. How, he wondered,
had his brother, and possibly his sister-in-law, come to the conclusion they
had about himself and Kathryn? They had only observed them on one or two
occasions. Could he have given them the impression that he was in love with
the lady?

Darcy could not be certain.

Thinking over their association, he wondered about his feelings, and the
more he wondered, the more he became convinced that he had probably failed
to see something that was plain to others.

Kathryn O'Hare was a charming young woman with a very particular
appeal that Darcy had not found in others of his acquaintance. Aside from her
looks, her conversation was unfailingly intelligent, her interests more diverse
than those of most ladies he knew, and he was to admit upon reflection, that it
would be very easy to fall in love with her.

He mused, if his brother Edward, who noticed very little outside of his own
professional business, had perceived it, would not others have done so too? It
was, he had to admit, a distinct possibility that they had.

This line of thought changed his attitude to his brother's letter altogether, for it now appeared that, by drawing his attention to it, Edward had forced him to acknowledge something he had ignored for some little while.

It was therefore with a new interest that Darcy now looked forward to his return to Pemberley at Christmas.

It would be good to meet Kathryn again, he thought, and decide for himself whether there was between them that extra spark which denotes the beginning of feelings warmer and more enduring than mutual admiration and good company.

❦

Having finally persuaded himself that despite the foul weather, it was important to brave the cold, wet streets of London, Darcy addressed himself to the business at hand. There were papers to be read and breakfast to be eaten. He was in the midst of these essential activities, when the doorbell rang and Mr David Fitzwilliam was admitted.

Darcy's surprise was obvious—almost, he feared, to the point of rudeness—although he hastily assured his cousin that he had not intended it to be so.

"Why, David, what are you doing in London? Not bearing more bad news from home, I hope?" he had said, and seeing his cousin's astonishment, he relented and assured him he was very welcome.

Swiftly sending for more tea and toast, Darcy tried to make amends, "I do apologise, David, I did not mean to appear inhospitable or rude, I was just so startled to see you, I thought something dreadful had happened at home in Derbyshire and you had been sent to break it to me. But since that is obviously not the case, you are very welcome indeed. I do hope you are staying a few days, I should like to take you into the Commons and let you hear the debates."

Several cups of tea and much hot buttered toast later, it emerged that David Fitzwilliam had come up to London not so he could see the nation's leaders at work, but in the hope of obtaining his cousin's advice on what he termed "a delicate and very confidential matter."

Darcy was interested, "Is it a business proposition?" he asked, thinking immediately that his cousin had been offered a position in a firm and was concerned about its suitability. But David was adamant it was a far more important matter.

"Oh no, no," he said, "it is much more worrying than that. Seriously, Darcy, I do need your counsel; I cannot afford to make a mistake. "

Puzzled, Darcy urged his cousin to tell all, and when he did, was all aston-ishment at what he heard.

Unbeknownst to most members of the families at Matlock and Pemberley, an interesting new association had developed, mainly in Manchester, where David now spent a good deal of his time.

A certain Miss Lucinda Longhurst had been appointed to work as a teacher at the small private school started by David's sister Isabella Bentley for the children of the area, and David, who had met the lady socially and admired her greatly, confessed that he had reached the conclusion that he was in love with her.

"I have been pondering these last few months what I should do. Should I speak to her of my feelings? How is she likely to respond? Or must I wait until I have obtained some more lucrative employment before I approach her? I need some sound advice, Darcy; what do I do?"

Darcy was amused as well as surprised, not only because his cousin seemed so totally unready for the experience, but also because of the strange parallel with his own situation.

Although he was some years older than Darcy, David, the son of Colonel Fitzwilliam and Caroline, being a somewhat solitary young fellow after the death of his older brother Edward, had often turned to his younger cousins for counsel as he faced the challenges and hazards of growing up.

Edward Gardiner had been too busy with his medical studies, but Darcy had felt some sympathy for his cousin, and as their fathers and grandfathers before them had become close friends, Darcy Gardiner and David Fitzwilliam had looked to each other for friendship and company.

For his part, Darcy had disregarded the difference in their ages, finding in David a more congenial if occasionally rather naïve companion than his own brother Edward. Thus it was that he now turned his attention to what might be called David's love life, although he was quite sure David would be far too shy to call it any such thing!

While Darcy remembered well their governess Miss Fenton, he had only a very hazy memory of her niece, Lucy Longhurst, who had for a short time been governess to his siblings, James and Laura Ann, before she had moved to Manchester to live with her aunt. He had therefore to rely almost entirely upon David's description of her appearance and character.

"Darcy, she is quite beautiful! I am astonished that she is not already engaged, especially in view of her sweet nature, sound education, and exceptional talents," he said, and the superlatives flowed easily.

"My sister Isabella regards her very highly. 'Lucy is a little miracle!' she says. 'She is so good with the girls; she has them all learning their letters and sewing handkerchiefs and fashioning pincushions and Lord knows what else… they do not waste a single minute of the day.'"

David was clearly impressed, too, for he declared that he had seen Miss Lucy Longhurst at work with the children of Isabella's school and had been amazed at her proficiency.

"And all this she accomplishes without a single harsh word and no sign whatsoever of the dreaded cane! Darcy, she is an angel!" he declared, adding, "It seems so strange that she has not been spoken for!" David appeared genuinely puzzled.

"Could it have something to do with the lady's lack of a fortune?" his cousin asked quietly.

David seemed very shocked at the suggestion. "Could it? Do you believe that is the case?"

"Well, David, I wouldn't know, but some men, and I exempt you, of course, may believe that a young woman who must make her living as a school teacher is not sufficiently well endowed. Many young men today are seeking to wed a woman of substance, with property, shares, and influence even. They rate this above looks and education—certainly above talent and the ability to teach young children to read and sew."

David looked so revolted, Darcy had to smile.

"Darcy, are you serious? Do you mean to tell me that most men, even you, would so regard a lady that her beauty, however uncommon, her good nature and accomplishments would rate lower in their estimation than her fortune?"

Darcy laughed but spoke more gently this time. "No, my dear fellow, I certainly would not—but many would. In London society today, there are several young men from well-established but impoverished families, who are very short of money to support their extravagant habits. They would not marry a young lady without a fortune. Oh they would certainly admire her and even flirt with her, or worse, but marriage would not be considered prudent unless there was some prospect of money or a thriving business involved."

"And love?" asked David, with a degree of innocence that touched Darcy.

"Ah yes, love; well, David, I think we have to accept that some men only believe they are really in love with a lady after they have glimpsed the gleam of gold."

"That is disgusting!" said David and proceeded to declare, "But I do not care a fig about fortune!" as he rose from his chair and walked about the room, clearly agitated and unhappy, expressing his outrage at the conduct of others of his sex, "I love her and that is enough."

"Then," said Darcy, "you need not worry at all. If you love Miss Longhurst and believe she returns your affection, all should be plain sailing. There is no more fortunate man than one who loves and is loved in return."

David, still shaken but a little more confident, confessed that he had considered the matter very carefully, and while he was quite certain of his own feelings and had hopes of their being returned, he had not wished to propose to the lady until he had secured his own future.

"I must have some occupation—a secure position somewhere, before I can make her an offer. Do you understand, Darcy?"

Darcy agreed, "Indeed I do, and I am in complete accord with you. A man cannot propose marriage to a young lady unless he has something to offer, apart from himself, of course. Tell me, have you spoken of this matter—of your feelings for Miss Longhurst—to your sister or your mother? What has been their response?" Darcy asked.

His cousin shook his head and said ruefully, "No, I have not. To tell you the truth, Darcy, I have been reluctant to speak too openly of the matter to anyone, lest it become common talk and be conveyed to Miss Longhurst herself or her aunt Miss Fenton. I should not wish her to know of my feelings, except from my own lips, once I have ensured that I have a reasonable offer to make and secured my parents' blessing."

While he thoroughly approved of this sensible attitude, Darcy was now at a loss to understand how he could further assist his cousin. Unless David was hoping he could help him secure a position in London, he could not perceive what more he could do for him.

"David, may I ask how you wish me to help you in this matter?" he asked, sounding rather more tentative than before.

At this, David sat up straight in his chair, looking quite surprised at the question.

"Why, Darcy, I do believe you have helped me already. Speaking about it with you has made me see my situation more clearly. I now know what I must do; my chief concern now is, how shall I do it?"

Darcy Gardiner was generally a patient man, but his cousin's meanderings were beginning to exasperate him. He recalled the many times they had talked in similar vein, when David had been determined to pursue a career in the cavalry. It had taken many hours of argument and a few persuasive lectures from his uncle Julian Darcy to make David realise the futility of his ambition.

Not the most decisive of young men, though in many ways an amiable and charming fellow, David needed firm handling and wise counsel. Often he needed only to be prodded in the right direction and would readily follow good advice.

Darcy decided it was time to be firm.

"David," he said in a voice that brooked no interruption, "I think you need to go away and think things over very carefully and sensibly, before you approach anyone. Having done so, you should then advise your sister and parents of your intentions towards Miss Longhurst and your desire to secure a stable position with an independent income, after which you could call on the lady and declare your feelings with confidence."

David, having listened very earnestly, said, "Do you not suppose that in the meantime, she will begin to wonder at my silence? Were I to say nothing, will she not believe me to be indifferent to her?"

Darcy's patience was almost at an end. "My dear fellow, I cannot speak for Miss Longhurst, but most young ladies of good sense and sensibility are well aware of being the object of our admiration and conscious of a gentleman's interest in them. If your Miss Longhurst is as clever as you say she is, she will have guessed that you have gone away to consult with your family and will be back anon."

"As indeed I am and I will. Thank you, Darcy, I see it all in quite a different light now, and everything seems much clearer," he said, rising and moving to the door. "I had better be gone; there are things I must do."

"Exactly," said Darcy, much relieved. "Go to it and I wish you luck with your quest. Should you succeed, and I see no reason why you should not, I look forward to wishing you both happiness in the near future."

As David hurried out, thanking him again as he went, Darcy just managed to conceal a smile, as he said, "I shall never forget your kindness, Darcy; thank you again, and remember, you must call on me if I can be of any help, at any time," and disappeared down the street.

Returning to his room, Darcy realised that despite the aggravation it had caused, the strange conversation he had just had, had not been in vain.

He too had begun to see things more clearly as a result of considering his cousin's predicament.

His own feelings for Kathryn O'Hare were now at the very centre of his concerns, following upon Edward's presumptuous letter and David's naïve and often incoherent musings; it was no longer possible for him to deny it.

Picking up his brother's letter, he read it through again; it irked him and he felt impelled to write a sharp reply, but postponed acting upon the impulse, lest he be tempted into immoderate language which may betray his true feelings. The longer his brother and sister-in-law were kept in ignorance of his intentions the better, he decided.

Shortly afterwards, he was dressed and ready to leave for Whitehall, when a letter was brought in—it had been delivered by express.

Seeing the handwriting, Darcy opened it hurriedly.

It was from Jessica. She wrote:

Dear Darcy,

I have just heard from Cousin Lizzie that you are expected home on Christmas Eve and wondered if I may trouble you to do me a very personal favour.

I have little opportunity here to look for something particular, that I wish to get Julian for Christmas, and wondered if you would select for me a little token of my affection, which I may be able to give him as a gift on Christmas Day.

We have as yet no news if he is to be home for Christmas; I hope with all my heart he is, but if he is not, I shall send it to him in the post, with my love.

I know I can trust you to get something tasteful—Julian abhors anything flashy, as you know—perhaps a plain pin or a watch chain. I shall leave it to you, confident of your excellent taste.

Thank you and God bless you,

Jessica Courtney

Enclosed was some money, which had tumbled out of the folded note.

Darcy stood quite still, her letter in his hand, moved by the simple honesty of her words. They had come as he was contemplating his own situation and served to confirm his feelings. By afternoon, Darcy had decided that he could no longer avoid making a decision about his future. Impelled first by David's rambling revelations and then Jessica's lucid expression of love for Julian, to consider his own situation, Darcy had concluded that he must talk to Kathryn, tell her of his feelings for her, and discover if she cared for him. If she did, he would ask her to marry him.

When he left Whitehall that evening, having bade good-bye to his colleagues and friends, he felt quite elated. Visiting a shop he knew well, he selected for Jessica a plain gold watch chain, of a design he knew would suit Julian Darcy, whose distaste for ostentation was well known. He purchased also a simple diamond ring, which he had packed and put away privately among his things.

Returning to his apartment, he collected his things, packed a portmanteau, and called a hansom cab. At the station, he bought a ticket to Derby and boarded a north-bound train. It was still a few days to Christmas, but London with its crowded, cold streets held little attraction for him.

Once the excitement of the election victory had passed, he had found his political work rather more tedious and far less rewarding than he had expected. He saw less of Colin Elliott and others of his friends, who were now in the ministry and busy with the minutiae of legislation to disestablish the Irish Church.

There was much less now of the fine talk of personal liberty, the doctrine of John Stuart Mill and plans for the reform of the civil service and the introduction of a system of public education for all children. They seemed to have receded into the background, while matters of the Irish Church occupied the government.

Disappointed, if not entirely disillusioned, Darcy Gardiner was tired of London. Home, he decided, was where he wanted to be, and the person he most wished to see was Kathryn O'Hare.

Chapter Eleven

CHRISTMAS SEEMED TO ARRIVE in a great rush that year; there being so much to do, everyone had been very busy.

The children's choir had been practising at the church, and Jessica believed that they had, with Kathryn's help, achieved a very good standard indeed. Their appearance at Pemberley on Christmas Eve was keenly anticipated.

"The rector is very pleased and I am confident the children are going to be in excellent voice on Christmas Eve," she said as they walked back to Pemberley House one afternoon.

Kathryn agreed, "It's due mostly to your own hard work, Jessica. I did not believe it was possible to train them to sing so well in the time we had."

The two young women had become firm friends as they had worked together at the school, and there was between them a good companionship, as well as a warmth of affection, they both appreciated. Jessica benefited from Kathryn's erudition and her understanding of the arts and sciences, while Kathryn admired the enthusiasm and energy her young friend brought to all her activities. She had admitted to herself that her enjoyment of their work at the school had far exceeded her expectations of the position.

That afternoon, Jessica had persuaded Kathryn to stay over at Pemberley and help her decorate the saloon for the party on Christmas Eve—a tradition carried on over many years for the children of the staff and tenants of the Pemberley Estate. They were carrying baskets of holly and greenery collected in the woods, to make into garlands. The weather, which had been quite forbidding all week, had improved somewhat, and though there were still some clouds hovering above the peaks, it did look as though Christmas Eve would be fine.

"Are you expecting visitors at Pemberley?" asked Kathryn, as the entrance to the house came into view, "because it does seem that one of them has already arrived."

In the drive stood a hired vehicle, from which a gentleman in travelling clothes had alighted and was paying off the driver, while two servants collected his bags and carried them indoors.

As the vehicle drove away, he turned and saw them.

He had time only to say her name, before Jessica, recognising Julian, dropped her basket and without a word, ran straight towards him and right into his arms, which closed around her.

Astonished by this turn of events, Kathryn gathered up the fallen garlands and waited, reluctant despite the cold to approach the entrance to the house, where the couple stood in an embrace that could only have meant one thing.

Everyone—Kathryn, the footmen, the gardeners, and Mrs Grantham, the housekeeper, who stood transfixed at the top of the steps—must now know that Julian and Jessica were either already engaged or were very soon going to be.

Looking down from her favourite window, Mrs Darcy saw them too and smiled. Clearly she had not been mistaken in thinking that the regular correspondence she had noticed between her son and Jessica was a sign of something more than a mutual interest in his research into tropical diseases! How much she had guessed, she would not immediately reveal, but she was certainly not displeased with what she saw.

When the pair reluctantly broke apart and moved to enter the house, Jessica turned to her friend and, taking Kathryn's hand, drew her forward to meet Julian Darcy and share their joy. There was no doubt in Kathryn's mind then, that the couple was deeply in love, though how Jessica had concealed it from her and, it seemed, from everyone else, she would never know. Eager now to take everyone into their confidence, Julian and Jessica made no further effort to hide their feelings and went upstairs directly to tell Mr and Mrs Darcy their news.

With this duty done, the family gathered downstairs, and the rest of the evening was spent in telling them how it had all come about and laughing together over the fact that they had so successfully concealed their intentions until Julian returned from Africa.

"I think we both knew our feelings were engaged, even before I left for France, but decided quite separately that it would be best to wait until my return from Africa to let the family into our secret," said Julian, and Jessica, her heart too full to let her speak, smiled and agreed.

Kathryn, noting Mrs Darcy's smile, realised that they had probably not been entirely successful after all, but it did not signify, since Elizabeth was so obviously delighted with the outcome. Indeed, Mrs Grantham confided to Kathryn that she had not seen her mistress look so happy in a long while.

"Mrs Darcy took it very badly when Mr Julian's wife left him and their son; I don't believe she has ever forgiven her. Miss Jessica has been like a second daughter to her and Mr Darcy; it feels right that if Mr Julian were to marry again, then she should be the one to make him happy," she said.

Seeing them together, Kathryn had no doubt of it either.

The following day, a carriage was summoned to convey Kathryn home to Colley Dale and take Julian and Jessica to Kympton Rectory, where they would ask Reverend and Mrs Courtney for their blessing. This was given with much pleasure, and by dinnertime that day, the pair were formally engaged.

Thereafter, they went together to Camden House, where the delicate task of breaking the news to young Anthony Darcy had to be undertaken.

Once the engagement had been revealed to her and Richard, it fell to Cassy to tell the child, who had been in her care, since Julian had brought him to her three years ago, that his life was about to change again.

He was upstairs playing with his cousin James, when Cassy went to tell him that his father had arrived with presents for Christmas and some important news. A cheerful and unspoilt little boy, Anthony Darcy had long forgotten and possibly forgiven the neglect and pain of his early childhood, when his unhappy, confused mother and shattered father had seemed to abandon him.

The years following had been spent not in lonely isolation but in the warm and wholesome atmosphere of the home of his aunt Cassandra and her husband,

Dr Richard Gardiner. In his cousin James, the boy had found a playmate, and the general acceptance of him into the family by all its members and the entire staff had given him the security and affection he had craved.

It wasn't too difficult therefore for Julian and Jessica to explain that they were to marry and suggest that he would from now on have his own family as well as the home he had shared with his cousins at Camden Park.

The boy's response was understandable, if a little disconcerting.

"Will I have to leave Camden House and Jamie and Aunt Cassy?" he asked, quietly adding, "and what about the Little Major?"

The Little Major, Cassy explained quickly, was his pony, a birthday gift from his grandfather Mr Darcy.

Jessica was swift to reassure him, "No indeed, Anthony, you will not have to leave here—your papa and I will be going back to Africa to continue his work for a year. When we return, we shall look for a place to live, and you can come and visit and decide if you wish to live there or remain at Camden Park," she said.

"Will there be room there for the Little Major?" he asked and then, as if afraid of the answer, added quickly, "I think, if I may, I should like to stay here with Jamie and Aunt Cassy, but I would like to visit from time to time, if you wanted me to."

Tears stung Jessica's eyes, as she saw the uncertainty on his face. The words were spoken artlessly by a child, who had lost everything that made a home and then, found comfort and love with the Gardiners.

It was the only true home he had known and he was reluctant to leave it.

Cassandra and Richard had loved and cared for him as if he were their own son, and Anthony had responded to their kindness and love.

Putting her arms around him, Jessica said quietly, "Of course your papa and I would want you to come to us, whenever you wished to. Once your papa's work in Africa is done and he returns to England, we could meet and do lots of things together. It might be fun. Would you enjoy that?"

"Could we go fishing? Jamie and I go fishing," he said, and Jessica turned to Julian; she knew he had probably never gone fishing in his life. It was a difficult moment, but Julian rose to the occasion superbly, saying without any hesitation, "Of course we could, and you and Jamie could show me how to bait a hook and throw a line?"

The boy nodded, his eyes gleaming, clearly pleased at the prospect.

"That's settled then," said Julian. "I shall look forward to my first fishing lesson. And when we've done that, perhaps we could ride in the park or walk in the woods or…"

"Or swim in the lake?" suggested Anthony, making quite certain his father knew his range of activities.

They laughed together at the thought of Julian swimming in the lake at Camden Park or Pemberley! At least the child was accepting of their plans, and it would not be difficult to restore the bonds and, perhaps, one day make a family again.

Cassy, seeing them together, smiled. She had long suspected that Jessica Courtney was in love with Julian, but apart from an occasional mention of their young cousin in his letters, she'd had no indication of her brother's intentions. Now it was clear, and she wondered what would happen to Anthony. Would they wish to remove him from Camden Park?

Before she had time to speculate, Julian reassured her, "Cassy, Anthony and I have just been planning how we shall spend some of our time together when Jessica and I return from Africa. We intend to have some fun together—but if you are agreeable, I would wish that you continue your care of him. Neither Jessica nor I would wish to disrupt the remarkably happy life he has with your family and the excellent tutoring he shares with your Jamie. Would you and Richard agree?"

Cassy was so relieved, the tears she had held back fell uncontrolled as she embraced her brother. The child had come to mean a lot to her—it would have been hard indeed to give him up. Yet she was conscious that Julian had his rights as the boy's father.

"Will you not wish to take him to live with you, when you return to England?" she asked, half hoping he would say no.

"Not permanently, and certainly not against his will. Anthony's home has been with you, and when he grows up, it will be at Pemberley, where he must learn his duties as master of the estate. It was a responsibility and a source of joy which I surrendered, when I relinquished my inheritance and gave him into your care.

"No, my dear Cassy, it is to you he turns for guidance and you who will best prepare him, with Papa and young Darcy of course, for his future role.

Certainly, he must come to us when Jessica and I are married and he will be most welcome in our home, but only when he wishes to come."

Jessica and Cassy embraced, both women understanding the effort it must have taken for Julian to say those words, yet admiring his courage in saying them. Neither had any doubt that he was absolutely right.

When they returned to Pemberley in time for dinner, Mrs Grantham, who had in her time at Pemberley seen many engagements and weddings, remarked that she had never before seen a matter settled so swiftly and with such good prospects of success. It was a sentiment with which it was difficult to disagree.

~❦~

On Christmas Eve, Darcy Gardiner arrived at Pemberley to find the pair engaged and, with concealment no longer necessary, keen to share their happiness and claim from him the felicitations he was pleased to offer.

Despite his prior knowledge of their feelings, Darcy was surprised at the speed with which their engagement had come about. He was however, delighted for them, knowing how deeply Julian had been wounded by the disintegration of his first marriage and the tragic death of his wife, Josie.

As for Jessica, he knew for how long she had loved Julian and her present felicity was so profound, it seemed to enhance everything that was pleasing and lovely about her. She went about the house making her preparations for Christmas, carrying out a myriad of ordinary tasks with a look of such rapture on her face, that it was impossible to believe other than she was utterly and overwhelmingly happy.

Finding her alone, decorating the Christmas tree, Darcy went to her and took the opportunity to give her the package he had brought and express the hope that it would suit.

"Oh, I am sure it will, Darcy, I have every confidence in your good taste," she had said, thanking him for the favour.

He had congratulated them both that morning, but returning to the subject, said, "Jessica, I need not tell you how very happy I am for both of you..." and she turned to regard him with a transfiguring smile that made him stop in mid sentence.

"Why thank you, Darcy, you are very kind. Yes, I do believe we will be happy. I know Julian says he has been thinking of nothing else these last few days, as he made his journey home to England, but I have dreamed of this moment for years," she said, still smiling.

"I know, and you told me you would go with him to the ends of the earth. Will you?" he asked.

"Of course," she replied. "We are to be married after Christmas, and in the Spring, we leave for France and South Africa, so Julian can complete his work. It is far too important to leave unfinished or delay for long."

Darcy could see how real her devotion was. He knew that to Jessica, it would mean nothing to leave the comforts of Pemberley and accompany her husband to Africa, if that was where he had to go. She had once told him she would rather remain single than marry anyone else. Seeing her now, Darcy had no reason whatsoever to disbelieve her.

That brought him to a delicate subject.

"Jessica, there is a question I have to ask you... Please do not be offended... I do not mean to pry but I must know, did you ever tell Julian about me... that I had once hoped...?"

She placed a finger over his lips to silence him and said, "No. You have no need to ask, Darcy. I have not and will not, not even to Julian. Did I not give you my word at the time?"

Darcy was relieved.

"Then Kathryn does not know either?"

"Of course not. Would I do such a thing? No, you are quite safe there."

She smiled and added, "Will you let me give you a word of advice? If you wish to court her, do so now; she likes you, very much, I know that."

"Does she?" he was surprised, "has she said so?"

"Not in so many words, but I could draw such a conclusion from speaking with her. She is, however, modest and will not assume your interest, but I am confident that if you approach her correctly, you will not find her indifferent."

Her reply was promising, if a little circumspect. She was being gentle with him, as she had been before, and he marvelled at the maturity of her understanding. Julian was fortunate indeed, he thought.

Grateful for her advice, he was excited to learn that Miss O'Hare may favour him, but he was as yet unready to proceed, waiting first to observe how the lady would respond when they met again. He knew he would see her at church and later at all the Christmas festivities. Jessica had indicated that

Kathryn and her sister Elena had been invited to dine at Pemberley on Boxing Day. He decided it would be best to wait until then.

～❧～

The weather worsened on Boxing Day, and several of the guests who were to dine at Pemberley were delayed by snowdrifts that blocked the roads and the threat of a blizzard on the moors. When neither the Courtneys nor Kathryn and Elena had arrived by late afternoon, it was decided to send a carriage for them, and Darcy volunteered to go. Jessica, who had observed his rather nervous state all day, managed to get him alone and whispered, "Now, Darcy, you must not forget that Kathryn is not likely to promote herself and seek to gain your attention. It is you who must take the lead, if you wish to woo her. She is well read and accomplished but will not presume upon your feelings. Darcy, I truly believe your happiness is entirely in your hands."

Darcy, not a little surprised by her forthrightness, asked, "And do you suppose she will welcome my addresses?"

He was well aware that the two were close friends and wondered if he had ever been the subject of their speculation. But in this he was to be disappointed as Jessica replied with transparent honesty, "That, I cannot say, because we have never spoken of it as a definite possibility, nor discussed you in those terms. I do know, however, that she has great regard for you, she values your qualities of strength, respects your generosity of spirit, and admires your dedication to matters of principle, as I do, Darcy. Whether she loves you is for you to discover."

Darcy was disconcerted, not knowing for certain whether Kathryn's regard meant that she thought of him only as an interesting though indifferent acquaintance, with whom she could quite happily spend a few hours in social conversation, or if it signified the beginning of a deeper, more intimate attachment.

Sensing his disappointment, Jessica added archly, "Speaking from my own experience, I might say that, undertaken in the right spirit, such a voyage of discovery can be quite a delightful exercise."

Darcy smiled and promised he would do his best.

He had to know, for the more he thought of her, the more he was convinced that Kathryn was exactly the woman who, in character and disposition, would suit him. Her understanding and intelligence would complement his own, and they would share a range of interests so diverse as to ensure they would never be bored with one another's company.

Besides these estimable qualities, he was certainly not indifferent to the sweetness of her voice and the loveliness of her face and figure, which, since he had encountered her so suddenly in the park at Pemberley, he had not seen surpassed by any other woman of his acquaintance. Viewed in this context, Darcy decided, discovering whether she did love him as deeply as he would wish might well prove to be as pleasurable as Jessica had predicted.

Arriving at Colley Dale, where it had been snowing since early afternoon, he found both Misses O'Hare ready and waiting, but reluctant to undertake the journey to Pemberley in their modest little gig.

"We were afraid we might be stranded in the snow," said Elena, obviously delighted to see him. Having helped them in, Darcy proceeded to the rectory at Kympton, and with the Courtneys ensconced in the carriage as well, they set off for Pemberley.

The company gathered there were celebrating the engagement of Julian and Jessica when the late arrivals entered, and while Jessica's parents were accepting the congratulations of their family and friends, some eyes were on the handsome pair that had followed them into the room.

Lizzie Carr, for one, observed her brother closely as he escorted Miss O'Hare into the saloon and later took her in to dinner.

Throughout the evening, he seemed so engrossed in conversation with her, not only did he neglect to ask any other young lady to dance, he even appeared to sit out some of the dances with her, and she seemed not to mind this at all. Certain symptoms, Mr Carr remarked to his wife, of a man stricken with love and a lady who had correctly diagnosed his affliction.

As for Darcy, while members of his family speculated, he was enjoying the exhilaration of discovering that the woman he loved was sufficiently welcoming of his attentions, to let him hope that she returned his affections. While not presuming that she had fallen in love with him to the same extent, he had been convinced by her responses that she was certainly not indifferent to him.

All evening, even when he was not at her side, or she had been claimed by others in conversation, he was conscious of Kathryn and could not stay away from her for long. When he did ask her to dance, he was delighted that they matched their steps so well, and when she danced with some other gentleman, he was so distracted, he found himself quite unable to take the floor with anyone else, waiting only till she was free again. That she seemed to accept all this with some degree of equanimity gave him more hope.

At dinner, after they had been temporarily separated by the insertion of Colonel Fitzwilliam between them at the table, Darcy was delighted when the Colonel was called away to meet some distinguished visitor, thereby allowing him to spend the rest of the meal seated next to Kathryn, engaging her in conversation.

When, on trying to discover the gist of her exchange with the Colonel, it turned out that the Colonel was an admirer of Thomas Paine, Darcy was relieved to be able to claim, quite truthfully, that he had read *The Rights of Man* while still a student. To his surprise, Kathryn then drew him into a discussion of the subject, confidently revealing her knowledge of the radical author's life and work.

"My father always spoke of Tom Paine as a man of great principle and integrity, who, in spite of much provocation, even by those he tried to defend, continued to live by his principles," she said gravely.

The serious tenor of their conversation was plain to those opposite, who wondered at the subject of their discourse, until Kathryn, whose sense of humour was never in abeyance for long, remarked, "Mr Gardiner, I do believe we are being much too solemn. It is Boxing Day after all, and I fear that we may be punished for our gravity by having to participate in charades," at which he laughed and replied that wild horses would not drag him into charades, which he claimed to hate with a passion, declaring that he would much rather pay a forfeit instead.

Overhearing this rash declaration, his sister Lizzie demanded that he should indeed pay a forfeit and, when dinner was over, insisted that he should sing.

She followed up her demand by going to the piano, opening up the instrument, and announcing to the company that her brother Darcy would entertain them with a popular favourite, whose introductory bars Lizzie began to play.

Drawn unwillingly into the limelight, Darcy threw Kathryn a look that begged for help, and to his huge relief, she responded with kindness and joined him beside the piano.

As Lizzie played and they followed, their voices blending pleasantly together, Jessica, who was sitting with Julian in an alcove at the end of the room, whispered, "What do you think? Do you believe they are in love?"

His response was immediate. "Of course they are, but I doubt that either of them is aware of the extent of it. Darcy is probably unaware how deeply his feelings are engaged."

"Do you say this from observation alone or from personal experience?" she teased, to which he gave an answer that was bound to please.

"From my own experience, surely; as you well know, Jessie, I never knew my own heart. I was fortunate that you were both patient and loving."

Jessica smiled, well satisfied with the answer she had extracted, and pressed on. "And having disposed of Darcy's affliction, what is your diagnosis of Kathryn's condition?" she asked.

Julian was more cautious, "Oh dear, there I must be more careful, I am not as familiar with the lady as I am with Darcy; but since you ask me, I think I will have to say that, like all women, she must be aware that the gentleman is falling in love with her, but, being both intelligent and sensible, she is unwilling to allow herself to follow suit, unless and until she is quite certain of his intentions."

"That sounds very sensible indeed; not all of us are as circumspect when we commit to loving someone…" she began, but he would not let her continue.

"I will not let you say it, Jessie. I knew soon enough that I loved you, but was too afraid to let you see it, lest you should recoil from me—wary of my failure as a husband and father—no, let me say it, my dear. I never believed I deserved you, I was afraid you would say no and am profoundly happy and grateful that you said yes."

Pleased with all his answers, Jessica troubled him no more on the subject, content instead to observe the course of love, as yet unacknowledged, while enjoying the certainty of her own.

⁓❦⁓

The snow fell all evening.

It was still falling at midnight and some of the guests had not left, for fear of being stranded on the roads.

When news arrived that the bridge on the road between Pemberley and Matlock was blocked by a wagon that had lost a wheel, arrangements were made to accommodate overnight those of the party who remained. The staff bustled around making preparations and while Elena regarded this as a great adventure, Kathryn seemed concerned that her parents and in particular her mother may be worried about them.

Trying to allay her fears, Darcy promised to send a rider over to Colley Dale early the following morning to reassure them.

"Pray do not be anxious, Miss O'Hare, I am confident we should be able to get a man on horseback through early tomorrow, to take a message to your parents. Indeed, it being Sunday, Reverend Courtney will certainly wish to return to Kympton at the earliest opportunity, even if none of his congregation makes it to church."

She smiled at this, and he added, "When he goes, I shall arrange for a groom to go with him, who can then proceed to Colley Dale. Please do not be troubled; you may rest assured everything will be done to assure them of your safety and that of your sister."

Whether it was his genuine concern that moved her or her own anxiety which had suddenly overwhelmed her, she could not tell, but without warning Kathryn felt her eyes fill with tears and she was embarrassed that she could not conceal them from her companion.

And Darcy, seeing them, was concerned that he had not been able by his assurances to assuage her fears. He spoke quietly but with great earnestness. Producing a clean handkerchief, which she accepted, he said, "Kathryn, I am sorry, but if it will help, I shall ride over myself at first light, to set your parents' minds at rest," he began, but she turned to him at once, upset that he had misunderstood her tears.

Involuntarily placing a hand upon his arm, she said, "I do beg your pardon; please do not think me ungrateful. Believe me, I am most thankful for all that is being done; you must not misunderstand my distress. It was probably a result of the relief I felt at your suggestion to send a man over tomorrow... I was temporarily overcome... Indeed it was your kindness that brought it on... Please, Mr Gardiner, you must not even consider going yourself, that would worry me a great deal more... A message sent tomorrow morning should be quite sufficient."

She was speaking quickly and not always coherently, trying desperately to convince him that she had not been unappreciative of his concern. She had resolved to be sensible and yet, she had not succeeded.

Seeing her thus, uncertain and vulnerable, Darcy was quite unable to contain his feelings. His previous determination set aside, he spoke with a sense of urgency that surprised her.

"Kathryn," he said, speaking her name as he had done some moments ago, "please do not distress yourself; there is no need. I well understand your anxiety and will do everything I can to alleviate it," and when she turned to look at him as he spoke, he added in a gentler, more serious voice, "and if you will permit me, I should be honoured to continue to do this and more for you, for the rest of my life."

Then, seeing her eyes widen with surprise, he said, "Dearest Kathryn, I love you. Will you marry me?"

Nothing had prepared Kathryn O'Hare for his proposal.

So sudden, so precipitate, and yet so deeply sincere, coming in the wake of the chaos of a night of wild weather, yet, amidst the ordered elegance of Pemberley, she did not know how to respond. For a few moments, she said not a word.

Seeing her expression, which suggested some surprise and uncertainty, ambivalence even, Darcy spoke quietly but urgently. This was not how he had planned it; he had hoped to find her alone, when they could share their thoughts and hopes unobserved; he had expected to ask her calmly and with style, but circumstances and his own feelings had overtaken him.

"Kathryn, I do not expect an answer now. I understand you will wish to think it over and perhaps talk to your parents before you respond. If you will only assure me that your mind is not set against me, that you will consider my offer seriously, I shall be perfectly content to wait for my answer."

Kathryn was astonished at his modesty. She was unaccustomed to gentlemen who believed that they may be rejected by a woman to whom they had made an offer of marriage; arrogant men, of the ilk of Hartley-Brown, expected that no woman could refuse them anything. When she spoke, deliberately and with care, she made certain he understood her true feelings.

"Mr Gardiner, I am most honoured by your proposal. Please believe me, it is not any lack of regard for you that precludes me from giving you an immediate answer. I confess I was not expecting this, and there are matters I must consider, apart from the inclinations of my own heart. They are matters of a practical nature."

Her words gave him hope, yet he wished to know more.

"And after you have considered all these matters, when might I expect to receive your response?"

"If you would be so kind as to allow me a few days, a week at most, I should be most grateful. I do not mean by this delay to suggest…"

He would not let her continue. "Please say no more; there is no need for you to explain; you need time to consider and I am indeed happy to agree. A week it shall be, although I must admit it will be the longest week of my life."

It was difficult to believe that she would make such a request if she was intending to turn him down, he thought, not with any vanity, but with hope.

Kathryn thanked him. Her thoughts were in confusion, but her feelings, well, they were as clear as she could ever remember them to have been in all her life. She knew with absolute certainty that she had known no other man for whom she could feel such high esteem and warm affection.

Not long afterwards, the ladies were invited to retire upstairs to the rooms that had been prepared for them. Elena, still greatly excited at the prospect of sleeping overnight at Pemberley, came to call her sister away, and having bade good night to Darcy and other members of the family, who lingered in the rooms downstairs, they went.

They were attended by a maid, sent by Mrs Grantham to assist them with their toilette and provide them with suitable nightclothes. The girl could barely suppress her excitement at the engagement of Jessica and Julian, seeking their response to the news. It had obviously pleased the staff at Pemberley. Kathryn smiled, savouring the pleasure of her own secret.

What would they say, if they only knew? she wondered.

Neither Elena nor Kathryn could sleep that night, though for quite different reasons. The younger sister's excitement lay in all she knew she would have to tell her family and friends of Pemberley and its treasures, while Kathryn's mind was too full of a myriad of thoughts and feelings to let her sleep for long. No longer were her concerns of her parents' anxiety at their not returning to Colley Dale last night—Darcy's plan to send a servant with a message had quieted that worry. It was the matter of his proposal, his declaration of love and all that it implied, which absorbed her now, and the fact that she could not share her secret with anyone served only to increase the strain.

In the morning, the sun, when it rose, looked upon a much quieter scene. The blizzard had blown itself out, leaving some devastation in its path, but it had stopped snowing.

Some of the men had already ventured out to see what damage had been done, and Darcy Gardiner, together with a couple of workmen, had ridden out to the boundaries of the estate to inspect the condition of the road.

When they returned, he was able to confirm that the road was almost clear of debris and soon one of the smaller carriages from Pemberley could depart, taking Reverend and Mrs Courtney to Kympton. If Kathryn and Elena so desired, they could travel with them and proceed to Colley Dale.

"One of our grooms will ride with you all the way, to ensure that you reach home safely," he said as Kathryn thanked him.

She had had some trouble persuading her young sister, who had fallen into a deep sleep towards daybreak, to rise and be dressed early, so they could leave with the Courtneys if the road was clear. She approached Jessica, who had joined them at breakfast, and asked that their thanks be conveyed to Mr and Mrs Darcy.

"I should have very much liked to have thanked them myself, but I realise it is too early for them. Please be so kind as to say how very much we appreciated their hospitality and kindness."

Jessica agreed. The two friends embraced before parting and there was a special warmth between them, though no further words were exchanged.

It was as though each knew the other's feelings, though unable to speak of them.

Jessica had not been able to get Darcy alone to discover how matters stood between them, but had noted that he seemed perfectly at ease that morning, when he had come in to breakfast. No sign of the disappointed suitor there, she thought. Quite the contrary, in fact.

Had he proposed? She could not be certain, and Kathryn was certainly giving nothing away, though again, Jessica had noticed the colour rise in her cheeks when Darcy entered the room.

As they left the house and entered the courtyard where the carriage waited for them, Kathryn turned to Darcy, who escorted her to the vehicle.

"Mr Gardiner, I must thank you once more for your kindness last night," she began, and he, determined that she should not misconstrue his ardour, said quietly, so none of the others could hear, "Kathryn dearest, please believe me, it was not kindness; I love you dearly and will await your answer with earnest hope."

Elena had already run ahead and entered the carriage. Handing Kathryn into the vehicle, he held her hand in his for a moment longer than was customary and indicated in a low voice, so only she would hear, that he would call on her parents at Colley Dale before the week was ended.

She smiled and nodded her agreement, before sitting back to let the man-servant secure the door.

As the carriage drove away, perhaps for the first time in her life, she had experienced the deep pleasure that for a woman comes only with the recognition of feelings usually well concealed, which rise to the surface of her consciousness. That the source of those feelings was a man, much admired and loved, was undeniable. Last night, in a moment so unexpected it had left her momentarily speechless, he had declared his love for her and asked her to be his wife.

As the carriage bore them towards Colley Dale, there was no longer any doubt in her mind that she would accept him.

Chapter Twelve

DARCY GARDINER HAD NOT stopped to consider when, or at what particular point in their association, his feelings for Miss O'Hare had deepened from a warm admiration for her looks, her vivacity, and many accomplishments, to the deeper, more ardent attachment he now recognised as love.

He could recall feelings of pleasure whenever they had met and exchanged views on a variety of subjects, almost always thought provoking, frequently amusing; he remembered also his outrage on learning from the landlord at the inn at Bakewell of Hartley-Brown's claim to have known the lady. There had been an anger there, which had been inexplicable at the time, but had seemed, on reflection, to indicate a proprietory interest in her.

Beyond that, he was not able to fix upon a date or an event, when he had become conscious of a change in his feelings towards her.

On being reassured by Jessica that there was no clandestine arrangement between Hartley-Brown and Kathryn O'Hare, he had experienced a feeling of immense relief, but then, when Kathryn had admitted that she had, some years previously, allowed herself to be persuaded into a secret engagement with him, Darcy had suffered great disappointment and anger. Yet, his indignation had been directed not at Kathryn, but at the man who had dared to importune and wheedle, hoping no doubt to get his way with her. But he comforted himself with the knowledge that Kathryn had, in the end, rejected Hartley-Brown and returned to Colley Dale. For Darcy, that was the material point.

Since then, all Darcy's efforts had been bent to protect her from the blackguard who continued to threaten her. His outrage at the conduct of both Hartley-Brown and Lady Denny had increased his contempt for them and others of their ilk, who battened upon the good nature or naiveté of young women. The more he had heard of their activities, the greater had been his revulsion.

Darcy had to acknowledge, if only to himself, that he had over the past months grown to love Kathryn with an ardour that he had not felt ever before, for any young woman of his acquaintance. There had been those whom he had admired for their looks or their spirit, but none approached her. He knew that when he told her he loved her dearly and wished to marry her, he had spoken with the deepest sincerity.

He had longed to declare his feelings with greater intensity and sought an opportunity to express, in the most ardent terms, the warmth and strength of his affections, in order to convince her of his love, but had deemed it would not have been seemly to do so, without obtaining her father's consent to his proposal.

To this end, he prepared himself for a meeting with Mr Daniel O'Hare on the following Saturday.

Darcy Gardiner could not explain why he found the prospect of meeting with Mr O' Hare so daunting. An educated young man with excellent family connections, well versed in the ways of the world, he had settled into a rewarding position at Pemberley, with possibly the chance to enter Parliament if he so chose. He had influential friends and was universally liked, yet he was apprehensive of asking Mr O'Hare for his daughter's hand in marriage.

He wondered whether Mr O'Hare would ask a lot of awkward questions and how he would answer them, if he did. He had spent the entire week in a state of mild panic, in which he had been grateful for the understanding and sympathy of his cousin Jessica. Having discovered that he had proposed to Kathryn and had not been rejected outright, Jessica had set about preparing him for his visit to Colley Dale.

"You will need to impress Mr O'Hare with your prospects," she had warned, "I gather he still harbours some suspicions about young Englishmen, especially good-looking ones with little money in their pockets. The O'Hares are not wealthy, but like many self-made men, Daniel O'Hare has acquired property here and in Ireland, from which both of his daughters are likely to benefit. It means Kathryn's father knows she will always have money to live on and will not need to marry in order to survive," she explained.

Darcy was perplexed. "Do you think he will expect me to make a settlement upon Kathryn when we are engaged?" he asked rather nervously. "I understand Colonel Fitzwilliam did that, when he was engaged to cousin Caroline."

This was a subject about which he had no knowledge, and he wondered if perhaps he should have spoken with his brother-in-law about it. To this Jessica had no direct answer, but she did suggest that he should be prepared for such an eventuality.

It was a prospect that filled him with dismay. He knew little of such matters and hoped very much that it would not come to that. If it did, he would promise anything, he decided rather rashly.

When Darcy finally arrived at Colley Dale, he found to his surprise that no such ordeal awaited him there. Instead, when shown into the parlour, he found Kathryn and her mother waiting for him. They plied him with tea and talked for a while about the weather and the prospect of floods in Spring; then quite suddenly, Mrs O'Hare excused herself and left the room.

She had barely closed the door behind her, when Darcy turned to Kathryn, but before he could ask the inevitable question, she said with a smile, "Mr Gardiner, I have told my parents of your proposal and informed them that I have decided to accept it… they have said…" but she got no further before he leapt up from his chair and took her in his arms.

Darcy blessed Mrs O'Hare for leaving the room; he had wanted to do this for quite a while, yet this was the very first time they had been alone together for long enough.

Though at first she did nothing to deter him, Kathryn had more to say and, when she was free to speak, continued, "They are very happy for me and have said how much they admire and respect you and your family. They wish us every happiness, of course, and when we see my father, you may tell him that we are now engaged."

Despite his delight at her words, Darcy was a little circumspect, uncertain of the correctness of his situation.

"But, Kathryn dearest, I have not obtained your father's consent, yet…"

This time, she astonished him with her answer. "Nor need you. Darcy, I am twenty-five years old; it is I who must decide who I will marry and if I can be happy with you, not Papa. Of course I wish to have his blessing and Mama's, but my father is a man of the world; he understands my views on marriage; he knows I will marry only if I am in love and he will not expect me to heed his opinion over my own feelings. This is not to say that he has any objection to you, but if he had, it would not have changed my mind, once I knew for certain we loved one another."

Having taken a few more moments to demonstrate with feeling his appreciation of this statement, he then asked, "And does that mean you will return with me to Camden House and we may tell my parents the good news too?"

But he was to be disappointed in her reply.

"Darcy, there is just one thing I have to ask of you. There are some matters, arising out of my time at Lindfield Towers, which I must attend to. They concern one or two people for whose loyalty I am grateful, and I would ask that the announcement of our engagement be postponed until those matters are concluded. Do I ask too much?"

So overjoyed was Darcy at being accepted with so little fuss, he would probably have agreed to anything, but he asked, "May I not tell my parents? Or my sister Lizzie?"

"Not just yet, please, Darcy. I should very much wish that it were not known generally in the district for a while. But we could tell Jessica. I know that she has suspected something and would be delighted to be the first to be told. I had intended to tell her myself, but perhaps I shall leave it to you to give her the happy news. Our secret will be safe with her."

Darcy was keen to know when he could tell his family.

"Within a month at the most," she told him.

"A month!" he was appalled. "How shall I keep such a secret for so long? My manner will betray me, surely? I cannot pretend to be other than happy. Besides, Jessica and Julian are to be married and expect to leave for France and Africa in Spring. I should very much like to have it announced to the family before then," he said and was assured that his wish could be easily fulfilled. The matters she had to arrange would not take so long, she said confidently.

"I would not ask it of you, except that it is important to me that these matters be resolved. I can then enjoy more fully the pleasures of our engagement," she explained.

Concerned to help, Darcy asked, "Is there not something I can do?" but she assured him that they were simple matters and required none of his very special talents.

That settled, Kathryn took him upstairs to meet her father, whose amiable manner and obvious pleasure at the news was the very reverse of what Darcy had expected. Amused, he looked forward to telling Jessica how wrong they had both been about Daniel O'Hare. Here was a most amenable father-in-law to be—no sign at all of a money-grubbing skinflint!

Mrs O'Hare demonstrated her approval by inviting him to stay to dinner, and the rest of the day was spent so pleasantly that Darcy could not think why he had expected it to be so daunting in the first place. Elena too was told and sworn to secrecy. Her delight was even harder to contain.

When he said good-bye to Kathryn in the evening and left to ride back to Pemberley, Darcy went with the lightest heart and the highest hopes for happiness he had ever known. So absorbed was he in the contemplation of what the future held in store for him and Kathryn; so engrossed in his own aspirations, that he failed to notice a stranger on horseback, who crossed his path at the cross roads, as he took the road into the Pemberley estate.

At Pemberley, he found Jessica upstairs in the elegant little sitting room, which used to be Georgiana Darcy's. It was a pretty, restful room, and Jessica often retired there when she wished to be alone. She was sitting in the alcove that overlooked the rose garden, reading a letter, and had been unaware of Darcy's return. When he entered the room, she turned to him eagerly. She had known the purpose of his visit to Colley Dale and was keen to learn the outcome.

"Well?" she said, smiling, and even before he spoke, she could tell from the expression on his countenance and his air of confidence as he held out both hands to her, that it had gone well for him.

Darcy was a little tongue tied at first, but soon warmed to his subject and told her that his dearest hopes had been fulfilled. Kathryn had accepted him and both Mr and Mrs O'Hare had approved of their engagement.

"Indeed, they appear to have no concerns at all, except Mrs O'Hare asked how soon we expected to be married. It was a matter to which I had not given much thought, believing we would probably wait some months at least, but before I could speak, Kathryn, showing remarkable sensibility, intervened to point out to her parents that with the recent death of my grandmother, Mrs Gardiner, it would not be appropriate that we should be married before at least six months had passed. Of course, Mrs O'Hare was then very understanding, and no more was said on the subject."

Jessica nodded. "That is very like Kathryn; she is possessed of clearer understanding and better judgment on such matters than almost any other young woman I know. Oh Darcy, my dear cousin, I cannot say how very pleased I am for you both," she said. "I know you will be happy with Kathryn. She is a truly remarkable woman, warm, intelligent, handsome, witty—but you know all of this! You must want to go at once to Camden Park to tell your parents all about it, or have you been already?"

At this, his face clouded over a little and he sat down with her on the couch by the window and told her of Kathryn's request that news of their engagement be withheld from everyone except herself, for a few weeks.

"Apart from her parents and Elena, only you will know of our engagement," he explained.

Jessica frowned, puzzled by his revelation.

"Why so? Has she given you a reason?"

Darcy's answer did not entirely satisfy her, but she assumed that her friend must have a very sound reason for such a request and did not pursue the matter further. She was proud to be taken into their confidence and promised that no one, not even her dear Julian, would learn of it from her.

Darcy expressed his own regrets. "I should have liked to tell Mama, who I am sure will be pleased, as will my father. He speaks well of Kathryn's intelligence and wide reading. Mama likes her already and has said, as you have, that it is a pleasure to meet a young woman whose interests go beyond matters of domesticity and romance. Once she knows her better, I am confident that she will love her, too, as we do."

Jessica assured him that Sir Richard and Lady Gardiner would not be able to help themselves.

"I know that Kathryn's warm and generous nature alone would win their hearts," she said, "even above the obvious advantages of education and understanding, which they have already recognised. Your parents will see that in

Kathryn you have found a companion, who will match your affections as well as your aspirations. You are fortunate indeed, Darcy."

As they watched the sun sink low in the west, Darcy sighed, and for the first time, she noted a slight trace of sadness. When she looked at him, as if to ask for the reason behind this, he shook his head as though trying to dispel some lingering worry that teased his mind, but said nothing more.

Taking his arm, she suggested they go downstairs to dinner.

Neither Jessica nor Darcy could have known the real reason behind Kathryn's request for a delay in the announcement of their engagement.

Shortly before Christmas, Kathryn had received a letter from Mrs Ellis, the housekeeper at Lindfield Towers.

She was able, she said, to write openly and frankly because she was soon to leave Lindfield and return to her home in Ryedale, a quiet village in the county of Yorkshire, where she had been born and raised.

Her letter explained that she could no longer continue to work at Lindfield Towers, in view of the "goings-on in this place," which she described as "scandalous."

The mistress and Mr Hartley-Brown are now openly having an affair, in the absence of the master, unashamed and brazen, not caring who knows it. It is widely gossiped about among the servants and in the village. Worse still, there have been one or two visitors, friends of Mr Hartley-Brown, whose shocking behaviour has become quite intolerable.

...she wrote, describing one man in particular, a loud, unpleasant fellow called Bellamy, whose harassment of the housemaids had already led to one of them leaving the household and returning home.

He is a thoroughly unpleasant fellow, ma'am, the youngest son of a titled family with more money than brains and no manners at all, she explained, concluding her letter with greetings and good wishes to Kathryn and her family.

Then, on a separate scrap of paper, there followed a postscript, which seemed to have been hurriedly inserted prior to the letter being posted. It informed her that Hartley-Brown had been heard to assert in the hearing of one of the footmen that he intended to find Miss Kathryn O'Hare and bring her back to Lindfield Towers, where he and Lady Denny would persuade her to honour the engagement she had entered into with him.

It was suggested that he was still clearly incensed at being "jilted by that young minx," whom he considered to be beneath him by birth and social status and appeared determined to enforce his will upon her, by any means at all. His friend Bellamy, the footman had said, had urged him on, offering to help him find her and return her to Lindfield.

Mrs Ellis wrote to warn Kathryn to beware of any strangers who may visit the area, for, she said, they may be friends of Hartley-Brown, and if so, *they are not to be trusted, being quite ruthless and not above abducting you to compromise your virtue and character for their own evil purposes.*

And with this chilling piece of advice, the note ended abruptly.

Dismayed, Kathryn had put the letter away. It had made her uneasy and nervous; she had re-read it in private at least a dozen times.

She knew not what to do or whom to turn to. It was of no use to tell her parents, it would only cause them anxiety with no prospect of helping her resolve the problem. As for Darcy, she was quite determined he would not be drawn into this; she had hoped her unfortunate association with Hartley-Brown was now a closed chapter between them.

To bring it up again at the very moment when they had declared their love for one another would, she feared, sully their joy.

The arrival of her brother from Manchester to spend Christmas at Colley Dale had suggested a possible alternative, but it soon became clear he had very little time to spend at home with the family, and she had not wished to take up any of it with problems from the past, of which he was ignorant.

No, Kathryn decided, she had to resolve this matter herself.

To this end, she had written to Mrs Ellis, directing her letter to the village in Yorkshire, where she supposed her to be by the New Year. Seeking more information about the activities of Hartley-Brown and his clique, she proposed a visit to Ryedale and asked for directions so she may travel there. Kathryn was unsure what she might achieve by such a journey, but it was at least a chance to meet and speak of the problem with the only person she could trust to keep the matter confidential. In all her dealings with Mrs

Ellis, she had found her to be honest and open; Kathryn hoped these very qualities may help preserve her from the nightmare of a further encounter with Hartley-Brown.

✢

Meanwhile, Darcy found himself busier than he had anticipated, being called upon to settle two rather unpleasant disputes, each of a very different nature, both of which took up a great deal of time and effort.

The first involved the surreptitious efforts of a pair of stock-jobbers, working as agents for a developer from London, to purchase land without the authority of the council. Alerted by his brother-in-law Mr Carr, Darcy had had the steward at Pemberley make enquiries. He had been shocked to discover the extent of the deception involved.

Several parcels of land on the fringes of the Pemberley Estate, some of it leasehold and therefore not available to be sold, had been selected by the developer, seeking to make a swift sale and quick money.

The investigation revealed corruption of council officers, bribed to turn a blind eye to the illegality of the transaction, as well as the peddling of influence by some local landholders.

When the truth became known, Darcy Gardiner was instructed by his grandfather to have the miscreants brought before the magistrate, which was no easy matter, for some of them were rich and others had useful connections in the county.

It had taken days of legal argument, threat, and counter-threat to finally convince the developer that he was not going to succeed, and his minions of their great good fortune, that men were no longer hanged or transported for such offences.

"Mere incarceration," said Darcy, "seems almost too mild a sentence for their misdeeds."

Worn out by interminable days spent in discussions with attorneys and police officers, Darcy returned flushed with a degree of success, to find a note from his mother awaiting him. She asked to see him and suggested he dine with them that evening.

Having taken some time to bathe and change before leaving for Camden Park, Darcy despatched a note to Colley Dale. It had been almost a week since he had seen Kathryn and he had meant to visit her that evening.

His mother's urgent summons prevented him from doing so, and he made his excuses in a note reassuring Kathryn of his affections and promising to call on her very soon.

Arriving at Camden House, he found his mother in a state of high anxiety.

Cassandra Gardiner was not a woman to panic or become unduly anxious; however, her current state of mind was entirely understandable. A letter had been received a day or two ago from her brother-in-law Robert Gardiner, stating that his wife Rose was travelling to Derbyshire with a party of friends, intending to use the house at Oakleigh for the Spring, since their plans to tour Greece and Italy had failed to eventuate. He took it for granted that there would be no objection, assuming that his mother's house was still as it had been when she died several months ago.

Cassandra handed her son the letter. Robert wrote:

It will be less expensive than taking a town house in London, though not as convenient of course. However, Mother's servants will suffice and Rose will not need to hire new ones. If I hear nothing to the contrary, I shall assume that arrangements may be made for Rose and her party to arrive next month.

Darcy was astonished. "What does he mean, Mama? Does not my uncle know that Oakleigh passed on the death of my grandmother to my aunt Emily Courtney? Is he unaware that with Dr Courtney being unwell and likely to retire from the living at Kympton soon, the family are to move to Oakleigh in the Spring?"

Cassandra shrugged her shoulders and did not hide her irritation.

"Darcy, it is the most vexing thing; he is not only well aware of it, I have written to Rose myself over Christmas, a letter in which I mentioned that Emily was looking forward to the move, because Jessica could then be married from Oakleigh."

Darcy recalled immediately that Mrs Courtney had been delighted at the prospect.

"Much as I love our little rectory, which has been my home for so many years, it is too small for a wedding party, and though I know cousin Lizzie and Mr Darcy have offered to host the wedding at Pemberley, I should love to have my daughter married from my home," she had said.

Considering that the late Mrs Gardiner had arranged her affairs with a view to achieving just such a result, it seemed churlish for Mrs Rose Gardiner to want to thrust herself and a party of friends into the house right now, on a mere whim, thought Darcy.

When he discussed the matter with his father after dinner, Sir Richard was quite adamant.

"There is absolutely no question about it, Oakleigh belongs to Emily; our mother's will said so and neither Robert nor Rose nor anyone else can come in and presume to occupy any part of it for any length of time, unless Emily invites them to visit."

"Do you believe she may have done so?" asked Darcy.

Cassandra was certain she had not. "I have spoken with Emily, though I have not mentioned this letter, and from all I could gather, she has sent no such invitation. Indeed, she is very busy packing in readiness for their move to Oakleigh."

Richard Gardiner shook his head; he understood his younger brother and his wife less and less. With each passing year, they seemed to become more selfish and remote from the rest of the family.

"I suggest, Darcy, that you write to your uncle and explain the situation clearly and draw his attention to the fact that the Courtneys are moving to Oakleigh within the fortnight," he said, and Darcy did not relish the prospect at all.

The unpleasantness that followed sapped his energy and enthusiasm, as he tried to resolve the situation. In a particularly nasty letter, Mrs Robert Gardiner had suggested that her sister-in-law Emily Courtney and her husband, being accustomed to the cramped conditions at the rectory, ought be able to use one of the vacant cottages on the Oakleigh manor for the duration of her visit in Spring. She wrote:

After all, it is not as if they have ever enjoyed palatial accommodation, though I know Emily did spend some years at Pemberley as a house guest— it seems fair that they should put themselves out for a very short time, in order that we should share just a little of what should rightly have been Robert's country house!

Nothing he had heard about the increasing selfishness of his uncle Robert Gardiner and his wife had prepared him for this, and Darcy had grown weary of their complaints long before the matter was finally resolved. It was achieved by Richard and Cassandra Gardiner offering Robert and his wife the use of Camden House for a month in early Spring, after Jessica's wedding, when the Gardiners expected to travel to Standish Park in Kent, as guests of the Wilsons.

"A month, no more," said Cassandra, and the offer was duly conveyed to Mr and Mrs Robert Gardiner. To the relief of just about every member of the family and all of the household staff at Camden House, it was abruptly refused. Rose and her friends were off to Bath instead, said Robert in a note that was barely polite.

Darcy's own relief was immeasurable as he looked forward to leading a normal life again. The practical problems of tenants on the estate and the possible onset of a recession in British agriculture paled in comparison with the unpredictable and so often unreasonable demands of Mr and Mrs Robert Gardiner.

Then there was his personal life, which, from a high point of happiness a mere fortnight ago, appeared to have gone into reverse.

He'd not had time to visit Colley Dale all week but had sent regular notes to his beloved Kathryn. At first, he received gratifying replies, in which she said she understood he had some intractable problems to deal with and would await their resolution, when they could meet once more. Then he had no communication for two days and wrote again. But when, on returning to his apartments at Pemberley, he found no word from her had arrived in reply, he became concerned.

Had she grown tired of his absence? Was she hurt or angry at his silence?

He began by asking Jessica if she had heard from her friend, but no, she said, since school was out, she had had no word either. Besides, Jessica was busy with her wedding preparations and their subsequent departure for South Africa. She confessed she had been too engrossed in her own plans to notice that there had been no message from Kathryn all week.

"It is unusual, but I have been busy and did not think to ask," she said.

Finally, Darcy, unable to settle down to anything, went himself to Colley Dale, only to find that Kathryn was gone and no one could tell him where!

Her mother, grave faced and anxious, received him in the parlour and declared that a letter had arrived for Kathryn, which had clearly brought serious news of a confidential nature. It appeared to have necessitated her sudden departure, but Mrs O'Hare could give him no indication of her destination. She could only hazard a guess, she said, because the letter had come from a Mrs Ellis, who had been the housekeeper at Lindfield Towers, that Kathryn may have gone to Lindfield.

Struck dumb with consternation, Darcy could not imagine why Kathryn would ever return to Lindfield and place herself in the power of the people she loathed. It was beyond belief.

So dejected was he, that he neglected to ask when exactly Kathryn had left, and had to go back inside again to enquire.

"She was going to catch the train from Derby on Saturday," was all her mother could tell him, and afraid even to think what might have caused Kathryn to depart so suddenly, without a word to him, Darcy walked out of the house in a mood of deep despondency.

He was about to mount his horse when he caught sight of Elena some distance from the house, obviously attempting to stay out of sight of her mother, within the shadow of a clump of trees by the gate.

Waiting until he approached, she darted out and handed him a note, folded over and enclosing another piece of paper.

He was about to ask her about her sister's whereabouts, when she said quickly, "Kathryn's gone to Yorkshire… she left this for you. No one else knows and you are not to tell anyone please, else she may be in great danger."

When Darcy tried to question her, she shook her head and ran back through the shrubbery towards the house.

Wanting desperately to open it, yet unwilling to do so in full public view, Darcy rode down to the inn and, having purchased a pot of ale, sat down to read his note. He first read it through very quickly and was relieved that it contained nothing that reflected upon their engagement nor had anything untoward happened to Kathryn. He then re-read it, trying to understand its purpose. It told him very little, except that she had decided to travel to Yorkshire to meet with Mrs Ellis, the onetime housekeeper at Lindfield, and would return to Colley Dale later in the month. She assured him she was quite safe and he was not to worry about her.

Contained within it was a note from Mrs Ellis to Kathryn, giving simple, clear directions to the village of Ryedale, including a small, roughly drawn map of the area.

When he had re-read them so many times, as to almost know them by heart, Darcy decided to proceed to Rushmore Farm and consult his brother-in-law, Mr Carr. He could think of no other course of action, so bewildered and dejected was he. His sole relief came from knowing that it was plain, from both the tone and the content of her letter, that Kathryn had not run away from him. As far as he could ascertain, she still loved him and their engagement was intact. That at least was a relief.

When he had met Mr Carr and shown him the letter explaining the circumstances in which he had received it, he asked, "Can you think of any reason why Kathryn may have gone to meet Mrs Ellis?"

Darcy had no answer, except that Kathryn had spoken well of the housekeeper and trusted her. He was in turmoil, unable to understand her problem and therefore to devise a plan to resolve it.

What was he to do, he asked. Should he follow her to Yorkshire? Or remain here and look to her return, as promised in her note?

Mr Carr persisted. "Could Mrs Ellis have been the bearer of bad news regarding a mutual friend, perhaps? Is that why Miss O'Hare has gone to Yorkshire to see her?" he asked.

"In which case, there must have been another letter, one she received before this one with the map... one which detailed the bad news..." Darcy mused and then Mr Carr said, "I see it now—of course, Mrs Ellis has already left Lindfield and returned to Yorkshire. Having done so, she has written to Kathryn, giving her some significant news. Perhaps she is in some trouble and needs help. It is this that has prompted Kathryn to go off to Yorkshire to see Mrs Ellis, perhaps to help her in some way."

"But what could she have told her that has made her race off like this? Who is it about and what of Elena's warning that I should not reveal this to anyone else, or Kathryn might be in some danger? What do you make of that?" asked Darcy, to whom the situation was not much clearer. The most vexing thing was his complete ignorance of Kathryn's predicament.

They pondered these matters for a long while but came up with no credible answers. Darcy was about to leave, when a young lad he had seen helping the innkeeper with his chores, appeared running up the road to the farm. He approached Darcy and handed him a note. He had followed him from the inn, he said, missed him at the crossroads and doubled back to Rushmore Farm.

Thanking the lad and giving him some coins for his trouble, Darcy tore open the note. Together, he and Mr Carr read it aloud.

The innkeeper, who had been known to the families at Pemberley and Oakleigh for many years, had seen fit to inform Darcy Gardiner that a certain Mr Bellamy of Lindfield in Sussex, with references from Mr Hartley-Brown, had been staying at the inn and asking several questions.

I thought it wise to draw this to your attention, Mr Gardiner, sir, because he introduced himself as a close friend and associate of Mr Hartley-Brown, who was here last year and became a source of some concern to you, as I recall.

Furthermore, Mr Bellamy has also been asking about the family of O'Hare and has been heard to mention the name of the same lady—Miss Kathryn O'Hare.

It is not possible to believe that this is simply a coincidence, sir.

He added in closing:

Mr Bellamy has paid for his room in advance and expects to stay at least a week.

This communication threw them into even greater confusion, since neither Darcy nor his brother-in-law Mr Carr had heard of Mr Bellamy, nor knew how he might be connected with Kathryn's departure for Yorkshire.

"How is it possible to resolve a problem, if the problem itself is hidden from one?" Darcy asked helplessly. "I cannot comprehend it at all."

It was Mr Carr who, after some thought, made the first practical suggestion.

"Darcy, since you have been given the map and directions by Miss Elena, on the instructions of her sister, one may assume that the lady would not be displeased if you turned up in Yorkshire. How would it be, then, if you were to go there yourself, find Mrs Ellis, and discover if Kathryn is there with her?" he asked, and his friend's eyes lit up at the suggestion.

"If this were the case, I am sure she would explain everything to you, which she may not have been able to do in a letter or at her home in Colley Dale, with her family present overhearing your conversation."

Darcy agreed it was a plausible proposition.

"And, while you are gone, I could set a watch over the activities of this Mr Bellamy and should he in any way whatsoever transgress or break the law, I'll have the police after him. If he is an associate of Hartley-Brown, he must be here as his emissary and is probably waiting for an opportunity to approach Kathryn, unaware she has left the area. He may try to visit her family at Colley Dale or approach them in the village. If he does, I'll have him! Once we have him in custody and before the magistrate, he will tell us everything—his kind generally do, they're no heroes," said Carr.

Darcy thought this over and concluded it was probably the best idea they'd had, but so many unanswered questions swirled through his mind, he was prevented from thinking clearly. He wanted time to consider it and promised to return to Rushmore Farm on the morrow. Tired and downcast, he was at the end of his tether and his brother-in-law bade him good night and let him go, urging him to get a good night's rest.

It was into this unhappy state of affairs that Darcy's elder brother Edward Gardiner intruded again, with yet another letter; this time addressed to their mother.

Cassandra Gardiner arrived at Pemberley, shortly after breakfast, to see her son, knowing that he had spent the previous two weeks in a continuing state of anxiety and aggravation. She was aware that the unpleasantness generated by her brother-in-law Robert Gardiner and his wife Rose had taken its toll on the generally amiable and obliging young man. Darcy had found it particularly difficult to confront the couple, whose self-indulgent behaviour was totally at odds with his own standards and those of the other members of his family. His mother was well aware of this.

Which was why, on receiving Edward's letter, Cassy had decided to come to him, instead of summoning Darcy to Camden Park again. She hoped for some explanation, which might set her mind at rest. She had, for the same reason, refrained from disclosing her concerns, and the contents of the letter that had raised them, to her husband. Instead, she had chosen to let Darcy see his brother's letter first.

Edward Gardiner, successful and married well, advancing both his personal happiness and his professional status simultaneously, was not averse to giving members of his family, and especially his younger brother Darcy, the benefit of his opinions.

His sister Lizzie, having married the man of her choice without feeling the need to consult her elder brother, was immune to his gratuitous advice.

Not so Darcy, who by reason of his amenable and open nature was often the target of Edward's homilies.

On a previous occasion, he had written to counsel his brother against making an unsuitable alliance, but since he had made no specific reference to the lady concerned, Darcy had chosen to ignore it. This time, however, writing to their mother, he had gone further, much further than before, and whereas the previous letter had sought to advise, this one was clearly meant to admonish.

When Cassandra Gardiner found her son in his apartments at Pemberley, he was completing his toilette, prior to coming downstairs to breakfast.

There was no mistaking either his astonishment at seeing her or the seriousness of her countenance as she entered his room.

"Mama! What has happened?" He was immediately concerned, it had to be bad news... some dreadful accident... he could think only of Lizzie or his father. But before he could say anything, she held up a hand and spoke quickly to allay his fears.

"Have no fears, Darcy, no one is ill or hurt or anything at all. I am sorry to have intruded upon you at this early hour, but there is a matter of some importance, which you must know of... your brother Edward has written a letter in which..."

"Another letter from Edward? What does he say?"

Darcy wiped the residue of shaving soap from his face and came forward as his mother seated herself in the chair that stood to one side of his bed.

"Here it is, you can see for yourself... and then perhaps you will explain to me what this means and if I have any reason to be concerned..." she said as she handed him the letter.

He stood in front of her reading it, half aloud, and from the way his voice changed as he read on, Cassandra could see that he was deeply shocked by what he read.

Edward wrote:

My dearest mother,
You will, I know, understand that I write this letter with some
degree of reluctance. I am not inclined, as a matter of general principle,
to interfere in the personal affairs of my brothers and sisters. However, in
this instance, I do not believe it is right that I should remain silent (and
in this my dear wife agrees with me) lest it be said in years to come that
I did not do my duty as your eldest son and draw your attention to the
possible damage that may result from the actions of my brother Darcy.

Notoriously longwinded, Edward went on for a paragraph or two, extolling the virtues of family loyalty and personal integrity, before getting to the point of his letter. When he did, he left no doubt of his intention.

Pardon me, dear mother, but I digress. The chief purpose of writing to you
was to express my very real unease about my brother Darcy's close asso-
ciation with a certain young woman, a Miss Kathryn O'Hare of Colley
Dale, with whom you are no doubt acquainted. I gather it is now common
knowledge in the district that they are on terms of very close friendship
and are often seen walking together between Pemberley and Colley Dale,
engaged in long and intimate conversations.
Now, while I understand there is as yet no talk of an engagement, it
is impossible to believe that one is not in prospect. If this were to eventu-
ate, I should view the matter with great alarm, since it is unlikely, in
view of what is presently known of Miss O'Hare, that we (by that I
mean my dear Angela and myself) would be able to receive her into our
house. Given her lowly antecedents and dubious previous employment,
it would be difficult to understand what Darcy sees in her—though I
grant you she is handsome and well spoken. It would be difficult enough
to see my brother marry the daughter of a former Irish horse trainer, if
she were not also the former governess at Lindfield Towers, where it
is said she was an intimate friend of Lady Denny and her cousin Mr
Hartley-Brown, whose misconduct is widely known and talked about
in London society.

While I am well aware that my brother would probably not admit of any interference from me into his private affairs, I have hopes that you, dear Mother, and perhaps my father also, will be able to make him understand the unsuitability of this connection.

I do not believe for one moment that Darcy would have entered deliberately into an engagement with the lady without acquainting you and my father with his intentions and obtaining your approval. However, I fear that being of an amiable and compliant nature, he may have been drawn in too far already and formed too deep an attachment to retreat, despite the fact it is a situation of which his entire family must surely disapprove.

There was more in the same vein, but Darcy had no desire to continue. He folded the letter and handed it back to his mother.

Cassandra looked at his face and wondered at the depth of anguish reflected upon it. Saddened, she was about to ask a question, when he sat on the bed and faced her squarely,

"Mama, may I ask what it was in Edward's letter that so perturbed you, that you came in all this haste to see me? Was it the thought that I may be in love with Kathryn O'Hare?"

Cassy answered with a question of her own, "Are you?" and received the only answer he could give, "I am."

"And is your brother right? Are you already too deeply committed to her to retreat?" she asked.

At this even Darcy's mild nature, riled beyond bearing by his brother's words, rebelled and unable to repress any longer the anger that the letter had provoked, he spoke his mind with candour and an unusual bitterness.

"My brother is quite wrong about Miss O'Hare—on several matters of fact as well as in his opinion of her."

"In what way?" asked his mother gently, not wishing to provoke him any further.

"In a most shameful way!" he retorted. "To the extent that he has cast aspersions upon her parents, who are eminently respectable people, well liked in the community; he has not only insulted her, but has demeaned us all, including myself, my cousin Jessica, Mr and Mrs Darcy, and yourself, for have we not all been guilty of encouraging Miss O'Hare in her endeavours, appointing her to teach at the school and inviting her to our homes?" He looked at her but did not wait for an answer.

"But far worse are his insinuations against Kathryn's character," he raged, "the suggestion that as governess to the children of Lord and Lady Denny, she is somehow tainted, because of Lady Denny's notoriety, beggars belief. It is the kind of guilt by association that gave rise to the terror in France after the revolution—it presupposes that one must be condemned as corrupt because one's employers are so accused. His views are thoroughly abhorrent to me, Mama, and, I would have thought, to yourself and my father."

Horrified by the comparison, Cassy protested, "Darcy! Surely you go too far?"

"Do I?" he would not be contained, so great was his indignation. "Consider this, Mama, both Jessica and I are fully aware that Kathryn accepted the position at Lindfield with the Dennys upon the specific recommendation of persons whose status and standards Edward and his wife would endorse without question. We know also that she left Lady Denny's employ voluntarily, having discovered and disapproved of the situation in the household and the position in which she found herself.

"Kathryn has never spoken openly of what she knows because she is disinclined to speak ill of a former employer, even when such criticism may be justified. She considers it unseemly to gossip about matters to which she was privy, as a member of their household. But privately, she has left me in no doubt of her opinion of the activities of Lady Denny and her cousin Mr Hartley-Brown."

Cassandra nodded, clearly agreeing with the sentiments expressed, but Darcy, who had been walking about the room in a state of great agitation, had not quite finished.

"But that is not all, Mama," he said. "I resent deeply my brother's assumption that I am incapable of judgment or discrimination, that I am so easily bewitched by a pretty face or a clever wit, that he chooses to write to you to ask that you counsel me against a match with a lady whom he, upon the most superficial evidence, condemns. It is quite intolerable, that he should be so presumptuous, so overbearing!"

Cassandra, realising it was useless to defend her elder son, decided to use a different approach.

"Am I to understand that you wish to marry Kathryn?" she asked, and this time her voice was so gentle, so completely free of any pejorative overtones, even Darcy, incensed as he was, could not resent her question.

He looked at her and said with great sincerity, "Yes, Mama, I do, and before you ask, I *have* proposed to Kathryn and she has accepted me. I intended to tell you and Papa, but as you know, we have been exceedingly busy this week with many other matters…"

She stopped him in mid sentence. "Darcy, what other matter would so absorb my attention as to prevent my listening, had you spoken of your wish to marry Kathryn? Why have you left me in ignorance, to the extent that I was so unprepared, your brother's letter, when it came, threw me into such confusion and distress? I should have liked to have known something of your intentions."

Darcy apologised at once; he understood her distress. The delay was not of his making, but because he did not wish to divulge Kathryn's present troubles, he accepted the burden of guilt.

"I am sorry, Mama, I had hoped to bring Kathryn to see you and tell you our news, but, since she is visiting a friend in Yorkshire, I thought it best to await her return. Forgive me, Mama, it should not have been revealed like this, but that is the consequence of Edward's actions and circumstances quite outside my control. When Kathryn is back, I promise I shall bring her to visit you. As for my brother's insufferable letter, let me write an appropriate reply and tell him what I think of his snobbery and prejudice."

But Cassy laughed, "Oh no, I shall not encourage you to start some petty feud with your brother. No, I shall wait until your engagement is announced and write a suitable reply, giving Edward my opinion."

Darcy understood why his mother had such a high reputation for integrity and generosity within and outside of their family. Not for nothing was she Mr Darcy's daughter.

They embraced warmly, and before she left, stopping to look in the mirror and straighten her hat, she said, with a twinkle in her eye, "You need not lose any sleep over her family connections; after all, your sister Lizzie married the grandson of an Irish stable boy; I cannot see that the daughter of an Irish horse trainer is any less acceptable."

Darcy beamed with pleasure, confident now that he had his mother's approval and certain there would be no adverse repercussions from Edward's ill-informed letter.

It was one piece of good news in an otherwise dismal week.

Chapter Thirteen

I T DID NOT TAKE Darcy Gardiner long to decide that he should follow his brother-in-law's advice and travel to Yorkshire immediately.

His predominant desire now was to find Kathryn.

To this end, he made his plans and went first to Rushmore Farm to consult Mr Carr. There, he discovered that his brother-in-law had already contrived a simple scheme that would enable him to claim that he had estate business to attend to in Sheffield, from where he would take the train to Yorkshire. "I will send my most trusted man with you, so that you can send me word, if you need my help. Meanwhile, rest assured that I will have a very close watch kept over Bellamy; I shall see Mr Hand at the inn tomorrow— Bellamy will not move without my knowing it. One false step and we will have him."

As they parted, Darcy wondered how he would ever repay his brother-in-law for all he was doing. Their friendship had deepened as they matured. The grandson of an Irish stable hand, Carr had made good in America and returned to England some years ago, when the two men had become firm friends. Later, to Darcy's delight, his sister Lizzie and Michael Carr had fallen in love and married. Darcy had great affection for his brother-in-law and would have trusted him with his life.

The journey to Sheffield and thence to York by train took the better part of the following day. Watson, the man who accompanied him, made all the necessary arrangements and proved an excellent traveling companion.

As they journeyed north through the vale of Pickering, Darcy recalled similar journeys to Scarborough in Summers past, when, as children, they had looked forward to arriving in the grand old town, with its mineral spa and pump room, which engaged the adults, while the younger members of the party wanted only to race out to the cliffs and watch the boats coming in, their nets laden with fish—sole, plaice, skate, and many other strange sea creatures besides.

They were simple days, filled with innocent fun, that seemed a lifetime away. Deep in his nostalgic reverie, Darcy dozed off and had to be shaken awake when they reached their destination.

They alighted and saw that they were almost at the edge of the moors and the familiar, verdant countryside through which they had passed had given way to the rough grey-green folds of the moorland and the hard edge of bare ridges against the sky; not an inviting prospect at all.

Locating Ryedale did not prove too difficult. The pony trap that transported them from the train station was driven by a man who did not need the rough map Darcy produced. Though his speech was almost unintelligible, he knew the area well.

Mrs Ellis' detailed directions proved adequate to allow them to find the place, which had all the usual features of a Yorkshire village. Shaded by a giant yew tree was a village green, to one side of which stood a smithy, a cobbler's shop, and a small but clean hostelry as well.

It seemed the only promising place in which to spend the night, and Darcy, who had taken the precaution of dressing less formally than usual so as not to draw too much attention to himself, paid off the driver and went into the inn to ask for rooms for himself and Watson.

It was, in truth, a fine old inn, catering mainly for the locals and a few itinerant travellers. With no one around apart from the landlord and a couple of early drinkers, Darcy had the business done quickly, stored his things away upstairs and went out to enjoy the last of the sunshine.

Looking at Mrs Ellis's map, he could not tell in which direction he should proceed. Should he follow the road across the bridge or take the path by the river? He assumed this was the Rye, which sprang from among the rocky outcrops on the moors above Pickering and ran down into the valley. But he could not be sure.

Fortunately, Mr Carr's man Watson was in the yard already and had been talking to a couple of the local lads. From them he had gathered that the main road only led north to Pickering, whilst the path beside the river broke intermittently into a maze of footpaths, crossing the fields and moors and linking the stone cottages and farmhouses to the village.

As to finding the way to Mrs Ellis' cottage, there was nothing for it but to strike out across the paddock behind the inn and ask as one went along, if there was someone out there to ask. Darcy was grateful for the company that Watson, a cheerful man with a beard and a deep booming voice, provided. Alone, he would have been hopelessly lost.

They set off together, Watson carrying a thick, heavy stick and a lamp, in case they were overtaken by darkness. He kept urging Darcy to mind where he put his feet, for the path was very rough, having been trodden into humps and hollows by thousands of hooves and many feet.

They passed two boys leading a cow and its calf home from the fields and asked directions, then crossed the shallow stream at the ford and walked as briskly as the condition of the path would allow. They came to a stile, climbed over it, and ignoring the sleepy-looking sheep in the paddock, made for a distant pair of ancient elms standing on rising ground, lonely sentinels in an otherwise bare and unwelcoming landscape.

It was the landmark on Mrs Ellis' map they were looking out for and they were glad indeed when they loomed into view.

When they reached the spot, they could see a small cluster of cottages below them—the only sign of human habitation. Beyond lay the darkness of the moors.

Accustomed to the soft, friendly greens and gold of the woods around Camden Park and Pemberley, Darcy found the scene bleak and forbidding. Making their way towards the cottages in the dale, they noticed two women working in the garden of one of them. One, a young woman with a scarf that hid her hair, was busy tilling the soil in a vegetable patch, while the other, an older woman, worked with a hoe between the rows.

So intent were they upon their tasks, neither woman saw them come up the path, clearly unaware they had visitors, until Watson leaned over the gate and rang an old cowbell that hung beside it.

Both women turned together in some alarm, and since neither knew Watson, they looked puzzled and not entirely comfortable with the prospect of confronting a large, strange man at their gate.

However, when Darcy, who had been hidden from their view, stepped up to the gate, the younger woman put a hand to her mouth as if to stifle a cry, and her apprehension changed to joy, as she pushed back her scarf and cried, "Mr Gardiner!" as though he were the last person on earth she had expected to see.

Darcy was through the gate and into the garden in a trice, and as Watson and Mrs Ellis looked on a little awkwardly, they met and embraced, leaving no one in any doubt of their feelings and their utter relief at seeing one another again. Darcy was clearly the more relieved of the two, since he'd had no inkling of Kathryn's whereabouts for over a week. There had been the added anxiety caused by cryptic messages from Elena, about her sister being in grave danger. Kathryn was glad to see him, too, though she said afterwards that she had always known he would come. She had enclosed the map and Mrs Ellis' instructions hoping he would follow her meaning.

All these and other explanations were given as they went indoors and Mrs Ellis bustled around getting a pot of tea ready for her visitors. As they talked together, Watson slipped outside to smoke his pipe and Mrs Ellis went upstairs, ostensibly to change her work clothes, leaving Kathryn and Darcy alone.

Darcy was impatient to ask so many questions.

"Kathryn, why did you run away without a word to me?" he asked at the first opportunity, "I was at my wit's end with worry. I had no idea where you were," he complained, but she was to explain it all.

"I had to go, there was no time to waste; I had heard from Mrs Ellis that Hartley-Brown was to send Mr Bellamy on an errand to persuade me (and, if I refused, to compel me) to return to Lindfield. I had to leave Colley Dale before he arrived, else I'd never have got away. Mrs Ellis was the only person I could trust, which is why I came here to Ryedale. No one knows where I am but you."

"But, dearest, could you not have come to me? I could have arranged for you to stay with Lizzie at Rushmore Farm, as before."

"And expose all the business with Hartley-Brown to the scrutiny of your family? I do not think so, Darcy. They may never have understood. Believe me, this was the best way. Besides, I needed to get away and think of a way to defeat them. It is not enough to hide from them, we have to fight them."

"And how do we do that? These men are ruthless, Kathryn, and persistent as well, they will resort to anything," he said, and he did not sound very confident at all.

But Kathryn was adamant, though Darcy could not yet see upon what foundation her determination was based.

"Indeed, and they are greedy as well. That is exactly their weakness—let me explain, and you will understand, I think. Mrs Ellis has some very useful information which, if judiciously used, can put them back where they belong very quickly."

"In jail, I hope?" said Darcy quite viciously, and she laughed, a low merry laugh, for the first time in days, delighting him as he heard it.

"Not at first, perhaps, but yes, eventually when all the facts are known and they are brought to justice, Mrs Ellis is confident they will both be in deep trouble. You see, Darcy, not only is Hartley-Brown Lady Denny's lover, he is also purloining many valuable trinkets and silverware that lie around the rooms of Lindfield Towers and selling them through a well-known fence in London. And who do you suppose takes them to London and returns with the proceeds?"

"Not Bellamy?"

"The very same—he is his friend's bagman and partner in crime. Mrs Ellis has a long list of missing items, taken from the bedrooms and cabinets upstairs—snuff boxes, silver salvers, candlesticks, and hair brushes—all missing in the last year, during which time Hartley-Brown has been frequenting the house, often staying there for long periods when Lord Denny was from home."

"And Mrs Ellis is prepared to expose him?"

"She is, and that is how they can be foiled. We have to get a message to the chief constable and also send a letter enclosing Mrs Ellis' list to Lord Denny, who is currently in Scotland. Mrs Ellis, with our help, will do this. Lord Denny trusts her implicitly—she has served his family for almost thirty years. Indeed, he does not know that she has left Lindfield, nor the reason for her departure. When he learns the truth, he will not be best pleased."

Darcy agreed that this was certainly a good scheme and would, if it were successfully carried through, help put the pair in jail or have them transported to the colonies for a considerable period. But before he would proceed with it, there was something he insisted upon; Kathryn had to return to Derbyshire, with him.

He put his case with strength and conviction, "Dearest Kathryn, it is of no use for you to stay here, for the longer you stay away, the worse it will get. People will begin to ask where you are and why you have gone away, and very soon the entire county will be gossiping about you. I urge you instead to return with me," he pleaded. "If Mrs Ellis will be so good as to accompany you, it will be perfectly proper for you to travel with us, when we return tomorrow," he argued.

Seeing some doubt in her eyes, he went on, "We could go directly to Colley Dale and put your parents' minds at rest.

"I know your mother is exceedingly anxious, no doubt your father is too, and Elena was in tears when I saw her last. You owe it to them to let them see you are safe and well."

This argument seemed to convince Kathryn, and Darcy continued, more certain now of her agreement.

"Once you are safely home, I shall proceed to Rushmore Farm and ask my brother-in-law to alert his contacts in the constabulary and have Bellamy apprehended. With him in custody and Mrs Ellis' evidence, they will probably get Hartley-Brown as well. They can both be brought to book and will trouble us no longer," he said, and though Kathryn still seemed doubtful, she had to agree that she had no better plan.

Mrs Ellis came downstairs to ask if the gentlemen would stay to supper.

Her son was not back from the market at Pickering, she said, and if they could wait, he could take them back to the inn by the main road on his cart. But Darcy and Watson declined, saying they had to be back at the inn before nightfall. However, they promised to return very early on the morrow, having persuaded Mrs Ellis to accompany them, and arranged that they would be ready to leave for Derbyshire.

Back at the inn, Darcy was weary. It had been an excessively long day.

But before retiring for the night, he revealed to Watson some of the information he had gained from Kathryn. Watson was quite hopeful that with the evidence of Mrs Ellis, both Bellamy and Hartley-Brown could be arrested, but warned that they were both "toffs" and likely to use every possible advantage at their disposal to evade punishment.

"They will deny everything and lay the blame upon one of their servants," he said, and sadly, Darcy knew this to be true.

Too often had he seen cases in which the rich and infamous got away with far more heinous crimes than the indigent or the petty thief, who was inevitably less likely to be believed.

"If Mrs Ellis is supported in her story by Lord Denny or one of his men, then justice might be done!" said Watson, and Darcy was inclined to agree.

"Unless, of course, they are caught red-handed!"

At which both men laughed, knowing that was not very likely.

Darcy slept well that night, despite the fact that his bed was hard and the blankets rougher than he was accustomed to. Tiredness and relief worked together to induce a deeper sleep than any pill or potion.

He was awakened shortly before dawn by the sounds of early preparations in the yard below. Watson had already gone downstairs and procured a tray with tea and breakfast for Darcy, which arrived as he was shaving.

He opened the windows to a morning that was fresh and air that was cool and bracing. A veil of mist clothed the ridges of the distant hills, and damp grayish lumps of it lay all over the moorland.

But the sky was clear and presaged a fine day to follow.

Darcy hastened to finish his meal and went downstairs to find Watson waiting for him, eager to get started on the business of the day. They set off at once for Mrs Ellis' cottage, where both women were ready and waiting. Kathryn was impeccably attired in a sober travelling gown, and Mrs Ellis looked a most respectable chaperone indeed.

This time they took a larger hired vehicle, which the landlord had procured for them, and made the journey in half the time. Taking the train to Sheffield, they travelled in comfort, since there were very few other passengers in their first-class compartment.

Kathryn took the opportunity afforded her by their proximity, as well as the discretion of Mr Watson and Mrs Ellis, who allowed them as much privacy as was possible, to reassure Darcy of her feelings and apologise for the haste with which she had left Derbyshire, while he, as lovers often do, resisted the temptation to reproach her in any way for what had occurred, choosing instead, to lay the blame upon the villains, of whose culpability he had no doubt and vowing that they would be brought to justice.

In so doing, they avoided any recriminations and swiftly restored the trust that had been such an important part of their association. Throughout their journey, though they conducted themselves with perfect decorum, their affection for one another and their relief to be together again were plain to both their companions, who, sympathising with their predicament, left them mostly alone

By the time they were at the end of their journey, there were no further issues of contention between them. Mrs Ellis, who had seen and heard the sadness and sighs of Miss O'Hare during the past week, saw with pleasure the return of her good spirits. Watson, on the other hand, was simply content that the mission on which Mr Carr had sent him had been successfully accomplished, with hardly any aggravation at all. He hoped his master would be well pleased.

Hiring a vehicle at the station, they directed the driver to Colley Dale. It was late evening and they had expected the house to be quiet, but to their amazement, they found it all lit up, with two members of the local constabulary in the hall, while Mrs O'Hare, attended by her maid, wept in the parlour. Seeing signs of confusion and alarm, Kathryn rushed indoors to her mother, believing it was all on her account. She was mistaken.

To her horror she discovered that the news was much worse than she had imagined. Elena, her young sister, was missing!

Hearing her exclamations of fear and dismay, Mrs Ellis and Darcy had followed her into the house and found Mrs O'Hare weeping, as she told how her younger daughter had set off as usual for the local library at Kympton, and when, after several hours, she had not returned, her father had insisted on sending for the police.

Meanwhile the servants had searched the surrounding area and sent a party as far as Kympton and back, but to no avail. No one had seen her.

Elena had disappeared without trace.

Darcy could think of no rational explanation.

The O'Hares, who lived soberly and quietly, were well respected in the area, and Elena was a popular young lady, whose love of reading and regular attendance at the local church and library was well known. How was it possible for her to have disappeared in an area with which she was so familiar? What could possibly have happened?

Darcy was completely mystified.

Though he was loathe to leave Kathryn, he decided that the only sensible thing he could do was to go to Rushmore with Watson and consult Mr Carr. Making his excuses to the O'Hares and assuring Kathryn he would do everything in his power to find her sister, he returned to the vehicle, and leaving the kindly Mrs Ellis to assist the family, they made with speed for Rushmore Farm.

There, a strange scene met their astonished eyes.

In the main yard, to the left of the house, stood a police wagon and several members of the local constabulary, who appeared to be guarding two men. One was a rough-looking young man in country clothes who had been handcuffed and was being guarded by a policeman with a vicious-looking dog on a lead. The other, standing at some distance from the first, was well attired in the best city style, yet he too was being restrained and guarded, though without the aid of a dog, by an officer carrying a heavy truncheon.

Neither Darcy nor Watson knew who the men were.

As they alighted and went indoors, they were greeted in the hall by Mr Carr, whose first question concerned Kathryn.

"Have you found Kathryn? Is she safe?" he asked.

Darcy greeted his friend warmly, assuring him that indeed they had found Miss O'Hare and brought her home with them.

"She is quite safe, but presently very anxious about her sister Elena, who has unaccountably disappeared! Michael, please tell me, what on earth is afoot here? Who are those men, and what is half the constabulary of Derbyshire doing in your yard?"

Mr Carr laughed and then hastened to explain.

"That at least I can explain—but before I do, let me go to Lizzie and tell her that Kathryn is safe at home in Colley Dale. Her sister Elena will be greatly relieved to hear it, too."

Darcy frowned, confusion now worse confounded.

"Did you say Elena? What is she doing here? We have just come from Colley Dale, where her poor mother is well nigh demented with fear, because Elena has not been back from Kympton and Mr O'Hare has called in the police. How is she here?"

"That," said Mr Carr, "is a long story, but I must tell Lizzie and Elena the good news first."

He ran briskly up the stairs and was gone but a few minutes, during which Darcy went out again to take another look at the two men. He had never seen them in his life before, but something like recognition moved in his mind as he looked at the man who now stood in the shadows, sullen and silent, beside his guard. There was something about him that led Darcy to believe that this was Mr Bellamy, who'd come from Lindfield to do his friend's bidding and take Kathryn back with him.

He went back indoors just as Mr Carr came downstairs.

"Michael, there is something I must know. Do those two men out there have anything to do with Elena's disappearance?"

"Indeed they do—or should I say they would have done, had not their plans gone badly awry. Darcy, do sit down and let me get you a drink while I explain; you are plainly exhausted from your journey."

Darcy admitted that he was and did as his brother-in-law suggested.

"Well?" he prompted, and his friend detailed a most extraordinary tale.

"Those two men are Bellamy, friend of Mr Hartley-Brown, and his accessory, Hodges, a petty thief from Bakewell, only recently returned from the penal colony of Van Dieman's Land. They attempted this afternoon to abduct Miss Elena O'Hare as she was arriving at Rushmore Farm."

"What? Abduct Elena?" Darcy was so shocked, he could not say another word until he had heard more of Mr Carr's explanation.

"Exactly," said Mr Carr, continuing his story. "The man Bellamy is a fool. He had obviously been sent here by Hartley-Brown to persuade Miss Kathryn O'Hare, by whatever means, to leave her home and return to Lindfield. However, it transpires that Bellamy, when he failed to find the elder sister, because she had already left for Yorkshire, decided on an impulse to take the younger one instead."

"Good God!" Darcy exclaimed, so astounded, he could scarce believe a word of what he was hearing, yet Mr Carr was quite serious.

"He had stalked Elena for two days, presumably hoping to catch her alone and unattended and then to abduct her. Perhaps he intended to take her to Lindfield and use her to blackmail Kathryn into following them there herself. Who knows what vile plans he may have had—the police are yet to question him; when they do, we shall know more."

"The villain!" Darcy exclaimed, then asked, "How was he foiled?"

"Well, as I promised you I would, I had Bellamy watched and followed every time he left the inn," Mr Carr explained, enjoying the telling of it.

"The landlord has been most helpful; each time he went walking or hired a gig or a pony cart, we had him in our sights.

"When Elena, unaware of the threat posed by Bellamy to herself and her sister, decided on her way home from Kympton to call on Lizzie and ask if there was any news of Kathryn, she quite unwittingly set a trap for him, making herself the bait."

As Darcy listened, speechless, Carr explained how Bellamy, having hired the man Hodges from Bakewell to drive a small closed vehicle, had followed Elena at some distance as she walked home from Kympton; then when she turned off the main road into the private lane leading to Rushmore Farm, he had closed in upon her, leapt out, and attempted to seize her and force her into the vehicle.

"Needless to say, she struggled and screamed in terror, alerting two of our workmen and bringing my man, who had been following Bellamy on horseback at a discreet distance, to her assistance at once. Bellamy alone was no match for all of them, and they soon had him overpowered and bound—an indignity he resented very much and complained of quite loudly, I have to say," said Carr laughing as he recalled Bellamy's indignant protests at his mistreatment.

"He tried to make out that Elena had stolen his watch, when he laid it on the counter in the library, where he had followed her that afternoon. A likely story indeed! Well, he was taken into a barn, restrained, and held there, until the police were fetched. I must say his partner in crime was far more forthcoming and willing to tell all. As you saw, they are now in police custody and will presently be taken to Matlock, to be produced before the magistrate and charged."

"And Elena? Is she well?" asked Darcy anxiously.

"Well enough, though she was very frightened—almost hysterical, the poor girl. She must have been startled out of her wits. But she has suffered no injuries; indeed, she inflicted some upon Bellamy, I believe, when she struggled with him—his face and hands are deeply scratched. She has been with Lizzie since and is much better for knowing that Kathryn is safe.

"Now, Darcy, you must go to her and reassure her that her sister is well and back at home. It has been her constant anxiety all week, she says."

"I can well believe it." said Darcy, "I have had not an hour's peace of mind since I learned she had gone. Thank God, and you, Michael, for your help, else I never would have found her. Watson was excellent. I am completely unfamiliar with Yorkshire, but I did not have to worry about anything at all. He is a treasure."

"He certainly is that and very discreet, too," Mr Carr agreed as Darcy went upstairs to Elena and Lizzie.

In the yard, the police officers were preparing to take their prisoners away to be held in confinement and produced before the magistrate. They would take statements from Miss O'Hare and Mrs Ellis on the morrow, they said.

A short while later, Darcy came downstairs with Elena, who, even though she had recovered from the shock of her ordeal, was still pale and shaking.

"May I use your carriage to take Elena home to her family? They will be relieved to see she is well," Darcy asked.

Mr Carr smiled, "They will indeed. I have already sent word that she is here with Lizzie, so they will know she is safe, but I have said nothing of her terrible experience. I thought it best to let Elena tell her sister first and decide together how much they will reveal to her parents. There was nothing to be gained by alarming them, now the man Bellamy is locked up. You can certainly use my carriage, and you may return to Pemberley in it afterwards. I must be in Matlock about mid morning to make my statement to the magistrate."

Darcy thanked his brother-in-law again for his discretion as well as his help in saving Elena from a dreadful fate. He shuddered at the very thought of what might have been. The man Bellamy must have taken leave of his senses to have attempted such a crass outrage!

Darcy did not wish to think further about the consequences that would flow from the strange events of this day. He was glad it was finally over and both Kathryn and her young sister were safely back at home.

When Elena was reunited with her sister and parents, there were tears of joy and relief and a great outpouring of gratitude for Darcy Gardiner and his brother-in-law Mr Carr. Mrs O'Hare, who had feared a fate worse than death for one or both of her daughters, was immensely gratified to have them both safe home with her again.

Darcy took his leave of Kathryn and returned to Pemberley more exhausted than he had been in a very long while, but too relieved and pleased to be overly conscious of it.

There would be time enough to marshall the forces of Law and Justice against the culprits and confront them with all of their misdeeds. This time, they *had* been caught red-handed; there would be no escape. There was much satisfaction to be gained from the thought. But, that could wait.

For tonight, Darcy was content that Kathryn was safe, free from persecution, and her tormenters were in custody.

That she had also assured him repeatedly that she loved him and promised to marry him as soon as ever he wished was an added source of pleasure—though of a far more deeply satisfying kind.

END OF PART FOUR

POSTSCRIPT FROM PEMBERLEY

Part Five

Chapter Fourteen

I N A WEEK THAT began with a summons and ended with a celebration, Michael Carr was, without any doubt at all, the man of the moment.

His practical advice to his brother-in-law, his shrewd plan to have Bellamy tracked and watched, and his prompt action in summoning the local constabulary to arrest the miscreants had all been proved right, leading to an exceedingly satisfactory conclusion. He was, that morning, appearing before the magistrate as a witness.

While her husband was busy giving evidence against Bellamy and Hodges, Lizzie Carr was brought to bed with her first child. Over several hours, during which she asked many times if her husband was back from Matlock, she was delivered of a very healthy son.

Before the news was given to Mr Carr, he'd had the satisfaction of seeing the conclusion of their efforts to apprehend and punish the culprits. Hodges, the stupid bumpkin, had escaped with a lighter sentence, having admitted his guilt and turned against his co-conspirator, who he claimed had deceived him, never revealing he was to be involved in a criminal abduction of a young lady. Bellamy, on the other hand, was treated to a severe dressing down by the magistrate, who took an exceedingly dim view of his conduct and sentenced him to a long spell in jail.

The magistrate expressed his particular disappointment that transportation to Botany Bay or Port Arthur was no longer available to him, the practice of sending felons to the antipodes having but recently ceased.

"I should very much have preferred to have sentenced you to be removed altogether from this country and sent to Van Dieman's Land for your most heinous crimes; there you would have learned the error of your ways more swiftly, I think," he said, regarding Bellamy with a look of extreme censure, and warning him never to re-offend or he may face the ultimate penalty.

"Men have been hanged for less. I must warn you, that if you ever re-offend and appear before me, there will be no mercy."

For Mr Carr there was a special commendation from the bench, for his sound common sense and dedication to the cause of law and order.

Well pleased with the results of his work, Michael Carr emerged to find Darcy Gardiner waiting for him with the good news, ready to drive him to Rushmore Farm to celebrate the birth of his son.

He was so pleased as to be rendered speechless, wanting only to get home to his dear wife, from whom he had been separated on this, most important of days. That she had borne him a son brought him to the very zenith of his happiness, marred only by his being away from her at the time.

Still, by the time they were halfway home, he cheered up considerably.

"I must say, Darcy, that we did well today, with both villains going down. 'Twas a great pity we did not get Hartley-Brown though," he said.

"I understand from Watson that the police can find no trace of him—they think he has probably gone into hiding, hoping to flee to Europe or America, where he can disappear into the population more easily. They have been watching the ships at all the ports in the south, but I am not hopeful—he is the kind of villain who will use every trick in the book to escape the consequences of his actions. Though quick to use the law against others, these men are no respecters of the law themselves."

Darcy agreed, but added with great satisfaction, "At least the scoundrel Bellamy will not escape with him."

Arriving at Rushmore Farm, all thoughts of villains and their machinations vanished, as Mr Carr raced upstairs to hold his wife and son in his arms. Darcy, following his brother-in-law more sedately, could not fail to be touched by the very real devotion of the couple. It was almost impossible to believe the pert young miss who had been his little sister had been transformed as she was into a warm and loving young mother.

❧

Many months were to pass before they discovered that Hartley-Brown had indeed fled to America to escape the wrath of Lord Denny, who on receiving Mrs Ellis' letter had returned forthwith to Lindfield, ready and able to despatch Mr Hartley-Brown not just to prison but to meet his maker!

As for Lady Denny, reports reaching Mrs Ellis suggested that her Ladyship was presently sunk in a state of deep depression since the sudden departure of her "cousin" and the return of her husband. Doubtless, her continued indisposition would keep her confined to her bedchamber, but without the congenial company she used to prefer therein.

With his sister Lizzie and her husband now devoting most of their time to cherishing each other and their son, Darcy decided it was time to announce to his family his engagement to Miss Kathryn O'Hare. Jessica's wedding day had been fixed, and with Mr and Mrs Darcy in an especially good mood, it would be, he thought, an appropriate time to break the news.

His first visit, accompanied by Kathryn, was to his mother at Camden House. With Cassandra already aware of his intentions and happy to welcome Kathryn into their family, it seemed that nothing her elder son Edward had said had influenced her judgment of the young woman whom Darcy had chosen to be his wife.

She greeted her warmly, and when Sir Richard arrived to join them, he likewise made his pleasure at the news plain. They both saw Kathryn as a woman of good sense and education, well able to match their son's intelligence and aspirations in life. No adverse reports of any kind had reached them, and if they had, it is unlikely they would have been given much credence.

When, after an hour or more of pleasant conversation, the pair left to return to Colley Dale, the Gardiners spoke frankly of Miss O'Hare.

"Kathryn is a most personable and intelligent young woman, yet there is a pleasing degree of modesty about her manner," said Cassy. "Mama has made comment upon it too, which must bode well for her acceptance at Pemberley."

Richard agreed, "Certainly, but I do believe, my dear, that if Darcy and Miss O'Hare wish to marry at Easter, as has been proposed, they ought be seeking to settle in their own place, independently of Pemberley. I know Darcy has been happy there, but I doubt that it would be sensible or fair to impose such a situation upon a newly wed wife. Pemberley can be quite daunting to a young woman who has lived most of her life in fairly simple circumstances. Do you not agree?" he asked.

Cassy, upon contemplating the question for some moments, was inclined to see her husband's point of view. "You are quite right, Richard. There may well be some awkwardness with the staff, too; they are unused to the presence of two married women in the household; even though Kathryn would not seek to establish a position for herself, it may not be quite comfortable for her."

"Exactly," said her husband, "it is the type of situation that can lead to embarrassment for a newly wed pair, which is why some alternative arrangement must be found. They are both of an age when they may be expected to set up and run their own establishment."

Remembering the discomposure her late sister-in-law Josie had suffered, Cassy understood precisely her husband's concerns; yet, she could not immediately see how the matter might be resolved. Neither Darcy's present income, nor the short time available between now and Easter, would allow him to locate and lease a suitable property in the area. Most would be either out of his reach or too large for their requirements.

"How is it to be done? There is so little time, and besides, if Darcy is to continue to manage the estate at Pemberley, surely it would not do for him to live at too great a distance from it?" she asked.

"I agree," said her husband, "but there is no reason why he should. Not if they take our house at Matlock. The current lease has expired, and Thomas has been approached already by one or two people wishing to inspect the place with a view to taking out a lease for the New Year, but I have held them at bay, in the hope that Darcy may wish to consider it. It is vacant now and it could be made ready by Easter with very little expense."

Cassy was surprised at the forethought that had gone into his suggestion.

"Do you mean to let them have it rent-free?"

Richard shook his head. "Not entirely, but it would be a considerably smaller sum than they would pay elsewhere. I think it would suit them well; besides, we were very happy there, and it would be appropriate to let one of the children enjoy it, do you not think, my dear?"

Cassy remembered well their days in the house, which had been their wedding gift from Mr and Mrs Gardiner, and in which all of their five children had been born and raised. They were good, wholesome memories filled with fun, love, and much hard work. It had been a singularly happy home, and she had been loathe to leave it, even for the gracious, more spacious Camden House, purchased for them by her father, Mr Darcy.

She rose and went to her husband. "I do, and what's more, I think you are the most thoughtful, generous man in the world," she said, declaring her complete agreement with him in a manner that pleased him very well.

Meanwhile, Julian Darcy, visiting the library at Pemberley, had been persuaded by his mother to take tea with her in her private sitting room.

It had been many years since they had had anything approaching a private *tête-à-tête*, and Julian was understandably nervous. He knew that his mother could be brutally honest in her comments on one's conduct, and he wondered what she had in mind. It turned out that he had no cause for apprehension, although he still had something to learn.

Jessica had told him of her intention to suggest to Mr Darcy that Kathryn O'Hare be entrusted with the responsibility of running the parish school when Julian and she left for Africa.

"I have already mentioned it to Kathryn, but she has not given me a definite answer; no doubt she wishes to consult her family. Once I have Mr Darcy's consent, I shall ask her again. I am very confident of her agreement," Jessica had said, adding with an arch look, "She is an excellent teacher and in view of her association with our cousin Darcy; it would be the perfect thing, would it not?"

Julian, though willing to believe that Miss O'Hare was capable and qualified to carry out the task, was not entirely sure of his parents' response.

Joining his mother for tea, it was the matter he took up first, hoping it would lead to some general discussion.

"Jessica believes Miss Kathryn O'Hare will be able and willing to take over her duties at the school when we leave for France," he said, and Elizabeth answered without so much as a raised eyebrow, "Well, Jessica is probably right, I understand Kathryn is an excellent and popular teacher. But, Julian, they will miss Jessica very much, as will we all, when you take her with you to France and Africa."

At this, Julian looked across at his mother and saw the slightest suggestion of tears in her eyes, which astonished him. He had not anticipated this response.

"Mama, surely you do not disapprove?" he began, unable to comprehend her objection, if there was one, but Elizabeth interrupted him, "Disapprove? Of course not; why would I disapprove? Jessica is ready to marry you and go with you to Africa because she loves you and, even more importantly, because she has a genuine interest in your work. That is a great blessing, Julian, and I thoroughly approve, but nevertheless, I shall miss her. She has been like a daughter to us, and Pemberley has become her home. She loves it as we do."

Then moving over to sit beside him, she said, in a voice that was both grave and appealing, "You must promise me, Julian, that you will take good care of Jessica. Do not leave her too long on her own. She is an intelligent girl, with plenty of sound common sense, and she will want to share your enthusiasms and learn about your work. So you must not go chasing after some tropical bug and forget that your wife needs your attention, too. Remember, some women do like to learn about these things; not all of us are averse to talking of matters that may seem like the province of men alone."

Julian was aware of a deepening tone in her voice. "I know that Josie never did care about your research; she was bored and that made things difficult between you..."

He tried to intervene. "Mama, please, I cannot let you blame Josie. I have long admitted to myself, the mistakes and shortcomings which destroyed our marriage were mostly mine; Josie was not responsible..."

"I do not mean to blame her, Julian, but what I have said is not only true, it is materially relevant to your chances of happiness with Jessica.

"I am happy indeed to hear that you accept some responsibility for the problems that beset your marriage to Josie, and I do not intend to plague you with a reiteration of them. I am sure you were aware of my views at the time. But it is also important that you understand that Jessica Courtney, who has been raised within a family to whom service to others is second nature and selfishness is unknown, is quite a different young woman to Josie Tate. I do not mean to suggest that one is superior to the other, simply that they are completely different and must therefore be treated differently.

"Marriage to Jessica may be more tranquil than marriage to Josie, but it will require you to share your life, your work, and your ideas and aspirations with her, as well as your bed and your table."

Elizabeth's voice was serious as she continued, "Unlike Josie, Jessica comes to you without any great ambition for fame or reputation for herself, but I know her well enough to say that she will love you and support you in everything you undertake." As Julian listened, she went on, "Jessica has loved you faithfully for many years, well before you became aware of your own feelings for her; now that her life is linked with yours, she will ask no more and no less than to share it equally. Her happiness, indeed your mutual happiness, will be enhanced, the more closely your lives are woven together."

Elizabeth took her son's hand and said quietly, "I do not mean to lecture you, Julian my dear, I want only to protect you from the kind of heartbreak that you endured before. I know I said little then, but I suffered with you, more than you know. This time, I pray that you and Jessica, whom I dearly love, may enjoy the same happiness your father and I, and your sister and Richard, have found together."

Julian listened, astonished at how much his mother had known of his own pain and of Jessica's feelings for him. He had never believed that either she or his father, had understood how deeply he had been hurt by the disintegration of his marriage to Josie Tate.

They talked frankly thereafter, Julian admitting he had failed in his marriage to Josie, because he had never succeeded in making her love him as he had loved her and did not know how to show her he cared for her.

"I was too young, too self-conscious, unaccustomed to speaking openly of my feelings. I thought it was enough to encourage and praise her work and hope it would all come right. It did not, of course.

"With Jessica it is different. She knows instinctively how to love deeply and to let me love her. She has brought me new hope; I know in my heart that we will be very happy together."

Elizabeth, remembering her own experience, recognised that here indeed were the beginnings of a deeper, more satisfying love and the prospect of a genuinely happy union. Her once shy, tongue-tied, awkward son had, at last, found words to express his deepest feelings. She was content, glad she had spoken and more at ease with him now; confident he would recognise and, even more importantly, nurture the happiness that Jessica could bring him in marriage.

He told her then that they wanted only a very quiet family wedding with no grand celebrations, and she agreed.

As Julian rose to leave, Elizabeth rose too, and they embraced, she assuring him of her love and prayers, he pledging his devotion and gratitude.

"Have no fears, Julian; I know this will be a good, strong marriage," she said, and this time there were no tears.

It was the closest they had been since he was a very little boy, and both mother and son were deeply moved by the encounter.

~✱~

Earlier, on that same day, Elizabeth had spent time with Jessica, who had, amidst a few tears and some laughter, confessed that she *was* a little apprehensive about going to Africa with Julian, but quite undaunted by the prospect of marrying him.

"Dear cousin Lizzie, if you only knew how long and with what little hope I have loved him, you will understand why it seems the most wonderful thing in the world to me," she had said, in answer to Elizabeth's enquiry if she was not a little concerned after Josie's unhappy experience with Julian.

"You do know his dedication to his research is certain to continue? Are you not apprehensive?"

Jessica's answer had been unequivocal. "How can I be apprehensive of something I have longed for, over many years?"

Elizabeth had held her hands in hers and asked again, "Are you not daunted, Jessie, even a little, by all that has gone before? You must know he blames himself for much of it."

"No indeed, I am not daunted. I do not mean to say that they were not matters of concern to me. They could be quite serious and worrying to those who neither knew nor understood the two persons involved. I did not know Josie well, but I did learn from Mama that she had often been lonely and unhappy, thwarted in her ambition to write and be published. It must have been difficult for her to abandon all her hopes for marriage. I have no such unfulfilled ambitions, no deep frustrations to complain of; I have been richly blessed in my family and friends, whose love and affection have sustained me. I have enjoyed my work at Pemberley, and all my dreams were of Julian. My only sorrow, that he did not even notice my existence."

Elizabeth laughed. "My poor Jessie, and now, he loves you dearly," she said.

"He does indeed, and it has transformed my life! I never knew, until he told me he loved me, that one could be completely absorbed in one's feelings for another human being and need little else for happiness. I had thought that it was good to love someone, even if they did not love you. But to be loved in return..." She could go no further, her voice failed, and she hid her face, her cheeks burning.

Jessica, overcome with emotion, had not the words to express her feelings.

Elizabeth, whose memories of love remained bright, had put her arms around her young cousin, sharing a moment of honest emotion that both women felt intensely.

Elizabeth spoke softly. "Julian loves you; I know he does, and yet, he needs your help, because he is often shy and sometimes fearful of deep feelings. Even as a child, he was diffident and could not always respond to affection, unlike my dear William..." This time it was Elizabeth who could not proceed.

Jessica looked up at her face.

She had never known William Darcy; he had been killed in an accident many years before she was born, but Jessica had learned from her mother Emily how deep the wounds were that Elizabeth and Mr Darcy bore as a result of his untimely death. Only to those she loved very dearly would Elizabeth speak of him, while Mr Darcy could scarcely bear to mention the boy at all, so utterly devastating had been their loss.

Tightening her arms around her, Jessica held her close and thanked her.

There was no more to be said.

Mr Darcy, returning with his grandson, found his wife in a pensive mood.

She told him Julian had left to meet with Jessica and the rector at the church, where they were to discuss plans for their wedding.

Mr Darcy poured himself a drink while young Anthony played at being a highwayman, holding up the footman on the stairs and demanding he surrender the silver.

"Have they fixed upon a date yet?" Mr Darcy asked.

"I think they have, because Julian must be in Paris next month to complete preparations for their departure to Africa," said Elizabeth, and as he nodded, understanding her drift, she added, "I believe they are quite determined it will be a quiet wedding. They insist they will ask only family and their closest friends, and want no celebratory banquets and fireworks."

Mr Darcy put down his glass and declared that it seemed a very sensible decision.

"I am very glad to hear it, Lizzie; it shows both personal modesty and good sense. I cannot see the point of extravagant wedding parties in these straightened times, not unless one is determined to demonstrate that not only has one more money than one's neighbours, one is also more inclined to fritter it away!"

Elizabeth, who could recall the lavish celebrations of Georgiana Darcy's wedding and their own daughter Cassandra's marriage to Richard Gardiner, wondered at the way Mr Darcy's perception of such matters had altered over the years. Time was when Pemberley set the standard of magnificence on such occasions; it would have been considered a betrayal of the family tradition and its standing in the community to have done less. Clearly, her husband no longer saw it in the same light.

He no longer regarded Pemberley as a symbol of his family's status in the county, and though devoted as ever to the maintenance and preservation of the great estate, it had become more a matter of his responsibility to the entire community, than of pride in himself and his inheritance. It was a change that had come about gradually, over the many years of their marriage and the influence of his partnership with Mr Gardiner.

Almost imperceptibly, the Master of Pemberley had become the custodian of a great heritage, whose worth he counted not only in the value of its splendid properties and commercial assets, but in the prosperity and contentment of its people. It was a change of which Elizabeth thoroughly approved; one her father Mr Bennet would have applauded.

Though he personally deplored ostentation, Mr Darcy had always accepted the place of "pomp and circumstance" in a family such as his own.

In the past, there had always been an appropriate place for it.

However, with Julian having relinquished his inheritance in favour of his son Anthony, much of the management of the estate had fallen at first upon their daughter Cassy, who was Anthony's legal guardian, and passed to her son, Darcy Gardiner, since his appointment as manager of the estate. Both were dedicated and hardworking; neither had any taste for ceremony or display.

Despite his other interests, in fields far removed from Pemberley, Darcy Gardiner's commitment to Pemberley was no less than his grandfathers and many had been surprised at his success in the role. The people of the estate, tenants and labourers alike, acknowledged that they had rarely known such a conscientious manager. Their well-being and prosperity had increased with his application of new ideas and techniques that had vastly improved the productive value of the estate.

Julian, on the other hand, had shown no interest in the place, except as his childhood home. Now he was going away to Africa, taking Jessica with him; it was obvious he felt no strong attachment to Pemberley.

To his mother, it was almost a relief, removing the incipient tension that was inevitable had Julian remained at Pemberley while taking no part in its management.

As she remarked to her sister Mrs Bingley, who with her husband had come over to dine with them, "Mr Darcy seems completely comfortable with the prospect that it will be Darcy Gardiner who will manage Pemberley and make most of the decisions about its future, until Anthony is required to take up his inheritance and is of an age and competence to do so."

"And God willing, Lizzie, that will be many years away," said Jane, noting that her brother-in-law was a good deal fitter than her own husband Mr Bingley, who was some four years his junior.

"Indeed," said Elizabeth, "and it is an indication of the trust and confidence he places in young Darcy, that my dear husband has no reservations about it at all."

So saying, Elizabeth took her sister's arm, and the two went out to the terrace in time to see Mr Darcy and his grandson, the very young man they had been speaking of, walking together towards the house.

As they entered the saloon, it was plain from his countenance that Darcy Gardiner had brought good news. Indeed, he had come to ask Mr and Mrs Darcy to join the family at Camden Park on Saturday, when his parents were giving a dinner party to celebrate the engagement of their son to Miss Kathryn O'Hare.

Finding the Bingleys there, the invitation was immediately extended to them, and it was a case of congratulations and felicitations, as Darcy was complimented upon his engagement to the handsome and accomplished Miss O'Hare.

Both Jane and Elizabeth were determined to tease him for having kept it such a close secret so successfully for so long!

"Why, Darcy, you did not need to be so secretive about it," said Jane, but his good nature soon foiled their efforts, as he confessed that he had waited until Julian and Jessica had named the day for their wedding, and for this piece of considerate behaviour, he was further commended.

"It is fortunate that you have such a plausible reason Darcy," said his grandfather, "else you would have had a difficult time convincing the ladies that there was not some great conspiracy afoot."

At this Darcy coloured and tried to conceal his confusion with laughter. "Indeed, sir, I can see that," he said as Mr Bingley joined in with a joke about a Mr O'Hare, who was an Irishman, banished to Australia and there became a "bush ranger."

"Which, I am told, is, in common parlance, none other than a highwayman!" he explained to the great delight of the ladies. "Will Camden's son, George, recently arrived on board a ship from Australia, tells the story very well. Apparently, O'Hare is a great big fellow, with a red beard and red hair, and very popular with the ladies, to whom he is unfailingly courteous and charming, even as he robs them of their jewels! All very droll indeed," said Mr Bingley.

Elizabeth found her brother-in-law's colourful tale most diverting. "Are you quite certain, Darcy, that your Miss Kathryn is not connected to this famous highwayman?" she asked, and Darcy had no difficulty at all in assuring them of the truth.

"As certain as I am that the sun will rise tomorrow, ma'am, Miss O'Hare has no relatives who were transported to Australia. Of that I am absolutely positive."

By this time everyone was at pains to assure Darcy that they were only teasing him and no one would ever believe his lovely Kathryn was associated with any such villains, whether in Australia or anywhere else.

The invitations being happily accepted, Darcy politely declined another glass of wine and made ready to depart. Despite his affection for all those in the party and his general good humour, it was one occasion upon which Darcy Gardiner was relieved to be leaving Pemberley.

All that talk of criminals and conspiracies had been a little too close for comfort. He was glad indeed to get away.

Chapter Fifteen

THE BINGLEYS, AS WAS their wont, stayed over at Pemberley after dinner. It was too late to make the twenty-mile drive to Ashford Park; besides, there was still so much the sisters wished to talk about, it was generally accepted that they would stay.

With Mr Bingley asleep quietly in his favourite armchair by the fire and Mr Darcy having settled down to read while finishing the last of the port, Jane and Elizabeth went upstairs to Lizzie's private sitting room, where they were ensconced for an hour or more.

Elizabeth always looked forward to these talks, but on this occasion, Jane had some very particular matters to discuss, which were unlikely to bring her sister much pleasure. She had a letter, which she had received a day or two ago, and as they sat sipping their tea, she produced it apologetically for Elizabeth to read.

"I am sorry, Lizzie, but I have waited all evening to show you this letter. I did not wish to upset my dear brother-in-law with its contents..." she said, and Elizabeth could see at once that Jane, always unwilling to hurt anybody's feelings, was very anxious indeed.

The offending letter was from their sister Lydia, now a widow, living with her unmarried daughter, Fanny, in a cottage on the outskirts of Meryton, not far from Longbourn, their childhood home. Always short of money, yet unfailingly extravagant, Lydia often wrote to her sisters to ask for help to pay her bills, and Elizabeth supposed this to be just another such letter. However, on reading it, she frowned as the meaning sank in, and she looked at Jane in some alarm.

"She wishes to attend Julian's wedding?" she said, as if unable to believe her eyes.

Jane nodded, apprehensive and uncomfortable. "She does, and, Lizzie, do read on, she wishes to bring her daughter Fanny with her to stay with us at Ashford Park! What ever shall I say?"

Elizabeth's eyes expressed her horror at the prospect.

Lydia Wickham was not only unwelcome, she would wreak havoc upon Julian and Jessica's hopes of a quiet wedding, for no occasion that Lydia attended could ever be described as "quiet"—of that both sisters were certain.

Lydia's capacity, nay her active desire to make a spectacle of herself, to speak in a penetrating voice as her mother used to do, expressing her opinions, however uninformed, on a myriad of subjects and persons, to laugh loud and long at anything and everything, and above all, to appear dressed in execrable taste, would ensure that she was the centre of attention, the cynosure of all eyes, causing pain and embarrassment to all of her family, a consequence of which Lydia would be blissfully unaware.

Elizabeth knew she would cringe with shame, and Mr Darcy, while he had mellowed and overcome his earlier habit of leaving a room whenever one or other of the Wickhams entered it, would not enjoy the prospect of seeing Lydia at the wedding.

As for Julian and Jessica, their wedding day would be ruined by Lydia's presence, and for Elizabeth that was the material point.

"Jane, you must write at once and discourage her—I cannot imagine why she wishes to invite herself. I do not believe either Julian or Jessica would wish to ask her. Neither of them knows her except by hearsay."

Jane looked thoroughly disconcerted. "But, Lizzie, how shall I prevent her if she insists upon coming and means to attend the wedding? What can I say to dissuade her?"

Jane was at a loss to know how to act. Naturally obliging and gentle, she could not be rude, try as she might, and however well her errant sister deserved to be censured for her past conduct and her continuing stupidity, Jane would not find it easy to castigate her and refuse her hospitality at Ashford Park.

Through the years, both before and after the death of Lydia's husband, George Wickham, whose feud with Mr Darcy had precluded Elizabeth from ever receiving them at Pemberley, Jane and Mr Bingley had extended the occasional invitation to Lydia. At least once a year, she would arrive, with or without the rest of her family, announcing her intention to stay but a few days and frequently staying a fortnight or more, enjoying the salubrious surroundings, good food, and ample hospitality of the Bingleys. When she finally left, they would heave a sigh of relief and give thanks for the return of peace and serenity to their home.

This time, however, the matter was further complicated by Lydia's clear determination to attend her nephew's wedding.

She had written:

Dear Jane,

I have always had a soft spot for Julian and indeed once hoped he might favour my daughter Fanny. I always knew he would not be happy with Josie Tate—she was such a stuck-up little thing and no great beauty either. I suspect he was inveigled into it by Josie's mama, Becky Tate, who must have had visions of her daughter becoming the next mistress of Pemberley!

Poor Julian, I am delighted he is to marry again, even if it is to Jessica Courtney, who is a bit of a mouse herself; but if she is as good natured and capable as Emily, she will probably make him a good wife.

Dear Jane, I am very eager to see them wed and wish them happy. I have bought them a little wedding gift, of course, and... and I must get new clothes for the occasion. I am going into town again to see if I can pick up a nice hat; mine is too old and out of fashion to be seen at Pemberley. I shall not give Lizzie a chance to say I disgraced her by wearing some old thing...

...and so she went on and on.

Elizabeth sighed, irritated by it all.

"It's so like Lydia, is it not? Empty headed and trivial, so full of herself—oh Jane, what shall we do? There seems to be nothing that can keep Lydia away, short of a timely epidemic of chicken pox or floods in the southern counties!"

The sisters retired for the night, without having resolved their dilemma.

Unwilling to trouble her husband with their problem, Elizabeth waited until Mr Darcy had left for his early ride around the park before confiding in Jenny Grantham, her housekeeper, who had that morning brought in her tea tray, intending to consult her mistress on some domestic matter.

Mrs Grantham could understand and sympathise with her mistress' unease. Having been with Elizabeth since her arrival at Pemberley as a young bride, there was little Jenny Grantham did not know of the family's problems, and the conduct of Mrs Wickham was not easily forgotten.

Besides, Jenny loved Elizabeth dearly and was keen to help.

"If only we had some means by which she could be persuaded to stay away—oh Jenny, I would gladly pay a large sum of money to ensure that she did not turn up and ruin Julian and Jessica's wedding day!"

Mrs Grantham having listened a while, had an idea. "Could we not send one of the lads to fetch Mrs Wickham in a carriage, which might lose a wheel or lose its way somewhere between Ashford Park and Oakleigh, ma'am? If they did succeed in getting it repaired or finding their way back, it would probably be too late to get to the wedding, would it not, ma'am?" she asked, and Elizabeth, bereft of ideas herself, clutched at it as though it were the proverbial straw and she a drowning man!

"Jenny, that sounds like a really good idea," she said, "but how shall we convince Mrs Bingley? I cannot see my dear sister readily agreeing to such a naughty scheme, can you?"

Jenny Grantham seemed fairly sanguine. "That is true, ma'am, but leave it to me, I am sure we can think of a way. Let me talk to my nephew Dan first—he would be the best one to send over to Ashford Park with the carriage. Once I have explained matters to him, we can advise Mrs Bingley that a vehicle will be sent over to convey her guests to the wedding. She need be told no more than that."

As it happened, there was little need to convince Jane, since she had already begun to worry that there would be no room in their landau for Lydia and her daughter, since two of her own daughters, Sophie and Louisa, would be traveling with them too. She had told Elizabeth that the girls had begun to be concerned that their gowns might all be creased in the crush!

Elizabeth, seeing a sign of providential intervention here, asked her sister not to trouble herself, for she would send a vehicle from Pemberley for Lydia and her daughter.

"Then are you resigned to the fact that they will attend the wedding?" Jane asked, surprised at this change in her sister's attitude.

Elizabeth sighed dramatically, "Sadly it does look as though, if Lydia insists, she cannot be stopped. Mr Darcy can hardly call out the local constabulary to keep my sister away from Julian's wedding! Well, Jane, as our dear sister Mary would have said, what cannot be cured must be endured, and we must endure Lydia and Fanny as best we can. At least she will not inconvenience you and Mr Bingley—we will send the brougham to Ashford Park to convey her to the wedding, and your family can have the landau all to yourselves."

Jane smiled, glad to be rid of the problem of transporting Lydia to the wedding at last. It had weighed heavily upon her mind for days.

"Lizzie, I think our sister will enjoy that—she will feel quite honoured to be so grandly conveyed to the wedding in a carriage from Pemberley. It is very kind of you, I am sure," she said with that look of innocence that characterised Jane's nature, and Elizabeth had to struggle to suppress a mischievous smirk.

Afterwards, she discussed the detail of their plan with Mrs Grantham.

It was quite simple: her nephew Dan would take the brougham, which was unlikely to be required on the day, and proceed to Ashford Park on the previous evening. On the morrow, after breakfast, he would leave with Mrs Wickham and her daughter and, as instructed, would arrange to stall the vehicle somewhere between Ashford Park and the Gardiners' place.

"Dan is good with the horses, ma'am; he could very easily discover that one had lost a shoe or gone suddenly lame and needed attention," said Jenny reasonably, as she proceeded to explain that Dan would then set off to get help and delay his return until it was past midday. At which point, it was hoped, Mrs Wickham, realising it was too late to attend the wedding, would choose to return to Ashford Park. Indeed, Dan would suggest that he drive them there, where they could take some rest and refreshment and await the return of the Bingleys.

It sounded to Elizabeth like a capital scheme.

"Are you sure it will work?" she asked with almost girlish glee. "Dan will not get cold feet?"

"No indeed, ma'am," Mrs Grantham replied. "It is simple enough, and Dan is no fool—he knows he will be rewarded for his trouble."

"Does he know that I am aware of the plan?"

Jenny was appalled. "Certainly not, ma'am, he believes it is entirely my wicked idea, because I know how unhappy both you and the master will be if Mrs Wickham turns up at the wedding uninvited. He is not unaware of her previous conduct and her low standing in the family, ma'am. I have led him to believe she can be a difficult guest."

"We shall have to ensure he says nothing to anyone," Elizabeth warned. "If Mr Darcy were to learn of it, he would be very cross indeed, and as for Mrs Wickham—Lord help us all if she were to discover my part in this. I may tell my husband later, but that will be after the wedding and no great matter."

Mrs Grantham assured her mistress that Dan could be trusted with their secret.

⚜

Jane Bingley's relief had been short-lived.

Under normal circumstances, the arrival of one or two unexpected guests at Ashford Park would not have been cause for concern. The Bingleys were sufficiently well placed to accommodate such persons without additional strain upon their resources or their staff.

Besides, Mr Bingley was a genuinely hospitable man and welcomed visitors with great cordiality. Nothing was too good for those he entertained in his elegant home. However, when the uninvited persons were Lydia Wickham and her family, it was quite another matter.

Having, by various means, discovered the date of the impending marriage of Julian and Jessica, Lydia had been determined that she would attend. Claiming that as Julian's aunt and Jessica's cousin she had a dual interest in the proceedings, she was unlikely to be deterred by distance or the lack of a formal invitation.

In truth, Lydia cared less about the couple who were getting married and more about appearing at a family function, at which she hoped to advance her cause. A widow since the death of her husband George Wickham, from the consequences of an ill-spent and intemperate life, Lydia had made a practice of appealing to all her relatives and some of her friends for assistance. She had deemed that a wedding such as this one, at such an elegant venue as Pemberley, would afford her a rare opportunity to pursue her object of obtaining for herself and her daughter a regular allowance contributed to by all her sisters and their husbands. She considered them to be more affluent than herself and therefore duty-bound to assist her in maintaining her own somewhat perilous lifestyle.

Lydia's arrival at Ashford Park some days before the wedding was both unexpected and inopportune. Mr Bingley had been troubled by a persistent cough since the beginning of Winter, and Jane was concerned that she may need to send for the physician if he did not respond to the usual remedies. So concerned was she with his condition, she had quite forgotten about Lydia, expecting that she would write before leaving Meryton for Leicestershire. However, arriving without prior warning, Lydia had secured for herself and her daughter a ride in the hired vehicle of a gentleman she had met on the train, who happened to be travelling in the direction of Ashfordby and had kindly offered to take the ladies to Ashford Park, a few miles from his own destination.

Jane, returning from a visit to the apothecary, who had given her a potion to be used to relieve Mr Bingley's cough, was surprised to hear from her housekeeper that Mrs Wickham and Miss Fanny Wickham had arrived already and been lodged in the rooms prepared for them, where they were resting after their long journey.

Her surprise was even greater when the maid who had been sent to assist them revealed that she had unpacked two elaborate gowns, which were clearly to be worn to the wedding.

"They are ever so grand, ma'am," she said in awe—her mistress always dressed simply and in impeccable taste, and Nellie was not accustomed to seeing such elaborately beaded and embroidered ensembles.

"Oh dear, oh dear!" said Jane as she went upstairs. "Lizzie will hate it, I am sure, and Mr Darcy will look very grim indeed if Lydia appears at the wedding dressed like a duchess at a coronation. Jessica was so particular that they should have a simple family wedding... oh dear me!"

At dinner that night, Lydia could not say enough in praise of the man who had let them share his carriage.

"He was so well mannered and polite, he insisted that we should not get out at the gate and walk up your long drive, Jane. He had the driver bring the gig right up to the entrance and was most gallant in the way he helped us out. I wish I could recall his name—he did tell me on the train, but I am afraid it has gone right out of my head!" she said as she chattered on throughout the meal, leaving poor Jane feeling very tired indeed. How they would get through the week and the wedding with Lydia for company, she could not imagine.

But Jane's kindliness and general tolerance overcame her irritation, and she gave orders that everything be done to make her sister and niece comfortable, before retiring to her apartments on the other side of the house, where she set about attending on her husband, whose ill health had enabled him to make an early retreat.

She had only two prayers for the Almighty that night: that Mr Bingley should recover quickly, shaking off his cough, and Lydia should not make too much of a scene at the wedding. It was useless to pray that she would not make a scene at all—Jane knew not even heavenly intervention could achieve that.

On the morning of the wedding, Elizabeth, awaking to a fine Spring day, experienced a sense of almost childish excitement, the reason for which she succeeded in concealing from her husband, who put her general good spirits down to her pleasure in seeing their son Julian genuinely happy again. He was certainly right in assuming that it was the root of her happiness, but Elizabeth's determination to avert the disaster of Lydia's unwelcome attendance at the wedding had even overshadowed the preparations for the function, as she checked and re-checked the details of the plan with Mrs Grantham to ensure that nothing went awry.

Jenny Grantham assured her that everything was proceeding according to plan. Dan had been duly dispatched the previous evening and would probably be preparing the brougham to start the journey from Ashford Park about now, she said, and Elizabeth thought no more of it. She did not expect to see or hear anything more about it until they returned to Pemberley that evening, after the wedding.

By then, she supposed, Lydia would be safely back at Ashford Park.

She was glad that no one else knew anything of the plan she had hatched with Jenny Grantham. Certainly not Mr Darcy, who was busy entertaining two illustrious academic friends of Julian's, who had made the journey from Cambridge to support their former colleague and had stayed overnight at Pemberley. They had heard of its many treasures, and their host was pleased to show them around his library and gallery.

Julian, meanwhile, had repaired to his rooms to dress, and Jessica had gone home to her parents at Oakleigh, where preparations were well in train.

Her mother Emily Courtney, now the mistress of Oakleigh, to the great chagrin of her sister-in-law, Rose, had with her own staff and others lent by her sister Caroline done her daughter proud. Jessica and Julian had wanted a simple family wedding, and Emily aimed to provide exactly that. But, at Oakleigh, with much of her late mother's tasteful furnishings, chinaware, and napery to help her, she had produced an impressive function which happily combined simplicity with elegance.

The parties from Pemberley, Camden House, Matlock, and Ashford Park had all arrived well in time, and the village church was almost full.

As is customary on such occasions, no one was in any doubt that the bride was the loveliest young woman to walk up the aisle in years and the groom, whose usually serious countenance was transfigured with delight when he saw her enter the church, was universally acknowledged to be a most fortunate fellow. Around them, Elizabeth noted with satisfaction, was not a single contrary face in sight, nor one discordant voice to be heard.

Only Jane was concerned that Lydia and her daughter had not as yet arrived at the church.

"I cannot imagine what has happened to them, Lizzie," she said as they made their way to the house after the ceremony. "I saw their gowns made ready, and the brougham from Pemberley was waiting in the drive for them, although I did not see Lydia before we left for Oakleigh, I was sure they would not be far behind."

Elizabeth urged her not to worry. "Perhaps Lydia was late having breakfast—you know how much she enjoys her food—or maybe she could not fit into her gown!" she said lightly. Jane laughed, but then went on to say how very grateful they were that Elizabeth had sent the vehicle from Pemberley to transport the two ladies.

"Louisa and Sophie were especially pleased. With Lydia and Fanny both being quite stout, there would not have been room in the landau, and we would surely have been crushed, if they'd had to squeeze in, too. It was a very sensible idea of yours, Lizzie, to send the brougham," she said, and Elizabeth swiftly gave the credit where it was due.

"Do not thank me, Jane; it was Jenny Grantham's idea—she planned it all," she said to her sister's surprise, "and it has worked out rather well. I cannot imagine what I would have done without her help."

By the time the wedding party was over and the wedded couple had been driven away to their secret destination, it was late afternoon and the guests were beginning to disperse.

There was still no sign of Lydia and Fanny, a circumstance that affected Jane and Elizabeth in two completely divergent ways.

The former was worried that her sister, who had been so determined to attend the wedding, had not appeared at all, and this must mean something dreadful had happened to her; while the latter was confident that it meant everything had gone exactly to plan. Lydia, she decided, must by now be back at Ashford Park, in a state of high dudgeon at having missed the wedding, but probably partaking of afternoon tea!

While some younger family members were inclined to continue celebrating, others with less stamina left for home. The Darcys and the Bingleys returned to Pemberley together, while Sophie, Louisa, and their families proceeded to their respective homes. It had been, they all agreed, a perfectly simple family wedding, just as Julian and Jessica had wished.

Arriving at the entrance to Pemberley House, the party of Darcys and Bingleys were surprised to see a rather irritable-looking young woman in a somewhat crushed velvet gown, sitting outside. She got to her feet and glared at them as they alighted from their carriage.

No one knew who she was except Jane, who recognised her immediately.

"Why, Lizzie," she cried, "that's Fanny—Lydia's girl. Now what on earth could she be doing here, and what could have become of Lydia?"

"I cannot imagine," whispered Elizabeth, and then Jane said with a gasp, "Good Lord, look, there's Lydia!" and indeed, standing beneath the great Palladian entrance, like some grotesque figure in a comic opera, all dressed up in finery that had begun to look rather tired at the end of a long day, was none other than Lydia Wickham.

She looked and very soon sounded furious!

As Jane alighted from the carriage and went towards her, she screamed, as though in mortal agony, "Why, Jane, you horrid, horrid creature, why did you not tell me that *the wedding was not at Pemberley?!*"

There followed a moment of absolute silence, after which Mr Darcy turned to his wife and asked in a tone of voice that defied description, "Lizzie, have you any idea what this is all about? What is she doing here?"

Elizabeth answered truthfully, "No, I do not know what on earth Lydia is doing here."

Her husband's look of exasperation spoke volumes, but he said nothing.

Jane found her voice in time to say, "Good God, Lydia, I thought you must have known—everyone knew cousin Emily wanted Jessica to be married from their family home at Oakleigh. All the invitations said so. Oh Lydia, I am sorry. What happened? Did you lose your way?"

At that Lydia grunted and harrumphed and went back indoors, followed by her daughter, who had burst into tears.

Mr Darcy had turned away in disbelief, leading Bingley into the saloon, while Elizabeth, unable to contain her mirth, hurried upstairs, where Jenny Grantham followed her to explain.

It was a long story and one that had to be told with some caution, lest it be overheard. It transpired that Dan had carried out his instructions to the letter, bringing the brougham to a halt some ten miles out of Ashfordby, on a track which afforded them shade and privacy, but very little hope of assistance.

Having claimed that the horse had thrown a shoe and was in danger of going lame, he had set out ostensibly to get help, leaving the ladies sitting in the carriage. When he had returned an hour or more later, they were gone, having disappeared without a trace. After spending some time searching the woods, he had returned with the vehicle to Pemberley, only to discover that Mrs Wickham and her daughter had walked to the cross roads, waved down a vehicle, and begged a ride to Pemberley from a complete stranger, clearly believing the wedding was being held there. The gentleman had conveyed them to the gates of the estate and driven off in the direction of Lambton, claiming he was late for an important appointment.

On arriving at the house, Lydia had found the place deserted, it being then early afternoon. Making enquiries such as, "Where is everybody? Is the wedding breakfast over? Have the guests gone already?" she had discovered that the wedding *was* probably over, and in any event, it had been held some five miles away at Oakleigh Manor! With no other vehicle available to convey her thither, hot and hungry as a result of her recent exertions, Lydia had vented her anger upon anyone and everyone who appeared, abusing her sister Mrs Bingley in particular, for what she claimed was her deliberate deception.

"Mrs Wickham believes Mrs Bingley tried to prevent her getting to the wedding, ma'am," said Jenny Grantham, and Elizabeth was shocked.

"Jenny, that is so unfair; my sister would never do such a thing!" she protested, and Jenny agreed, "No, ma'am, we have told Mrs Wickham so, but she was quite convinced it was so."

Lydia's disappointment and fury had abated somewhat when the servants, taking pity upon her and Fanny, had provided them with food and tea, letting them rest in the sitting room until the family returned.

Though she had continued to fulminate, Jenny was certain Lydia had no inkling at all of the part played by Elizabeth and herself in the sequence of events, which had caused her to miss the wedding. She laid the blame squarely at the feet of her innocent sister Jane.

The obliging stranger who had conveyed them there turned out to be none other than Mr Jennings, the Gardiners' attorney, who, having left them at Pemberley, had proceeded to Oakleigh, where he had arrived at the church, only just in time to do his duty as a witness.

Never having met Mrs Wickham before, indeed scarcely knowing of her existence, Mr Jennings had not for one moment imagined that the highly bedecked and coiffured ladies he had picked up at the cross roads and conveyed to Pemberley could have had any connection with the simple ceremony at Oakleigh.

When, apologising for his late arrival at the church, he had related his story to Caroline and Emily, who'd had no idea that Lydia was even expected at the wedding, they were as bewildered as he was. It was very much later that they discovered the identity of the ladies concerned and shared their story with the rest of the family, many of whom continued to be puzzled as to how Mrs Wickham had been stranded at the cross roads and ended up at Pemberley!

The story was told and re-told around the families; embellished and enhanced, it remained for many years a matter for both conjecture and mirth.

In years to come, Elizabeth would reveal some of the truth about this diverting episode to selected members of her family—perhaps even to her dear Jane and Mr Darcy. No doubt, Jane would be appalled; having been so occupied with alleviating her husband's cough, she'd had little time to speak with Lydia before the wedding. She would probably blame herself for the omission and castigate her sister for being so mischievous, but in the end they would most likely agree that it had been done in a good cause.

After all, they would both agree, the intention had been to carry out the wishes of Julian and Jessica to have a simple family wedding, without the fear of disruption by Lydia, and in that endeavour they had succeeded without question.

Of Mr Darcy's reaction, Elizabeth was less certain. She knew he would have been relieved that Lydia had not turned up at the wedding, yet it was likely he may have frowned upon the subterfuge employed to achieve that end. She would have to tread cautiously there.

For the moment, however, on the clear understanding that no one but she and Jenny Grantham knew the whole truth, Elizabeth was able to enjoy the success of their scheme.

Everyone, including young Dan, who was amply rewarded for his services, had been satisfied with the outcome, except Lydia.

Most importantly, Julian and Jessica had had their tranquil family wedding, free of any unpleasantness and embarrassment, and that, thought Lizzie as she prepared for bed, was exactly as it should have been.

Chapter Sixteen

UNHAPPILY FOR JANE, HER problems with Lydia did not end with her non-attendance at the wedding.

After spending many hours grumbling and fuming about the debacle that had cost her a splendid opportunity for self-promotion, Lydia proceeded to exercise the skill she excelled at, retailing rumour and gossip. Neither family nor friends were left unscathed; no one was immune from the poison she purveyed with such relish.

Jane, who had to listen to her, was often aghast at the tales she told. One or two in particular caused her great concern.

On the day following Julian and Jessica's wedding, Lydia, having risen too late for breakfast, was consuming a plate of food specially prepared for her in the middle of the morning. She still ate as heartily as she had done when she was a young girl at Longbourn, noted Jane, whose abstemious diet had shocked her younger sister.

"Jane, I do not know how you stay alive with so little food!" she had exclaimed at dinner, while reaching for a second helping of roast gammon.

This morning, however, it was not food upon which she concentrated her attention. Making an oblique reference to Caroline Fitzwilliam's son David, she observed, "Ah well, I suppose there will soon be another wedding in the family. I understand David Fitzwilliam is likely to be tying the knot, too."

Jane, who did not know the extent of Lydia's knowledge about David's personal life, feigned ignorance. "I am not so sure you have been correctly informed; Lydia, we have heard nothing of an engagement..."

But her guest was not so easily diverted from her quarry.

"Have you not? Oh la, that is odd, seeing as you are so friendly with Caroline and the colonel. Come now, Jane, I am sure you would know more than you are willing to tell. You need not worry about keeping secrets—after all we are family and in any case, it's all over town. My boys George and Phillip have heard it all."

Jane was so surprised she dropped her guard and asked, "Why, Lydia, what have they heard? I know David spends a lot of his time in Manchester; he works for Mr Gardiner's company now. I suppose he must have some new friends there."

"Ah yes, of course he does," said Lydia archly. "And who else do you suppose is in Manchester?"

Hardly waiting for an answer, she proceeded to swallow a morsel of food and place some more in her mouth before saying, "I am surprised Lizzie hasn't told you, because she must know. I believe it's all been agreed between them and they were waiting only for Julian and Jessica to be married before announcing it. Mark my words, Jane, David Fitzwilliam will be engaged to Lucy Longhurst within the month."

She looked at her sister, expecting a response, and when Jane simply regarded her blankly, she went on, "Lucy Longhurst, do you not remember her? She was the orphan girl whose father disappeared and no one knew who he was. Well, she is now a school teacher and soon to be Mrs David Fitzwilliam—oh la! how people's fortunes change!"

At this, Jane's usual restraint deserted her, and she exclaimed, "Lydia, you have no right to say such a thing, particularly when you know it to be untrue; I shall not listen to such nonsense."

"You may please yourself, Jane," Lydia replied with a degree of insolence that shocked her sister and ill became her. "Does that mean you *do* know something of the matter? If you do, perhaps you would care to tell us who her father really was?"

Furious at having been ambushed into this conversation, Jane left the room, but returned moments later to admonish her sister.

"Lydia, you shall not speak of anyone in those terms in this house. Mr Bingley will be most unhappy. Besides, in the case of the lady in question, what you claim is not true at all. Lucy Longhurst was Miss Fenton's niece, her sister's daughter. She was raised and cared for by her aunt and her grandmother after the death of her mother when Lucy's brother was born. Their father, a respectable man in the community, was heartbroken at the death of his wife. He joined a merchant vessel that sailed to the Caribbean and was lost at sea when the ship was attacked by pirates in the Indies. I had it all from Miss Fenton herself, when she was governess to Cassy's children." Jane's outrage rose, giving her both eloquence and nerve.

"It is both unfair and cruel to spread such wicked lies about a young woman who has done you no harm. You shall not besmirch Lucy's name, and it is no matter whether or not she is engaged to David, she is a respectable young person, and I will not have it said that you spoke ill of her in my house."

Shaken by the vehemence of her usually gentle sister's words, Lydia was quiet for a while, finishing her food and rising from the table.

Then she asked, "And was Lucy Longhurst at the wedding?"

Jane's irritation showed. "I confess I did not see her, and that was because I was worried about you and Fanny… because you had not arrived. I thought something had happened on the way… some accident."

That almost re-ignited the complaint that had filled most of the previous evening, and Jane decided to escape from it all to her private apartments, where Lydia could not follow her.

Two days later, Jane was in the morning room, writing to her daughter Emma, who had recently returned from Italy with her husband James.

The Wilsons had consequently missed Julian and Jessica's wedding, and Jane was writing to tell her all about it, when Lydia entered the morning room, plainly idle, bored, and looking for someone to talk to. For a while Jane carried on writing, hoping she would leave, but it was a vain hope.

Peering over her sister's shoulder, Lydia asked, "Who are you writing to? Is it Charlotte Collins?"

Jane almost snapped, "It is not!" then added, "I am writing to Emma; why do you ask?"

"Oh, nothing," Lydia replied, picking an orange out of a bowl that stood on the table and beginning to peel it, "except I wondered if you had heard from Charlotte since she had a visit from our cousin Robert Gardiner and his wife Rose last month."

Jane was confused. "Robert and Rose were visiting Longbourn last month? I thought they were in France at Christmas."

"They were indeed, and a jolly old time they'd had, too—but they were in Hertfordshire at the New Year, looking at properties in the area, and they came to tea with Mrs Collins. I happened to be visiting Charlotte at the time and stayed on to chat with the Gardiners. Rose is looking remarkably well, and she had on a splendid chapeau—purchased in Paris, although poor old Robert looks older and more put upon each time I see him. She runs him ragged, I do believe."

Jane shook her head. "Oh, Lydia, you are hopeless; you must not say these things about people. So Mr and Mrs Robert Gardiner are looking to buy a property, you say?"

Lydia warmed to her subject. "They are. I am told they were exceedingly cross with Aunt Gardiner for leaving her house and estate at Oakleigh to cousin Emily. Rose was quite insistent that it had been as good as promised to Robert."

Jane looked askance, wondering if this was another of Lydia's rumours.

"I am sure that is not true, Lydia; besides, why should they want it? Robert and Rose were well provided for by our Uncle Gardiner in his will, while Emily, with Mr Courtney retiring from the living at Kympton, has no home to go to. Should anything happen to James Courtney, God forbid, Emily will be on her own with young Jude. Cannot Robert and Rose understand that his sister, who has given up so much of her life to serve the community, needs a home? Can Robert not persuade his wife to be generous, even when his money is not involved?" she asked.

Even Lydia, to whom concepts of service to the community were strangely unfamiliar, could not disagree. She shrugged her shoulders and said, "Well, I agree that Emily deserves a home of her own, and I wish her well, but, Jane, it is all very well for you to say it, 'cos you can afford to be generous. Rose says that Aunt Gardiner promised Robert the use of Oakleigh. She believes it was Richard and Caroline who changed their mother's mind, because they knew that if Mr Courtney dies and Cousin Emily has no home to go to, they will have to take her in and look after her to the end of her days."

Jane's look of contempt said it all. "That is nonsense, Lydia, and you know it. Emily will be cared for by her family, whatever her circumstances. She is the kindest, most warm-hearted person in the world, and no one would mind her having Oakleigh except Rose, who has always made it clear that she wanted Robert to have it. Indeed, she seemed impatient to be rid of Aunt Gardiner herself! But my aunt had decided that Emily should have the place a long time ago. I know, because Mr Bingley had it from Mr Darcy; Aunt Gardiner simply wanted to ensure that Emily would have a home."

Lydia was undeterred.

"But if Robert and Rose had the use of it, I think Rose would have invited Emily to stay at Oakleigh and help run the place."

Jane could not believe her ears.

"Did she tell you so herself?"

"No, but I think she would have. After all, Rose has never been mistress of such a large place, and she would have needed the help. Besides, she and Robert are away a lot, and I suppose Emily would have been a godsend. Rose as good as said so."

"What? To be a housekeeper for Robert and Rose in what was her mother's home? Oh Lydia, how could she even suggest it? Has Rose no sensibility at all?"

Lydia shrugged her shoulders again, sensibility was not her strong point.

"Well, what else could she do? With Reverend Courtney's heart disease worsening, she may have an invalid husband to look after and quite often, these people live forever—she may be stuck with him for years..."

"Lydia!" cried Jane. "I think that will quite do. Reverend Courtney is not dying, so we shall not speak of him as though he is. I cannot imagine how you get these cruel ideas!"

Lydia's callous talk had so shocked Jane, she picked up her writing things and retired to her room, where she completed her letter to her daughter.

Dearest Emma, forgive me if I sound despairing and miserable when I ought be cheerful and happy after the wedding, but I have had your aunt Lydia to cope with these past few days, and believe me, my dear child, it has been a dreadful imposition upon us all.

There is nothing that I can do to avoid her chatter and gossip, of which we are all so weary that your father now will not come downstairs for longer than half an hour at the very most before dinner. Mercifully Lydia is not an early riser, so we are spared her company at breakfast, but every other meal has become a sort of penance, though what manner of sin your dear father and I have committed to deserve such a harsh sentence, I do not know.

It is however a great joy to know that Julian and Jessica are happy, and your aunt Lizzie could not stop smiling all through the wedding, though I do believe there were some tears at the end before the couple left on their honeymoon.

They are gone to Wales and Cornwall, I believe, though this is a secret which no one is supposed to know. Jessie admitted to me that she was dying to see Tintagel Castle!

Now your aunt Lydia has turned her attention to young David, cousin Caroline's eldest son—that is, he is her eldest now, since dear Edward's death, of course—and she will not stop probing, trying to discover by one means or another if he is engaged to Lucy Longhurst. Do you remember Lucy? She was such a pretty little girl, sadly orphaned early in life and brought up by Miss Fenton, who used to be governess to Cassy's children. Well, I do believe she is just as pretty, is now a school teacher, and David Fitzwilliam is in love with her. I understand he has admitted as much to Darcy Gardiner.

I think it is wonderful, but Lydia does go on about her being an orphan and not knowing who her father was, so I have to pretend I know nothing of the matter.

If they are engaged, and perhaps they soon will be, then I hope James and you will be able to come to the wedding, which will probably be at Matlock or Pemberley.

But, despite Jane's hopes, David Fitzwilliam's wedding was neither in Matlock nor at Pemberley. Neither Lydia Wickham nor Emma Wilson was able to attend, the former because she was not invited and the latter because Mr Wilson was engaged in hearing a complex case of fraud in the county courts and could not undertake the long train journey from Kent to Manchester.

Being both rather shy and unaccustomed to the limelight, David and his bride to be had decided they would be married in the small church in the little parish in which they planned to live, and only those friends and relations who could brave the journey west were there to see them wed.

The Darcys, Fitzwilliams, and Bingleys attended, and Miss Fenton was there, of course, but perhaps most touching was the sight of Lucy Longhurst arriving at the church, escorted by her young brother, now a naval lieutenant. The boy, whose birth had caused the death of their mother and, consequently, the despair which led to the demise of their father, had returned to play his role at his sister's wedding.

It was, by all accounts, a most affecting moment and many tears had been shed.

The bridegroom's sister Isabella and her husband Mr Bentley were host and hostess for the day and did their family proud, wrote Jane to her daughter Emma.

I think, Emma, no one can doubt Isabella's happiness now. Caroline tells me that Mr Bentley has proved a most devoted and loving husband and takes great care of young Harry too. David cannot speak too highly of his brother-in-law, Caroline says.

Our cousin Robert Gardiner did attend, but he came alone, as Lizzie predicted he would. Rose and her parents were invited, but felt they could not cope with Lancashire weather at this time of year! A pity, because it was an unusually fine day!

Emma my dear, I suspect Lizzie and Mr Darcy have quite lost patience with Robert and Rose and her parents. Lizzie believes that Robert is increasingly dictated to by his wife and father-in-law, while his mother-in-law, Rosamund, who used to be an amiable young woman before her husband succeeded to his title, has acquired a host of airs and attitudes, and behaves more and more like a dowager duchess. I cannot believe she is the same pleasant person we used to meet at Pemberley every Christmas.

No doubt they felt the wedding at the little parish church in Manchester was not sufficiently grand to tempt them to brave Spring in Lancashire county!

For myself, I would not have missed it for the world. Lucy was lovely in her wedding gown, and David, though he is not as handsome or as tall as Darcy Gardiner, looked very much the proper gentleman. I have never been able to think of him without remembering how he loved to dress up and play at soldiers. I know Caroline is very glad that he has given up all

ideas of going into the cavalry and is making a very good fist of his job in
Uncle Gardiner's Commercial Trading Company.

I understand that David and Lucy are to travel to Sussex to spend a
few weeks at Lizzie's farm, and will call on you and James at Standish
Park. I am sure when you meet, you will agree that they make a fine
young couple.

Concluding her letter, Jane went in search of her husband, whose reluctance to encounter his sister-in-law had almost made him a recluse in his own
home over the past fortnight. She found him in the library, which was one of
the few places into which Lydia was unlikely to venture, and persuaded him to
accompany her into the garden.

Bingley had taken an interest in the gardens at Ashford Park, and his wife
knew it would do him good to get out into the warmth and fresh air.

She had good news for him, too—her maid had informed her that Lydia
and Fanny were planning their departure. Jane knew he would be glad to hear
it. "I think, my dear, they may require the carriage to take them and all their
luggage to meet the coach at Ashfordby," she said a little tentatively.

Bingley's countenance was transformed with the prospect that peace would
return to Ashford Park. He responded quickly, "Of course, they can have the
carriage, my love, it can carry them all the way to London if need be. Please, do
give orders that it be made ready forthwith," and dropping his voice he added
mischievously, "before they change their minds."

It was about as far as Mr Bingley, who was generally a polite and amiable
host, would go, but his wife understood his meaning exactly and went at once
to do as he had suggested.

Chapter Seventeen

THE HAPPINESS OF JULIAN and Jessica was enhanced by the prospect of their imminent departure for France and Africa. Her contentment complete in a marriage that had already exceeded her expectations, Jessica's wishes now centred upon their forthcoming journey. She looked forward to it with an almost spiritual fervour, savouring the knowledge that she would be helping her beloved husband accomplish a long-held ambition, while at the same time fulfilling her own desire for new horizons. Marriage had brought both intentions so close together in her mind, as to be inseparable.

For Julian, her excitement and interest in his work made for a blending of professional achievement and personal delight such as he had never experienced, nor believed possible. That with Jessica, he could give and receive the deepest love, without compromising anything he valued, was to him uniquely satisfying. Left feeling bruised and guilty by his previous attempt at marriage, he had been apprehensive at first, even disbelieving such an intimate communion was possible.

To find it so simply seemed, to him, close to miraculous.

Meanwhile, Darcy Gardiner and Kathryn had the pleasure of announcing their engagement considerably increased when Dr Gardiner handed his son the keys to their home. A modest but elegant Georgian house on a property of moderate size, beside the river Wye, situated halfway between the village of Bakewell and the dales of Matlock, it had been Darcy's parents' first home and the place that held all his most treasured childhood memories.

A wedding gift from Mr and Mrs Gardiner to Richard and Cassy, it had been an exceptionally happy place, occupying one of the prettiest sites on the river, where a pleasing combination of tumbling water, rocks, and green meadows created a delightfully soothing prospect. Kathryn fell in love with it at first sight, and both she and Darcy were deeply touched by the generosity of his parents.

Spring was always a busy time at Pemberley.

It was even more so this year with the introduction of new equipment and farming practices, as well as more efficient management methods on the property. There were rumours abroad of a rural recession, and Darcy, together with his grandfather and their chief steward Mr Grantham, had been involved in planning for the new year, hoping thus to avert disaster.

For Kathryn, too, it had been a hectic period, as she prepared to take over Jessica's work at the school. She had thought at the start it might be fun, but soon found it took up a lot of her time, as she worked assiduously to complete their plans for the New Year.

Indeed, they had not as yet decided upon a date for their wedding.

"I think we have had enough weddings for one season," Darcy had quipped in answer to a question from his grandmother. "Kathryn and I are both content to be engaged for a while, while we get on with our work. We are happy as we are and look forward to making our plans over the Summer. Perhaps, we may make up our minds on a date in the Autumn."

Elizabeth was a little surprised at his casual attitude and said so to her daughter, but Cassy, who had already spoken of the matter with her son, had no concerns.

"I believe, Mama, that Darcy and Kathryn are taking some time to consider their future," and seeing the astonishment upon her mother's face, she added quickly, "I do not mean to suggest that they are uncertain of their desire to have a future together—quite the contrary, I believe they are very deeply committed to one another—but before they marry, Darcy must decide where he will finally settle. He will not admit it, but I do believe he still misses the cut and thrust of political debate and sometimes speaks as though he might wish to enter Parliament one day. But, at the same time, he knows he has a role here, with us and with Pemberley, as Papa's manager and as Anthony's guide and mentor. It is a duty he takes very seriously."

Elizabeth shook her head; it had never occurred to her that her grandson might have such a conflict to resolve. She had assumed, when he accepted his position as manager of Pemberley, that like her husband he had made a decision for life. She had believed then he had done with politics, and privately, Elizabeth had been relieved.

"Do you think he is likely to leave us then?" she asked, and Cassy heard the note of concern in her voice. "Your father does depend upon him a great deal, and he is well liked by the men and the tenants. Cassy, has he spoken of this intention to you?"

"Not in so many words," said her daughter, "but I am aware from Lizzie and Mr Carr that he has mentioned the fact that after years of waiting for the Whigs and Reformists to win an election, he regrets missing the opportunity to contribute to the policies of the government. It is something he and Kathryn must resolve before they are married. Much will depend upon their decision."

Cassy knew a little more about her son's dilemma, but was unwilling at this early stage to trouble her mother with it. There was every possibility that it would all be resolved soon.

She gently steered the conversation towards more mundane matters. One of the maids had been taken ill and had to be removed to the hospital, she explained, as she poured out more tea. Elizabeth was concerned that the children had not been exposed to any infection and needed to be reassured that it was not a contagious condition. Cassy was quick to reassure her mother. "Richard is very particular; he is sure it is not a serious infection and she will soon be well again," she said, to Elizabeth's relief.

Elizabeth could have wished that she would be similarly reassured about young Darcy's future plans, but as it happened, any resolution of Darcy Gardiner's future political ambitions had to wait, when a far more pressing issue intervened and immediately claimed much of his attention.

His aunt, Emily Courtney, returning from a visit to the local church, had found her husband feeling very poorly. Doubled up in pain and unable to give any reason for it, he was so plainly distressed, she had had to call on a servant to help her carry him into an ante-room where he could rest, before sending urgently for her brother Dr Gardiner.

Richard attended upon Reverend Courtney as soon as he could and, having examined his brother-in-law, decided that he should be removed to the hospital forthwith, where he would be kept under close observation. He suspected a heart condition, but could not be sure. He wanted a second opinion. He was unwilling also to leave him overnight at Oakleigh without any medical supervision.

"If his condition were to worsen, the time taken to reach him might make the difference between life and death," he explained, and Emily agreed at once that they should go.

Fortuitously, Darcy had been visiting his parents and had accompanied his father to Oakleigh, for it was the end of the week and the workmen and labourers on the farm had to be paid that evening. Emily appealed for his help, and Darcy agreed to look after matters for her. Having shown him where the cash box and accounts were kept, Emily accompanied her husband and Dr Gardiner to the hospital.

It transpired there was very little money in the cash box to pay the workmen and some outstanding bills. Darcy began by using some of his own money to settle those that required immediate attention. Opening the books in order to record his payments, he began to understand the seriousness of his aunt's situation and, as he went further into the accounts, became somewhat alarmed at the parlous state of her finances.

Having made some notes, Darcy opened a drawer and was about to put away the books and lock the desk, when he noticed two letters lying open in the drawer. Since they were clearly business rather than private communications, being written on formal letterhead paper, Darcy had no reservations about glancing at them, lest they were matters that required his immediate attention.

He could see the one on top came from the office of an attorney in Matlock, a Mr Maxworthy, whom he knew to be associated with his uncle Robert Gardiner. It contained a proposal to either buy outright or accept as security for a loan, the entire property of Oakleigh. The sum of money proposed to be lent was certainly far less than was the generally accepted value of the estate, but it was still a considerable sum. Darcy read further, moving to the window for better light.

He was intrigued and even a little alarmed by what he saw.

In making the proposal, Mr Maxworthy declared he was acting for Mr and Mrs Robert Gardiner, who, he claimed, "had an abiding interest in the said property, being part of Mrs Gardiner's deceased estate."

Darcy could not understand what had occasioned this offer, until he picked up the second piece of paper, which had lain beneath the letter. This was a copy of a letter written by his aunt Emily to her brother Robert, asking if he would be willing to assist her set up a school for girls, on the lines of one run by Mrs Charlotte Collins at Longbourn in Hertfordshire.

She placed before him, openly and honestly, the facts pertaining to her husband's ill health and retirement, their now quite inadequate income, the meagre savings she had kept "for a rainy day," and her own determination to do all she could to care for Reverend Courtney and ensure his return to health. The proposed school, she hoped, would be an additional source of income. It was this proposition that Robert had passed on to his attorney, who had responded with a counteroffer to either buy or accept a mortgage on the Oakleigh estate. He had pointed out that while Mrs Courtney would need the consent of two of her siblings to sell the property, a mortgage would require no such condition, and the money could be used to set up the proposed school.

So alarmed was Darcy Gardiner at what this might imply, he made several notes of the facts and figures involved and decided to place the information before his parents as well as Mr Darcy, as soon as he could.

He could not imagine that they would, under any circumstances, approve such a deal. Yet, clearly something had to be done to help Mrs Courtney, something that would not put the future of Oakleigh Manor in jeopardy.

On the day following, having first ascertained that Reverend Courtney was no worse, indeed he had passed a comfortable night at the hospital, with no further sign of a heart attack, Darcy determined to take the information first to his father, Dr Richard Gardiner. Finding him at home in his study, while his mother was out walking in the park with James and Anthony, Darcy placed all the facts before him, together with the notes he had made.

"I thought it was essential that you and Mr Darcy should be made aware of the situation, sir," he said quietly. "It is very much graver than I thought at first. Aunt Emily needs help and she must be extricated from this impossible situation."

Richard Gardiner's countenance reflected his astonishment and his sense of betrayal. Darcy could see that his father was deeply shocked and hurt by the revelation that not only was his sister Emily in financial trouble, but their younger brother Robert was scheming, unbeknownst to the rest of his family, to entice Emily into selling or mortgaging, without any hope of reclamation, the home she had inherited from their parents.

Richard rose from his chair and walked away to the end of the room, then returning to his desk, read again the notes Darcy had placed before him.

"Darcy, you are quite certain of this? There is no possibility that you could have been mistaken?" he asked, almost hopefully.

"None, sir, I read both papers over carefully. I cannot begin to tell you how very shocked I was, it took a while for me to fully comprehend the matter.

"Aunt Emily's appeal was quite straightforward; but, when I realised what was being proposed by my uncle's attorney Mr Maxworthy, I knew I had to get the information to you and Mr Darcy as soon as possible, before my aunt was persuaded to sign anything," he said by way of explanation.

Richard praised his son's prompt action and sound sense of rectitude. "You did absolutely right, Darcy; I am indebted to you and I know Mr Darcy will be too, when he learns of this outrageous offer."

Darcy did, however, remind his father of the facts. "But, sir, it must be remembered that the matter was initiated by Aunt Emily. While Mr Maxworthy may be culpable, indeed he could be accused of having attempted to take advantage of her situation, we must not forget that Aunt Emily still needs to find the money for her school," he said and was surprised to find that his father was quite adamant on that point.

"That is out of the question," he said firmly.

Darcy looked askance at his father, wondering at the speed and determination with which he had rejected the idea.

"But, sir, she has planned..." he began, when Richard interrupted him gently. "Darcy, your aunt Emily has only the best of intentions, but it is unlikely that she could ever organise and administer a school such as exists at Longbourn under the control of Mrs Charlotte Collins and Mrs Jonathan Bingley. To begin with, Anna Bingley, who does most of the teaching at Longbourn, is an eminently qualified practitioner in both art and music; she has studied in France and Belgium. Emily will need to hire a suitable teacher. There is also not the same demand for such a school in this part of the country as there obviously is in the southern counties. The daughters of most of our tenants either look to be married to a farmer or shopkeeper, while many others seek to enter domestic service or work in the factories. Those young ladies fortunate enough to be educated in seminaries or by a private tutor, as your sisters were, would have already acquired the skills required to paint or play an instrument."

Darcy listened as Dr Gardiner continued, "Secondly, and this is far more important, your aunt does not know it yet, but she is going to have her hands full, caring for her husband. Reverend Courtney's condition, though grave, is not yet critical, but one false step and he would indeed be in peril. When he returns home, Emily will need all our help to care for him and ensure his recovery. She will have neither the time nor the energy left to organise and administer a school for ladies."

Dr Gardiner's voice was very grave, and Darcy could see his father was quite serious.

"But what is to be done to help her?" he asked, in some desperation.

His father's answer demonstrated the difficulty of the problem. Richard had sat down at his desk again and picked up Darcy's notes.

"I think it is best that we take this information to Mr Darcy, forthwith. I am neither sufficiently familiar with the resources available to assist Emily, nor am I confident that my judgment will be completely unbiased. As a cautious medical practitioner, I should like to obtain a second opinion on the problem, and Mr Darcy's is the very best there is. Besides, as the brother of both Emily and Robert, I may be more prone to prejudice than someone less directly connected to them, such as Mr Darcy," he explained.

When his son had the temerity to suggest that the close friendship between Mr Darcy and Mr and Mrs Gardiner might constitute a similar obstacle to impartiality, Richard retorted, "Darcy, I would place my life in your grandfather's hands with complete confidence in his fairness and honour. I know no other person of whose integrity I could be so completely satisfied, and I am quite certain your aunt Emily would feel the same."

Not long afterwards, they left Camden House, and Richard, having taken a few minutes to acquaint his wife with the nature if not the detail of their errand, called for the curricle, and the two set off for Pemberley.

On the way, Darcy, having been quiet for a while, asked another question that had been on his mind since the previous day.

"If you will forgive what may be an obtuse question, sir, I have wondered why Aunt Emily has not asked William for any help. He is by all reports doing well at his chosen profession, as yet unencumbered by a wife and family; one might have expected her to turn to him rather than to Uncle Robert. I am aware that musicians are not very well remunerated, but one of his talent and reputation must have some means, and I should have thought he would wish to help his mother in any way possible."

Richard smiled. "That is certainly not an obtuse question, Darcy, but the answer is a rather long and complex one and will have to wait for another occasion. Suffice it to say that Emily believed she had a sacred duty to encourage and develop William's musical talent and ensured that he was never denied anything he needed, not even when her situation was quite difficult. Mr and Mrs Darcy have helped him, too, as have the Grantleys—so Emily is unlikely to trouble him for financial assistance except in the most desperate circumstances."

They were approaching Pemberley, and Darcy, though puzzled by this answer, decided to ask no more questions. He hoped on some other occasion to return to the subject and perhaps glean some further information about the circumstances of his cousin William Courtney.

At Pemberley, Mr Darcy had dressed for dinner and, since they were not expecting company, had decided to indulge his passion for the arts by spending some time in the gallery, where the light at this time of year was just right to allow one to fully appreciate the group of fine Italian masterpieces that were the pride of his collection. A Canaletto, which he knew had been coveted by Prince Albert himself at the time of its purchase, was a personal favourite of his.

The unexpected appearance of Richard and Darcy Gardiner alerted him to the possibility of something being amiss. That one or the other should arrive unannounced would not have raised a question, but that both should appear, without prior warning, especially after the sudden illness of Reverend Courtney, gave him reason to worry and he hurried forward to meet them.

However, since they did not look as though they were bearing grievous news, he greeted them cordially and said, "Richard, Darcy, this is an unexpected pleasure! Are you here to announce another special celebration at Camden House? A wedding perhaps?" looking directly at young Darcy.

Darcy seemed a little confused, and Richard laughed, though not very cheerfully, "No, sir, sadly we are not. I am sorry to disappoint you, but we have a somewhat unexpected problem and hope you might help us resolve it."

"Indeed? An unexpected problem, which calls for three heads instead of one or two? This is a question of some complexity then?"

"It is indeed, sir," said Richard, "and I think you will agree, when you have heard the detail of it, that it requires careful handling."

Sensing the seriousness of the situation, Mr Darcy took them into his study and, sending for a footman, asked for drinks to be served to his visitors. In the interim, he went to find his wife and advise her that he may be late for dinner.

Elizabeth was curious. "Richard and Darcy Gardiner are both here? What can possibly be the matter? Not some problem with Darcy's engagement to Miss O'Hare, I hope?"

He was quick to reassure her. "No, my dear, it certainly did not appear to be a matter of the heart as far as I could tell. But be patient, Lizzie, and I am sure all will soon be revealed."

Returning to his study, Mr Darcy shut the door and poured himself a drink.

"Well now, what is this conundrum that has you so concerned?"

Richard had already placed the relevant notes upon the desk, and as Mr Darcy picked them up, his grandson explained how he had come by the information they contained.

To say Mr Darcy was shocked and grieved would be a complete understatement. His brow was furrowed, his mouth tightened with anger, yet he said nothing as he read through the notes.

Then, turning to Darcy Gardiner, he asked, "And have you any idea, Darcy, if your aunt Emily has already responded to this proposal?"

"No, sir, I cannot be certain, but I do not believe it likely that she has had time to respond. The letter is dated just three days ago, and if it had arrived yesterday, there would have been insufficient time to respond," he replied.

"And was there any other indication that she may be willing to accept Maxworthy's offer?"

"No, sir, none at all, except that it does seem as though Mrs Courtney's finances are in a parlous state, and if she has no other means, she may be tempted by it. She will need to do something to balance the books."

Mr Darcy nodded. "I agree, but that does not have to involve the sale or mortgage of her parents' home! Oakleigh meant a great deal to Mr Gardiner—it was much more than a property acquired at a good price for commercial advantage.

"Mr Gardiner bought it to fulfil a promise to his wife, who, as you both know, was born and raised in the district and loved it dearly. Your father, Richard, was delighted when he was able to purchase such a fine place for her, and I think it would have broken their hearts to think its sale would even be contemplated by one of their children.

"I am aware that since Mr Gardiner's death, there have been offers to buy the place or to subdivide and sell portions of it for development, but Mrs Gardiner did not wish it, and I advised against it. If I were asked today, I would do the same again. Oakleigh Manor is an excellent, profitable estate and ought be kept in your family."

He sounded so determined, both Richard and Darcy realised that even if Emily had wished to pursue the deal offered by Mr Maxworthy, Mr Darcy, as joint trustee of the estate together with Richard, would not have consented to it.

"I think we are agreed then, sir, that Aunt Emily should be advised against accepting the proposal," said Darcy Gardiner, "but we do have to find some means of helping her overcome this financial crisis."

"Indeed, we must," said his grandfather. "Emily is always in danger of being exploited, because she thinks so little about her own needs. Her concerns are primarily for others—her family or the community."

"Can I assume then that you do not support the idea of a school for ladies?" asked Darcy, curious to know his grandfather's view of the proposal.

Mr Darcy smiled and, when he replied, was somewhat ambivalent on the matter. "While I can see why Emily is attracted to the idea and I can understand the value of such a school, there will always be the problem of funding it. The income from the estate goes into the trust, which your father and I together with the attorney Mr Jennings administer. Emily may draw upon it for her own expenses and the maintenance of the property, but she is not authorised to use it for any other purpose, certainly not for setting up a school," he said.

Young Darcy raised his eyebrows and looked anxious. "That would certainly present a problem," he said.

"It would, and Emily knows this well, which is why she has appealed to Robert's generosity, which she alone must believe in, for I confess, I have seen no evidence of it!" said Mr Darcy, adding with a smile, "And, it would seem that in his usual fashion, Robert has passed the proposal on to Maxworthy, who is no fool. He has jumped at the idea of a mortgage, knowing, on the basis of Emily's own figures, that she will never be able to repay the full sum plus the

POSTSCRIPT FROM PEMBERLEY

interest. Now, while a sale is not permitted under the conditions of the will, a private mortgage may well be another matter."

"Could my aunt take such a mortgage on the property without the consent of the trustees?" Darcy asked.

"In theory, yes, because she is the immediate inheritor according to the terms of Mrs Gardiner's will, and if she does so and cannot repay the sum on demand, the trustees will be notified; the matter may then go to court and the court may order a sale. I leave you to speculate who will benefit most from such an eventuality."

Both Darcy and Richard looked horrified at the prospect.

"Do you believe, sir, that my uncle Robert is capable of foreclosing upon Aunt Emily in order to acquire the estate? Is it possible?"

Mr Darcy's eyes narrowed and he looked very grave indeed.

"Darcy, you are yet to learn that in matters of property, anything is possible. Families have been thrown onto the street or sent to the workhouse, because an avaricious lawyer has taken advantage of the situation of one relative or the greed of another. Robert, you must remember, is not the only protagonist here—Maxworthy is probably deeply involved as well. It is he who will provide the money for the loan. It is unlikely that Robert can find even half that sum."

"And how might we prevent this, sir?" asked Richard, clearly shocked by what he had heard.

"Only by explaining to your sister the perils of the scheme proposed by Maxworthy and providing her with a sensible alternative," replied Mr Darcy.

"With what you have told us, it may not be difficult to achieve the first objective, but how on earth is the second to be accomplished? If Emily's financial affairs are so dire, what alternatives are there?"

Richard, having had very little time in the course of a busy medical career to be involved with business and property matters, was completely at sea.

Mr Darcy went to his bureau and took out a cutting from a recent edition of the *Matlock Reporter*, which he handed to Richard.

It was an advertisement inserted by a businessman, wishing to start a flower farm and looking to lease a piece of enclosed, fertile farmland for the purpose. He was open to offers and gave an address in a village not far from Matlock.

Richard was intrigued.

"A flower farm? Do you believe this is a possible alternative, sir?" he asked.

"It may be, but there are others like it, which could well provide a simpler, far more certain source of income for Emily than a school. Better still, there would be no need to borrow any money for capital expenses; instead she would begin to earn an income from the lease, immediately the contract was signed," Mr Darcy explained.

"And the trust would have no objection?" asked Darcy Gardiner.

"No, because there is no risk to the estate at all," replied his grandfather cheerfully. "Indeed, it might be said that this would constitute an improvement to the value of the property. There are many acres of good farmland at Oakleigh, enclosed in earlier times and left fallow, which may be used in exactly this way, without impinging upon the home farm. We have similar areas within the Pemberley estate, too, which I would like to look at with a view to making them more productive."

Young Darcy was most impressed and enthusiastic.

"It is a capital scheme, sir, but I wonder how it may be recommended to my aunt. How is she to be persuaded that it is in her best interest to lease part of her land to some flower farmer?"

At that his grandfather laughed, a very cheerful laugh. "Well, Darcy, that piece of diplomacy I believe we must leave to you; with your experience in the political sphere, persuasion should come easily to you. It should not be difficult to explain how it was that you discovered the information and to convince her that such a scheme as this one, or some other like it, would be far preferable to Maxworthy's perilous proposal for a mortgage, which she has no chance of repaying!"

"But what about her school—will she agree to give it up? Aunt Emily can be very single minded," said Darcy.

Richard intervened then to explain, "I think not in this case, not when I have explained the situation in relation to James Courtney's health and the care she will need to give him, if he is to have a chance of recovery. She will see, I am sure, that the school is not a practical proposition."

Mr Darcy nodded, seeming quite sanguine. "Well then, go to it and make sure you have her convinced, before she is persuaded by Robert or Rose or that old fox Maxworthy to sign something that may cause her and the rest of us a whole lot of unpleasantness," he said. "I do not trust Maxworthy; he is a cunning fellow; I once caught him trying to persuade a tenant farmer of mine to sign over his entire crop over several years, in return for a fixed sum of money. The man needed it to get his son into the Navy and was prepared to do anything to get it. Fortunately, Mr Grantham got wind of it, and we put a stop to it. We found him the money and sent old Maxworthy off with a flea in his ear!"

Laughing together, they went downstairs to join Elizabeth, who tried to persuade Richard and Darcy to stay to dinner. But both father and son were tired and keen to be home.

"Mama expects me to dine at home today; I shall not be popular if we are late again," said Darcy, and his grandmother, whose affection for him was unconditional, conceded.

"Ah well, I daresay, I must give way to your mama occasionally," said she. He was a great favourite with her. She was, however, still keen to discover the reason for their sudden visit and the time they had spent closeted in her husband's study.

"And what have you three been plotting together?" she asked, to which Mr Darcy laughed and replied lightly, "Only a little matter of a flower farm, my dear; nothing of any major consequence."

"A flower farm? Where?" Elizabeth asked, more curious than ever.

"That is what young Darcy intends to find out, Lizzie. When he does, I am sure we shall all know about it, am I not right, Darcy?"

Picking up his cue swiftly, Darcy replied, "Yes indeed, sir, I shall be back with all the relevant information," and before Elizabeth could ask another question, they moved to the entrance, where the curricle awaited them.

No doubt she would ask Mr Darcy again and probably later, when they were alone, he would tell her more about it; but for the moment, with the servants milling around lighting the lamps and preparing to serve dinner, the topic was closed.

Chapter Eighteen

Prior to visiting his aunt, Darcy Gardiner went to Ripley, to meet the man who wished to lease land for a flower farm.

Having discussed the prospect with his mother, he had taken her advice that it would be best to ascertain more about Mr Mancini and his plans before taking it to Emily.

Cassandra had been quite enthusiastic about the scheme. "What a good idea; no doubt there is a growing demand for blooms in the cities, and if they can be transported on the railway, it might prove very profitable," she said, clearly pleased with the suggestion.

"Enough to pay Aunt Emily a reasonable sum on a lease?" Darcy asked.

"Certainly; look how well Colonel Fitzwilliam has done by leasing the lower meadows on his property for cattle pasture. It used to be idle land—too wet for sheep and too poor for crops. It brings him a good return now, with very little effort or expense," she said, adding, "Trust my father to come up with a sensible proposition."

Mr Mancini turned out to be an Italian piano tuner turned farmer. He had married a young woman from the village of Ripley and settled in the area, where he had a small mixed farm. He told Darcy, his father had been a stall holder at the Covent Garden markets, and while he was content and happy with his lot, he'd always yearned to follow in his father's footsteps and grow flowers for the London market. With his family grown up and engaged in their own businesses, he had time and money on his hands, he said, and talked enthusiastically of growing and marketing roses, lilies, and baskets of lavender.

"But I have not enough land here," he said. "All I need is an enclosed piece of fertile land, not too far from here," and when Darcy proposed that he take a look at the land available at Oakleigh, the man was eager and willing to come at once. Indeed, it was with some difficulty that Darcy persuaded him to wait a day or two, until his aunt had agreed to the scheme.

They discussed terms, and both men appeared satisfied, and though nothing was concluded, there seemed to be a level of trust between them, which was reassuring. Mancini certainly did not lack the money or the energy needed for the enterprise, thought Darcy.

He did, however, press Darcy for a quick settlement of the matter.

"I cannot delay too long," he said. "If the land is suitable, I must prepare the soil and set the bulbs for next Spring, before the ground is too hard. The roses too must be in well in time. There is much work to be done in the early Winter," he explained, and Darcy assured him he would have an answer very soon.

As he left the village, he felt a sense of relief; if his aunt agreed, it seemed as though Mr Mancini may well help save Oakleigh from the machinations of his uncle Mr Robert Gardiner and his lawyer Mr Maxworthy.

Before going on to Oakleigh, Darcy called at Colley Dale, hoping to find Kathryn at home. He was told by Mrs O'Hare that she had gone in to Matlock with Elena to purchase supplies for the school. Disappointed, since he had not seen her in several days, he promised to call in later and was invited to stay to dinner.

At Oakleigh, he found his aunt Emily Courtney alone with her young son Jude, who was studying at the dinner table while his mother struggled with her accounts. When Darcy arrived, she closed the books and pushed them away and greeted him gladly, but he could feel the weariness in her. She was younger than her sister Caroline, but looked a good deal older, and he could not fail to see the lines of anxiety that marked her countenance.

Yet, she smiled and offered him tea and thanked him for his kindness in helping her pay out her labourers.

"It was good of you to advance the money, Darcy; we have been a little short of ready cash this month. There have been many unforeseen expenses and

I am very grateful. I promise you will be repaid very soon," she said quickly and without any embarrassment.

Determined to do his best to persuade her to reject Maxworthy's offer of a loan, Darcy made light of the matter of the money, but proceeded quickly to the subject of the letters he had discovered by chance in her desk. He revealed apologetically that he had read them, believing they were business matters, which may have required his attention in her absence.

"Believe me, Aunt, I did not realise until I had read both documents that it was a response to a request from you to my uncle Robert. I did not mean to pry into your affairs, and I do beg your pardon."

He said nothing of his having taken the matter to his father and Mr Darcy, waiting for her response, expecting her to express some degree of surprise or disapproval even and wondering how he would get on thereafter.

But no such thing ensued.

Instead, when he looked at her, expecting a mild reproof, he saw tears in her eyes, and moments later, she rose, and taking young Jude with her, rushed from the room, leaving him alone, wondering what was to follow.

Would she return? Was her departure a sign of anger, and did she expect him to leave? he wondered.

He waited, and some ten minutes later, Emily returned to the room, having taken her son upstairs to continue his work there. She brought with her the two letters he had mentioned and placed them before him on the table.

In a voice that was still unsteady, she said, "Please read them again, Darcy. I cannot tell you how relieved I am that you did discover them."

He picked them up, and she continued, "I have sat here day after day, since Mr Courtney was taken to the hospital, filled with regret and shame—all because of those wretched letters."

She looked miserable, and Darcy was very remorseful as she continued, "Now, I know you have seen them, at least I can talk about them to you. Darcy, ever since I understood what Robert had done, bringing in Mr Maxworthy, and I realised what I had become involved in, I have been so unhappy…" she said tearfully.

Darcy Gardiner was appalled. He could not comprehend it; his aunt was weeping, ashamed, and unhappy, yet it was she who had initiated the matter, by her appeal to her brother for help with the school. It was a perplexing situation, which he found difficult to unravel.

Yet, as she sobbed, he could not bear it and, rising from his chair, went to her side, trying to comfort her.

Seeing her obvious distress, he asked gently, "But, Aunt Emily, how was it you came to be in this situation?"

The explanation, given through a series of sad and often incoherent sentences, told him something of the anguish she had borne, mostly alone, since discovering the truth about her husband's health and the desperate state of their finances. The realisation that Reverend Courtney would have to retire and, without the stipend he received from the living at Kympton, his modest annuity and that the money they derived from the farm would be quite inadequate for their needs, and the acceptance that she was responsible for most of their forlorn circumstances, since in her enthusiasm for charitable causes, she had given away most of her patrimony, had been the genesis of her idea for a school.

"I had heard how well Charlotte Collins had done with her little school, and I felt it was a good thing to do. I could use a part of the house—we do not use even half the rooms downstairs—and I would work at home, being always here to care for Mr Courtney when he needed me. I knew it would require some money to be spent at the outset, which is why I appealed to Robert for help. I was not asking for charity—I hoped he would see it as an investment in something good and wholesome, a scheme that would earn us some money and help the community, too.

"Darcy, I did not expect him to send my letter off to his attorney, nor did I dream that they would offer to buy me out or take a mortgage on the property. Ever since Mr Maxworthy's letter arrived, all laid out so coldly, I have been so ashamed. I could see Mama's face—I have wondered how she would feel, would she ever forgive me?"

She broke down, and he put an arm around her shoulders. "Did you not think to ask my father or even Mr Darcy for help?" he asked, and she dried her eyes and shook her head.

"How could I? They have both done so much for us. Mr Darcy was my father's dearest friend and partner—I did not know how to face him; what would he think of me? Besides, it is to Mr Darcy and Cousin Lizzie I have turned whenever we had a problem, and they have always helped. This time, I thought it was my duty to find a solution myself."

"And Papa?" he pressed her further, and she replied, "I did contemplate it, but Richard is very busy and always so kind. He has been so good about attending upon Mr Courtney at all hours, I had not the heart to trouble him with my financial problems. Besides, I know he is not very interested in matters of business. He was not keen to be involved in Father's company either. I thought Robert might be more interested, but clearly, I was wrong."

Again she lapsed into a state of depression and seemed surprised when Darcy asked, "Have you yet communicated with Mr Maxworthy or my uncle Robert?"

Emily shook her head vigorously and said, "No, I have sat here scribbling, trying to write a dozen or more letters, and I have torn them all up. What could I say? I was afraid if I said bluntly, no, Robert would be angry with me, because I had asked for his help and then wasted his time…"

"But you do not intend to take up Maxworthy's offer of a loan, do you?"

"Certainly not; how would I ever repay it? Besides, should he foreclose, what would I tell your father and Mr Darcy? They would be appalled!"

"Indeed, they would, I am sure, but what about your school?" Darcy wished to discover how committed Emily was to the school, before suggesting that she should abandon the idea.

At this she looked truly unhappy and said, "I don't really know. I had hoped it would help me earn a little extra money, whilst also helping to improve the lives of some of the girls in the area; there are many young women from decent families, who get no education and no chance in life, because they are too poor to have a governess and there is no school for older girls here. They are most often condemned to work as servants or in those ghastly factories in the Midlands. I had hoped to teach them to speak and read and conduct themselves in society, so they may have some hope of advancement in life. But, if I cannot find the money, I cannot help them or myself."

It was at this point that Darcy decided 'twere best to tell his aunt the plain truth about his visit.

"Aunt Emily, when I came here today, I came to tell you of something you *can* do, which will help you make some extra money, without the need for borrowing money or taking on more work yourself."

Emily sat up quite straight and looked at him in disbelief.

"Darcy, I am too old to believe in fairy tales. I trust you are not teasing me with some silly investment scheme."

"No indeed, I am not. Before I tell you more, tell me, has my father spoken to you of Reverend Courtney's condition and what needs to be done for him?"

"Yes, he has; Richard explained it all to me at the hospital," and her voice fell to a whisper, even though there was no one to overhear her words. "I know he will need a great deal of care. I have said nothing to Jude or Jessica yet, but I do realise it is going to be a very difficult time until he is fit again."

Darcy sighed, grateful for his father's timely intervention. That at least would make his own task easier.

"What is it you came to tell me?" Emily asked.

He began by showing her the cutting taken from the *Matlock Reporter* by Mr Darcy and then proceeded to explain the scheme proposed by Mr Mancini. "I have been to see him. He is genuinely eager to do business; I have ascertained what he is prepared to pay for a lease on a piece of enclosed farmland, with access to the road, to enable him to transport the flowers to the railway…"

"Flowers? Did you say he wishes to grow flowers on this piece of land?" she asked, interrupting his explanation.

"He does—he says his father sold flowers at Covent Garden. He wishes to grow them and send them to the markets in the cities."

Emily listened, staring wide-eyed at her nephew, astonished not only at the simplicity of the scheme proposed, but also at the astute business sense he had demonstrated. Emily had never been particularly keen on business; service and charity had been her strengths.

When he had explained it all, she nodded, understanding what he had meant when he said it would require no money and no extra work on her part.

"Is it really possible? Will this gentleman, this Mr Mancini, pay me a monthly sum on the lease and spend his own money on the rest—repair the fences, prepare the soil; the land has been idle for many years and will need much work if he is to succeed—and will he hire the labour to do the work?" she asked, almost disbelieving.

"He will; he is himself a farmer—he runs a small mixed farm and market garden outside Ripley and to judge by his house, he must be a fairly successful farmer. I believe he will attend to everything and pay you for the privilege of doing so," he said, and Emily could scarce believe it. Rising from her chair, she embraced her nephew and thanked him from the bottom of her heart.

"Darcy, I shall write tonight to refuse Mr Maxworthy's offer, and I shall take great delight in doing it," she said with a smile that lightened her countenance, for the first time, since he had arrived at the house.

Agreeing that it was a sound decision and having arranged a convenient time to meet with Mr Mancini, he left to return to Colley Dale.

He should have been pleased, filled with a sense of achievement; instead he felt only fatigue and deep relief. It had been an exhausting afternoon.

❧

At Colley Dale, Kathryn's family made him very welcome.

Mrs O'Hare protested that he had not dined with them in a fortnight, and Elena declared it was almost seven days since he had come to visit. Kathryn smiled but said nothing. Darcy, looking and feeling abashed, made his apologies. "It has been an extraordinarily busy week," he said. "This is always a hectic time of year. As well, the new rector of Kympton, Frank Grantley, and his wife and baby have arrived to take up residence. And we had to help them settle in."

Mrs O'Hare was interested. "I understand the new rector is your cousin, Mr Gardiner."

"He is indeed; Frank is the younger son of Mr Darcy's sister Georgiana, who is married to Dr Francis Grantley, a very distinguished dean at Oxford. Frank's wife Amy is also my cousin, from the Gardiner side of the family; she is my aunt Caroline Fitzwilliam's daughter, and of course, Aunt Caroline is married to Colonel Fitzwilliam, who is Mr Darcy's cousin!" he explained, and everyone thought this was very droll indeed.

"Oh dear, I wonder how you keep track of them!" exclaimed Mrs O'Hare.

As the rest of the family chatted and laughed over dinner, Darcy noticed that Kathryn seemed especially quiet and put it down to her being tired from her journey into Matlock that morning. It had been unusually warm, and the long walk could have been quite enervating. He recalled that she had once before suffered similarly, and said nothing, not wishing to embarrass her.

After dinner, Mr O'Hare stayed only a short while before retiring upstairs, having bid their guest good night, but not before saying, "If you see any of those Liberal politicians, Mr Gardiner, tell them I am bitterly disappointed that they are intent on spending so much time arguing about the Anglican church in Ireland—they have done nothing yet for the poor working men and women they promised to help. A pack of liars all of them; I don't believe a word they say. Yes, even Mr Gladstone—the people's William, they called him—he has let them down!"

There was no mistaking the anger and cynicism in his voice, and Darcy felt he was only echoing the views of many other people all over the land.

He knew there was a great deal of grumbling going on about the priorities of Mr Gladsone and his government, even among the Reformists who had supported him.

It was still another factor in his generally depressed state of mind, and not even Kathryn's presence could free him from its bondage. She was looking charming as usual, if a little pale, that evening, though he did notice, as they were alone together when Mr and Mrs O'Hare had left the room and Elena had gone to order tea, that she seemed a little unsettled, lacking her usual vivacity.

They had spoken quietly but not privately as they sat at the dinner table and yet they had not been alone together for almost a week.

When Darcy rose to take his leave, Kathryn accompanied him to the door as usual and stepped outside with him as he moved towards the vehicle which stood waiting for him. Turning to her, he took her hand and raised it to his lips, and then, in the only indication of intimacy she had had all evening, he kissed her lightly, said, "Good night, my dear Kathryn, you seem tired tonight; sleep well," and was gone.

After he had left, there was still sufficient light in the sky to let her take a turn in the garden alone. Kathryn was feeling disconsolate and melancholy, quite unlike her usual self. She could not altogether account for her state of mind, but she knew it was related to Darcy Gardiner's present demeanour. She could not define it, yet she knew something was amiss. As she walked about in the darkening garden, with the scent of thyme and camomile crushed underfoot, she was unable to say what it was. She could not accuse him of discourteous conduct, nor even of neglect of her, for he was always particular in everything he did and said, to pay her and other members of her family every courtesy.

But neither could she forget how it had been some months ago, before they had announced their engagement. Darcy Gardiner had been one of the most exciting and spirited young gentlemen of her acquaintance. His mind and manners were remarkable; imbued with the charm and energy of an intelligent man, with a keen interest in ideas, he had the skill to articulate them and the will to pursue them, unlike anyone she had known before.

When she had become aware of his interest in her, she had pulled back a little, until she was certain of his determination, and that was never in doubt when he was wooing her with ardour and spirit. She recalled the warmth of his words, the tenderness of his concern when she had been in some danger from Bellamy, and remembered even now, with pleasure, how passionately he had claimed his right to protect her when she had run away to stay with Mrs Ellis in Yorkshire. Then she'd never had cause to doubt the depth of his love.

Yet, in the past few weeks, things had seemed to change. While there was neither indifference nor coldness, she felt he was often pre-occupied and, sadly, did not seem to want to share his concerns with her, as she had hoped he would. When they used to talk together as mere friends, they'd found such a remarkable coincidence of views and ideals, and she had imagined how easily they might share their thoughts and match their hopes. She had hoped for this above all else.

A sensible and practical young woman, Kathryn did not expect that the young man she was engaged to would spend all day, every day, at her side. She was well aware that he had his duties as manager of the Pemberley estate and other family obligations, as did she, with the school and at home.

However, seeing him that evening after several days' absence, she had hoped for a warmer, more affectionate encounter, and when, even as they had been quite pointedly left alone in the sitting room, he had not come to her as he used to, she was left feeling deeply saddened.

Had he told her the cause of his changed mood, explained that he had been busy, distracted by a matter of business or some family problem, she would have understood. That she could have borne—not this.

She feared, unreasonably, that he may have had second thoughts about their engagement or, worse, begun to doubt her word. It was not impossible, she thought, a young man with ambition and the possibility of a seat in Parliament may well be wary of making a marriage that might bring embarrassment later in life. Her brief association with Hartley-Brown may have the potential to damage him and ruin their chances of happiness. Could it be that his family, having learned in some way of her past foolhardiness, was even now persuading him to abandon her? Tormented by a sense of guilt, Kathryn could not hold back the tears. Glad of the gathering dusk, she remained in the garden awhile longer.

Hearing her mother and Elena come back into the sitting room, she went indoors. Hoping they had not noticed her discomposure, she claimed she had a headache, said good night, and went up to bed.

Quite unaware of Kathryn's injured feelings, Darcy returned to Camden Park, where he reported to his parents that Emily would accept Mr Mancini's offer and would meet him very soon to sign an agreement. There were congratulations and much praise for him from both Richard and Cassy. They were justifiably proud of their son, who had demonstrated both compassion—a rare enough commodity—as well as sound common sense in dealing with the matter of Emily's financial problems.

He told them that he had given her his word, that he would be there to advise and assist her whenever the need arose, which, he said, seemed to give her some comfort.

Cassy, who knew how easily Emily was moved, understood how reassuring his words would have been to her.

When Darcy went to bed that night, he was feeling a good deal better than he had felt in a very long time, despite the long and tiring day.

Chapter Nineteen

T HE AGREEMENT BETWEEN EMILY Courtney and Mr Mancini was duly
signed after the latter had arrived at Oakleigh Manor, where he had
inspected and selected a satisfactory piece of land—some ten acres,
which he declared was exactly the right size and position for his proposed
flower farm.

Darcy Gardiner, who with the attorney Mr Jennings had witnessed the
signing of the lease, which promised to deliver to his aunt an agreed sum of
money on the first day of each month, was surprised at the ease with which it
was accomplished. Mr Mancini, having decided on his plot of land, had asked
if he might have the use of a barn where he could store his tools and supplies,
which request Mrs Courtney had readily granted.

When it was over, they repaired to the house and partook of sherry and
small cakes, specially baked for the occasion, before Mr Mancini left, having
paid the first month's rental in advance.

It had all been so simple, Darcy wondered why there was not more of it.
Perhaps, he thought, it may be successfully applied at Pemberley too, where
some older tenant farmers could no longer make a living from their land. With
talk of a rural recession in the air, few men wanted to plough more resources
into their land; perhaps, leasing it to those who could work it profitably might

provide a solution and some income for the tenants. He decided to raise the matter with his grandfather at the earliest opportunity.

When he returned to Pemberley, feeling pleased with what they had achieved for Mrs Courtney, a message from his mother awaited him, inviting him to dine at Camden House that night, "because we are expecting some very special guests who have asked particularly to meet you." Intrigued, unable to think who they might be, Darcy assumed they would be colleagues of his father or even old family friends. He was in two minds whether to accept, but not wishing to displease his mother, decided to go along.

Earlier he had called at the school to see Kathryn. Recalling that she had not seemed well on the last occasion upon which they had met and anxious to ascertain if she had recovered her spirits, he was disappointed to learn that she had already left with Jessica.

Darcy remembered then that Julian and Jessica had returned some days ago from their honeymoon and were soon to depart for France and Africa. It was understandable the two young women, who had become close and affectionate friends, should wish to spend some time together. He had hoped to see Kathryn, but since this was clearly not possible, he despatched a note to Colley Dale, arranging to call on her the following evening and expressing the hope that she was quite recovered from her temporary indisposition.

Arriving at Camden House, he discovered that the mysterious guests were none other than his friend and political mentor, Mr Colin Elliott, MP, and his charming wife, Anne-Marie. There was yet another man, who was introduced to him as Mr Howell, and who, he was told, had worked very hard at campaigning for the extension of the franchise. He too was a member of the rather loose coalition of Reformists and Liberals who were trying to persuade the government to take a more active role in social reform.

"Mr Howell has expressly asked to meet you, Darcy," said Colin Elliott, and Howell, who had a cheerful, rather loud voice that made a booming sound as though he were using a loud hailer, said, "I have heard a good deal about you, Mr Gardiner, and the considerable amount of work you did to advance the cause of reform prior to the last election. I have to say I am most impressed."

Darcy was pleased to be singled out for praise, but Mr Howell's next statement took him completely by surprise.

"We have a proposition for you, one which we think you will find exceedingly attractive."

"Indeed?" said Darcy. "And may one ask what it is?"

"Certainly you may; it is a quite simple proposition. There is a strong possibility that there will be a by-election in the Autumn, caused, we believe, by the ill health of one of our older members from the West Riding of Yorkshire. We think you might wish to stand for the seat and would like to put your name up to the committee. You will get the support of the Liberals and Reformists, of course, and while it is likely the Tories will put up a candidate against you, he is unlikely to trouble you in that seat. It is one of our safest." Looking directly at Darcy, he asked, "What do you say? Will you stand?"

So astonished was Darcy by this unexpected proposal and the casual manner in which it had been put to him, he was at first quite unable to say anything at all. He looked from Howell to Mr Elliott, trying to discover if this was a serious suggestion. Then, recovering sufficiently to say he was honoured by the offer, he added that he would need time to consider it.

Anne-Marie Elliott, who had been seated with Cassy, within earshot of the gentlemen, turned to her hostess and asked, "Do you suppose Darcy will agree to stand for a seat in the Commons? My husband thinks he is the perfect candidate."

Cassandra looked somewhat unsure and replied, "It will depend very much on what Darcy wishes to do. I know he has an abiding interest in reform politics, but at the moment, he is occupied with his work at Pemberley, where he manages the estate for my father. Besides, and I do apologise for not writing to your father about this, Anne-Marie, but it may not be the right time; I believe Darcy and Kathryn may have plans to marry in the Autumn. I cannot imagine he would wish to be campaigning for a by-election at the same time!"

Darcy Gardiner had not heard his mother's response to Mrs Elliott, but his thoughts had followed similar lines. He was not ready, however, to reveal his personal plans for the future to a complete stranger. When he answered, he made it clear that he was honoured to be asked and thanked both Mr Howell and Colin Elliott, but added, "I have several commitments which I have made here and at Pemberley, which I cannot abandon. I shall need time to think it over."

Urging him to consider it seriously and reminding him of the importance of good representation for the people of Yorkshire, the guests went in to dinner. Darcy was grateful to find himself seated beside Anne-Marie Elliott, and to his relief, the topic of conversation soon changed from the politics of the Parliament to the problems of the Queen. Her self-imposed isolation from her subjects since the death of her beloved consort was causing problems, Anne-Marie told him; there had been rumblings in the Royal Household and government about it. Though Darcy had little interest in the Queen's private predicament, he was glad of the diversion.

He was quite certain that Colin Elliott, who knew how dedicated he had been to the cause of reform, would try to persuade him to accept. He was flattered, of course, but hoped he would be able to resist the lure and the persuasive arguments that would be put to him.

When dinner was over, he decided to return without delay to Pemberley, where he hoped to have a meeting with his grandfather Mr Darcy after breakfast on the morrow.

Meanwhile, Kathryn had spent a pleasant evening with her dearest friend, who had called to say good-bye. Julian and Jessica were leaving on the following morning for Derby and thence by train for London and Paris, from where they would depart for Africa. Jessica could not leave without seeing her friend one last time.

When she had first called at the school, Kathryn's delight at seeing her had been so excessive, Jessica had been genuinely surprised.

"Why, Kathryn," she had exclaimed, as they had hugged one another and wept like schoolgirls, "it has only been three weeks! My dear friend, what will you do and say when we have been gone three years?"

Kathryn was unapologetic and wholehearted in her appreciation. She had felt Jessica's absence keenly.

"Jessica, my dear, dear friend, how I have missed you! Is it really only a few weeks? It feels as though you have been away for so much longer! But let me look at you—oh my word, how very well you look; marriage certainly agrees with you."

Jessica, upon whose complexion there was now a deep blush as well as the lovely bloom that Kathryn had noted and admired smiled and, with her arms still around her friend, whispered confidentially, "It is a state I would happily recommend to you, Kathryn, and if your Darcy were to ask my dear Julian, I have no doubt at all he would concur."

As she moved away and regarded her friend, she added, "Oh Kathryn, if you had told me a year ago that I could be so utterly happy and contented, I should have laughed you to scorn. Yet look at me now!"

Looking at her, Kathryn could not doubt her words.

There had always been about Jessica an indefinable quality of quiet serenity, as though she coveted nothing in the world beyond what she held in her hands at the moment. Yet now, she appeared to be aglow with delight, and Kathryn could not mistake it for anything other than the happiness she had found in her marriage with Julian. If only, Kathryn had thought, if only such profound pleasure were given to us all.

This time, Jessica insisted that she had wanted to spend some time with her friend, and Kathryn invited her back to Colley Dale. From Pemberley they proceeded in one of the smaller carriages to Colley Dale, where the rest of the evening was spent as friends who were as close as sisters would spend their last evening together before parting for almost three years. They talked and laughed a great deal, wept a little, and made much of comforting one another, promising to write regularly and tell each other every significant thing that happened in their lives.

Jessica insisted that she must know all the news. "Now, Kathryn, when you write, I want you to tell me all about the preparations for your wedding. Have you fixed upon a date?" Jessica asked as she put on her bonnet, preparing to leave. When Kathryn admitted that they had not, she feigned shock.

"Kathryn, why must you delay? Pray do not waste another month of your lives—if you love each other, as I know you do, it is sinful to spend so much time apart being miserable, as I know you must be, when you can be so much happier together! This is most unsatisfactory—I think I shall speak to my cousin Darcy about this."

Kathryn, who had not the heart to tell Jessica of her present melancholy state and the reasons for it, had laughed lightly and said, "Well, Mr Gardiner has sent me a note saying he intends to call on me tomorrow. Perhaps something will come of it then."

Jessica was confident. "There you see! I knew it. Well, as soon as ever you have fixed a date, you must write to me; will you promise? And when you do, I shall pray as hard as I can that you will both be as happy as we are. Dear Kathryn, I cannot promise you more."

She was still smiling as they went to the door and she entered the vehicle that waited for her there.

Seeing her thus, Kathryn could not help but envy her friend's felicity.

~❦~

The following morning, young Darcy, returning from a morning ride around the park, met with Julian and Jessica as they waited in the saloon for their luggage to be loaded into the carriage that would take them to meet the train at Derby.

Although they had met on their return from London, he had not spent much time with them; they had all been rather busy. Now they were about to leave and would be gone, he realised with a shock, for almost three years. He went to them and, casting formality aside, warmly embraced first Julian and then Jessica, wishing them a safe journey. As he did so, unexpected tears flooded his eyes. They had both been a part of his life since childhood, and he felt their departure keenly.

Jessica did too and whispered so only he could hear, "Darcy, pray do not delay too long; when you go to Kathryn today, do decide upon your wedding day. She loves you dearly, and every day that you spend apart is wasted time, when you might be so much happier together. Please believe me and do as I say."

Startled by her forthright advice, he drew back and looked at her. Seeing only honesty and warm affection in her eyes, he embraced her again.

"Thank you, Jessica, I shall," he said.

Then Julian came to say the carriage was ready to leave. He took his wife's arm and helped her into the vehicle.

Moments later, with a wave and a last good-bye to the family and servants gathered in the hall, they drove away from Pemberley and into the life they had chosen. It would not be an easy life, but they hoped their dedication to the work and their love for each other would sustain them.

Watching them depart, Darcy experienced a sudden sense of loss. He knew he would miss them. Their marriage had marked for him, as it had for his grandparents, a renewal of faith. Following the tragedy of Julian's failed marriage and the death of Josie, there had been at Pemberley an atmosphere close to despair, which even the bright presence of young Anthony Darcy could not always dilute. Much as they all loved the child, he remained, to many in the family, a reminder of what had been lost.

It was as though Pemberley had been emptied of hope.

But, with the marriage of Jessica and Julian, there had been a perceptible change. Darcy had seen it start with their engagement, as the warmth of their affection and Julian's improved disposition seemed to pervade the household. There could be no doubt of their felicity, and it seemed to enhance the contentment of Mr and Mrs Darcy, too.

Back briefly from their honeymoon, their love quietly yet so unambiguously expressed, they had made Darcy yearn for a similar degree of certainty.

Now, Jessica's parting words, "She loves you dearly, and every day you spend apart is wasted time, when you might be so much happier together..." nagged at his mind.

However, before he could decide upon a course of action, he had to see Mr Darcy. There were matters to be decided, important to them both, relating to Pemberley and his own future.

Colin Elliott and Mr Howell had made Darcy an attractive offer—to support his candidacy for a seat in the Commons. It was no vain promise, but a tangible proposal with the very real possibility of preferment in a future political career, if he accepted.

Could he, Darcy wondered, afford to turn it down? What would Kathryn say? She knew of his interest in politics and had encouraged him in it.

Would it not seem like a wasted opportunity, and might he not regret it in years to come?

These thoughts crowded in on him, and yet he had to admit to himself that, unlike a year ago, when he would have grasped such an offer with eager hands, today his enthusiasm for politics was on the wane. A political career was, in his eyes, no longer the pinnacle of achievement. A degree of disillusionment, even mild cynicism, had begun to erode the once bright idealism of his support for the cause.

He recalled the words of Mr Daniel O'Hare: "Tell them, Mr Gardiner, how very disappointed I am... they have done nothing to help the working men and women.... A pack of liars, all of them..." They were hard, angry words.

He could not deny that neither Mr Gladstone nor any of his senior ministers had shown any inclination to deal with the policies and imposts that had made the lives of millions of ordinary people harder and more miserable than they needed to be. They had promised change but had taken no immediate steps to effect it. Ireland's aggravating tenancy laws and the disestablishment of the Irish church, esoteric subjects that touched the lives of none but landlords, clergy, and politicians, had taken precedence over the important reforms they had espoused.

By the time he met with his grandfather, it was midmorning and Mr Darcy was taking coffee in the morning room. Darcy was keen to discuss matters of business, and his grandfather invited him to partake of a cup of the popular beverage. The subject of their discussion turned to proposals for subletting parcels of farmland, which had remained idle for two years or more.

"We could encourage the tenants to follow the example of Mrs Courtney and Colonel Fitzwilliam; it could bring them additional income and make better use of the land, which is being degraded while lying idle. Would you have any objection to it, sir?" he asked.

Mr Darcy thought for a moment before answering, "No, not in principle, but only if you can assure me that no tenant of mine will be compelled or pressed into subletting his fields or farm to some greedy neighbour or developer who will override his rights."

There was no doubt where Mr Darcy's interest lay.

Darcy sought to reassure his grandfather.

"I would certainly not permit it, sir. It would only be arranged by mutual consent and under my supervision, where the tenant farmer could obtain a clear benefit and the land would be worked with due care."

He added what he thought would surely please Mr Darcy.

"With the talk that is around of a rural recession, it could be just what we need to get the men working and the farms profitable, sir," he said, and Mr Darcy agreed. "Very well, go to it, then. But I should like to be kept informed of every new agreement before it is finally signed. It is not that I do not trust you, Darcy—I would trust you with every penny I have—but I must be certain some sharp businessman does not bamboozle my tenants into surrendering any of their rights. Some of these families have been settled on the estate for several generations. We owe it to them to protect them from exploitation or injustice. But, yes, I do agree, it could be useful at a time when cropping is unprofitable and small holdings are being swallowed up everywhere."

Darcy was delighted. "Then may I make a start, sir?"

"Certainly, but remember, the rights of my tenants and their families must come first. They need certainty and continuity as we do. Our prosperity is dependent upon their well-being and vice-versa."

Darcy smiled. "Yes, sir, I shall not forget that." Then, changing the subject, he added, "There is just one more thing, sir—I would like you to know that last night I was offered a chance to stand for Parliament, at a by-election for a seat in the West Riding of Yorkshire."

"Were you? I suppose this was one of Mr Elliott's schemes to lure you back to Westminster? I did wonder what Mr Howell's interest was. Your mother mentioned that he was exceedingly keen to meet with you."

"Yes, sir, and he was very flattering, but I have decided to turn it down," said Darcy.

His grandfather seemed very surprised. "Is that not rather precipitate? Such a valuable opportunity may not come your way again; safe seats in the House of Commons are not offered around every day of the year, you know."

"Indeed, sir, I know it is an honour and a rare opportunity, but I intend to refuse it just the same. I believe my place is here, sir."

"Not, I hope, because of your sense of duty to me and Pemberley? Noble as that may be, I should not like to think we had stood in the way of your political career if that was your desire."

Mr Darcy's expression betrayed his anxiety. Clearly his grandson was making a very serious decision, one that could change his entire life and shut him out of a once coveted career. He knew well Darcy's dedication to Mr Gladstone and the Reformist cause.

When he spoke, his voice was grave. "Darcy, if you are doing this because it is what you want to do, I would be the first to applaud and encourage you, but if you are acting purely out of a sense of loyalty towards me, I should ask you to reconsider your decision. Remember, it will affect the rest of your life."

Darcy spoke up immediately, "I am aware of that, sir. I am very conscious of my duty to Pemberley, to you, and to my family, but that is not the only reason—indeed, it is not even the chief reason for my decision. There is another, even more significant matter that I must consider."

As he stood up and walked over to the window, he seemed, to Mr Darcy, taller and more self-assured in his manner.

"The by-election is to be in the Autumn, and the elected member will be expected to take his seat at Westminster for the next session of the Parliamentary year; I do not believe I will be available, sir."

"Will you not?" Mr Darcy seemed puzzled, but his grandson smiled and said, "Sir, I expect and hope that Miss O'Hare and I will be married and on our honeymoon by then."

At this declaration, Mr Darcy's face creased into a smile and he began to laugh, clearly appreciating this new development.

"Now, that is certainly a good reason, Darcy. I cannot argue with your priorities there. I take it you already have Miss O'Hare's agreement to this plan?"

Darcy coloured slightly and confessed, "Not yet, sir, but I intend to remedy that when I call on her this evening. I shall ask her to set the date for our wedding, and I intend to suggest that it should be in the Autumn."

His grandfather was clearly delighted. "Very well then, let me wish you success and I shall await your return with the young lady and the good news! I look forward to telling your grandmother all about this—she will be delighted, I am sure."

They shook hands and parted in excellent spirits.

Chapter Twenty

When Darcy Gardiner went to Colley Dale that evening, he took the curricle. He took also the keys to the house at Matlock. Work had been completed that week, making it ready for refurbishment, his mother had told him, urging him to see it for himself.

Kathryn greeted him in the hall. She seemed a little nervous and uncertain as to his mood, but not for long. Within moments of his entering the house, it became apparent to her that his mood and manner were entirely changed from what they had been before. Having greeted her with a degree of warmth that she had missed recently, he asked if she would like to fetch a wrap, because they were going to be driving out.

Surprised, she asked, "Driving out? Are we going far?"

"No, not far, but I am concerned that the late evening air may be cold."

His voice was kind and solicitous, and she did as he suggested.

Hastening upstairs, she collected her bonnet and wrap and told her mother they were driving out. Mrs O'Hare also urged her daughter to protect her throat, else she may catch cold, but otherwise seemed happy enough to see her go. She had begun to express some concern lately that no date had been agreed for the wedding, and her satisfaction probably reflected her hope that this evening's drive may bring some resolution to it.

Darcy helped Kathryn in and, having ensured she was comfortable, drove on. At first, she was quiet, anxious that he may yet be troubled by something she had no knowledge of and wishing he would confide in her. So uneasy did she become, that after a while, she could hold out no more and had to ask, "Darcy, will you not tell me the purpose of this journey? Are we only to drive to the top of the hill to look at the prospect, or had you something else in mind?"

He looked at her briefly and smiled. "We are going to look at the house we are to live in after we are married. The men have completed their work, and now you must decide on drapes and furnishings and such matters. We had best get started, else it will not be ready in time."

His voice was so matter of fact, as though he expected her to comprehend his meaning exactly.

Kathryn, though she thought she knew, said nothing at first, forcing him to ask, "Have I surprised you, Kathryn?"

She was reluctant to admit it, yet it could not be denied. "Indeed, you have. I must confess I had no notion at all of your intention to drive out to the house," she said.

"But you have no objection to going?" he asked quickly and, when she said she had not, added, "I thought it a particularly good opportunity. With the workmen gone, we shall have the place to ourselves. We can see it at our leisure and decide on its refurbishment. However, we shall have to make haste, especially, if it is to be ready for occupation in the Autumn."

"For occupation in the Autumn?" she asked, simply repeating his words, turning them into a question.

They had reached the entrance to the drive. He turned in and took the vehicle up to the house, pulling up at the porch.

When he was helping her out, he asked, apropos her last question, "Would you consider that too soon, Kathryn?"

"Too soon?" she asked, as though she were not certain of his meaning.

"Too soon for us to be married?" he said with a smile.

He opened the door, and they were in the hall. He had kept hold of her hand, and she had to look up at him directly. She saw that his expression was remarkably like it had been on the night he had proposed to her as the blizzard had raged around Pemberley.

As the memory returned, she was uncertain where this conversation might lead and decided to lighten the mood. Resorting to the playful tone she would often affect when they were courting, she asked, "And have you brought me here to persuade me?"

Taking his cue from her, Darcy replied, "And if I confess that was indeed my intention, might I hope to escape your censure, were I to plead in mitigation that I felt you may need some persuasion?"

Sensing that he was on the defensive, she was determined to tease him. "Why would you believe that?" she asked.

He was a little slow to respond, appearing to search for an answer. "Perhaps because in recent times, I may have appeared to have neglected you a little."

It was the first time he had made mention of the awkwardness that had come about between them in the last few weeks, and Kathryn was curious to discover his meaning.

"In what ways, especially?" she asked, and though she was quite genuine, he believed she was still in a mood to taunt him and, throwing her an injured look, pleaded, "Must I? Dearest Kathryn, pray do not torment me. Will you not forgive me and spare me this penance? Let me only ask you, please, to name the date for our wedding. I think we have waited long enough and should like very much if it could be in the Autumn."

Surprised by the sudden excitement in his voice, conscious also of the re-kindled warmth and passion in his manner as he reassured her of his love, she realised then, not least from the heightened response of her own heart, that nothing had really changed; they were as much in love as they had ever been.

Her answer, that she would gladly marry him in the Autumn, on whatever day he wished to choose, brought an entirely predictable response.

There is no reason to give an account of what followed, for each pair of lovers will discover what delights them most. Suffice it to say, that neither had known such profound and tender feelings ever before as they now acknowledged to each other. Darcy was as surprised by the intensity of his ardour as by the warmth of hers, for Kathryn, knowing she was so well loved, had no reason to tease or dissemble, and let him see how well she understood him and how deeply she cared, sweeping away any doubts that may have trammeled up their present contentment.

Later, as they wandered through the house, he told her of Colin Elliott's proposition. She was surprised and seemed somewhat concerned, until he remarked, almost casually, "I do not intend to accept, of course."

To which she said, "But, Darcy, is it not what you have always wanted?"

His reply surprised her. "I once assumed it was, but no longer... I have thought about it long and hard and reached the conclusion that my place is here, with you, with my family and Pemberley."

Seeing her astonishment, he asked, "Tell me, my love, what do you think I should do?"

Her answer was honest and unequivocal. "Darcy, you must do as your head and your heart direct you. Had you decided to go to Westminster, I should not have tried to change your mind—but it would have cost me dearly. While I love you with all my heart, I do not believe I could walk away from the school after the solemn undertaking I have given Jessica to carry it forward until her return. Nor would it have been easy to leave Mama and Elena again to care alone for my father. He finds such comfort from my presence and was so pleased that we would live in the neighbourhood; had I moved to London, it would have broken his heart."

"And yet you would have come with me to Westminster?" he asked.

"Of course, whenever you wished me to be there. I should not have married you and asked you to give up your ambition for me."

Darcy drew her to him and held her, his hands clasping hers. "Nor would I ask it of you, dearest Kathryn. I love you too well to impose such an unreasonable demand upon you," he said.

"I am honoured and delighted that you think so," she said, and her voice trembled, betraying how deeply she was moved by his words. "It is indeed my preference that we should share our hopes and dreams and accommodate each other's wishes. But I should never presume so far as to insist that you abandon yours for mine. That would be unpardonable arrogance. Surely such self-indulgence cannot sit comfortably with love."

"Indeed, it cannot," he said, gathering her into his arms again, even as the darkening sky outside alerted them to the lateness of the hour.

They had lost count of time, but well aware of their responsibility to their families, they returned first to Colley Dale to tell her mother of their decision to wed in the Autumn, and thence to Camden Park and Pemberley to share their happiness with the rest of the family.

Mrs O'Hare was truly delighted and expressed her satisfaction in the warmest terms. "I am so pleased my dear Kate and Mr Gardiner have fixed the day at last," she said to her husband and Elena after the couple had left. "I confess I was beginning to be concerned. Not that I did not trust Mr Gardiner implicitly, but because I was anxious that we should have sufficient time to prepare for the occasion. It is not every day that one gives a daughter in marriage."

Turning to Elena, she said, "But now, I am sure all will be well… We shall probably have to make dozens of lists—of guests to invite, food to prepare, and things to buy… It will be a most exciting time, Elena, and I shall need you to help me."

Mrs O'Hare was clearly exhilarated by the prospect of giving her eldest daughter in marriage and plainly happy with the gentleman to whom she was to be given.

When Darcy and Kathryn arrived at Camden House, Dr Gardiner had just been called out to the hospital to attend upon a child with croup. It was ever thus, said Cassandra, who nevertheless received their news with much pleasure.

"Dr Gardiner is always being called away, and since his campaign for better hospital sanitation and hygiene has won the support of Miss Nightingale herself, he is much in demand at meetings of the profession and all the hospital boards," she explained. "He will be very happy to know the date of your wedding has been fixed."

Turning to her son, she added, "Darcy, your papa will be very pleased—he was saying only a few days ago that it was time you and Kathryn started on the refurbishment of the house; you will find the rooms upstairs in very good condition, but the drapes downstairs may not be to your taste. Should you wish to change them, Mr Grantham will recommend a woman who will do the work for you at a very good price. We had her do the work for Laura Ann's bedroom and have been very satisfied."

Promising to discuss all these important domestic matters further, they had gone finally to Pemberley, where Mr and Mrs Darcy were both unambiguously delighted with their news.

Elizabeth had but one complaint: "I do love an Autumn wedding—but why will you not marry at Pemberley?" she asked, adding, "The park here looks splendid at that time of year; you could not ask for a prettier setting."

Darcy had explained that Mr and Mrs O'Hare would probably prefer that they were married at Kympton, which was their parish church, and of course, the wedding breakfast should be at Colley Dale.

"Besides, I have asked Frank Grantley to marry us; it will probably be his first wedding in his new church," he said.

Mr Darcy, sensitive to Kathryn's feelings, said it was no matter anyway, since the living of Kympton was part of the Pemberley estate and Frank Grantley was his nephew, which would make it almost as good as being at Pemberley. His wife, taking her cue from her husband, agreed and said that they would hold a dinner party for the happy couple before their wedding, so that everyone could meet Kathryn.

Darcy was clearly pleased, and Kathryn appreciated their kindness and their ready acceptance of her. Time was when the marriage of any member of the Darcy family to a son or daughter of an Irish horse trainer would have been considered a *mésalliance* of tragic proportions!

It was late when Darcy had taken her home to Colley Dale and, following a reluctant and prolonged leave-taking, left promising to call on the morrow, which was a Saturday, so they could begin their preparations for the wedding. Kathryn, still feeling a sense of unreal elation, partook only of a cup of tea before going upstairs, where she found her sister waiting up for her. Elena had waited several hours for her sister to return and was keen to ask a few questions of her own.

"Dear Kate, I am so happy, and I am sure you are going to be very happy with your handsome Mr Gardiner; shall I be your bridesmaid?"

Kathryn was touched and embraced her young sister. "Thank you, and of course you shall, just so long as you do not insist on wearing pink. It is a colour I abhor!"

Promising faithfully never to wear pink ever again, Elena then proceeded to ask where they would live, how many servants would they have, and many more questions until Kate, beginning to feel very sleepy, begged to be excused.

Still bright-eyed at two in the morning, Elena had one more question. "Kate, when you are married, do you suppose your Mr Gardiner could ask his grandfather if I may have permission to read in the library at Pemberley? I have never seen such a wonderful array of books! There must be thousands of them!"

Kathryn laughed; she knew well her sister's enthusiasm for reading. "Dear me, that I am afraid we shall have to wait and see, because it is not in my Mr Gardiner's power to give you permission to use the library. However, I am sure he will apply to Mr Darcy on your behalf, and if you promise to be very quiet, Mr Darcy may well let you in!"

Promising to be quieter than a mouse, Elena went to her room to dream of the delights of the Pemberley library, while Kathryn was left to ponder the events of the day as she prepared for bed.

The weather changed suddenly on the morning after and a low mist hung over the moors and rolled into the dales, interfering with their plans.

Darcy, who had been invited to dine at Colley Dale, was late arriving, and Kathryn was feeling tired after the excitement and activity of the previous evening.

Which being the case, they spent most of the afternoon in the comfort of the warm parlour talking, rather than making plans. When Elena brought them in some cake and tea, Darcy asked if she would like to attend the May festival at Pemberley on the following Saturday. The invitation was gleefully accepted by Elena, who had never been to a May festival before.

"Shall we all go?" she asked eagerly, and Darcy thought that was a good idea and said so.

"Why ever not? It will let Kathryn meet some of the people on the estate. Would you like that?" he asked.

Kathryn had some reservations and needed to be persuaded. "Would it not be as good as announcing our engagement to the entire population of the district?" she asked nervously, and Darcy, not wishing to embarrass or discomfit her, asked, "Would that worry you, Kathryn?"

She thought a while before replying, "No, not if you were with me."

He was quick to reassure her. "Which I will be, of course. Have no fears, my love; I have heard not a single word against you on the estate, and since you went to work with Jessica at the school, there have been so many compliments from the mothers of the girls you teach. They were afraid that when Jessica married, the school would suffer, but you have done so well, they are most grateful."

Inclined after that solemn speech to tease him a little, she asked, "And does that mean they appreciate Miss O'Hare the school teacher, or do they like me for what I am?"

"I would declare that they do both, for you are indeed an excellent teacher and yet I defy them not to love you; how could they not?"

At this, she looked at him, thinking he was teasing her in return, but, seeing the look in his eyes, saw that she had no longer any need to wonder at the strength and consistency of his love for her.

Yet there was one subject that had not been spoken of which had lain hidden in her heart. When the rest of the family had withdrawn, she asked the question that had troubled her for several weeks and to which she had as yet found no answer.

"Darcy, I must ask this if only to set my heart at rest; pray do not be angry; I mean no offence, but I must know the truth. It will not do for me to pretend it is of no importance, because it has troubled me greatly.

"During the past four or five weeks, there were times when you stayed away for several days at a time, and when you did come to see me, you seemed preoccupied and grave, as though you had some weight upon your mind.

"I had hoped you would speak of it to me, but you did not, and I have been concerned that you said nothing. What was it caused you to be so distracted and perhaps even indifferent to me?" she asked.

As she spoke, Darcy's expression changed. He had hoped he would never have to explain the circumstances that had occasioned his unusual behaviour, but there was no avoiding it now.

"Dearest Kathryn, I will answer you, but promise me, you will not misunderstand my words or my motives when I do."

She did, and he went on, "I admit I have been preoccupied of late, but it was not indifference, nor any change of feeling on my part. What transpired was caused by the intervention of our old enemy, Mr Hartley-Brown."

"What? I believed him to be in America!" she exclaimed, shocked at his words.

"So did I, but having returned from the United States, where he apparently found no favour, he seems to be as vicious as ever. The passage of time is clearly of no significance to a man as evil as he is. Sometime last month, I received in the mail a letter in an unfamiliar hand. I opened it, never suspecting that it contained a poisonous accusation and a threat to send similar documents to my father and Mr Darcy. The blackguard had obviously discovered that we were engaged and was trying to turn my relations against you."

"Against me? What did it say?" She was pale with apprehension.

Her hand trembled as he held it and said, "It is of no consequence now, because, my dear Kathryn, it has all been dealt with. I would never have mentioned the matter had you not asked the question, but since you have, I thought it best to be open with you."

She was deeply distressed. "If you will not reveal what it said, then will you not at least tell me how it was dealt with and who else among your acquaintance and family knew of it?" she asked, concerned that her reputation may have been sullied.

"Certainly, if it will put your mind at rest. But you must not be upset, since it was a vile lie, wholly untrue and proven to be so. In order to expose it and its author, I had to make a couple of journeys, outside the county and once to London. With my brother-in-law Mr Carr, who is the only other person in my family to whom I have spoken of this matter, I returned to Yorkshire to see Mrs Ellis. She gave us a sworn statement about Hartley-Brown and his activities at Lindfield, which enabled us to enlist the help of Lord Denny and the police. They tracked him down to a lodging house, where they apprehended a man who was not Hartley-Brown but a former confidant of his, who readily gave information against him. He was finally arrested in Worthing, among some of his cronies, and taken in for questioning. When confronted with the evidence of his crimes, he confessed to writing the letters and many other things besides," Darcy explained.

"Where is he now?" asked Kathryn, apprehensive that the man was still able to pursue and torment her.

Darcy was quick to reassure her. "He is soon to be arraigned and prosecuted for this and other offences, including the theft of his Lordship's property. Needless to say, Lord Denny is particularly pleased with the result, and so of course should we be. He has admitted that the accusations he made against you were totally false and were made not so much out of jealousy, as I had thought then, but to extort money from me. He meant to blackmail me into paying for his silence. He thought he could gull me into believing his lies. When Carr and I called his bluff, he was easily destroyed. Hartley-Brown will trouble us no more; the villain is likely to spend quite a long spell as a guest of Her Majesty!" he said with some satisfaction.

"So you see, dearest Kathryn, it was while this matter was in progress that I stayed away. My apparent preoccupation was real enough—I was trying to find and prosecute this blackguard, during which time I had to keep my distance from you, lest I gave something away in an unguarded moment and placed our entire plan in jeopardy."

Her disquiet was so apparent, he took both her hands in his and asked, "Do you understand now, my darling? It was never a question of a change in my feelings for you—if anything, they have grown stronger over these weeks when I was trying to protect you. And no other member of my family has heard or will hear of these matters. My brother-in-law has given me his word that not even Lizzie will know. Perhaps I should have explained earlier; I am sorry to have caused you concern; please forgive me."

While learning the truth had certainly made Kathryn feel better, she began to experience feelings of guilt for having doubted him. What she had thought was indifference, was in reality the very opposite. He had been engaged in defending her good name from a malicious attack by Hartley-Brown. Even the thought of it made her shudder.

Knowing now how deeply Darcy loved her, she wished to reassure him. "Darcy, of course I understand, and what is there for me to forgive? Your actions were beyond reproach. It is I who am sorry for having thought otherwise. You were not neglecting me; indeed, the reverse was true."

There were tears in her eyes as she continued, "How shall I ever thank you enough for what you have done? Your actions have preserved not only my reputation, but protected my entire family from scandal. Had Hartley-Brown been able to spread his slander, they should all have been tainted, and I would have been to blame. Even young Elena would have suffered from the disgrace.

"My parents know nothing of my earlier, foolish association with him! It would have horrified and shamed them. Darcy, you have spared us all this, truly; I do not know how to thank you."

Assured that she had no need to do or say any more than she had already, that he had acted as he had because he loved her, Kathryn was eager to make amends, and Darcy was content to let her affirm her love and esteem for him in the warmest, most generous words she could find.

With every question between them thus resolved, he suggested that they take a turn in the garden, to which she readily agreed. The low cloud that had earlier obscured the view had lifted, and the late evening light softened the outlines of the hills. A brisk shower had left the air clean and sweet.

Walking together in the avenue to the west of the house, watching the light fade from a reddening sky, there was nothing more significant to occupy them than the enjoyment of their present delight and the contemplation of their future happiness.

END OF PART FIVE

Kathryn is both beautiful and intelligent, a rare enough combination today when beautiful girls seem to feel it is their role to behave as though they had forgotten how to think and intelligent women are regarded, in general, as having no appeal whatsoever, save in their mastery of the mathematical tables! Kathryn is educated, charming, and devoted to my grandson. My dear Charlotte, I cannot imagine a happier circumstance.

Most other members of the family were agreed that it was a happy match between two particularly agreeable and popular young people.

Jane Bingley, whose opinion was never far from her sister Elizabeth's, declared she was delighted and was sure they would be very happy, while Caroline Fitzwilliam, who had always regarded Miss O'Hare as a modern, intelligent young woman, told her nephew he was a very fortunate fellow to have secured her affections.

"There are not many young women who could lay claim to your Kathryn's looks, education, and style, yet would wish to live in the country. Most often, they become bored and seek the kind of society one can find chiefly in London, Paris, or Bath, as your uncle Robert's wife Rose and the Bingley sisters have done," said Caroline, and Darcy, who valued her good opinion, did not dispute it. He was well aware of his own good fortune.

For Lizzie Carr, her brother's choice came as close to perfection as she could imagine, for she held Kathryn in very high esteem, while her husband, knowing something of Darcy's earlier tribulations in matters of the heart, was well pleased to see his friend so content at last. Mr Carr and his wife both agreed that Kathryn was a more appropriate bride for Darcy than the lady he had failed to win. While they all loved gentle Jessica Courtney, it was Kathryn they had come to admire for her style and intelligence, and they were convinced that she suited young Darcy best.

Perhaps most happy was his cousin David Fitzwilliam, himself now a happily married man, who owed much of his own present satisfaction to Darcy's timely advice. Arriving from Manchester to stand beside his cousin as his best man, David proclaimed his opinion to anyone who would listen. "I think Darcy is just the luckiest fellow to be marrying one of the handsomest, most charming ladies I have met," he declared, as though defying anyone to contradict him. None who knew the couple did.

An Epilogue . . .

IT WAS PROBABLY AN indication of the popularity of Darcy Gardiner that almost everyone had a view on his forthcoming marriage to Kathryn O'Hare.

His parents were both pleased and relieved, having begun lately to worry that their second son appeared to have none of the ambition that drove his elder brother and few specific plans for his future. That he had decided to remain in Derbyshire rather than move to Westminster pleased his mother very well, and her fondness for Kathryn increased her satisfaction considerably.

After the couple had been seen together at the May Festival, news of their engagement spread quickly through the district, and congratulations were generally forthcoming from friends and relations alike. The family at Colley Dale were deemed by all their neighbours to be exceedingly fortunate, for was not young Darcy Gardiner regarded as the most eligible young gentleman in the district? Kathryn O'Hare, they declared, had made a very good match. Mr and Mrs O'Hare were clearly delighted that their daughter was also likely to be very happy in her marriage.

Mr and Mrs Darcy had made it clear to anyone who cared to ask their opinion that they approved entirely of the choice their grandson had made.

They had a very high opinion of Miss O'Hare.

Writing to her friend Charlotte Collins, Elizabeth was generous:

There were others, however, within and without the family who did not agree and were not averse to expressing their reservations. Notes and letters were swiftly and sharply exchanged between some of those who, having had very little opportunity to form an opinion on the matter, being wholly disconnected from the couple, presumed to do so, just the same.

Darcy's brother Edward's wife, Angela, always particular about matters of reputation and social status, had declared in a letter to Rose Gardiner that:

Despite her obvious attractions, there is something lacking in Miss O'Hare's background, which must surely make one pause when assessing her suitability as a wife for a young man from such a reputable family. You would not have believed that Darcy Gardiner would consider such a person as Daniel O'Hare suitable to be his father-in-law and grandfather to his children in the future!

To which remark, Rose had replied with equal aplomb:

Indeed you are so right, Angela, Kathryn O'Hare does lack something. My dear mama thinks the wild Irish background of her father is the cause; after all he was no more than a horse trainer at the Camden stud. Mama is amazed that the Gardiners have permitted the match and wonders why Mr Darcy did not forbid it!

Rose Gardiner's dear mama had not counted on her ill-advised remarks being conveyed to the Gardiners and Darcys. Consequently, she found to her consternation that no invitation to the wedding was forthcoming for herself and her husband Sir James Fitzwilliam. Cassy, having learned from her son Edward of Lady Fitzwilliam's low opinion of Kathryn's family, had decided that if this were the case, she should be spared the distress of attending the wedding, at which the O'Hares were unavoidably present.

Having removed their names from her list, she remarked mischievously, "Mama, I cannot believe that their disappointment at being left out will be greater than my satisfaction at not having them attend," and to her delight, her mother had agreed.

"I think it very unlikely they will be missed," said Elizabeth, who had long since abandoned any hope of reclaiming her former friend Rosamund Camden, whom she had known and liked when she was the daughter of a simple farming family. Though only recently elevated to high status through her husband's unexpected accession to a title, she nevertheless took it very seriously and had adopted a loftiness of manner that greatly vexed Mrs Darcy.

Consequently, when the families gathered at Kympton on a fine, Autumn morning to see Darcy Gardiner wed Kathryn O'Hare, Sir James and Lady Fitzwilliam were notably absent. Robert and Rose Gardiner did attend but had little to say to anyone except Edward and Angela Gardiner and, after an initial formal introduction, scrupulously avoided the company of the O'Hares. Having survived the service at the church, they left, ostensibly returning to London, to the immense relief of the rest of the party.

"I could not imagine them sitting down to the wedding breakfast at Colley Dale," said Lizzie Carr to her mother, whose expression betrayed her own satisfaction at their early departure.

"Neither can I, but their rudeness is unpardonable. This must be Lady Fitzwilliam's doing. It beggars belief that the acquisition of a title can so alter the values and manners of anyone as much as they have changed Rosamund Camden. Mama says she used to be a very agreeable young woman," Cassandra remarked, to which her daughter replied blithely, "Who has certainly turned into a most disagreeable old lady!"

Conspicuously absent, too, was Lydia Wickham, who, alas, had heard the news too late to procure a suitably grand gown and hat for the occasion and sufficient funds to make another journey to Derbyshire.

Visiting Charlotte Collins at Longbourn, she had bemoaned her inability to attend.

"If only I had known sooner, I should certainly have attended; young Darcy is quite a favourite of mine, for he is a pleasant, well-mannered young fellow, not as high and mighty as his grandfather," she had said regretfully, unaware that Charlotte had heeded her friend Eliza's pleas and not revealed the date and details of Darcy Gardiner's wedding to Lydia.

Dear Charlotte, I do not think any of us could cope with another dose of Lydia! Elizabeth had written and Charlotte had understood.

Unable to undertake the long train journey to Derbyshire, Charlotte herself would have to rely upon her niece Anna Bingley and her granddaughter Anne-Marie Elliott to bring her reports of the wedding.

Elizabeth was disappointed. "I do wish Charlotte could have been here," she said to Jane. "She writes that her rheumatism is worse and prevents her making long journeys. I am glad that Catherine intends to visit her mother on their return journey to Kent—I am sure Charlotte will enjoy that. She says she is looking forward to hearing all about the wedding."

Charlotte's eldest daughter, Catherine Harrison, whose husband the Reverend Dr Harrison had the dubious distinction of being the longest serving incumbent at the parish of Hunsford, had already arrived for the wedding and was staying at Pemberley, at the invitation of the Darcys.

She had explained that, sadly, Dr Harrison, who suffered from intermittent palpitations of the heart, had on the advice of his doctor felt unable to undertake the journey from Kent to Derbyshire.

Catherine, who remained a remarkably active and handsome rector's wife, came accompanied by her younger daughter, Lilian, a quiet-spoken, gentle girl, whose attachment to a certain Mr Adams, curator of the Rosings Park Estate, had only recently been revealed to her mother. It was not generally known, and Catherine and Lilian had agreed that, in view of the fact that the gentleman had not as yet applied to her father, nothing would be said of the matter to anyone else, for the moment.

Both Elizabeth and Mr Darcy had commented upon the extent to which Catherine Harrison resembled her mother in disposition and manner, though she was certainly handsomer than Charlotte.

"Yes indeed, and by some stroke of good fortune, there appears to be little trace of their lugubrious father in any of the Collins' daughters," said Mr Darcy. Elizabeth could not but agree.

"In Catherine, there is, in addition to Charlotte's sound common sense, a natural grace and dignity, which does her great credit, and it seems she has passed some of that on to young Lilian."

While young Lilian was in raptures about the bride's beautiful lace gown, her mother was more impressed with the dedication of the couple to the people of their community and the decision Darcy Gardiner had taken to forego a career in politics to remain at Pemberley.

"I understand young Mr Gardiner will not stand for Parliament after all," she had remarked to Elizabeth. "I have no doubt his friends at Westminster will be exceedingly disappointed."

Elizabeth had explained the reasons Darcy had given for his decision, and Catherine continued, "And Miss O'Hare, Cassandra tells me she is a most remarkable young lady; I believe she has undertaken to run the parish school at Pemberley."

Once again Elizabeth agreed, "She has indeed, and the young girls of the area, who have no other means of learning to read and write, love her dearly for it."

Catherine was very impressed. "Such significant service to one's community is rare indeed," she said and added, with a note of regret in her voice, "Had Lady Catherine de Bourgh agreed to let us start such a school at Hunsford, we might well have had the opportunity to do likewise. Mr Harrison and I had great plans, but sadly, Her Ladyship was of the opinion that educating the girls of the parish would only give them ideas above their station and make them discontented with their lot in life."

Anne-Marie, who with her husband Colin Elliott had joined the group outside the church, was quite shocked and said so. "I could not possibly agree with such a preposterous assertion. It presupposes that they must accept that a life of drudgery is their lot. My husband is very disappointed indeed that Darcy will not stand for a seat in Parliament, but he does admit that the work he does at Pemberley is very valuable. As for Miss O'Hare, her resolve to carry on Jessica Courtney's work in educating the girls of the village, I absolutely applaud."

Colin Elliott did not disagree with his wife, but he had been unable to hide his deep disappointment when he had sought out his friend on the afternoon before the wedding to offer him his sincere felicitations.

"Darcy, my friend, I am sorry that some tardiness on the part of our government in fulfilling the pledges made to the people has turned you against them. I should have liked to see you take the issues that are so dear to your heart into the Parliament and fight for them there," he had said.

It was then that Darcy had admitted there were other reasons for his decision than his disillusionment with the performance of the government.

"I must be frank with you, Colin; it is true that I have found the entire debate on the Irish church tedious and unproductive; the tenancy laws have only increased sectarian bitterness in Ireland and are likely to create more, not less conflict between Catholics and Protestants—they are divisive and ineffective," said Darcy, continuing on a familiar theme. "But most of all, I have sensed a lack of resolve on the two issues most vital for the people of England; there is no plan to reform the thoroughly inadequate systems of health and education, and no more than a hint that something substantial will be done in the future.

"They were the concerns that made me a Reformist and a supporter of Mr Gladstone, not arcane issues of church and state! These may engage the minds of politicians at Westminster and deans at Oxford, but they will in no way improve the lot of the people, who continue to suffer at the bottom of the social ladder. I have lost patience with them."

He had spoken with great passion, and Colin Elliott had listened intently before asking, "But, Darcy, if this were all, I still believe we could have persuaded you to join us and fight for these causes from within."

Seeing Darcy smile, he added, "I'll wager any amount you care to name, there is another reason for your refusal."

Darcy responded quickly, "Save your money, my friend, I am not a betting man. I will concede, I have other concerns as well."

He then revealed the reasons, which they had never discussed before.

"My family needs me here, Colin. You know that my mother is Anthony's legal guardian until he attains his majority; she needs my help to prepare the boy for his inheritance. But even then, he may not be ready to take over all his responsibilities for this great estate and its people. And if, God forbid, he is called to it earlier by my grandfather's untimely death or incapacity, their need of me will be the greater. I have lived here all my life. I know all these people; I understand their problems, and I have given my word to Mr Darcy, from which I will not resile."

After this passionate speech, Colin Elliott had felt impelled to draw his friend's attention to certain simple facts.

"Darcy, you do not need me to remind you that, despite your very noble dedication to Pemberley and your grandfather's family, you will never be more than the manager of this estate. Whenever young Anthony Darcy succeeds to his inheritance, he will be the Master of Pemberley. Your role will not change. Are you happy with such a situation? Do you not wish to be your own master and achieve something in your own right?"

Darcy threw back his head and laughed, "Colin, surely you do not mean to suggest that I could be my own master in the Parliament?"

"No, but you will have influence on policy..." Elliott protested.

"Will I?" Darcy's voice had betrayed his scepticism, and then he had smiled, in that disarming way that always unsettled his opponents. "Colin, you are a very dear friend and a valued colleague; I have no wish to quarrel with you. I owe you a great deal and ask you to believe that my decision has been made only after much thought and is dependent upon what I believe to be in the interest of myself, Kathryn, and my family.

"I have no unrealistic ambitions for myself. I know I cannot inherit any part of the estate, but I too have received a legacy from Pemberley whose worth cannot be estimated in mere monetary terms. I have enjoyed my life here and am grateful to be the beneficiary of its great traditions and feel the need to give something in return."

Colin Elliott had appeared a little nonplussed, unable to comprehend his meaning, and Darcy had explained, "I have no profession and no estate. Were I to enter Parliament now and leave it in ten years' time, I should still be no better qualified than I am now. Pemberley has given me both the opportunity and the means to do something worthwhile with my life. "

"And you cannot accomplish this in the Parliament?" asked Elliott.

"Not at this time—I can see no better way for me to accomplish something useful for the people of this estate, for my grandparents and myself, than to remain here and continue the work I am engaged in. I have plans that may help see us through this rural recession, which everyone predicts is upon us. If it is indeed true, then hundreds of families will be grievously hurt and disadvantaged; I feel the need to work to avert or at least alleviate their hardship. I have discussed my ideas with Mr Darcy and have his consent to try; it is my duty and my genuine desire to do so. If I succeed, that will be my lasting legacy," Darcy replied.

"Are you determined then never to stand for Parliament, or is it possible you will reconsider it at a later time?" Elliott asked, unwilling to believe that his friend had abandoned politics for good.

Darcy shrugged his shoulders. "Who can tell what may be possible at some later date? I am not able to say. But I can tell you quite sincerely that I will always retain an interest in Reformist politics—I shall not abandon you and my other colleagues in the party. Indeed, I shall be watching your work with great interest and will support you whenever and however I can."

So saying, he had parted from his friend to meet again at the church on the morrow. Colin Elliott was deeply saddened and disheartened. He had set his heart on seeing young Darcy Gardiner in Parliament.

It seemed it was not to be.

Darcy had been too preoccupied with preparations for his marriage to be troubled by regrets or recriminations. Since his conversation with Colin Elliott, his thoughts had turned almost completely to the anticipated happiness of sharing his life, his hopes and successes, and perhaps even the occasional, inevitable failures with the young woman he had come to love so well.

Kathryn had become pre-eminently important to him. Once he had recognised the depth of his feelings for her, he had realised that nothing and no one in his life had meant more; no cause had evoked greater passion. While her beauty and charm had captivated him at first, now every aspect of her nature and character attracted and inspired his affections.

In the delightful weeks following their engagement, he had come to a greater understanding of her disposition and saw in her a woman possessed of exactly the qualities of strong feelings and quiet resilience he had always admired. When he had feared he could lose her, he had understood how dearly he loved her. With the certainty of her love, he was confident that they would have a passionate, rewarding marriage and was eager it should begin.

For the lovers, the morning of their wedding day could not come too soon; it had seemed like an eternity of waiting. Their families and friends had hastened and bustled to prepare for the day, which seemed to rush towards them, leaving too little time to get done all that needed doing.

Flowers had been gathered to fill the church and the house with sweet scents, gowns had been fashioned and fitted, while hats of every description had been procured and trimmed.

At Colley Dale, tables covered in crisp white cloths groaned under the weight of platters filled with food, while the cellars had been scoured for the best wines. Daniel O'Hare and his wife had certainly striven to provide a banquet that was bountiful without being ostentatious. Their pride in their lovely daughter was apparent in all their arrangements.

There was entertainment, too, for all. Genteel music played by a small chamber ensemble charmed those who sat down to the wedding breakfast, and afterwards, a group of more vigorous Irish fiddlers and dancers performed on the lawn, to the delight of the gathered guests.

"Thankfully," said Cassy to her daughters, "Rose and Robert have left early, else they might have been affronted by the performance. As for Lady

Fitzwilliam, I cannot imagine how she would have coped with seeing an Irish jig danced on the lawn! It is likely she would have had the strongest objections to such a spectacle!"

Whilst the guests were engaged in drinking, dining, or dancing, the couple whose union they celebrated could not wait to get away. Impatient to be alone together, they drove away on a journey that was to take them south to Woodlands, where they were to spend their honeymoon, carrying with them the heartfelt felicitations of their families and friends, as well as the blessings of an entire community.

Meanwhile, at Pemberley, a letter had been delivered for Mr Darcy, which, for obvious reasons, could not be handed immediately to the master, who was at Colley Dale attending the wedding.

The sender's name—a Mr Adams—was unknown to the young footman who accepted it. Assuming it to be a matter of no urgency which could wait for the morrow, it was put aside with the rest of the Master's mail, to be opened by Mr Darcy after breakfast on the following day.

No one could possibly have guessed at the significance of its contents.

Returning to Hertfordshire after the wedding, Colin Elliott wrote to his friend and colleague Jack Howell. *I am truly sorry to say that I have failed to persuade young Darcy Gardiner to change his mind about the by-election,* he wrote.

> *Not only has he the best reason in the world to remain in Derbyshire, having just married a clever and lovely woman, but he is also imbued with a strong sense of family loyalty and sees it as a sacred duty to guide the young heir to Pemberley, Anthony Darcy, towards the day when he will take over his inheritance.*
>
> *I know you will agree, Jack, that such a young man of principle and integrity would be an asset to us in the Commons. Perhaps one day in the future, we may try again, at a more propitious time, but for now, I fear the chapter is closed.*
>
> *Yours very sincerely,*
> *Colin Elliott*

꧁

Kathryn's letter to Jessica, written two days before her wedding, reached her friend several thousands of miles away in South West Africa some weeks later. Her husband was out in the field with his assistant, collecting specimens for analysis.

The southern Spring was almost warmer than Summer in England.

Seated in the shade of a flame tree, in front of a white-painted timber bungalow, protected from the heat of the sun by a large canvas umbrella and a wide-brimmed hat, Jessica read it eagerly.

My dearest Jessica, she wrote.

First, let me thank you and Julian on behalf of Darcy and myself, for your kind letter with its good wishes and your exquisite gift. I have never seen such a finely crafted piece of work; it shall have pride of place in our home.

Dear Jessica, how much more there is for which I must thank you. If I had never met you, I should not now be writing this letter to tell you how happily and with what degree of anticipated pleasure I look forward to our wedding on Saturday.

Even as I do, I think of you and wish you were here to share with us this special day, for you had no small part in bringing us together.

Darcy and I have spoken often of the circumstances of our meeting in the park at Pemberley. Had I not known you, had you not invited me to visit your school, I may never have come to know and love the man I am to marry tomorrow. He has taught me the value of love sincerely and honestly given, and I look forward to our marriage with more hope of happiness than I have ever known.

For all this and your dear friendship, I thank you with all my heart.

If there is one thing that stands in the way of complete contentment, it is your absence from England for the next three years. It seems such a long time—I can only pray it will pass sooner than I expect, for we shall miss you both very much.

Yours ever,

Kathryn O'Hare

In a brief postscript, added on the morning of her wedding day, Kathryn wrote:

It is quite early, and the air outside is cold and very still.

I am awake before the birds, before the dawn light has touched the sky, because I cannot sleep. Also, I must complete this letter and despatch it to the post, so you will know that on this happy day, my thoughts were of you.

Dearest Jessica, I shall miss you so today, I hope we shall meet again soon.

I pray daily for your safe return to England.

Your loving friend and soon to be your cousin,

Kate

Returning from their honeymoon, both Darcy and Kate were quickly plunged back into life in Derbyshire with difficult decisions to be made at Pemberley and much hard work to be undertaken at the school. Both were equally committed to the responsibilities they had accepted, but neither were so imprudent as to let the demands of others put in jeopardy the warmth and strength of their marriage. Young and deeply in love, they ensured that their lives were filled with both the rewarding satisfaction of work as well as the delightful pleasures of a passionate union.

Darcy claimed truthfully that he never missed the cut and thrust of politics, while Kathryn confessed that she missed only the presence of her dear friend Jessica to make her perfectly content.

Then, by one of those happy coincidences that come but rarely in life, Kathryn's prayer was answered when, a year later, Dr. Julian Darcy was invited to address a distinguished gathering of scientists in London and accept an award for his work on tropical diseases.

It brought him and Jessica to England for a few weeks, during which time the families travelled to London, and afterwards, the two young couples, with Elizabeth's blessing, journeyed to Woodlands where they spent a fortnight together.

It was but a brief period of shared happiness, all the more enjoyable because it had been unexpected. At Woodlands, amidst the mellow loveliness of the

Albury Downs in late Autumn, there was time enough to enjoy their friendship and understand the value of the work they had each undertaken in life. With many hours of lively conversation and interludes of quiet enjoyment, it was, except for the inevitable sadness of parting, a time of unalloyed pleasure.

No one argued, not one intemperate word was spoken, and while they were certainly not always in agreement, they resolved their differences with such pleasing affability and reasonableness, that no one was ever out of temper.

For Julian and Darcy it was a chance to discover and speak of many matters other than the business of Pemberley; much had happened since they had last been together in Derbyshire. There was both good and sad news to tell, and both men had matured in experience and understanding.

As for Jessica and Kathryn, not surprisingly, they indulged in that most fascinating pastime of young women, recently wed—exchanging confidences. Closer now than even sisters could be, they shared their hopes and spoke of their dreams without inhibition or fear of ridicule, encouraging each other's aspirations and making light of their occasional fears. Each confided in the other their expectations and confirmed their deep contentment in their marriages.

It was a very special time.

At the conclusion of their stay, with Winter approaching in England, they parted reluctantly, each to return to their chosen world.

Julian and Jessica would travel to the bright heat of Africa, where more work awaited them, while Darcy and Kathryn returned to Derbyshire and the people of Pemberley, whose warm affection and esteem would ease the cold of a northern Winter.

Appendix

A list of the main characters in *Postscript from Pemberley*:

Julian Darcy—son of Mr and Mrs Darcy of Pemberley
Jessica Courtney—youngest daughter of Reverend James Courtney and Emily
   (Gardiner) of Kympton rectory
Cassandra Gardiner—daughter of Mr and Mrs Darcy of Pemberley
Dr Richard Gardiner—Cassandra's husband, son of Mr and Mrs Gardiner
Darcy Gardiner—son of Cassandra and Richard Gardiner, grandson of Mr and
   Mrs Darcy of Pemberley
Edward Gardiner—his elder brother, a medical practitioner
Angela—Edward's wife
Lizzie Carr (Gardiner)—sister of Darcy and Edward Gardiner
Mr Michael Carr—her husband, owner of the Rushmore Farm and Stud
David Fitzwilliam—Darcy's cousin, son of Colonel Fitzwilliam and Caroline
Kathryn O'Hare—daughter of Mr and Mrs Daniel O'Hare of Colley Dale
Elena O'Hare—her younger sister
Sir James Fitzwilliam—Mr Darcy's cousin
Lady Fitzwilliam—his wife (Rosamund Camden)
Rose—their daughter

Robert Gardiner—her husband (also brother of Richard, Emily, and Caroline)
Colin Elliott, MP—friend and political colleague of Darcy Gardiner, husband
    of Anne-Marie (daughter of Jonathan Bingley of Netherfield)
Jonathan Bingley—son of Mr and Mrs Bingley of Ashford Park
Anna—Jonathan's wife (Faulkner)
Lord and Lady Denny of Lindfield—Kathryn's former employers
Gordon Hartley-Brown—Lady Denny's cousin

⚜

From the pages of *Pride and Prejudice:*

Mr and Mrs Darcy of Pemberley
Mr and Mrs Bingley of Ashford Park
Col Fitzwilliam and his wife Caroline (née Gardiner)
Mrs Gardiner—aunt of Jane and Elizabeth
Mrs Charlotte Collins—Elizabeth's friend, widow of Mr Collins of Hunsford

Acknowledgements

The author wishes to thank all those kind readers whose encouragement has been greatly appreciated. Their views and comments are sufficient reason to be convinced of the worth of *The Pemberley Chronicles* series.

Special thanks are due to Ms Claudia Taylor, librarian, for her research and advice; to Marissa O'Donnell for the artwork; to Ben and Robert for technical help; and to Rose for keeping everything on track so effortlessly.

Thanks also to Beverly Wong for her work on the website, for where indeed would the shades of Pemberley be, if they were not so well served?

Heartfelt love and gratitude, of course, to Ms Jane Austen.

— Rebecca Ann Collins, www.geocities.com/shadesofpemberley, www.rebeccaanncollins.com

About the Author

A lifelong fan of Jane Austen, Rebecca Ann Collins first read *Pride and Prejudice* at the tender age of twelve. She fell in love with the characters and since then has devoted years of research and study to the life and works of her favorite author. As a teacher of literature and a librarian, she has gathered a wealth of information about Miss Austen and the period in which she lived and wrote, which became the basis of her books about the Pemberley families. The popularity of *The Pemberley Chronicles* series with Jane Austen fans has been her reward.

With a love of reading, music, art, and gardening, Ms. Collins claims she is very comfortable in the period about which she writes, and feels great empathy with the characters she portrays. While she enjoys the convenience of modern life, she finds much to admire in the values and world-view of Jane Austen.

The Pemberley Chronicles

A Companion Volume to Jane Austen's Pride and Prejudice
The Pemberley Chronicles: Book 1

REBECCA ANN COLLINS

"A lovely complementary novel to Jane Austen's *Pride and Prejudice*.
Austen would surely give her smile of approval."
—BEVERLY WONG, AUTHOR OF *Pride & Prejudice Prudence*

The weddings are over, the saga begins

The guests (including millions of readers and
viewers) wish the two happy couples health
and happiness. As the music swells and the
credits roll, two things are certain: Jane
and Bingley will want for nothing, while
Elizabeth and Darcy are to be the happiest
couple in the world!

Elizabeth and Darcy's personal stories of love,
marriage, money, and children are woven
together with the threads of social and political
history of England in the nineteenth century.
As changes in industry and agriculture
affect the people of Pemberley and the
surrounding countryside, the Darcys strive
to be progressive and forward-looking while
upholding beloved traditions.

"Those with a taste for the balance and humour of Austen will find a
worthy companion volume." —*Book News*

978-1-4022-1153-9 • $14.96 US/ $17.95 CAN/ £7.99 UK